HAWTHORNE

DRUID SPIRIT CHRONICLES BOOK ONE

Kevin Fury

BANSHEE PUBLISHING L.L.C.
COLORADO

Wishing you Magic!

Kevin

D1028210

Hawthorne
By Kevin Fury

Print ISBN: 978-0-692-562437
eBook ASIN: B01774NM74

Cover Art, "Grip on Life," by Alan M. Clarke.
Used with permission.

Published in the United States
by Banshee Publishing L.L.C.

Visit me at:
www.kevinfury.com

To Naomi,
for making all my dreams come true.

Acknowledgements

My love of stories started at a young age, with the seed planted by Mom and Dad. Grandparents and teachers watered it for many years. Some of those teachers taught me through their books. J.R.R Tolkien, C.S. Lewis, Terry Brooks, Neil Gaiman, Jim Butcher, and Kevin Hearne, all taught me to love fantasy stories and inspired me to try my own hand at writing one.

This book would not be here today without the support and guidance of many people, including my editors Lorin Oberweger and Todd Barselow, Alan M. Clarke, who painted the cover, and Jim Pinto who designed the cover. I'd also like to acknowledge the Rocky Mountain Fiction Writers organization, who puts on a wonderful conference every year and where I learned a lot about the business and craft of writing.

Most of all I'd like to thank my family and friends for their patience and support through the many years that it took to finish *Hawthorne*. For my best friend, Scott Kietzmann, who brainstormed and offered honest feedback. For my sister, Colleen, for being the one person who really knows where I'm coming from. For my Mom and Dad, who read many drafts of this book and never once grew exasperated and always shared their enthusiasm even with my early drafts. For my wife, Naomi, who has been untiring and unwavering in her support of this project of mine. She has read the book many times and given me endless good ideas and detailed editing. Your support truly helped me make the final push to get this book into the world, making my dream come true.

Chapter 1

A scent of sage washed over Rhiannon O'Neil as she put on her glasses and sat up. A drop of water fell from the tent's ceiling and spattered on her sleeping bag. She lay back down and shifted away from the leak, knocking into CuChulain, her big malamute, who lifted his head and looked at her. She reached out a hand, stroked his white fur, and watched as he closed his eyes.

She tried to fall back asleep, wondering what had woken her. A stone made itself known to her ribs as she tried to settle in. *Why do you keep doing this to yourself, O'Neil?*

But she knew the answer. The discomforts she experienced were a small price for the peace of the wilds. The pure air, the forests, and the streams made her feel whole, even if only for a short while. The rugged terrain and long hikes in the Colorado mountains could be conquered. They were manageable. Her life was not.

Coming to the wilds had its risks, she knew. After the fae killed her mother, she was never completely safe or at ease. Her uncle protected her from faerie attacks, but there was always the chance something might get through.

Back home she immersed herself in her school projects, working on her PhD in Celtic Studies. Her hunger for knowledge helped to push down her fear and when she had the time, like now, she escaped to the wilderness. Here, in her favorite place—Eagle's Nest Wilderness—she could go for days without seeing a single person. Her fiancé didn't always understand her need to have alone time, but she didn't let it stop her. It was risky coming out here, but it was worth it.

She told herself that she was being proactive, keeping her body and mind sharp by her choices, that she wasn't running from her past, hiding from its dangers, but it was a lie. The insanity of being afraid of faeries, creatures that few people even knew existed, haunted her. Seeing her mother killed by them had left a deep scar. She required the healing power of nature regularly. She desperately desired to move beyond just being able to limp along. She longed to finally be rid of her fear, to be able to live again.

She shifted, trying to find a comfortable spot on the hard ground. Nearby she heard CuChulain's collar jangle. He reached out and nosed her hand. She gave him a fond rub, grateful for his presence.

Feral cries suddenly erupted from the darkness, breaking the peace.

Her body stiffened. She grabbed her revolver. "What was that?" she whispered to the darkness.

The howls grew closer. CuChulain stood and growled.

Rhiannon rustled out of her sleeping bag, cursing the noise it made. "Be quiet, CuChulain," she whispered. "Maybe whatever it is will pass us by."

The cries grew nearer, creeping forward, retreating, then coming nearer, faster this time. A predator hunting its prey.

Rhiannon's heart hammered in her chest as she fumbled to get her boots on. She unzipped the sodden door and peered outside, needing to see what was happening. A chill, far deeper than the crisp mountain air warranted, crept up her spine. She pointed her gun into the bleak darkness.

Eyes glowing purple, backs hunched with muscle and fur, a pack of creatures slunk out into the open, no longer hidden behind the trees downhill. The moonlight illuminated them—at least thirty strong. They looked like coyotes raised on a diet of steroids and evil magic.

She felt the magic in her well up, instinctively rising to protect her. She willed a protective shield around her, like she had been taught. Nothing happened.

Her breath caught in her throat, stifling a scream. Before she could move, CuChulain pushed past her. He stood protectively in front of her, hackles raised, a snarl rumbling deep in his throat. The pack turned toward them, and with terrible speed, rushed up the hill, their claws tearing up huge clods of earth.

She stepped outside, fighting the primal urge to run, knowing that she would be easy prey with her back turned. She had to stand and face them. Blood pulsed in her temples.

With shaking hands, she raised the gun and pulled the trigger once. The noise ruptured the mountain night, and the flash of the muzzle temporarily blinded her. When her vision cleared, she realized with satisfaction that her bullet had struck the closest beast in the shoulder. The physical force made it stumble, neon purple eyes flashing, but it was back on its feet. The leader bared its black jagged teeth and pressed forward.

Adrenaline rushed her system. Time slowed and her vision narrowed. Almost without thought, she called on her magic.

"Oh Taranis, mighty thunderer. I call on your power. Drive back these beasts with your fury. Hear me, sky father, and hold true to your word."

The sky rumbled, as if indeed hearing her. Lightning flashed, and a blinding gout of pure energy struck the ground. Heat and light blasted her, knocking her off her feet.

She scrambled upright again, ears ringing. "Oh, my gods," she said, eyes wide. Spots filled her vision as she looked for the pack. CuChulain charged downhill. Thunder rumbled menacingly as three coyotes ripped into her beloved dog.

Anger flooded Rhiannon. "No! CuChulain, come! Come!"

She fired the .357 again. The bullet struck true, killing one of them, but the other two pulled CuChulain to the ground. He struggled back to his feet, ripped the throat out of one, and broke the leg of another. The pack set upon him like a furred storm of teeth and claws.

He collapsed under the weight of the attack.

"Cu!" she cried out, her eyes stretched painfully wide.

Lightning struck again. The superheated air exploded, shredding five coyotes and setting fire to three more. In the brief flash, Rhiannon counted at least a dozen creatures left. She emptied her gun into the pack, but there were still too many. CuChulain stopped moving, and the pack turned all their attention to her.

Rhiannon stood frozen to the ground for an instant, but desperation forced her to move.

She dove for the tent opening as the coyotes rushed her. She fumbled with her daypack and pulled out the box of custom made hollow point iron bullets. Fae creatures were most susceptible to iron. Her hands jerked as one of the beasts grabbed her hiking boot and tried to pull her out.

Rolling onto her back, she popped the cylinder open and dumped the brass casings. Another coyote bit her other boot and yanked hard. She almost dropped the gun, but she loaded it. She fired the slugs between her feet. Grim satisfaction filled her as each bullet blasted into the creatures.

The Ruger was empty again. A cloud of smoke filled the tent. She reloaded blind and coughed as claws ripped into the fabric walls and the amassed weight of the coyotes snapped the fiberglass poles, bringing the tent down on top of her. Screaming, she kicked and punched blindly, trying frantically to get free.

Claws raked and teeth bit. Her thigh gashed, Rhiannon shouted and blindly poured bullet after bullet into the ravaging shapes.

The damage she dealt bought her enough time to scrabble free.

She spun in a circle. Jaw clenched tight, she scanned the ground for the dropped box of ammo.

Lightning struck again. Rhiannon dropped to her knees and closed her eyes to avoid a repeat of the first strike's effects. When she opened her eyes, two more dead coyotes lay before her, and the rest of the pack pulled back toward the trees. She found the ammo, reloaded and fired, shooting until the gun clicked empty and the last of the coyotes disappeared down the hill into the night.

She stood, sucking in deep breaths as she surveyed the damage before her. She remembered CuChulain. Racing to him, she found him lying still in the long grass. Her steps faltered as she reached him, and she dropped to her knees.

CuChulain's eyes stared lifelessly into the night. She touched his head gently, then closed his eyes. The feel of the soft fur on his ears, still so much like puppy fur, reminded her of his comforting presence through many dark nights. Rhiannon collapsed over him and let loose a wave of grief and anger. She hugged his body to her, yelling until her throat swelled.

Finally, she stood and left, determined to get to safety and to figure out why the faerie creatures had attacked her.

* * *

Rhiannon limped to the door of the truck, breathing heavily. She opened the door and waited for CuChulain to jump in. Tears came for the first time.

The faerie had killed him.

They had killed her dog.

She reached over into the glove box, took out another box of iron-tipped bullets, and reloaded.

She locked the doors of the truck and took out her cell phone. There were nine messages, two from a 353-91 area code, meaning Galway, Ireland, and seven from Logan. *Brighid, what now.* She hit the button to listen.

"Rhiannon, please call me as soon as you can," a wavering older female voice said. *"Something terrible has happened...please call."* Rhiannon knew it was Mrs. McBride, Uncle Brennan's housekeeper.

No, not him too. I can't take this; it's too much.

She threw the phone on the seat and rolled down the truck window. She wiped her hands on her jeans and took a breath. She picked up the phone again.

Her stomach clenched as she listened to the second message.

"The police have come to the house and...oh, Rhiannon, it's too terrible, please call. They couldn't find him..."

Rhiannon swallowed, knowing her worst fear was coming true. Her hands shook as she tried to put the keys in the ignition. She dropped them on the floor, pounded the steering wheel with a growl. She picked the keys back up and started the Ford Ranger.

A spray of gravel erupted from the truck as she stomped on the gas. She gripped the wheel and braced herself to listen to Logan's messages.

"It's probably nothing, but I got a call from your uncle's housekeeper, and she is freaking out. Give me a call." He paused and said, *"... and next time, take your damn cell phone with you."*

The reality of what was happening sank in. Rhiannon didn't need to hear anymore, but she listened to the next message anyway.

"Your uncle's housekeeper is worried that Brennan is dead. She doesn't have any proof. She only knows he's missing. She keeps calling me. I'm worried about you. Call me."

The words, "Brennan is dead," struck her like a club. She hit the brakes and nearly skidded off the road.

Okay, O'Neil, get a hold of yourself. Crashing into a tree isn't going to help things. She took a breath. And then she called Logan.

"There you are," he said, relief evident in his sigh. "Are you okay? What the hell is going on?"

"CuChulain is dead, and I barely made it back to the truck."

"Where are you? I'm coming there now."

"No need. I'm driving home."

"Tell me everything."

"A pack of overgrown coyotes attacked us. CuChulain fought them off as best he could, but there were too many. I had my pistol, and that saved me."

She hated not telling him everything about what happened. She had never told him about the faerie curse on her family, knowing that if their roles were reversed she would have never believed it herself. Nevertheless it felt like a betrayal, not being completely honest with him. She knew if she started explaining things now there would be more questions she didn't want to answer.

"I've never heard of coyotes doing anything like that. I mean, maybe attacking a poodle or something, but not a human and a big dog."

"It was terrible, Logan. I had to leave his body. He deserved better than that. I didn't dare bury him. I was out of bullets, and I had to get back to the truck."

"I'm so sorry."

"I need you to book me a flight to Ireland today."

"I guess I'll need a ticket too?"

Rhiannon looked back into the woods and tried to imagine saying no to him. She didn't want to endanger him any more than she already had. The faerie had a reputation for attacking loved ones, but she needed him at her side as she faced whatever awaited her in Ireland. His presence brought her hope that her life could one day be normal, that someday all the danger and strangeness would be gone and she could get on with her life. If Brennan was truly dead, she would be the last of her bloodline. That reason alone made her want Logan close. She loved him, and he would be the only family she had left.

She took a deep breath. "Yes," she answered. "Yes, you will need a ticket."

Chapter 2

Red and blue neon cast purple shadows at Hiccups Bar. AC/DC's *Back in Black* blared from the speakers, and the room smelled of stale beer and sweat.

Logan liked this place. Here, he could get lost in the crowd, hiding from those looking for him as well as his troubled thoughts. He put his phone into his leather vest pocket, grabbed his Coors, and drank it down.

"You know, Kohana, I didn't think I'd find you so easily."

Logan bristled at the sound of his Sioux name but didn't turn around. A hand settled on his shoulder. His stomach tightened, he turned on his bar stool, stood, and faced the person standing there. "Akecheta," he spat.

Older than Logan, the man had the same long black hair and clean-shaven face, but that was where the similarity ended. His dark eyes, framed with crow's feet, were hard and unforgiving. His tall, thin build made him look sharp as an axe blade.

"It would go easier for you if you agreed to come back with me, but we both know that's not going to happen."

Logan glanced around the room, packed with leather-clad bikers drinking beer and waiting for the next set to start. He knew more were out back smoking. "Not here," he said. "Let's take this to the parking lot."

"I don't think so. I don't want a repeat of what happened with your father."

Heat flushed Logan's body. He squeezed his beer bottle tight. "You and I both know that wasn't my fault."

"That's what you've said, so why not come back and prove it?"

"I have no proof."

Akecheta stepped closer and pointed his finger in Logan's face. "That's right, you don't, and that's because *you are guilty*. You murdered your father and you think you can escape justice by running away. But you're wrong."

All of Logan's muscles tensed, ready to attack. The blood rushed in his ears. He shoved Akecheta back. "Justice? You're the one who needs to answer for what *you* did." He gave the man another shove. "*You* betrayed him!"

A few people nearby took notice and stepped back. Logan realized Akecheta wasn't going to come at him, not in this place. With something close to regret, he grabbed his leather jacket off the back of the bar stool and headed for the door.

As Logan walked away, Akecheta shouted at his back. "You know, Kohana, now that we know where you are, we will find you again. Next time, you won't be able to just walk away. It won't be just me. I'll bring lots of help."

Logan stopped, pulled in a breath, and slowly released it before turning back. "Next time, I'll be ready for you. And my name is *Logan*."

Adrenaline coursed through him. He wanted to fight, hated to walk away, but it was too dangerous for him to lose control, especially with so many people around.

Logan zipped up his jacket and walked to his Victory motorcycle. Before he put the key in the ignition, Akecheta's reflection in the black paint of his gas tank looked back at him.

"You can't keep running forever, Kohana, and when you are caught, I will be there to see you go down. Then you can join your parents where you all belong. In the grave."

Logan's composure melted. It was enough that his parents were dead; his father brutally murdered and his mother dead giving birth to him. He didn't have to stand there and listen to Akecheta insult his family.

He pulled back his fist, silver rings glinting on his fingers, and swung. His hand met only air and a rush of black feathers as Akecheta shape-shifted and lifted up high in the air. The crow cawed and seemed to laugh at him as it disappeared into the sky.

Logan shouted, letting the anger pour out of him. *Someday Akecheta would pay*. Wiping the sweat from his palms, he put on his gloves and started his bike. He ripped open the throttle, and the roar of the engine vented his rage and frustration. He kicked the bike into first and thundered down the street toward home.

Let's see them find me in Ireland. His bike growled through the empty streets.

Logan sighed, his anger evaporating. His thoughts turned to Rhiannon. From the moment he met her, he sensed her magic; and it was one of the reasons he loved her. As he got to know her, a seed of hope began to grow. Maybe she could help him master his power, maybe she could help him finally prove his innocence. Now he had to decide how to tell her and how to make her believe him.

Chapter 3

Rhiannon turned the last corner, headlights blazing, and the Elizabethan manor house that had been her childhood home in Ireland loomed upward like a bastion of rock in a sea of trees. Beyond the circular drive with the fountain, it rose three floors, the red stone exterior accented with white borders at the windows, balconies, and roofline. The short trimmed grass was still green, despite the lateness of the year. Tall chimneys reached upward into the night.

The sight made her feel both relief and terror. She was home, but what was she going to find inside?

Rhiannon sped into the driveway and skidded to a stop, opened the door and dashed for the house. At the entry, she grabbed the bronze ring and pulled the heavy oak door open. She looked back to make sure Logan followed her and saw him grabbing their luggage.

They had taken the first flight from Denver and now, many hours later, Rhiannon felt desperate for answers. Her stomach churned, and she kept thinking about the worst-case scenarios. What if Brennan was dead?

The door creaked on its hinges, opening into the great room. Logan joined her, and their boots echoed off the hardwood floors as they approached the grand staircase ahead. The scent of oak and wood polish brought a rush of memories. This had been her home since she was nine, since her mother was killed. A rush of love for her uncle filled her, immediately overshadowed by her fear that he, too, was gone.

"Mrs. McBride. Are you home?" Rhiannon shouted.

They heard the opening of a door, followed by approaching footsteps. The stately lady at the top of the stairs looked to be more of a grandmother than a housekeeper. When Rhiannon got closer, she tried not to stare at Mrs. McBride's disheveled hair and the bags under her eyes.

"I came as quickly as I could," Rhiannon said, meeting the woman halfway up the stairs and clasping her hands urgently. "Tell me everything."

"Let me show you." Mrs. McBride's voice quivered.

Rhiannon and Logan followed her back down the stairs to a closed door. The woman looked at Rhiannon, grimaced, and nodded toward the door.

The familiar scent of the library—leather, paper, and peat—met her nose, again stirring youthful memories, but the view of the scene inside shattered all the good feelings. The tall bookcases were torn, with great swaths of wood ripped free. A confetti of shredded paper covered every flat surface. Brennan's heavy desk was overturned, and the leather chairs cut with what looked like razor claws. The scent of smoke replaced the paper smell as Rhiannon stepped over a pile of books.

"What about the rest of the house?" Logan asked.

"Fine. It's all fine, except for here, and for the fact he's gone."

"Did the police find anything?" Rhiannon scanned the room.

"No, they didn't. I'll leave you two alone. Let me know if you need anything."

Rhiannon put a hand on Mrs. McBride's arm. "Thank you."

Rhiannon took a breath and turned her focus back onto the room. This place, the library, was her uncle's inner sanctum, the heart of the house, and everywhere she looked, the books that had been her companions over the long summer months of her childhood met her eyes. They were falling apart just as her life was. With an ache in her gut like someone had kicked her, she leaned against Logan. His arm circled her waist and she looked up into his face, trying to draw what strength she could from his eyes, but then pulled away. She didn't have the luxury of weakness. Her uncle needed her.

She kicked at the debris around the room, looking for anything the police might have missed.

Nothing.

Rhiannon felt like she was going vomit. She ran a shaky hand through her hair. She had hoped that when she got here, she would find something, anything to tell her what had happened. She clenched her hands into fists and stared out the window.

"I don't know what to do. It doesn't make sense." She threw her hands up. "Brennan is powerful man. For him to disappear like this, with no explanation and no hint of where he went isn't right."

"Whatever happened here, there was surely a fight. Maybe he didn't have time to communicate anything."

"No, you don't understand. He should have seen an attack coming, he should have made preparations."

"Anyone can be surprised. Why isn't it possible he was?"

"It's complicated."

"Complicated? I'm listening. Maybe, I can help."

"There's nothing you can do." Rhiannon flinched at the unintended heat in her words.

Logan's face flushed and he looked at her. "Nothing I can do?"

"I'm sorry. That's not what I meant. Just having you here helps."

"You are right that I can't help if you don't let me know what is going on. What aren't you telling me?"

Rhiannon didn't know what to say. This was her opening to spill everything. Maybe he could help? Even if he just listened to her talk it out.

"There is something I've kept secret from you," she said. "Mostly because I was afraid of what you might think of me if I told you."

Logan nodded, listening.

Rhiannon rubbed her hands down her jeans. "My family has kept alive the ancient teachings of the Druids, passing them down through the generations. I am an apprentice Druid."

Logan's eyes widened. "What is a Druid?"

Rhiannon smiled. "The Druids were the priests, doctors, and lawyers in pre-Christian Celtic society. They studied herbs, memorized genealogies, and made laws but also worked magic."

Rhiannon looked into Logan's eyes and saw curiosity but no condemnation.

"Magic?"

"Yes, magic. We believe that, by using the energy of nature, we can alter reality in small ways and use our will to make changes."

"I've heard of it, of course. My people believe that people can use magic to change shape, to take different forms."

"That would be a powerful magic."

"Why are you telling me now?"

"Because of my family's Druid blood, we have attracted enemies. I'm telling you now because I believe Brennan was attacked by the fae." Rhiannon crossed her arms and waited, hoping for the best.

"As in faeries?"

"Yes, but not the Disney type. These faeries can kill."

Logan scratched his neck. "It's a lot to take in, Rhiannon. I can see why you didn't tell me."

Sweat broke out on Rhiannon's forehead. "Do you believe me?"

Logan swallowed. "Yes, I believe you. I know you wouldn't make up something like that. I've had some experiences I can't explain myself."

Rhiannon let out a long breath, feeling relieved, and slowly smiled. "What kind of experiences?"

"I've seen people shapeshift."

Rhiannon stared at him. "Really?"

"In my tribe, there are some people who can take animal shapes." Rhiannon had never seen anything like that but thought it could be possible.

"I would like to see that sometime."

"It's not all that pleasant to watch really."

"I can only imagine."

This was the first time Logan had ever mentioned a tribe. Who were these people? Why hadn't he mentioned them before?

Rhiannon brought a hand up and touched her chin.

"Tell me about this tribe."

"They are my extended family. I grew up with them, but we had a falling out and I had to leave."

"What happened?"

"It's a long story. I don't really want to talk about it now."

Rhiannon narrowed her eyes and crossed her arms. "Now who's holding back?"

"I know, I know." Logan held up his hands. "So if the fae attacked your uncle, what does that mean?"

Rhiannon raised an eyebrow and gave a small smile. "Okay, I'll let you change the subject, but I want to hear more about this shapeshifter later."

Logan nodded. "I will tell you, just not now. So what about the attack?"

"It means if he is gone they will be coming for me next."

Logan blanched. "Coming to kill you?"

"Yes," she said. She paused, looking at her feet. "I wish I knew what to do, but I don't."

"You know it's been a long day. Maybe some sleep will help?" said Logan.

Rhiannon rubbed her eyes. "Okay, let's call it a night."

With a sigh, she took Logan's hand.

"I think you're right. It's time for bed. Tomorrow, let's go back through the library to see if we missed anything, then we can check the grounds. Maybe when we are fresh, in the daylight, it will be easier to figure it out."

* * *

At the top of the grand staircase stretched a long hall with several white doors. Rhiannon walked to the first one to the right and opened it. As soon as she stepped inside, her body relaxed.

This was *her* room. Everything about it was familiar, from the sitting room with the fireplace to her queen sized four-poster bed with the wooden supports carved to look like tree bark and the green canopy of fabric above. She let the room wrap her up like a warm blanket. She needed to feel support, to regroup, and of all the rooms in the house, this room gave her what she needed.

Logan set the luggage on the trunk at the foot of the bed. Rhiannon reached into one of her bags, pulled out her books, and placed them on her nightstand. She smiled at the sight of her old friends: *Irish Myths and Faery Tales, Don't Be Afraid of the Dark: Blackwood's Guide to Dangerous Faeries,* and her favorite, *The Druid's Guide to the Faery Folk.*

Logan sat on the bed and pulled off his engineer boots. "I'm going to grab a shower," he said.

Rhiannon looked up from unpacking. He'd taken off his shirt, and his wolf tattoo, which covered his left shoulder and the side of his bicep, stared back at her. She held her breath for a moment and touched her throat, feeling a sudden warmth. She hadn't seen Logan much because he had been on the road.

Suddenly, the idea of him in the shower made unpacking seem unimportant.

"On second thought, I think I'll join you," she said, running her hand over his tattoo.

Logan smiled at her over his shoulder, turned, and kissed her. "That's the best thing I've heard all day," he said as he led her to the shower.

His hands felt good on her body, his strength reassured her. She kissed him and unbuttoned his fly and helped him out of his jeans. As he reached around and undid her bra, the heat of his kiss flared. She pulled her jeans down and her panties. Logan pulled her closer.

Her relief about finally sharing some of her past made her feel so close to him. He had not laughed at her, but instead listened and offered support. Rhiannon turned on the hot water and took her lover under its steamy embrace. She let the water and Logan's attentions wash the terror of the last day away.

Being with Logan did for her what nothing else could. He made her feel loved. Even if she couldn't share everything with him, she could have this.

* * *

Rhiannon awoke to moonlight streaming through the stained glass window, painting her comforter in pale blue, indigo, and sage. She shivered, pulled the blankets up tight around her, and wondered what had awakened her. She reached over for Logan, to feel his warmth in the dark, but her hand found only cool sheets. Unsettled, she grabbed her glasses and looked around the room. She was alone. She looked toward the bathroom, but it stood dark and empty beyond its open door. A shiver ran through her.

"Logan?" she whispered to the darkness, but only silence responded.

Rhiannon pulled on jeans and a t-shirt, and grabbed her Druid bag from the nightstand. She stepped out into the hall. All was quiet. She looked down the stairs and froze. Red and brown leaves carpeted the landing. The hair rose on her arms.

Brighid, what is going on?

She stared at the open doorway at the foot of the stairs. Blue moonlight flooded the house, and the dark wind gusted into all the warm places. Rhiannon blinked, seeing but not wanting to see. She closed her eyes tight for a moment. She wished for her revolver, but there was no way to bring it on the plane, and Brennan didn't own any guns.

Gods damn it. Where was Logan?

She hurried down the stairs, looking for any sign of him. When she reached the landing, she grabbed her coat. Cold permeated the fabric. Almost frantic now, she pulled on her boots, grabbed a flashlight from a drawer in the credenza, and ran outside. In the frost covered grass, a set of footprints led off into the darkness.

"Logan!" she called out, following the prints. Her panicked voice echoed back sharply.

The prints led to the garden. The wooden gate stood ajar, and she pushed it open and followed the bricks that edged the open area. The prints started again on the grass and led toward the bridge over the lake. He had gone to the island, toward the ancient hawthorne in its center.

Her heart raced faster now. Logan was nowhere to be seen, and she knew he never would have come outside alone without waking her.

Not of his own free will, anyway.

The tracks stopped at the tree and disappeared.

"Logan!" she shouted, but only the wind in the dying leaves answered her.

She hugged her arms around her, biting her lips as she slowly approached, feeling dangerous vibes pulsing from the tree. The hawthorne was trying to push her away.

Rhiannon held the light unsteadily when it met the tree at ground level. The shaking beam revealed that the tree was inexplicably split wide, like a gaping wound, yawning into the earth. The smell of soil mixed with the smell of the decaying leaves, overwhelming her nostrils.

She leaned forward, shining the light into the heart of the tree. Instead of wood or earth, her light illuminated a way in and down. Rhiannon barely felt the biting wind as she realized with horror what the crack meant.

Her mouth fell open. This could also be where Brennan had gone.

And now Logan had gone inside the tree too.

Rhiannon shivered and felt a pain in the back of her throat. She rocked back and forth, tugging at her hair.

There was no sign of struggle. Even more, Rhiannon was convinced that Logan had not been under his own control. He never would have come here alone, let alone enter the tree. The only explanation was that *they* had taken *him*. She had expected the faerie to come, but for her, not Logan. What the hell was going on?

She clutched her hands into fists, her nails biting into her palms.

"Gods damn it!"

She shone the light as deep into the crack as it would penetrate. All she could see was retreating darkness, pulling back deeper into the earth. Her breath misted the air as she fought to make sense of what was happening.

"Logan!" she shouted into the gap. Silence.

Suddenly, the tree shuddered. The fracture grew tighter, slowly closing, shutting out the moonlight. The menace she felt amplified as she took her first step forward, and the rift at the center of the tree now stood just wide enough for her to squeeze through.

Rhiannon took the deepest breath of her life. Moisture coated her palms, despite the glacial air. She looked back at the house and wished she could go inside and grab a few things to help, but she had no time. If the tree closed all the way, she would be locked out, and who knew when it would open again?

She had but a moment to choose.

"Oh Brighid, my goddess, protect me now," she whispered to the wind. She clenched her fists even tighter, firming her resolve, and stepped inside.

Chapter 4

A twisted tunnel led downward, with large roots forming a rugged staircase into the depths. The bright beam of Rhiannon's flashlight slashed the darkness, revealing fine strands penetrating the walls of the passage, like centipede legs. They reached out like probing fingers, waiting for Rhiannon to descend. Using the roots like a ladder, she took her first step. The rounded protrusions were slippery, and her knuckles turned white as she gripped each one tightly.

She climbed as fast as she could, leaving the faint outline of the entrance way above her. She had to believe Logan was not that far ahead. She had to believe, if she hurried, she would soon find him.

The tendons in her wrists started to burn from gripping so hard. Afraid that her hold might give out, Rhiannon stopped and shook her hands one at a time, hoping to get more blood flow into her forearms. The thought of the tree closing behind her, sealing her in, filled her with panic. She squeezed her eyes shut and pushed everything else out of her mind. She had to find Logan.

Rhiannon opened her eyes and climbed with new determination. Sweat ran into her eyes, and she tasted the salt of the soil from the stray particles that found their way to her mouth.

The giant roots gave way to granite boulders, and the tunnel widened into a cave. She paused, took her coat off, and wrapped it around her waist. The flashlight picked up flecks of white and gold in the boulders, hints of brightness in this dark world.

She sat and slid slowly down to the next boulder beneath her. The surface of the rock was smooth, and she searched for rough spots to place her boots for traction. The flashlight beam danced crazily as she struggled to hold it and move carefully forward.

Her downward climb continued, her jeans and hands gritty with dirt. Her mouth was dry, and she was out of breath. Rhiannon stopped and shone her light down the incline, breathing hard. The tunnel wormed onward, seemingly without end.

She turned off her light to conserve the batteries while she caught her breath. In the darkness, her eyes adjusted, and to her amazement and disbelief, a faint light glowed. Startled, she stopped and listened. It was dead quiet. Keeping the light off, she slid down a boulder, and then another, and soon the light grew and she could see her sweaty scratched hands.

Rhiannon kept moving, encouraged by the radiance. She stopped abruptly and her hand rose to cover her mouth. A single luminous lavender flower, unlike any bloom she had ever seen, glowed just ahead of her.

It reminded her of a starlight rose, but it was even more beautiful. Its petals were blue with light lavender highlights, with deeper shades toward the heart of the flower. She reached out and gently touched its velvet petals, amazed at its perfection.

More purple light shone up ahead. She crawled around the delicate blossom, careful not to crush it, and two more appeared. Sweet perfume, like a thousand bouquets of wild flowers, filled the air from the open buds. Rhiannon continued on, past more of the beautiful florets, and the cave grew more open and bright. Like a burst of sunshine through a heavy cloud, light enveloped her in a shimmering amethyst whiteness as she crawled free of the cavern at last.

Blinking in the brightness, she took in her surroundings. Green grass, ferns, leaves of all shapes and varieties; umber earth and tree trunks; more of the azure blooms, but now they were everywhere, lighting the scene as it opened up before her. She stood in a rock archway on the edge of the great brilliance. As her eyes adjusted, she glimpsed even more color, followed by distant shapes.

"Unbelievable."

A wave of euphoria washed over her as she tried unsuccessfully to take it all in and make sense of the sight. As far as she could see, a meadow filled with luminous foliage—poppies, daisies, columbines and roses—opened before her. A steady purple brightness curved above her; no sun or moon, light radiated from everything. Large stones covered with lichen and moss, like paint on rough clay sculptures, were strewn throughout the meadow.

Unlike anything she had seen in even the loveliest places she'd visited, the beauty of it filled her with awe. This was nature in its uncorrupted, original purity.

Rhiannon took a step forward, then turned to look behind her. Above the cave, a sheer wall led nearly straight up, until it vanished in the light. A clear stream of silver water fell off to the left, crashing into a clear pond.

What is this place?

She looked around for any sign of Logan. At first, she didn't see anything, but when she looked closer she spotted U-shaped indentations in the ground. The hoof marks scattered in all directions, but the heaviest concentration led straight away from the wall. Whoever took Logan now had him on a horse.

"Gods damn it!" she cursed. "How I am going to catch up with him?"

She rubbed the back of her neck and had an idea. She reached into her bag and removed her pendulum. A stone of blue lapis lazuli, swirled with gold, hung at its end.

She sat down and struggled to calm her mind. Finally she pictured Logan in her mind's eye and let the pendulum down. At first, it didn't move at all, just stayed neutral. Slowly, it began to swing.

Rhiannon breathed, opened, and watched the weight begin to move back and forth in the direction most of the tracks led. Satisfied, she stood and put the pendulum back into her bag. *Well at least I know which direction he went.*

With a determined sigh, she started running. Soon, she discovered a trail leading the same direction. Several routes branched off the main one as she ran, but she stayed on the first, trusting her pendulum had been right.

Slowing to a walk to catch her breath, Rhiannon studied her surroundings, still not quite believing it all. She also realized she wasn't going to be able to run all the way after Logan. As much as she hated to slow down, she knew she needed to pace herself.

Soon, the grassland rounded into a large hill, and the stream descended to the left, leaving the heights for a woodland below. As Rhiannon moved amidst the tall grass, she brushed something like a dragonfly wing and twitched her hand back in surprise. A burst of vibrating sound buzzed her ears. She spun, but whatever it was disappeared.

In a few seconds, it whirred again, farther into the grass. Translucent wings, like those of a humming bird, carried it away, but, just as quickly, another one appeared, and then several more darted among the butterflies. Their quick whirring movements made her a little dizzy.

Rhiannon watched them with trepidation.

They were faeries.

Somehow, when she used to think about where the faeries lived, she imagined a dark place filled with monsters, but this place was beautiful. Like everything else, the winged creatures gave off light. Each one had a unique color; some fuchsia with a touch of violet, others emerald green with a silver shimmer. They looked like petite, six-inch people with whirring wings. The quick flashes of light played carefree amidst the swaying thistles and daisies, like watching fireworks that never went out. The bright colors changed and waltzed without end.

Hair rose on her arms and nape. Rhiannon drew in her elbows, trying to make herself as small as possible. She held her breath and waited.

Like a flock of sparrows, the faeries rose up into a cloud and floated toward her.

Instinctively, Rhiannon drew on the Nwyfre, the life force around her, and summoned a protective shield. A blue sphere of light enveloped her and she gasped.

"Look at that!" she said, unable to keep from laughing.

That had never happened before. The circle had always been more of a mental construct, something that she called on instinctively when she felt endangered. But now it glowed around her. Brennan had taught her about Nwyfre and she had felt it flowing in her before, but she had never seen it. He explained the Nwyfre is the energy of life, the power of nature and that it could be drawn upon to help her. She breathed deeply and watched the swarm of faeries approach.

The swarm hovered around her and a few tested the blue sphere, kicking and punching at it. One purple faerie took out a tiny bow and fired an arrow at her. The dart fizzled.

"A fledgling Druid," the faerie said and laughed. It sounded like the tinkling of bells.

"Don't see one of those every day," said another, getting his bow out.

"Now, wait a second. I'm not here to be your target practice."

The first faerie laughed again, and the sound was amplified by a hundred as the cloud of fae jingled with glee.

Rhiannon couldn't help but laugh herself, which set them all laughing again.

"You won't need that shield today, young Druid."

"Perhaps, but I'll keep it just the same."

"Oh! A prickly one! I like her," said the blue faerie.

Rhiannon felt beads of sweat on her upper lip. She looked all around her at the faeries. Small as they were, there were so many of them if they should decide to attack her she would have little chance against their numbers.

"I'd introduce myself, but I can't go giving out my name to strange Druids, you know," said the purple faerie.

Rhiannon swallowed and took a breath. She knew names held power, and she knew that if she could befriend these creatures, maybe they wouldn't attack her and she could get some much needed information that would help her find Logan. Maybe they could tell her where the pathway led. "Perhaps we could trade names?" she said.

The purple faerie put his hand to his face while he considered. "Very well, let me in and whisper it in my ear."

Rhiannon wasn't sure how to do that, but she agreed and mentally thought to allow the one faerie inside.

A whisper tickled her ear. It said, "Thistle."

Rhiannon nodded and whispered her name so only Thistle could hear.

"I knew it," shouted Thistle. "It's Rhiannon!"

Rhiannon opened her eyes wide. *Wait. How would these faeries know me?*

The flock looked surprised and amazed. Bright laughter rang out from all of them.

Rhiannon put her hands on her hips and frowned at Thistle. "It thought it was a secret between us."

"It is," he said. "Farewell, lovely Rhiannon, and beware the stone ring!"

Before she could ask anything further, the faeries flew high into the air and disappeared. She let her shield down. Apparently, not all faeries were intent on killing her. In fact, it was hard to imagine how any creature from this bright place could kill.

Rhiannon wondered what Thistle meant, but before she had time to ponder it, the stone ring appeared. Just ahead and to her right stood a knoll topped with a ring of standing stones. She didn't know how she had missed it before.

The question now was, should she heed the faerie's warning? Maybe some important clue waited there. She knew that, in mythology, there were many different faerie mounds, and she decided this was one of them. Maybe an ogam inscription on the stones would tell her which mound she was in, and that might help her to know who lived here.

The hill called to her. Its ancient stones sang with secrets of ages past. Rhiannon knew she could stop climbing toward them if she wanted to, but the information she might gain could be too important to pass up. She needed to find Logan, but it would be worth it to just take a minute. Despite Thistle's warning, she could not resist the urge to examine the stones more closely.

As she climbed the slope to the top of the hill, she thought about Brennan. She knew he'd come here before, and she wondered why he hadn't brought her himself? Maybe he didn't think she was ready? Maybe he was protecting her? But surely it would have been better to come with him than to be left stumbling around in this unfamiliar place all alone and unaware of its secrets.

When she reached the top of the hill, she wondered if this was how Stonehenge looked long ago. She walked slowly, taking in the view. Fragrant forget-me-nots and tiny violets grew in bunches on the ground. Heavenly blue morning glories climbed the stones, with their blue and white trumpets glowing rich cobalt and an iridescent pearl. Large black and yellow bumblebees buzzed lazily amidst the flowers.

The energy of the place washed over her in waves. Inside, it was warm, and the sky above was brighter, if that was possible. Rhiannon took off her boots and felt the soft earth through the soles of her feet. She stood, enraptured by the place, then walked forward, dropping her coat from her waist.

She came to the center and turned around. Shadows lay under each lintel, with bright light in the spaces in between, like the rhythm of light and dark that spoke to her of the rhythm of the year's light trading with dark in an endless cycle, winter following summer, and starting over again. A vague thought came to her, reminding her to look for ogam inscriptions. She glanced around dreamily but found none.

A cool mist descended on Rhiannon, washing the fatigue away. She breathed deeply, fully aware of the air entering her lungs. Living sparks of fire, bright orange embers of light, swirled and flickered around her as she spun with the creatures, feeling their light and warmth radiating tranquility.

Peacefulness fell upon her, and she basked in it. *Why did I come up here again?* Her mind grew very still, and the sound of distant running water was all she could hear. As her eyes grew heavy, one last thought filled her mind.

Why are there bones at my feet?

Chapter 5

Logan's wrists burned beneath the ropes. Gravity sawed at his flesh as he tried to keep his balance on the fast moving horse. The light above baffled him. Just a few hours ago, he had been lying in bed with Rhiannon on a dark night. Now he would guess that it was close to midday, and the sky was purple.

Where the hell am I?

Just as he had emerged from the tunnel beneath the hawthorne, a group of men grabbed him. He fought them, and bloodied three before they took him down. It happened so fast he had no chance to think of shifting before they clubbed him unconscious.

He tried to remember how he had gotten to the tree, but it was like a dream. He remembered waking up to the sound of distant music, and compelled to find the source, he got out of bed and dressed quickly.

Like an irresistible call or a forgotten dream, the music promised all his heart's desires. He hadn't even thought to wake Rhiannon. Powerless to resist, he followed the music to the ancient hawthorne.

It wasn't until he'd emerged from the cavern that the spell lifted. Immediately, he turned to go back—he couldn't leave Rhiannon—but he'd been attacked and captured. Despite his predicament, all he could think about was Rhiannon. She would wake to find he'd vanished, just like her uncle.

The clear air shimmered, casting a brilliant light around the armored man leading his gray horse. The open ground of the field sped by under galloping hooves. Butterflies scattered as the advancing troop cut through the long grass and wildflowers. Ahead, a dark forest waited, and beyond that, a craggy ravine. Logan counted twenty soldiers in black leather armor. He had to find a way to get free.

"You've made a mistake," Logan shouted to the nearest man. "I'm not who you think I am."

The guard ignored him, but glanced behind.

Twisting painfully, Logan followed the man's gaze. A cloud of dust rose on the horizon.

Pursuers.

Logan wasn't sure if he should be grateful or afraid. Maybe the pursuers would let him go, but they could just as easily kill him. The black guard spurred their mounts to greater speed, racing for the cover of the trees. They would make it, but the riders behind rapidly closed the gap.

The ancient forest of oaks, birch, and ash loomed over Logan's head. Fallen trees covered the ground in a tangled mess of crisscrossed trunks, like a tree graveyard. A two-track path parted the tree cemetery, allowing two riders at a time to pass under the ancient boughs. The group slowed to condense their ranks.

The soldier, who was leading Logan's horse, went first. The rest of the troop followed, guarding the rear. The forest road led upward, winding back and forth.

The sheltering trees soon crashed up against the bastion of stone that marked the cliff-lined passageway, like broken waves upon the shore. Red stone vaulted upward, reaching for the ungraspable sky. Hardly any shadow remained on the cliff faces in the full glare of daylight. Sweat ran into Logan's eyes, and he tried to shake it off. It stung and made him blink. The red dust from the horse in front of him coated his moist face and hands. He shifted uselessly, feeling helpless, and his eyes darted.

The screams of a horse and rider sounded nearby. The leader did not look back. He didn't have to. Pounding hooves echoed from the canyon walls like thunder as they rode.

Suddenly, the big man in front drew up hard, and Logan's mount did the same. He would have been thrown if he hadn't been tied on. Behind a wall of boulders strewn across the bottom of the ravine stood a small army of blue-faced men with long mustaches. Dressed in armor, their spears were tipped with leaf-shaped blades.

Logan swallowed hard. He tightened his leg muscles around his horse and looked around frantically.

"Out of our way, dogs," yelled the black leader. "Or you'll taste the Queen's wrath."

"Give us your prisoner and we'll let you go."

"We can't let these dogs have him," the leader said. "Aghamore and Gothfraidh, come with me. Mannuss, take the rest, attack the blue faces, and bring me the leader's head."

Logan bit his lower lip and squeezed his hands into fist, trying to decide what to do. He knew he didn't want to be anyone's prisoner. He hoped that the blue-faced men might set him free, he knew his captors wouldn't.

Mannuss charged toward the blue-faced men, with the rest of the black guard following. Shouting and cursing, they spurred their horses to ride down the spearmen. Outnumbered and out positioned, Logan thought them foolish to charge the spear points. The spearmen had excellent cover, and the light cavalry closed in from behind.

The more of his captors that died, the greater his chance for freedom, Logan thought grimly.

The blue faces gave a shout as the first horse leapt over the debris and into the waiting ranks of foot soldiers. Logan craned his neck as he was rushed away, trying to make sense of the chaos, but it was impossible for him to see.

The tumult faded as the ground pounded away beneath him. Now it was just he, the leader, and two remaining guards. His jaw unclenched and he allowed himself a breath. With only three guards, he stood a chance of breaking free—if he could just get untied.

The leader led them back the way they had come and took a different route. Two of his guards were ambushed by more of the blue-faced fighters at the edge of the trees. By the time they reached the open grassland, only Logan and the leader remained. They rode hard, and soon, they left their pursuers behind. He wasn't sure if he was happy to be getting away.

Who was this Queen, and why were people willing to kill to take him captive?

* * *

Darkness settled in and they stopped. The leader, who was now alone with Logan, put a hood over Logan's head before untying him from the horse.

"Don't get any ideas about running off. I have ways to make you pay that even *she* wouldn't notice."

Logan licked his lips and swallowed hard.

"Who is *she*?"

"Ha! You will find out soon enough. Now be quiet or you'll regret it."

The kidnapper tied Logan to an oak tree, and his numb hands screamed as the circulation returned. He fidgeted against the rough bark, his mouth gone dry. Finally, his hood was removed and he was given water and coarse bread. He couldn't eat, but he drank the water greedily. As the light faded, Logan decided what he would do.

He waited until the soldier was asleep then wriggled quietly, pulling his feet in. He pushed hard against the tree, using the strength of his legs to scrape himself up the trunk. He hoped that as the tree grew narrower his ropes would get loose enough to pull an arm out. The friction scraped the skin from his back, but he got his feet under him.

He stood breathing fiercely through his nose. He clenched his stomach willing himself to be quiet, to slow his breathing. He watched his guard with keen attention, looking for the slightest movement. When his breath had slowed, he shrugged his right shoulder. It came up but not enough. He tried the left and realized neither was going to give. The ropes were too tight.

Using his legs, he pushed to circle the tree, hoping to get around the back side, out of sight at least, thinking that maybe the circumference was uneven and the little bit of give he had earned would open just a little more.

Sweat soaked him and his back burned from the grating, but he moved. He ran into a low branch that he hadn't seen. It stopped him cold.

The man in front of him scratched at his face and rolled over.

Logan felt his heart pounding so loudly he feared that alone would wake the soldier. He took a deep breath and reconsidered. He knew the chances of scraping himself back around without waking his captor were slim, plus he decided it was very possible another similar branch awaited him.

He was left with only one choice; to use his magic.

Logan looked down at the ground, feeling his head starting to ache. He didn't want to do it. He hadn't shifted since the night his father was murdered and he had promised himself he wouldn't do it again, at least not until he learned to control himself after he changed. Since he had first shifted, he had a problem of losing himself in the animal and his human consciousness being shoved down so completely that he had no control and no memory of what happened.

He weighed the pros and cons. If he didn't shift, he would be taken to this queen, a prisoner. If he did shift, he could break free and escape, but he would be breaking his word to himself. He also might kill the soldier. *When I made that promise, I never imagined I'd be in this kind of situation*, he thought.

He shook his head slowly and frowned.

He didn't like it, but he had to try to get free he decided. He would have to break his promise.

He swallowed hard and brought his feet together, unhappy with his decision but not really seeing an alternative.

Logan concentrated. First came the pain, as always. He felt the terrible pressure building in his skull and in his spine. He gritted his teeth, steeling himself for what was about to happen, but the ropes that bound him glowed and burned. The change stopped. He tried again. Still nothing.

Logan clenched his fists and cursed.

The soldier turned his head, suddenly awake. "We'll have none of that. *She* said you might try to go animal on us."

"Wait, I'm sure there has been a mistake. Maybe we can work something out?"

The brigand stood and laughed. "I don't think so."

The club came down and all went dark.

When Logan woke, he was back on the gray horse. His head ached, and the galloping made it worse, but a strange new hope overshadowed his misery. His ropes had somehow kept him from shifting; if they could do that, maybe this Queen knew something about shapeshifting.

Maybe she could help him?

Chapter 6

Garth leaned over the water basin and washed the blue paint from his face. Glancing in the silver mirror, he watched the blue disappear as the white of his skin returned. Washing the paint away helped him separate the warrior from the family man. How could the same face that earlier witnessed the painful grimaces of those he killed to keep his family safe look upon his young son? It was a small thing, the blue woad, but it helped him keep his boundaries.

He hefted the stone basin, now filled with blue water, and poured it out into the ditch just outside the door. Deirdre would want to see him first, but she would have to wait. The King must know he'd failed him.

Garth's armor lay scattered around him, and his sword leaned against the wall. Oren would take care of the armor, but he never went anywhere without his sword. He grabbed the iron and bronze leaf blade, pulled it free from its scabbard, and found some stray streaks of gore, which he cleaned off. He polished it with a soft sheepskin and oiled it before sheathing it again.

Next, he donned a white linen tunic trimmed in purple and belted it at the waist over his bracae. He added a gold torc and rings. Finally, he laced up his leather boots and put on his black and gold checked wool cloak with the dragon pin.

Garth double checked his clothes and left his arming house for the mead hall. He glanced briefly at his roundhouse, where he knew Deirdre would be waiting for him. He wanted to go to her, to have her help cleanse the horrors of the day away, but duty came first. He turned his gaze and feet toward the courtyard.

The open courtyard of the timbered fortress was full of activity. Warriors fresh from the fight ate roasted pork and fixed broken straps on their leather gear. Not everyone had the luxury of help to replace popped rivets and polish the bronze and iron plates. Some would say Garth had it good, but he knew the cost of his luxuries. Being a son of the king came with much responsibility.

Enticed by the delicious smell of meat, he cut a slice off a roast that Angus basted on a spit. Garth slapped him on the back and smiled at him. The pork was moist, and the juice ran down into his beard as he walked. He began to feel at home.

Garth walked through the center of the villages, dodging chickens and geese. He hiked down the dirt street, surrounded by roundhouses. The familiarity of their wattle and daub walls and tall, pointed thatched roofs eased his mind. At the end of the houses, he mounted the steps and climbed the hill to the great hall.

Four spearmen guarded the double doors. One of them nodded to Garth as he strode past unchallenged. The large round hall, often full of many tables and great platters of food, now overflowed with warriors standing in a crowd near the wooden dais of his aged father. Some of them he recognized as his father's inner council.

He stared up at the tree in the center of the hall which sat on a raised mound. Gnarled roots dug into the ground, like a hand grasping the earth itself, clinging desperately to life. Bark was stripped away in many places, exposing gray wood beneath.

The large tree stood guard over the proceeding, its trunk above and behind the king's throne, and its skeletal branches, mostly stripped of foliage, reaching out fingerlike forming a distant canopy over the chair. The hawthorne tree crouched over the men, as if it needed to be closer to hear what was happening. Its near leafless boughs reminded Garth of the nearly bald head of his father. Above, the roof opened up to let in the lavender glow of day.

The men parted to let Garth through to his father's seat, and turned their attention to the throne. He took a knee at the bottom of the stairs, lowered his head, and only rose when his father, Conor, gave him permission. Garth looked up, nodded to his father, and stood.

"Though we killed many of Morrigan's men, one was able to escape with the overlander you sent us for," he said, feeling that the hall had suddenly gotten too hot.

The King's eyes smoldered. "Tell me everything."

"We came upon them too late. They had already quit the

gateway and were riding fast toward the forest. I sent Aodhan and Cathaoir to pursue them with a dozen horsemen, but most came with me to the narrows where the road to Morrigan's land enters the canyon. We set up an ambush and waited for them.

"Morrigan's troops charged us in the rocks while three sidhe and the overlander escaped into the trees from which they had come. Aodhan realized what was happening too late but pursued them anyway. He caught and killed two of them, but the third escaped with the prisoner."

"This is grave news, Garth." The king's face turned red and the vein in his forehead pulsed.

Garth exhaled hard. The failure was his. He tilted his head down and frowned. He looked up again. "I will do what I can to make it right."

The king took a breath and his color returned to normal. "What is done is done, but perhaps there is a way." He paused for a moment, then turned his gaze to the assembled warriors.

"My friends, this is a dire hour," he said. "Morrigan has succeeded in capturing the overlander, and it will go ill for our people if he is won over to her cause. We will have to trust that he will see through the Morrigan's deceptions and know she is evil and corrupt. It is out of our hands now."

He stood from the throne. "However, now is not the time to be complacent. It is time for us to act! The hawthorne is dying, and we have waited long enough to try to restore it. With the overlander gone, our hope of his help is gone too. The Morrigan will be emboldened by her success and will soon attack. We need to find the Well of Wisdom and bring the Water of Life here to restore the tree."

Immediately, the room buzzed. A few nodded and shouted their support for the king, but the louder voices were argumentative.

"We've heard this before," shouted Dermot, one of the king's advisors. "What we need are more men and better arms."

"Silence!" shouted the king. When the roar quieted he spoke again. "Arms and might have indeed kept the way protected, I agree. But the ancient magic of our fore-bearers is fading and, without its help, we will be overrun."

Garth's stomach hardened and he clenched his jaw. This debate had been going on for too long. It was time they made a decision before it was too late. They needed to stop arguing and do what must be done.

Garth clasped his hands and took a breath. "The Morrigan grows in power, and soon we will not be able to stop her. We all know the truth though it hurts our pride. We are a strong and brave people, but without the tree Morrigan will kill us all. We need the Water of Life."

"No one knows where to find the Water of Life," said Bran. He paused and looked pointedly at Garth. "What we need is to teach Morrigan and her people that they are indeed prisoners here and that we will never let them leave, tree or no tree."

"Force of arms has kept the way blocked, but that is only because the hawthorne has thrived. But look at it now." Garth gestured upward. "It is fading before our very eyes."

"I say we plan a raid on Morrigan to teach her a lesson," said Bran.

Several in the crowd shouted their agreement.

Garth shook his head, his pulse quickening. *Bran always wants a fight*, he thought. *How can he not see the truth?*

"No one doubts your courage Bran, but your plan simply won't work," Garth said shortly.

"No one doubts your courage either, Garth, but why place our only hope on an old tale?"

"That old tale is why we are here. It is why we left the world above. It is our sacred trust to restore the tree."

"Much of what Bran says I agree with," said the king. "We must remind Morrigan who is in charge. Tree or no tree, we must hold Morrigan back." He paused, waiting for the room to quiet again. "However, Garth has the truth of it. I will not be the first king to dismiss our history and beliefs. While we will place most of our faith in the proven strength of our clan, we will also search for the Water of Life. We cannot spare many men to attempt this quest. It will take someone with some Druid learning to accomplish this task. Someone who will be able to read the signs to find the way. Are there volunteers?"

The crowd fell quiet. Men looked to Bran as the oldest son, and to Aron as the second oldest. The two merely kept their eyes on their father and remained silent.

Garth knew that, of his brothers, he was the most schooled in Druid lore. Bran was strong, but rash. Aron was more levelheaded, but no student of trees and their mysteries.

"I will go," he said. "It only seems right that I should be the one to make this attempt. To relieve the debt I owe for my failure today."

A murmur of approval passed through the crowd. No one objected.

Conor nodded. "You are right to take on this task. With your talents of strength, learning, and wisdom, I believe you are the only one who can see it done. Say no more of what happened today. This task relieves any mark on your honor, if there ever was one."

The hall murmured in quiet discussions, but Garth paid no attention, instead thinking about the Well of Wisdom. Legend had it that somewhere in the mound was a well, said to predate the creation of the mound itself, whose water could restore health to anyone or anything. But in all their years, no one had seen any hint that it actually existed.

Garth knew what his father said was true. If the hawthorne died, there would be no chance of his people fulfilling their ancient trust. The imprisoned faerie of Morrigan would be set free upon the world above, and with her power restored, she would kill them all on her way out.

Glancing around the hall, Garth studied the faces of his father, his brothers, his people. His hand tightened around his sword. He could not let them down.

I will find the well and restore the tree.

Chapter 7

Garth knew he should stay in the hall and help his father, but exhaustion from the raid was catching up with him, and he wanted a little time with his family. Bran and Aron could help Conor. No one would find fault with him wanting to spend the afternoon with his newborn son and his wife, especially since he would soon be busy making preparations for this quest. Determined to find his family, he left the mead hall.

Walking across the common area toward home, he took another slice of pork on his way, but did not pause or wander. He was almost to his door when Brennan appeared next to him. He was dressed in a green hooded robe and carrying a staff; a golden torc with matching dragon heads hung around his neck.

"Shouldn't you be with your father?" Brennan asked.

"Shouldn't you?"

"Perhaps we both should, but I wanted a word with you in private."

"Very well, come inside." Garth knew the Druid did as he pleased and didn't find it unusual that Brennan was not with the King.

Garth opened the heavy oak door that led into his house. A fire burned in the hearth, and the scent of fresh bread filled his nostrils.

Deirdre sprang up from her seat near the blaze and embraced him. Her tall, slender frame fit him perfectly, and he delighted in her laughing blue eyes.

"Well, you look none the worse for wear," she said, smiling. "I'm glad you made it back in one piece."

"You are not alone in that feeling," said Garth. "Where is that son of mine?"

"He's just fallen asleep, but I'm sure, now that you are

home, he won't be for long."

"I'm not really that loud, am I?" Garth asked with a laugh.

The laugh was proof enough as the baby stirred.

"You know Brennan, of course?" Garth asked Deirdre.

"Yes, of course," she said, nodding. "But I've never had the pleasure of a private visit from our Druid. I did not prepare much of a meal for such a guest, but you are welcome at our table."

"I won't be staying. I just wanted a word with your husband," said Brennan.

Deirdre left the two men alone and went to check on the baby.

"Why weren't you at the council?" Garth asked.

"I wanted it to be clear that the quest for the Well of Wisdom was your father's idea, not mine."

Garth raised a brow. "Did you think it wouldn't go over well coming from you?"

"Let's just say that Bran doesn't share your respect for the Druids and leave it at that."

Garth was curious what had brought the Druid to his home. He had always been a bit in awe of Brennan who held so much knowledge and power. Despite that, he genuinely liked the man. "So what's on your mind?" Garth asked.

"This quest you've volunteered for is no small thing. I know you feel that it falls to you, but it should not be undertaken lightly and without careful consideration."

Concerned, Garth nodded.

"You should enlist Niadh to help you."

Garth crossed his arms, his stomach turned to acid and his face flushed. "Niadh! That bastard? Never!"

"I know there is bad blood between you, but I want you to consider it," said Brennan.

"I can tell you now that it's no. I will bring some others, but not him," said Garth.

"I don't ask without good reason. I did an ogam divination about this journey. The clearest message is that deception and trickery will have a heavy influence on your success or failure. The signs said the best way to counter the deception is with an estranged friend who has been reconciled."

"We are not reconciled."

Brennan stared at Garth. "I don't ask you to decide now.

Just think on it."

"Could your reading have been wrong?"

"There is always that chance, but this reading was quite clear."

Garth widened his stance and clenched his fists. "You know I respect you, Brennan. Because of that I will consider it, but don't hold any false hope that my mind will change."

"That is all I can ask," said Brennan. "We will speak more later." He grasped Garth on the shoulder and took his leave.

Garth sighed. He had accepted an enormous responsibility and sacrifices would have to be made, but he never imagined bridging the rift with Niadh would be part of it. Garth rubbed the middle of his forehead to ease the sudden headache. On the one hand, he would feel relief to finally resolve things with Niadh, but on the other hand he didn't see how it was possible. Anger at what had happened between them still smoldered.

He walked into the side room and Deirdre stood there holding the baby. He wrapped his arms around her and his son, closing his eyes for a moment. Being with his family helped soften the impact of his conversation with Brennan. He explained all that had happened. "Can you believe what Brennan is asking of me?"

"It would seem you have already volunteered for it," she said, stepping back.

"You know what I mean, the part about Niadh."

"I'd say that's the least of your concerns. Did you give any thought to what leaving us behind might mean? You could be killed."

Deirdre stared at him, eyes softening. "I'm sorry. It's just that you've just come home from a dangerous raid, and now you are about to leave again. I know that restoring the hawthorne means more than just protecting our people. It means honoring our family's vow to protect the world above from Morrigan."

Garth held out his arms to hold his son. He looked into the blue eyes of little Wil and back at Deirdre. "*This*, right here, is the most important reason, keeping you and Wil safe. If I fail, the Morrigan will regain her full power, and on her way back to the surface, she will kill every one of us. She will swim in a sea of blood, our people's blood. She must be stopped, and I must do this."

"I think you have your answer about Niadh."

Garth looked his wife in the eye and nodded. "It's time to get ready. The sooner this is done, the sooner I can come back to you."

Garth grabbed an empty pack and left the roundhouse.

Chapter 8

Garth arrived late to the feast at the great hall, having lingered too long making preparations. The first thing he noticed was the smell of stew flavored with rosemary. It made his mouth water, but it wasn't yet time to eat.

The fires in the great hall changed how the atmosphere felt inside. The yellow and orange flames danced happily and lit the walls with a honey glow, a stark contrast to the daytime light. Garth took off his cloak, the temperature inside being too hot; even the open partition in the ceiling did little to cool the place down. Most men sat at tables throughout the hall, talking and laughing, while a few others stared into their cups.

He took a horn of honey beer from Breda, his friend Cathaoir's daughter, and walked through the crowd. The beer was frothy and good, but his thoughts were elsewhere. He didn't intend to stay long. Soon, he would leave on the quest for the Well, and many preparations remained.

Though Garth felt distracted, the feast was being held to honor the warriors who had died from the raid. It would have been remarked upon if he had missed it. He also wanted to talk to his father and ask his advice.

The Celts now packed the hall, dressed in their best clothes; tunics of linen and wool made with bright tartans, jewelry of gold and silver set with bright stones. Pitchers of beer were dipped in the communal bronze cauldron and carried through the crowd, filling every horn. Garth made his way to the head table where his father sat on a large throne with his faithful wolfhounds resting on either side. He reached down and scratched one of them behind the ear before he took the empty seat next to his father.

"I wondered when you might turn up," said Conor.

"I'm sorry, Father. I just have a lot on my mind." Garth

sank into silence for several moments, until he noticed his father watching him. "I know I need to go on this quest. Brennan says it must be done, and I've given my word that I will do so, but I don't know where to start. What if the Well doesn't exist anymore? What if it never did, despite what Brennan believes?"

"That may be true," Conor agreed. "However, it must be attempted. We can leave no path unexplored if we are to best Morrigan. I'm not the young man I once was, so it falls to you, my son, though I dread the thought of having you far from here during these dark times. Your brothers, though they are cunning and powerful warriors, would not be right for this quest. They have not sat by the Druid's fire as often as you have."

Conor sighed, his expression solemn. "You and Niadh are the best we have. Together, you once made a formidable pair. I hate to see your differences continue to divide you."

"I already told Brennan I'd think about it." Garth tried not to show his irritation. Clearly Brennan and his father had conspired together.

"This quarrel is just about a horse, isn't it?"

"Niadh helped raise my horse, Cadifor, and I won him in a tournament while he was out on patrol."

"It seems like a small thing," said the King.

"That is merely how it began."

"You would ignore the request of our Druid and your King, endangering all of our people, because of a horse?"

Garth felt his face turn red, and he took a long drink from his horn before answering. "I said I would think about it."

"For all your good qualities, your bullheadedness does you a disservice."

"I'm not being bullheaded." Garth looked away and took another swig from his gold-banded horn. Across the hall, torches flickered near the doors as more people entered, Niadh among them.

Garth thought back to the good days with his friend. They shared many adventures and too much ale. He frowned, remembering the bitter words spoken. What had started as a stupid thing turned personal, and he couldn't forgive the words said in haste. A duel would have settled it, but neither wanted the other dead. They just wanted the other to be wrong and admit it.

Platters of pork and fish were brought in, and the men set to with gusto. Garth ate his food mindlessly, his thoughts elsewhere. More beer came and as the fighters pushed back their benches, the entertainment arrived.

Six men with drums, pipes, and kilts took a spot on a small stage at the side of the hall. A young woman took up her place at the head of the musicians. Though she was a new addition, the drummers were welcome regulars, and Garth loved the thumping, pounding drive they made. He leaned back, prepared to listen.

One of the Bards in training, the girl began to sing, accompanied by a harp. Her song made Garth long for something far away. He could not name it, but it was a sweet longing, like a pleasant dream that melted in the light of day, a hint of some ancient memory that promised wisdom and fulfillment.

Her voice drifted away and silence filled the hall for a moment, before applause broke the spell. Next, the drummers erupted into a thunderous rhythm. They played vigorously while the crowd shouted and thumped along. Soaked in sweat, the drummers finally stopped for flagons of mead.

Conor stood from his high seat. "What is the code?" he shouted.

His men cheered, the question familiar. "Truth in the heart, strength in the arm, and honesty in speech!"

"You are the finest warriors and do this king great honor. Drink up, lads, to honor our fallen dead."

The men raised their cups and drank. A moment of silence followed.

"Let us mark the departure of our brothers with funeral games," said Bran.

"What shall it be, brother?" asked Garth. "A test of words, a test of arms, or a test of truth."

"I say a test of arms!" Bran replied.

Conor nodded. "I will offer a prize to make it more interesting." He hefted a bronze and gold helmet over his head so all could see.

A raised golden image of Cernunnos, the antler headed god, sat cross-legged just above the brow of the helm. The antlers spread high and wide across the whole front. The nasal guard and the cheek plates were decorated with bright golden knot work, while a black horsehair crest crowned the top. The horsehair fell down the back, creating a long tail. The warriors roared with enthusiasm at the magnificent prize.

Garth held in a breath and stroked his beard. He gazed at the prize and smiled. He knew he could win it and by winning the prize he could encourage more men to come with him on his quest. Maybe then Niadh wouldn't be so important.

"Surely only a strong person could win such a prize, and since it is a mighty prize, I propose three tests," said Conor. "The first shall be the testing stone; the next, the test of spears; and the last, the test of running. Anyone may enter, but failure in one means failure in all."

Finally shaken from his deliberations, Garth rose to his feet. He lined up with the other men and stood before a sand pit where the testing stone lay. Grim satisfaction overtook him when Niadh joined them. Here was a chance for Garth to prove he was the best of them all. Niadh often refused the games, but not this night.

Bran went first. He stepped into the ring, squatted low, and wrapped his heavily muscled arms around the slippery stone. Using the power in his legs, he lifted it high over his head and threw it back to the sand with a grunt. Aron went next, and then Garth. Garth smiled as he slapped Bran and Aron on the back; they had all lifted the stone.

The rest of them tried. Niadh easily lifted the awkward weight. Others did not do as well. Some let the stone slip and fall, and some simply did not have the strength to heft it overhead. Garth watched those who did not pass take their seats in quiet shame. He was proud to still be standing.

Next came the test of spears. A warrior, with shield and sword, stood in a waist-high hole in the floor near the sand pit while nine men surrounded the pit with spears at the ready. Each hurled his spear, either alone or a few at a time. If the warrior escaped without so much as a scratch, he was allowed to continue.

Bran again went first, and though many spears were cast at once, he was able to dodge and deflect with such speed that he showed not a nick. Triumphant, he started to boast. He realized too late that Garth had waited to cast his weapon. As Bran turned toward him, Garth launched the spear and nicked his brother's arm.

Bran roared with fury and clamored out of the pit. He grabbed Garth in a headlock. "Gods damn it, Garth. I knew it would be you if anyone would be wily enough to cut me."

Garth smiled and wrestled himself away. Bran would now try his best to retaliate, but first, Aron was up. Garth hurled his spear early and missed. Aron proudly emerged without a cut and was allowed to continue. He stood alone for the moment, waiting on the other warriors to finish.

Next in line, Garth kept a careful eye on Bran. Four spears were cast and Garth dodged them, and four more. Bran looked at Garth, smiled, and handed his spear to Niadh. Garth's palms grew sweaty, and he watched Niadh with narrowed eyes.

Niadh circled the pit and cast at Garth's torso, the hardest shot to dodge. Rather than ducking, Garth leapt high in the air and cleared the spear, which stuck in the wall of the pit.

"A mighty throw, *Niadh*!" said Garth, climbing out of the pit. "But you missed."

The bystanders laughed and slapped Garth on the back.

Garth laughed breathlessly and enjoyed the camaraderie with the others. He looked at the remaining men who had succeeded in the pit, all good men. The last test would be hard fought. Garth stood next to Aron, and around him the others— Niadh, Cailte, Aodhan, and Oisin—lined up for the last test.

"The last test shall be a foot race around the training course," announced the King. "Run through the loop in the forest and back to the hall. Each of you shall have two braids tied in your hair. If you finish first but your braids have been pulled by twig or branch, you will forfeit to the next man. You will start at the front gate with only tunic, kilt, and shoes, no weapons or armor."

"But I haven't got any hair!" shouted Aodhan as he rubbed his bald pate.

"Then you have the advantage over the others," laughed the king, who had little enough hair of his own.

Garth smiled, knowing Aodhan would take it hard if he won only because he had no braids. He was one of Garth's closest friends, and running was not his strong suit. But Aodhan would give it his all with his usual good cheer.

This test pleased Garth because he was fast, but he had good competition; both Cailte and Aron were fierce racers. And Niadh was not only fast, but cunning as well. Garth didn't know what to expect from him, but the others would try to tackle the faster ones and get ahead by throwing them down.

Garth left his sword with Oren and walked to the gate. By

now, many had heard what was happening and gathered around, including Deirdre. She smiled at her husband, and he knew she anticipated the honor he would bring to their family. She braided his blond hair at the temples and tied them tight. She didn't want to be blamed if the braid came undone.

The six fighters stretched and made sure their shoes were tied tight. Conor and Bran climbed the tower and looked down on the competitors.

The king hung the helmet from a long leather thong just over the gate. "The first one back will claim this prize. Ready yourself. When I strike the bell the race will begin," he said.

Garth smiled at his wife and little Wil. He looked thoughtfully at Niadh and wondered how they could get past their bitterness. He took a breath and focused on the race.

Conor struck the bell, and the men were off. They raced down the steep slope, and past the wheat fields. Aodhan made a grab for Garth, but Garth ducked away. He avoided the front of the pack and was glad to let Cailte lead. Garth knew from experience it was harder to run at the front at the beginning of the race and it tired you out.

Once they cleared the fields, they raced amidst sleeping cows. Niadh made a grab for Aron's braids and pulled them hard enough to frazzle them. Aron was done.

The five of them soon reached the edge of the forest. They ran over a small bridge and into the woods. A steep slope led them upward. Now the slower ones fell behind, while Garth, Niadh, and Cailte took the lead. Logs had been placed along the trail at different heights. Garth followed Cailte, and they jumped over ever-higher obstacles. Niadh raced just behind, and Garth had to make sure he didn't get close enough to snatch his braids.

At the crown of the hill, the slope turned sharply downward, and the men ran as fast as their feet would carry them. Sweat ran into Garth's eyes and, when he blinked, he nearly fell over a low boulder. Niadh gave a shout when Garth stumbled and Niadh surged forward, thinking he had the edge, but Garth pushed forward too, knocking Cailte aside. The former friends glared at each other and ran that much harder. Niadh was the faster sprinter, but Garth was better for longer distances.

A mud bog awaited them at the bottom of the hill. Niadh leapt to a boulder and over the worst of the mire, but Garth missed it and splashed down, knee deep, losing him precious seconds and bringing Cailte closer on his heels.

Free of the bog, Garth looked at the path ahead. The trees gave way to open ground, and the golden helmet glinted in the torchlight. He summoned all his strength and sprinted up the hill to raucous applause.

Niadh turned to see Garth gaining on him, and in that instant, tripped in a rabbit hole and went down. Garth knew he could easily leap over him and claim the prize, but a thought came to him. Maybe if Niadh won, it would help heal the wound between them. As much as he would love to have that helmet, he knew the quest was more important. If he could let Niadh win, if he could let go of his resentment, he could honor Brennan and his father's wishes.

He felt his stomach clench. He closed his eyes for an instant and let himself be tripped by Niadh's legs and fell into the dirt. Niadh untangled himself from Garth, leapt clear of him, jumped for the helmet, and grabbed it!

Garth lowered his chin to his chest and shook his head. He hoped his sacrifice was worth it.

Cheers and applause welcomed the champions back to the fort. Niadh held his prize high over his head and looked back at Garth.

Garth stood, brushed the dirt away, and nodded. "Good race, Niadh."

Niadh smiled broadly. Garth let out a huge breath and felt the tension drain from his muscles. He knew he had done the right thing. Maybe now the two of them could work together. Maybe the quest had a chance.

Chapter 9

Rhiannon forced her eyes open. She blinked hard and looked down to see the grass had grown over her feet. Confusion wrapped itself around her, and she fought to remember what happened.

She was still standing so that was a good sign, but how long had she been here? Bones lay scattered all around her, with many hidden in the deep grass. Her heart raced. How did all these bones get here?

The enchantment of this place must have captured many before her. They might have died in a blissful sleep, but they were still just as dead. Rhiannon wondered what brought her back, how she had been saved.

Instinctively, she brought her hand up and felt for her awen pendant through her t-shirt. Its shape always comforted her. She let out a little gasp when her finger landed on its face; it was hot to the touch.

Her pendant must have saved her. The gold medallion had been a gift from Brennan when she turned eighteen, and she never went anywhere without it. Whatever power Brennan put into it had clearly saved her. The others had not been so lucky.

An urgent prodding filled her mind, like she needed to do something, but she couldn't remember what. It rushed back at her. She blew out a series of short breaths, trying to regain control. Nausea gripped her as she remembered that Logan had been taken, that he'd already had a big lead on her before she had been trapped. Grabbing her shoes and coat, she stormed out of the circle.

From the safety of the path, Rhiannon looked back at the standing stones with regret. The cost had been steep, and she had learned nothing. There had been no inscriptions.

Her hope of catching Logan quickly was gone. He was on horseback, traveling much faster than she could match, and now she had been asleep. For all she knew, she had been just like Rip Van Winkle and slept for twenty years.

She rubbed the back of her neck and had an idea. She let her hair down from her ponytail and checked its length. Rhiannon laughed a shaky laugh. It was the right length. At most, it had been a week, though a week was far more time than she could afford.

Tears filled her eyes. *I'm failing.*

Logan had been taken right from her own bed, then she wandered senselessly into the ring of stones, despite being warned against it. If it weren't for Brennan's pendant, she would have died there.

O'Neil, you need to get your act together, now.

She wiped the tears with her shirt, set her jaw, tightened her fists, and continued down the path. Logan might be far ahead of her, and it might take her a long time, but she would find him.

The track of wet sand led downward, away from the high prairie. Yellow light, warm like sunflowers, poured through the air, covering the ground. In the distance, a forest rose up like a wave of green water about to crash on a sun soaked beach. She could see a dark opening punctured the frozen green crash, threading its way into the depths. Then the smell hit her. Something dead rotted nearby.

She edged closer, covering her nose, and found a corpse. A decaying soldier and his putrid horse lay in the grass. The man wore armor, and beneath the helmet, his face was beginning to decompose. A single sword cut sliced halfway through his neck.

Rhiannon swallowed hard, steeled herself, and peered closely. The man's ears were pointed, and his eyebrows arched too high for a human. His flat, unfocused eyes were a deep purple color.

She staggered away from the carnage, trying to keep from vomiting. Who was this dead warrior and who killed him? The man was clearly another kind of faerie creature. If he had been one of Logan's captors, maybe the killer had rescued Logan. It was too much to hope for, she told herself.

Rhiannon held her breath, took three steps forward, and took the man's sword. She buckled the scabbard to her waist. It was loose, so she cut a new hole in the belt with the sword point and cinched it tight. It felt strange to wear the sword of a dead man, but it made her feel stronger nonetheless. She strode way, leaving the dead man behind.

Ahead, the forest waited. Tall oaks rose up from the brown loam. Gnarled roots created a maze in the underbrush. Two enormous trees stood sentry-like over the path into the forest, forming an arch overhead. Craning her neck back, Rhiannon realized the top of the canopy was easily two hundred feet away. In the upper branches of the magnificent oaks, splashes of color moved amidst the boughs; bright gold, sky blue, and deep lavender spheres frolicked in the arms of the great trees.

Rhiannon rested her hand on the sword and stepped under forest's green canopy. The sword gave an unfamiliar comfort. She didn't know how to use it, but it was better than nothing. The dark ground quieted her footsteps as she walked. She watched continuously for a sign of Logan's passing, but found nothing. She wished CuChulain was with her, but she shoved that thought down before it gutted her.

The footpath continued, now winding through a sun-dappled grove. The brook suddenly turned from its course, heading left, leaving the path, and plunging into a deep furrow. The lushness of the foliage began to intrude on the pathway, slowing Rhiannon's progress.

The rocky path cut through wild raspberry bushes in full fruit, and years of leaves covered the ground. Rhiannon stopped and looked at the berries. Her stomach growled and she reached out, then pulled her hand back.

I know if I don't find Logan and Brennan soon I will have to eat, but not yet.

She knew from the old stories that there was a prohibition against eating food in the faerie mounds. In addition to the raspberries, all around her were medicinal herbs, chickweed, vervain, and lavender. She loved the bouquet of scents.

The light faded to a soft butternut. She looked around her and white bearded little men appeared walking amidst the tree roots and lighting lanterns, both on the ground and up in the trees. Beyond the small glen, forest spirits of every kind surrounded her. The gnomes gathered kindling and gazed up into the fading light coming through the canopy.

She approached one of them. "Excuse me. Do you know where this path leads?"

The grizzled creature shook a fist at her, turned his back,

and walked away. "Go away. Leave me alone."

Rhiannon followed him. "It's an easy question. Where does this path lead?"

"You know, you are lucky we are ignoring you. Go away before my brothers and I change our mind."

"Okay, okay." Rhiannon held up her hands.

I need to find someone who can give me information, otherwise I'm just flying blind.

The path meandered off into the forest, and Rhiannon followed it into the shadowy twilight, glancing at the trees and the luminous orbs that sparkled in the near dark. The trail climbed higher, and reddish brown stones rounded out of the earth, pushing aside bramble and creeper.

The lengthening shadow brought a chill to the moist air, and Rhiannon put her coat back on. Soon, she heard the distant roar of a waterfall. She quickened her pace. The purple light of twilight withered, and true darkness began to settle in. She could barely see the path now.

Thwack, Thwack, Thwack.

A sound echoed through the night. Rhiannon stopped and held her breath, listening intently. The pattern continued. What was that? After several moments, she steeled herself and pressed forward.

The chopping grew louder. Mighty whacks echoed through the tall pines and oaks. Rhiannon hugged her arms around herself. She wanted to turn and go back to the meadow and wait for the light, but she had delayed enough already. She must press on.

Body on high alert, she crept through the forest, toward the sound. In the dark, she could do little more than stumble from trunk to branch to fallen log. The self-luminous orbs and pixies above barely shed enough light for her to trip toward the noise.

Just as she considered using her flashlight to see, the din stopped. She heard crunching steps and the closing of a door. All was quiet. Her heartbeat sounded in her ears as she held her breath.

Rhiannon searched for the source of the sounds, listening and looking intently. Through the trees, a door appeared. Hope gave her a jolt.

The portal was enormous. She had never seen anything like it before. The handle itself stood taller than she, and the lintel reached more than twice that height. Strange hoof marks, the size of dinner plates, covered the ground.

Maybe this wasn't such a great idea after all, she thought, starting to turn. The door opened, and a splash of hot water hit her in the face. She jumped back with a curse, wiping the hot water from her eyes.

"What's this? What do I have at my door?" said a deep voice from within the cabin.

Rhiannon cleared her eyes enough to focus. Bad idea. A furry creature with a long snout, dark eyes, and horns loomed above her. Panic rooted her to the ground.

"You're no faerie." The voice turned hostile.

"No, no I'm not, but I mean you no harm," Rhiannon stammered.

"Ha, ha," roared the creature. "What harm could you do? Tiny as you are?"

Rhiannon bristled and put up her blue shield. The light erupted around her and the creature stepped back.

"Oh, so you are a Druid then, worse yet. Leave now," he growled.

Desperate, she dared to continue. "Wait," she said holding up her hands, "I just want some information, and then I'll be on my way."

"And why should I want to help the likes of you?"

"Good question." Rhiannon clenched her jaw.

I know the fae like to trade for things. What could I possibly offer him?

She spotted a nasty burn on his arm. "I could make you a poultice for that burn in exchange?"

"You would offer to help one of my kind?"

"Yes, in exchange for some information."

The creature stared at her and nodded.

"I'll need a few things. I'll be back."

Rhiannon remembered seeing some chickweed not far back, and she knew it would make a good poultice to help the burn. With her blue sphere lighting the way, she quickly found a good supply and walked back to the cabin and knocked on the door.

"Well, come in," he said. "It's warm inside, but it won't be for long if I keep the door open."

She stepped carefully into the cabin and glanced around

her. The creature's home intimidated far less than the creature itself. "I'll need a bit of fabric and something to grind up this herb," she murmured.

"Let me see what I have."

A dog lay near the roaring fire, and a pot steamed above. The dog lifted its head and stood, becoming the largest wolf she had ever seen. Rhiannon froze as it sniffed her and tried to jump up and lick her face. Alarmed, she stepped back.

The hoofed creature grabbed the wolf's scruff and held her. "Oh, Fao won't hurt you, at least not unless I say."

Rhiannon held her breath and stepped toward Fao, holding out her hand for the wolf to smell. She reached out and stroked the warm fur like she would have with CuChulain. The creature's back reached her waist, and Fao could almost look her in the eye. The wolf looked at her with more intelligence than she had ever seen in a dog, and though it was a kind intelligence, she doubted it was harmless.

"She likes you," said the creature. "You must not be all bad. Here is my mortar and pestle and a bit of linen."

Rhiannon risked a glance at her host in the full light. A huge, bullheaded minotaur, with black hair and skin stood regarding her. The hair lifted on the nape of her neck and arms. Her hands turned clammy and her shoulders tightened. She fought back the urge to run and focused on what she needed to do.

Rhiannon got to work grinding the fresh chickweed, and when she was done, she asked for a bit of hot water and mixed it carefully to make a paste with the right consistency. She tore a strip of cloth from the linen and used a square of what was left to make a pouch for the herbs.

"Okay, its ready. Let me see your arm."

The minotaur knelt down next to the fire, and Rhiannon tied the poultice onto his arm and put a bit of energy into it.

A green glow came from her hand and surprised her. Like her shield, her magic was amplified in this place. "There, that should help," she said, satisfied.

He looked at his arm and smiled. "It feels better already. My name is Tinurion."

"I'm Rhiannon."

"You're Rhiannon? But of course you are, the woods have been all aflutter about your arrival. Well, take a seat near the fire and ask me your questions. I'm true to my word."

"You know who I am?"

"The rumors are that you are one of Brennan's family from the overland and that you've come to help him."

A smile settled on her lips and she relaxed just a bit. "You know Brennan?"

"I don't know him personally," said Tin, "but I know of him."

"Do you know where I could find him?" A new lightness filled her chest.

"He's probably at the Fort."

"Fort? What Fort?"

"The place where the Celts live."

None of this made any sense. Celts? Fort? But Rhiannon didn't care. Her uncle was known here. "How far away is the Fort?"

"A few days travel from here," said Tinurion, gesturing in one direction. It was neither the way she'd come, nor the direction she thought Logan had gone.

She sat up straighter, remembering that her first priority was to find Logan. Brennan, if he was still alive, had magic to take care of himself, but Logan was out of his element. Her plan had to stay the same, find Logan, and when that was done she would find Brennan.

Tinurion turned and grabbed a huge ceramic bowl, which he filled with a golden liquid from a jug near the fire. "I'll not have it said that I don't offer hospitality to my guests. This is the finest mead in all the mound, if I do say so myself. Got to drink it slow is all, if you know what I mean."

Rhiannon nodded cautiously as she took up the basin the size of a large salad bowl. Full to the brim, mead sloshed over the side. She hesitated, recalling the warnings of ingesting faerie food, but it would be rude to refuse Tinurion's hospitality. Though there were rules that governed things like this, if she was his guest, she would be afforded certain privileges. At least it was true of the Celts. Besides, she was going to need to eat and drink something soon—finding Logan and Brennan was not going to be as fast as she had hoped.

"Go on, take a drink, it won't hurt you even if you are a Druid," said Tinurion.

Why was he so eager for her to drink it, Rhiannon wondered.

She held the bowl to her lips and pretended to take a drink.

"This is amazing, Tinurion," she said. "Do you make it yourself?"

"Ay, but the bees do the hard part."

"They must be happy bees to make honey this good."

"We get on pretty well here, I'd say. I insist you stay for a meal and the night. I'm sure you're ready for a bit of refreshment, as am I."

"You don't know how good that sounds. I'd be in your debt," Rhiannon said. She was careful not to thank him. She remembered from the old tales that saying thank you to a faerie creature was considered bad manners.

"Think no more about it. Besides, I doubt you'd make much of dent in me vittles, being as petite as you are."

"You are kind, and I'm grateful for your hospitality." Despite her words, she didn't let down her guard. Her host *was* a minotaur, after all.

He served up another large bowl, this time filled with the steaming broth from the crock over the fire. Rhiannon had watched her host closely after her supposed drink of the mead, to see if he was watching her too closely, but if he was waiting for her to collapse, he gave no sign.

Her need to keep up her strength, and her growling stomach outweighed her caution and she decided to risk the food. Rhiannon took the huge spoon she was offered and tried the stew. She found it delicious, although she wasn't sure what was in it. Mushrooms, leeks, onions, carrots, and barley floated in the broth, but there were other flavors she couldn't place. She discreetly removed what she thought were chunks of meat and put them in her napkin, not wanting her vegetarian tastes to offend him.

Tin also brought out fresh honey for the warm pan bread. After her first taste of the honey and the bread, she felt no compulsion to be a modest eater. She grabbed rough handfuls of bread and sopped it in the stew, and she chased it with the mead, barely looking up at her host.

"You do my cooking proud, young lass. I'd never guess you'd eat so hearty a meal."

"You're a fine cook and a gracious host," said Rhiannon.

"If you don't mind, I do have a few more questions." She put her spoon down and studied him. "My friend, Logan, came here, and I know he was brought against his will. I'm trying to find him. Do you know anything about it?"

"I seem to remember a war party riding through the woods a while back. I haven't seen nor heard anything lately that might be taken for unusual, except your arrival here, of course."

"Did you see this war party?" Rhiannon asked.

"I didn't see them, but from the tracks, it had to be Morrigan's troops. Unshod hooves and light riders are her way. It had to be at least a week ago, by my reckoning."

Rhiannon's hands instantly turned clammy. *The Morrigan?* "Tinurion do you mean the goddess, Morrigan?"

"That would be her."

It all made terrible sense now, the Morrigan, the phantom queen, goddess of the Tuatha de Dannan, was behind everything that had happened to her. She was responsible for her mother's death and the ruining of her life. Rhiannon had always stayed away from the Morrigan in her Druid work with cautious fear, like one stays away from a tornado. But now she realized she was on a collision course with the goddess of war and death. How could she even begin to hope to defeat a goddess? She bit her lip and took her first drink of her mead.

"Why would the Morrigan want Logan?" she stammered.

"That I don't know."

Her hands shook, and she set down the bowl of sloshing liquid.

"Are you okay?"

"No, I'm not. What you told me means that somehow my family and I have gotten tangled up in a feud with the Morrigan."

Rhiannon looked down at her hands and fought back tears. She tried to focus. "Then Logan is probably far from here by now?"

"That depends on where they were headed, but my guess is they were taking him to Morrigan's castle."

"I was afraid you were going to say that."

She had wanted information, and she got it, but it only made things worse, much worse. Rhiannon felt rooted to her seat, unable to move. She stared into the fire and wrestled with the enormity of what she learned. Her stomach felt rock hard and threatened to reject her dinner.

Trying to calm herself, she drank more mead and looked up at the minotaur. "I appreciate the meal," she managed to whisper.

Tinurion nodded and disappeared into the back room. He pulled out a thick warm blanket and set up a pallet of rugs and pillows near the fire. Fao disappeared into a back room with Tinurion, and soon, Rhiannon heard him snoring.

She watched the fire and thought about her situation. She knew she had no real reason to trust the minotaur, but the dead horseman suggested that Logan had come this way too. Taken together, there was a good chance she was on the right path. Though she had taken a chance coming to the cabin, in doing so she learned that Brennan might be found at a Celtic hill fort, which was good. But the fact that the Morrigan was behind the attacks on her family made her want to hide in a hole.

Rhiannon decided there was nothing to do but to keep trying to find Logan. She would then find Brennan and pray he would know how to defeat the Morrigan, or least protect their family. At first light, she would press on.

Rhiannon sat restlessly on the rough bedding, gazing at the fire and resigned to stay awake. Tinurion had been friendly, but he was still a faerie creature, and she didn't trust him.

Chapter 10

Rhiannon listened through the curtain windows to the trees swaying in the wind outside the minotaur's cabin. Her eyes red and near closing, she propped herself to stay awake. Despite the fact she had slept in the stone ring for what could have been a week, she still craved sleep.

A twig snapped. *It could be anything,* she told herself, sitting up straight nonetheless. From the next room, Fao growled loudly.

Rhiannon jumped up and approached the window. Suddenly, a fiery flash struck the curtain, and a torch rolled across the floor. Rhiannon leaped away and shouted, "Tinurion! Wake up!"

She grabbed a bucket of water and dowsed the fire from the torch, but another torch came hurtling inward through another window. "Fire!" she shouted.

Tinurion rushed in and grabbed a large axe from near the hearth. "Better keep your head down."

He peered out the window, and flames reflected on his dark skin. Smoke filled the room. She peeked out the door, but before she could see anything more than flames and shadows, three spears thudded into the door.

"We aren't getting out that way," Rhiannon said.

"Aye, but we can't stay here."

Another torch came through a third window, but they'd run out of water. Tin grabbed a leather tunic covered with bronze rings and pulled it over his head while Rhiannon snuffed the torch with a large rug. He grabbed another bag and threw things in it: a large block of cheese, a ham, and a wine skin. Finally, he tucked a small jar of honey inside his armor.

Rhiannon coughed. The smoke made it hard to breathe.

"Follow me and stay close," said Tinurion.

He pulled open the door and waited while more spears shot into the room. He ducked and ran toward the woods. Rhiannon drew her sword and followed closely behind.

Fao charged ahead and snarled as she leapt on an attacker. Tinurion jumped to the wolf's aid, swinging his heavy axe at the assailant. The spearman went down, but not before the two others threw at point blank. Fao yelped and Tinurion cursed as both were hit. Rhiannon's muscles tightened as she ducked and spun, looking for more spears. Tinurion's armor must have deflected the point. The weapon lay on the ground as the minotaur charged at the retreating forms, but Fao crumpled and lay still.

From the shadows, an armored man ran forward, sword raised. Rhiannon froze, her own sword like a lead weight, her hands clammy. The man swung at her head and she awkwardly parried the blow. She wished Brennan had taught her how to fight with magic. Being an accomplished healer did little for her now.

The man moved in closer and brought his hand back for another blow. Rhiannon gulped. She had to do something fast. This man was a trained killer, and she had never held a sword before today. She drew on the Nwyfre, and the blue sphere of light appeared around her.

Startled, the man stepped back. For a moment, she thought she should run, but instead, she lowered her shoulder and threw all her weight and the magic of her shield against her opponent.

Though she didn't weigh much, her momentum pushed him off balance and he stumbled back and tripped. Rhiannon fell on him, and her shield winked out as her concentration was broken. She felt, more than heard, the man strike the ground. She jumped up, ready to attack again, but he didn't stir. Confused, she spotted blood on a rock near his head.

Rhiannon felt sick. The soldier was dead. Nevertheless, she also felt a small measure of triumph. She wiped the sweat from her forehead and recast the blue sphere around her. As she caught her breath, she looked around for more attackers. She could see none. The fight had moved farther into the woods, and she decided her skills would be of more use trying to heal Fao than chasing after the big minotaur.

Rhiannon dropped to her knees beside Fao. A javelin jutted from the wolf's rib cage. She averted her gaze from the wound for an instant and rubbed her hands together nervously. Taking a breath, she lowered her shield, placed her hand on Fao's head, and stroked her fur. The wolf was still alive.

Over her shoulder, she heard Tinurion crashing through the woods and the shouts of combat. The cabin roared; the heat was unbearable. Rhiannon gently moved Fao away from the blaze, stood, and sheathed the sword, determined not to let Fao suffer the same fate as CuChulain. She took off her boots and socks and put her bare feet on the earth. She would need a lot more Nwyfre for what she was about to do.

She raised her hands, drawing in the power of the light and air above her and pulling it down into the ground. Her hands swept upward, drawing on the telluric force of the ground, imagining points of light and crystal caves inside the ground feeding into her. It took longer than she wanted, and she kept listening for the sounds of the fighting, praying they wouldn't come her way. Finally, she extended her senses as roots and limbs, connecting to all of nature, and power filled her.

Rhiannon placed her hands on the wolf and they glowed green again, like the night before. She concentrated on pouring Nwyfre into the wound. Fao looked up at her and snarled. She pulled her hands back.

This won't do, she thought. *The javelin has got to come out before I can help her.*

Placing her left hand on Fao's ribs, Rhiannon whispered, "Hold on, Fao. It's going to be okay."

She grasped the javelin shaft and quickly pulled it out. Fao howled and went limp. Blood poured from the wound. Rhiannon swallowed hard then quickly tore her t-shirt and pressed the fabric to the wound. She focused, drawing more energy in through root and branch. She placed her left hand over the throbbing wound and bathed it in green light, letting it pour into Fao. She felt life, but she felt death there too. There was no life without death, and the healer must be comfortable with both, Brennan had always said.

The energy dimmed. Rhiannon looked down at what she had done and hoped it had been enough. She felt her control slipping away. She had never performed such strong healing magic before. The sound of Tinurion's crashing grew fainter, and she thought she heard horses in the distance. Suddenly, the ground came at her in a rush and she could hold on no longer.

* * *

Rhiannon stirred, coming awake again on top of Fao. The cabin smoldered behind them. She peered up and Tinurion stood there, his face covered with soot and his axe covered with gore.

His eyes widened. "Thank the gods, you are okay," said Tin.

"Thank you for fighting them off," Rhiannon said, relief making her ignore her faerie manners.

Fao lifted her head weakly and tried to stand. Tinurion dropped to his knees and touched the bandage Rhiannon had torn from her shirt.

"I think she will be okay," Rhiannon told him. "I'm not sure what happened at the end, though. I must have blacked out."

"Are you ok?"

"I think so. Just feeling a bit dizzy."

Tinurion stroked Fao. The wolf sighed and dropped her head back to the ground.

"It looks like the bleeding stopped," said Tinurion.

Rhiannon sighed. "Good, I did what I could."

"I chased them off for now, but they could be back and in greater numbers. I'll carry Fao. We need to get out of here now. Can you walk?"

She nodded and slowly got to her feet.

Tin gently lifted the wolf in his strong arms. Rhiannon followed as best she could. Though slowed by the weight of the wolf, he still moved quickly through the darkened wood. Rhiannon tripped and stumbled but kept up.

After about an hour, Tinurion stopped in a tree-lined valley and pulled aside a tangle of roots and leaves, revealing a hidden cave. Inside, they found some firewood and dry bedding.

"We best stay here till first glowing." Tinurion carefully put Fao down on a soft bed of leaves and felt the wolf's side.

Rhiannon wrapped her arms around her waist and studied him. "Who were they, Tinurion?"

"Morrigan's soldiers."

Her mouth dropped open. "I'm so sorry if my presence at your cabin caused this attack. I didn't mean to endanger you or Fao."

"It's not your fault. It would have happened sooner or later. Morrigan's troops have been hunting for me too. I escaped from her prison and they've been after me ever since. Maybe they weren't after you at all."

"Why were you imprisoned?"

"To be honest, I was more of a pet to her. You see I…" His voice trailed off and he stared out into the woods.

"A pet?" Rhiannon prodded.

He met her gaze. "Morrigan has her games, and I was good at staying alive in them; too good, maybe. I had to get out of there before I had more blood on my hands. So I escaped."

Rhiannon gasped. "That must have been terrible."

She wondered what he meant by games, but she guessed it must have been like the old gladiator games in Rome. She didn't want to dig into his painful past needlessly. He was a faerie creature, and obviously very deadly, but he had befriended her when he had no reason to, and even now, protected her from Morrigan.

Tinurion turned his back to her and unpacked his bag. "I haven't been completely honest with you," he said, turning to face her. "I knew who you were the moment I met you, and I thought that if I turned you in to Morrigan, she would let me live in peace."

Unease chilled Rhiannon. "You were going to capture me?"

"I couldn't go through with it, and I decided before we were finished with dinner I could never live with myself if I turned you over to *her*, even if it meant my freedom. She is all rotten, and Faerie Queen or not, I won't be ruled by her anymore."

Feeling vindicated in her initial suspicion, Rhiannon now scanned the woods and wondered if she should be trying to get away.

"Don't worry now. I only told you because I don't want secrets between us."

She glared at him. "Why is that?"

"Because I'm going to help you and we are going to be friends."

Rhiannon smiled despite herself. She did need all the friends she could get. And why would Tinurion confess if he still planned to capture her? It didn't make sense. Besides, he had saved her from Morrigan's soldiers. She would still have to be cautious, of course, but maybe now she had a chance to help Logan and Brennan.

"Friends, huh?"

Tinurion smiled.

Rhiannon held out her hand and Tinurion clasped it.

At first light, she would continue her search for Logan with whatever help Tinurion was willing to offer. She might have a new ally, but an entire army of allies might not be enough to defeat the Morrigan.

Chapter 11

The hard ground and the growing light woke Rhiannon from her troubled sleep. She opened her eyes and tried to remember where she was. Dirt walls rose up around her, and purple light poured through the rough lattice of the cave's door. Her body ached from the fight from the night before.

Rhiannon rubbed the sleep from her eyes and looked over at Tinurion, who sat nearby working with a needle and thread. The mundane task seemed out of place with such a large creature and the surroundings, making her smile. He turned and looked at her when she stood.

"I found an old sack that I'm rigging for you to use as a backpack." Tinurion held up the pack with pride. He finished the last stitches and handed it to her.

"I found this for you too." He showed her an old cloak that he'd cut to her size. He wrapped it around her and pinned it on with a bronze clasp.

"Perfect. This will keep me from being seen too easily in the forest. And the pack will help too." Rhiannon smiled. She ran a hand over the forest green fabric and resisted the urge to thank him, remembering her faerie manners. She wasn't sure if minotaurs followed the same customs, but decided it was safer to assume they did.

"How'd you sleep?" Tinurion asked, handing her a hot cup of tea.

"Like I had a rock in my back," she said ruefully, rubbing her lower back.

Tinurion laughed. "Me too."

"While I wasn't sleeping, I had many questions going through my head. Do you mind if I start right in?"

"No, of course not." Tinurion sipped at his own cup.

"Who are the Celts you mentioned last night?"

"When the magic of the mound was created, the Druids decided to leave some people behind to keep an eye on things."

"Like guards?" Rhiannon asked.

"Yes something like that," said Tin. "The Celts built a Fort to protect the tree that is the source of the power to contain the Morrigan. They let her have her realm, but they guard the tree and make sure Morrigan stays away from the hawthorne."

"Why would the Morrigan need to be contained?"

"I would think you of all people would know that."

"Because I'm a Druid?" asked Rhiannon, trying to not take the comment personally.

"Yes, it was your kind that imprisoned *us*. Why don't you know this?"

Rhiannon clenched her jaw. Brennan had clearly kept a lot from her.

"Never mind that. Why was she imprisoned in the first place?"

Tinurion frowned. "I don't know for sure, but my guess is that after the war certain members of the Tuatha de Dannan were considered too dangerous and had to be imprisoned."

"I know the Morrigan is powerful and I think your guess is probably right." She thought back to what he had said earlier. "I got here through a hawthorne tree. Do you think it is related?"

"Yes, definitely. The tree at the fort is the source of the binding, but there are other hawthornes that seal off the passageways to the surface."

"So what happens if the tree is killed?" asked Rhiannon.

"Well, then Morrigan and all of the faerie creatures would be allowed to return to the world above."

Rhiannon stood and clutched her arms around her. "What? The Morrigan would be free?"

The implications made her mind hurt. Only the magic of a single tree kept the Morrigan imprisoned. What if the goddess were free to return to the world above? It could mean terrible things. She started to pace, more anxious to leave than ever.

"Yes, and so would I."

Rhiannon paused, studied him. "I didn't mean it that way," she said.

"Yes, you did." Tinurion narrowed his eyes.

She shifted uncomfortably. She always felt justified in her fear and hatred of the faerie, given the way her mother died. But the minotaur did have a point. Her experience in the mound with pixies and now with Tinurion was proving things were not so clear cut.

"I apologize, Tinurion. It was wrong of me to assume that all faerie creatures are evil."

He gave a short nod. "I can understand why you might think that, given your people's history. Apology accepted. You are right about one thing, though. If the Morrigan returns to the world above, there will be terrible destruction."

"I've got to stop her, Tin. It's a lot to ask, but would you help me?" She fingered her necklace nervously, waiting for his answer.

He paused, longer than she wanted. "I'm sorry," he said finally. "It's just that the Druids have been my enemy for so long. They imprisoned me here with many of my kind."

"You've done so much for me, Tinurion. I would understand if you didn't want to help anymore. After all, our people are enemies."

Tinurion stood, looked at her, and stomped out of the cave. Rhiannon was disappointed but could understand his difficulty. She wasn't sure herself if it would work out. She decided to follow him and see if he was leaving. Fao came with her.

Tin stood with his back to the cave and his hands on his hips. "It would take some getting used to, the idea that we can work together for our common good," he said, still with his back turned.

"It would be for *our* common good. Perhaps it will be a small beginning to a larger reconciliation?"

He turned and looked intently into her eyes as if trying to read her integrity. He nodded slowly. "No. I can't live with Morrigan as my queen, and she must be stopped. Even if it means helping the Druids, I must do what I can. I'll help you."

"Are you sure? The Morrigan's freedom would mean your own."

"True, but I rather like it here, and I have no desire to live above. Besides," he reached down and stroked Fao's head, "I owe you a debt for saving Fao. I'll help you try to find Logan and

maybe get some payback for what Morrigan has done to my home."

"You don't owe me anything, Tinurion. You took me in, and your house was probably attacked because of me."

Tinurion shook his head. "I was bound to be targeted sooner or later and if I'd been alone, who would have saved Fao? Besides, I don't really have a home to go to now, do I? I will go with you."

"I'm grateful." Rhiannon smiled up at him.

How ironic that a faerie creature would help her after all the years spent fearing the fae. Having his help would make a huge difference, though Rhiannon knew it was a risk to trust him. It was still possible the big minotaur was just waiting for the right moment to turn her over.

No, that didn't feel right at all. He could have alerted Morrigan's soldiers and maybe saved his home from being destroyed. She didn't like trusting a faerie creature, but he had protected her and fed her and clothed her. She would trust him, at least for now.

"The first thing I need to do is find Logan," she said. "After that, I need to find Brennan and try to come up with a way to defeat the Morrigan."

"I can show you the way to the Morrigan's castle, but if he is already there, it will be next to impossible for the two of us to get him out."

She pursed her lips and looked him in the eye. "I have to know for sure. He is here because of me. I won't lose someone else I love to *her*. I won't abandon him. If there is any chance of saving him, I have to take it."

"I understand. I will do what I can to help you."

"We are an odd pair, Tinurion, but together I think we will change things for the better."

"I hope you are right. Since we are now allies, you can call me Tin."

Rhiannon smiled. "Okay, *Tin*."

Fao woke up, stretched, and walked over to sit next to the minotaur. Tin fed her some dried meat and looked at her ribs. The only sign of the spear wound was a faint scar.

"That's quite the healing job you did."

"I'm pleased it worked."

The strength of her power amazed her. Ever since she arrived in this place, her magic had flourished. Whatever the reason, she was grateful. She would need every ounce of her power to survive.

Rhiannon and Tin gathered their things and left the cave again. Outside, the light was brilliant. Blue and yellow roses with open buds bloomed all around. Their sweet scent filled the air. Amidst the trees, pixies and gnomes went about their business. Rhiannon followed Tin, eager to track Logan.

The smell of charred wood met her nose before the blackened ruins of the cabin appeared. The huge timbers had collapsed in on themselves, and in places smoke still rose into the morning air. Tin kicked at the logs in frustration.

She took her glasses off, closed her eyes, and pinched the bridge of her nose. "I'm sorry, Tin. No matter what you say, I believe this was my fault. I will make it up to you."

"Morrigan will pay for this," he said with clenched teeth.

Rhiannon put her hand on his arm, he shrugged it off. She sighed and bit her lip.

Glancing down at her, he said, "I'm sorry. I'm just so angry, and it's not your fault. Why can't Morrigan let people alone?"

"I feel the same way. She killed my mother." Tears sprang to her eyes, her emotions overwhelmed by the words she'd never before spoken.

Tin knelt down and looked Rhiannon in the eye. "I'm sorry. I didn't know that."

She wiped the tears away. "Let's go, Tin. It's time we set things right."

Chapter 12

Fao ran ahead, and Tin and Rhiannon followed her down the trail. Seeing the wolf running and healthy when she should have been dead gave Rhiannon tremendous satisfaction. It was a small victory, but it was the first. By saving Fao, she had done something right. She stood a little taller as she hiked farther into the forest.

"We need to push it today," said Rhiannon. "I fear that with every minute, Logan is getting farther away."

"I agree. We can get some distance behind us if we don't run into Morrigan's soldiers. The trail stops ahead at a lake, then starts again at the edge of the swamp."

Sweat soaked her T-shirt as she tried to keep up with the long-legged minotaur. Hours passed before they emerged from the oaks onto the shore of a lake.

Rhiannon squatted down to get water. Leaves blanketed the bottom of the lake, not far below the surface. She washed some of the dirt off her face and hands and took a long drink.

"Tin, is following the trail the best plan if the Morrigan's troops are still hunting us?"

"The way will soon become impassable if we don't use the path. There is a swamp ahead, so we don't have much choice."

"Is there a way around?"

"Yes, but it's too far. If we want any chance of rescuing Logan before he's in the castle, we have to go straight and take the trail."

Rhiannon opened her mouth to speak but closed it again. She rubbed her neck and looked around her, hoping some flash of insight would reveal itself. To the right, above the tree line, a waterfall crashed. Tall, thin birches, willows, and alders ringed in the pool at the base.

"So it's straight into the swamp, with Morrigan's soldiers

probably waiting for us?" she asked.

Tin frowned. "I didn't say I liked it."

She took a breath, gathering her resolve. Around her, the timbers swayed in the breeze and gleaming light poured down from above, making the small waves at her feet sparkle. Gossamer winged pixies flew through the trees, and orbs of many colors danced under and above the clear water.

"Those are Daggerwing Pixies," said Tin, pointing toward the woods. "Beautiful but dangerous if they lose their temper."

Rhiannon's shoulders tightened. She reached down and put her hand on the sword. "How dangerous?"

"Dangerous enough. They usually stay neutral and keep to themselves, but Morrigan likes to use them as spies. She has been trying to win them all to her side, but I'm not sure how successful she's been."

Long pointed tips extended from the pixies' lower wings. Daggerwing described them perfectly. They looked like butterfly wings when they were still, but when they flew, they were all a blur. Though similar, none were identical, their hues as various as all the butterflies she had ever seen. They looked harmless, but Rhiannon knew from experience that small winged creatures could kill. She fought to keep that memory down.

"We better get going."

"I agree. There used to be a bridge here," said Tin, pointing across the water, "but it's long gone, so we will have to get our feet wet."

A small island protruded from the center of the lake. Old granite blocks jutted out of the water at regular intervals between it and the shore. On either side stood the remains of stone ramps leading to nowhere.

Rhiannon looked at the water and frowned. She hated hiking in wet clothes. She took off her boots and socks, undid her cloak, and put her shoes and socks inside. She rolled up her jeans and hefted the cloak over her head as she stepped into the cool liquid.

Rhiannon hoped Logan had come this way, but she didn't know. She felt responsible for what was happening and could only imagine what Logan must be thinking—to be caught in this place with no knowledge of the fae or Celtic myth would be terrifying. Her anxiety pushed her.

Fao splashed ahead, chasing and sniffing the orbs. They frolicked around the wolf, playing in turn with her. While it was not deep for Tin, Rhiannon soon found the water waist-high and her jeans quickly soaked.

Finally, they climbed up onto the island. On the other side, Rhiannon paused in the bright warm light and looked across to the other shore, which did not glow at all. Its dark shore was hidden from the brightness.

"We call it Darkin Wood," said Tin. "And you can see why. It's not the most pleasant place. It will take us three days to clear it and reach the far side. From there, it will be about another two days to reach Morrigan's castle. We better hope we find Logan before then." He scanned the island. "There are many dangers ahead. If we stay on the path, we should find our way through without too much trouble. I've hunted those woods many times and they are familiar to me, but it has been long years since I've crossed them," he said.

Rhiannon's stomach felt as hard as a rock at the thought of getting lost in the swamp. "What do you think our chances are of catching up to Logan before he gets to the castle? It has been a week and they were on horses."

"The swamp will have slowed them down, but even so, it's not much of a chance."

"You said it would be impossible to get him out once he's inside."

"It is a strong fortress and it is heavily guarded. There is no way the three of us could get inside and get out again with Logan."

"No way?"

Tin paused as if considering something. He turned his brown eyes toward her and studied her. "There is one way; the way I escaped. But I barely made it. There's a series of tunnels and natural caverns under the castle, inhabited by all kinds of evil creatures. Morrigan doesn't guard it because she doesn't have to."

"But it could be done?"

"Possibly, but only if there was no other way."

Rhiannon let out a breath and hoped they wouldn't have to resort to that route. "Let's go and hope we find Logan so it's not even a question." Rhiannon stepped back into the cool water and sloshed her way toward the darkened shore.

On the opposite bank, the forest was black and wet. Ponds

of still, fetid water surrounded them in the open areas. Fallen trees formed tangled knots across the trail at frequent intervals. Insects buzzed and bit, drawing blood from Rhiannon's tender skin. Small winged creatures with human features roamed the upper canopy of the trees. Their flitting made her nervous.

She put her boots back on and was glad for dry feet, even if it wouldn't be for long. Up ahead, a path disappeared into the dark of the forest. She recognized cypress and willows and tall black oaks. The low light made the hanging moss look like long gangly hair.

She took a deep breath. At last, a clear way stood before her. When she was ready, she set her jaw and gave Tin a curt nod.

The trail narrowed, turned difficult. Rhiannon followed Tinurion as he negotiated his way through the stunted bushes and low hanging branches, swinging his enormous axe to clear the path when it grew too thick. Fao stayed close to Rhiannon now, which comforted her far more than she would have expected.

The trail dipped down, descending toward a bog on the left, leaving a tall hill on the right. The ground lost its firmness, and black muck sucked at their feet, leaving behind water-filled footprints. They traversed the edge of the mire, stepping on jutting logs and rocks as much as possible. A black snake slithered across Rhiannon's feet, and she jumped back as the thing turned and flicked its black tongue at her before disappearing under a bush. Heart pounding in her ears, she took a breath and pressed on.

* * *

A stone's throw beyond a fallen oak in her path, a wallow filled with mud creatures came into view. With long, stick-like limbs, they moved awkwardly with backward joints, small heads bobbing atop glistening segmented bodies. A stench, like concentrated swamp rot, came off them in a yellow cloud. She shivered in revulsion and pulled her t-shirt up over her nose.

The creatures surrounded a small Daggerwing, whose footprints lead to the center of the bog.

"Get away from me, you muds! Or I'll blast you," shouted the pixie.

The muds didn't seem to understand or care, and they tossed globs of muck at the pixie. That enraged her, and she produced a tiny bow and fired sapphire-colored darts at the muds. The darts seem to hurt them, and they sank down into the mud to escape the stinging barbs, though some kept hurling mud. Rhiannon suddenly realized the muds plan to bury the blue faerie alive.

Without thinking, Rhiannon raced forward to help the pixie.

"No!" shouted Tin. "Come back here, Rhiannon. It's not safe."

Ignoring him, she pulled her sword free and raced through the mire, crossing many yards of swamp. Without hesitating, she swung the sword with the flat of the blade, smashing the muds down into the muck.

Fae or not, the small creature didn't deserve to die like that. She stopped swatting for a moment, focused her mind, and set a sphere of protective light around the pixie. She watched with satisfaction as the mud rolled off the shield. The pixie didn't pause to consider her good fortune, but kept firing her tiny arrows into the muds. Soon, the creatures had all sunk away into the mire, leaving the half-buried pixie alone.

Rhiannon knelt down to check on the creature. A gossamer wing hung useless at the pixie's side. "Let me take a look at that broken wing," she said. "I might be able to help you."

The pixie regarded her suspiciously. "Why would you want to help me?"

"Those things attacked you and I thought you might need some help. It looked like an unfair fight."

The pixie looked down at her mud-covered body and said, "Well, you're right. I did need a bit of help, but I can take care of myself now."

"I'm sure you can, but you'd be better off with that wing working so you don't have to walk all the way home."

"I don't need your charity," the pixie said stiffly.

"Fine," Rhiannon said feeling stung. "I don't see why I should go out of my way to help you anymore than I already have."

"Fine," echoed the Daggerwing. "I'll be off."

Rhiannon took a deep breath and watched the pixie try to walk away through the mucky debris.

No. In her heart, she wasn't hateful. It would be wrong to let her suffer needlessly. "It wouldn't be charity," she said finally. "Perhaps you know these woods well?"

The pixie stopped and looked over her shoulder. "I know them well enough."

"If I can fix your wing, perhaps you could show me and my friends the way through to the bridge on the other side of the wood."

The pixie paused to consider. Rhiannon thought it sounded like a fair deal. She knew it had been a while since Tinurion had been through the forest. The pixie could be a big help.

"Alright, you've got yourself a deal. My name's Flitania, and it will be a pleasure doing business with you. You won't regret it, I'll be true to my word. I'm the most honest Daggerwing you'll ever meet."

Rhiannon smiled as the words poured out of Flitania. The little pixie spoke like she flew—fast and bubbly.

"It's nice to meet you, Flitania. I'm Rhiannon."

"Wait, you're Rhiannon? Well, of course you are. I should've figured that out on my own. Stupid, stupid, stupid! I was sent here to find you."

Rhiannon gasped. "Sent by whom?" Was this one of Morrigan's spies?

"By Brennan, of course! Who else would it be?"

Her heart jumped and she smiled. "Brennan sent you?" *Could it be true?*

"Yes, and it seems that you found me instead of me finding you. How funny."

"So is he okay? I mean, I've been worried sick about him." She stumbled back a step, sat on log, and let out a huge breath.

"Yes, yes, he's fine. He discovered that Logan was captured and that you had come after him, and he was very worried about you and so he sent me."

She knows about Logan too?

"Thank you, Brighid," she said as she let her head fall back and closed her eyes. She wiped away a tear and a thought forced her eyes open. "Why didn't he come himself?" she asked.

"He wanted to come, but there is a crisis at the fort and he couldn't leave. He told me to bring you to him."

She thought for a minute and doubt crept in. What were the chances she would stumble across the one pixie Brennan sent for her? This was too much information all at once.

"What fort? The Celtic fort?"

"Yes, yes, it's the only one, but you didn't know that right?"

"No I didn't. He wants me to come now?"

"It's urgent you come, that's what he said."

Rhiannon put her finger to her lip, considering, and heard Tin approaching. She turned to him and explained what happened.

Tin frowned and put his hands on his hips. "Rhiannon, I know you are relieved Brennan might be okay," he said, "but remember what I told you before about the pixies."

Maybe this pixie is one of Morrigan's spies sent to discourage me from looking for Logan. She looked at her feet, trying to decide what to do. "Brennan must know I can't do that. Logan has been captured, and I need to try to rescue him."

"He didn't say anything about rescuing him. He only told me to come and find you and bring you back."

"Well you can bring me back, but it's going to have to wait until I find Logan."

The pixie put her hands on her hips and said, "Brennan wants you back now."

Rhiannon was torn. If the pixie really was a spy, would she be so willing to help them? What if Brennan really needed her to go to him? But she couldn't just abandon Logan. He was helpless in this place.

"Let's fix that wing," Rhiannon said, stalling for time.

She sat down near Flitania, took off her shoes, and let her toes sink into the mud. She closed her eyes and drew the life of the swamp up through her spine and out the crown of her head. She pulled down the energy of the light and air above.

Rhiannon concentrated, and a globe of light appeared between her hands. When it felt strong enough, she extended her hands and bathed the pixie in the green healing light. The power came through her, from the life all around them, and she let it do its work.

Flitania groaned as the light penetrated her broken wing. Rhiannon knew what it felt like. She'd broken her arm as a child, and Brennan had healed it. She remembered warm prickles and a sharp ache. Far from pleasant, it was much better than months of healing the slow way.

She kept the flow pouring into Flitania, and then it was done. The pixie looked at her wing and gently flexed it. She smiled at Rhiannon, tested the wing a bit more, and was soon hovering. Within moments, she darted through the air, humming happily.

"Very impressive! You fixed me right up." Flitania beamed. "You definitely have the Druid power! Brennan would be proud, I'm sure. You are just like him."

"I'm glad it worked and you are better now," said Rhiannon. Now she had to decide. She didn't know if she could trust the pixie, but she knew she couldn't abandon Logan. Brennan would have to wait.

"Flitania, if you will guide us to the other side of the forest, I would appreciate it. When we have Logan, then I will go find Brennan."

Tin scowled. "Rhiannon, I don't think you should trust this pixie to guide us. I know the way well enough."

Flitania flew around the minotaur's head, looking closely at him. "I don't think you should trust this minotaur," she said pertly.

"Listen, both of you. I trust you, Tin, and Flitania, I will be honest that I have my misgivings about you. But if you show us the way truly, you will prove your honesty."

"I'll not lead you astray. I give you my word, but Brennan will not be happy with me."

"I will tell Brennan it was my decision, and he will have to accept that."

"I don't trust her," Tinurion barked.

"It will be okay, Tin. We will know soon enough if she is true."

"There are a lot of things that can go wrong out here. If she betrays us, we could all end up dead."

"You know, I'm right here," said the pixie.

Rhiannon put her hands up to silence them. "It's my decision, and I say we trust her. You said yourself it has been many years since you've crossed the swamp. Plus I need to know if what she told me is true. If she proves her loyalty it might mean she is telling me the truth about Brennan. If it's too big of a risk for you Tin, you don't have to come. I'd understand."

Tin shook his head slowly. "I said I'd help you, and I will, but I'm not happy about this, Rhiannon."

"Let's go then," said Flitania as she flew down the path. Glowering, Tin followed.

Rhiannon tried to put the two of them out of her mind and

concentrated on Logan. With every step, she was getting closer to him.

* * *

Glowing green toads gave off a murky luminance, and downed trees and floating algae covered the surface of the water, hiding unknown dangers beneath. Squat trees sat with their roots pulled up, as if sitting in the dark water, and their gray limbs blocked all light.

Rhiannon swallowed uncomfortably and held her elbows tightly against her sides as she walked along the edge of the swamp. She hated the swamp.

The lifeless trees looked like rows of old skeletons, picked clean. Flitania rushed ahead, looking for a way through. An hour ago, they had lost the trail. It had just disappeared, like Darkin Wood just swallowed it up.

When they lost the trail, Rhiannon got suspicious. She wanted to believe the pixie was not misleading them, and more importantly, that she been sent by Brennan. Flitania probably worked for the Morrigan though. She sighed and tried to find a little faith. She reminded herself that Tinurion had not done any better finding the path either.

The fatigued trio followed the tireless pixie through the mire. They climbed occasional hills, and plodded back into the mud. Each step sucked at Rhiannon's boots. Her legs ached and her eyes stung.

She brushed her tangled hair out of her face and lifted her head. "Flitania! Flitania!" she called to the pixie. "Can we can we stop soon?

"Not here. On top of that hill should be safe enough," said Flitania, pointing just ahead to a hill rounding out of the swamp like a great knuckle.

Gray mist rose from the dank water around it. A few trees clung to its sides, but the top was covered, like a hairy mole, with dozens of willow trees.

They climbed up the slippery, moss-covered rocks to the low summit of the hill. Rhiannon sat down with her back to a willow and watched Flit disappear down the hill. She stared out into space and breathed a deep sigh.

Soon, the pixie's blue glow floated back up the hill. Rhiannon blinked in the sudden brightness.

"All's clear, as far as I can tell," said Flitania as she hovered near.

"I think this is a good place to stop, for just a short while," said Tin.

"I agree." Rhiannon was eager to keep going, but her wet clothes and her fatigue made a strong argument for taking a short break.

A horse neighed. Rhiannon's eyes widened, her skin suddenly tingling. She quickly hid behind a willow tree and then peered around it. Down below, a long line of Morrigan's troopers advanced through the trees toward them.

The almost bare hilltop would not conceal them for long as the mounted soldiers began to climb the hill.

"All's clear, ay Pixie?" hissed Tin as he raised his axe.

"I swear I didn't see them!" Flit squealed and ducked as if he intended to swing at her.

A rush of heat filled Rhiannon. She glared at Flitania and pulled her sword free. "I don't see how you could have missed them," she said in a heated whisper.

"Wait! You've got to believe me!"

"Give me one reason." Rhiannon pointed her sword.

"I can make it right. You can't fight them all. I'll pretend I'm a scout for the Morrigan and get them to leave," said Flitania with determined eyes.

"Not good enough," Rhiannon snapped.

"She's right about one thing. We can't fight them all," Tinurion said. "I don't think they have seen us yet. Let's go."

She gave hard shake of her head. "No, I'm not running, and I'm not turning back."

Tin put his hands on his hips and stared at her. "Rhiannon, it's suicide to try to take them on."

"You don't have to come, but I'm not leaving Logan."

"I didn't agree to throw my life away in order to help you, and besides you can't save Logan if you are dead."

"I don't want you throwing away your life either, Tin. We can go down the other side of the hill and see if we can get around them. If there are more soldiers, but they are spread thin like these, we can punch a hole in their line and fight our way clear."

Tin looked at her with wide eyes.

"Really, Tin. It can work." Rhiannon put a hand on the

minotaur's arm.

He took a deep breath, wide nostrils flaring wider. "Okay," he said. "It's crazy, but let's try it."

Rhiannon turned her attention to Flitania. "I don't know if you saw the soldiers or not, but now is the time for you to prove your loyalty, Flit. Come with us and help us fight."

"I'm with you."

Chapter 13

Garth bolted awake, covered in sweat. He gulped a huge breath of air and then lay back down in the bed.

"Nightmares again?" Deirdre reached an arm over his chest and snuggled close.

"Yes, curse them." Garth's heart still raced.

"Have you mentioned them to Brennan?"

"No. He will think I'm acting like a beardless boy to have such problems."

"Dreams can be important. You know that."

Garth turned and kissed her. "You're right. I will go see him in the morning. I need to get more information from him about the Well too."

Despite Garth's attempt to talk quietly, baby Wil woke and started crying.

Deirdre rubbed her eyes. "Can you bring him to me?"

"It's the least I can do, since I'm the one who woke him," said Garth.

"You seem to have a habit of doing that."

He heard the smile in her voice and smiled in return.

Deirdre breast-fed their young son, and Garth put him back to bed. He stared at the ceiling, not wanting to fall asleep again. First glowing finally came, and he rose, stoked the fire in the main hearth, and started water boiling for tea. Garth put more wood on the fire to heat the water in the cauldron then added barley, honey, and some milk.

He brought Deirdre a cup of tea when she sat at the table near the fire.

"I've decided to take Niadh with me," he said. "If he will go."

"Is that why you let him win the race yesterday?"

Garth felt his eyes stretch wide. "It wasn't that obvious, was it?"

Deirdre took a sip of her tea. "Only to me. If he finds out, he will be furious."

"I know, but I thought if he beat me, in front of everyone, the tension between us might lessen."

"It was a generous thing to do, and something no one will ever know about."

"Except you, of course," Garth said as he sat down at the table.

"I know it will be difficult to have him in your troop," Deirdre said after a moment.

"I don't want him along, but I must trust there will be a good reason for him to be on the journey. I need to leave today. I wish I had more time, but the tree is failing, and I don't know how long this will take."

"I wish you didn't have to go," she said, looking into his eyes.

He reached out and took her hands. "I know, my love, but duty calls. I go so that everyone can be made safe from Morrigan."

"What if the Morrigan comes after *you*?" said Deirdre with fire in her eyes.

"I pray the gods will prevent that. I'd have to fight her."

"At least *here* you have all of us together to face *her*. Alone in the wilds, you will have little help."

Deirdre bolted up and walked to the fire, turning her back to Garth.

"You can see why I have nightmares," Garth said, standing up and putting his hands on her shoulders.

Deirdre kept her back to him.

"How will you find it? Not even Brennan knows for sure where it is."

"I don't know, but I must try. Brennan said the Druids left clues."

Deirdre turned and put her arms around his waist and looked up at him.

"If anyone can find it, you can. You do our family honor to take up such an important mission. I'm sorry I doubted you."

"I have doubts of my own, but I must see this through."

* * *

Garth washed his face and put on a new léinte and his belt around it. Next, he draped a sheepskin brat over his shoulders and belted his sword at his waist. Finally, he added a heavy gold torc around his neck. He ran a finger around it, unconsciously trying to loosen it. He shifted his clothes around, unable to get comfortable. He kept thinking of Deirdre's words. What if the Morrigan found him alone? How could he stand any chance against her?

Garth picked at his breakfast, then kissed Deirdre and Wil goodbye. He walked the short distance to Brennan's home, trying to enjoy the cool air of morning. Garth knocked on the door and the Druid himself answered.

"You're up early," said Brennan.

"I apologize for the early hour, but I need to talk."

"It's alright, I was up. Come inside." Brennan pulled the door wide.

Inside the Druid's quarters Garth found all manner of things he had never seen anywhere else. Above a chaotic collection of ore, plants, and strange devices, smoke filled the rafters and slowly leaked out through the thatch. Everything smelled of herbs and smoke.

"So, what brings you here so early?"

Garth took a seat by the fire. "It's probably nothing," Garth began. "I've been having bad dreams, and I wake up short of breath and exhausted every morning. I hoped it would end after the raid, but it happened again last night."

"Are there any images from the dreams that you can remember?" Brennan asked.

"Yes. A wolf hunts me through a mist-filled forest. Whenever I try to throw my spear, it disappears. From out of the fog, it attacks me from behind, biting my neck. I wake up in a sweat, and I can't seem to get enough air."

"Hmm, that doesn't sound good. How long has it been happening?"

"It's been a fortnight at least," said Garth.

"You should have told me sooner. Here, take this valerian root. Make a tea with a knuckle of it before bed. It will help you sleep. In your dream, instead of trying to use your spear, try asking the wolf what it wants. That may help."

Garth took the root. It looked like a small uprooted tree with many thick tendrils hanging down from the main trunk. "I will do that. Thank you for not thinking I'm acting like a fool," he said as he put the root into his belt pouch.

"You know better than that, Garth. Dreams are important, and if you are not sleeping well, it will affect you."

He took a heavy breath. He wanted help with his nightmares, but even more than that, he needed information. "Tell me more about the Well of Wisdom."

Brennan was silent for a few moments and then began. "It is known by many names, the Well of Segais, Conla's Well, and Nectan's Well, among others. It is believed that the Well is surrounded by nine hazel trees, and from them fall the hazelnuts of wisdom. The nuts feed the salmon who live there and imbue the water with its properties."

"What power does it have?"

"The water from the Well will restore life, and some say, even bring back the dead. I don't know if that is true, but it is sacred water and must only be used for good. Morrigan is immortal and has no need of it, but I suspect she is aware of its existence. Let us hope she has not realized all our hope hangs on getting a vial of that water back to the tree."

Garth swallowed hard and cleared his throat. "Do you think she knows where it is?"

"I doubt it. The Druids would have hidden it carefully."

"Tell me more."

"Before Morrigan was imprisoned here, my Druid predecessors found the well. They decided the mound would be the perfect place to set up the hawthorne barrier because the Well could keep the hawthorne alive indefinitely. But they also knew it had to be kept secret or the restorative power could be abused."

Brennan studied Garth's face before continuing. "In the early days, the Druids made it a test to find the well—much like the tests you warriors go through. Before a Druid was made an elder and given the chance to become the high Druid of the grove, he had to find the Well of Wisdom. Hidden clues led a learned and resourceful Druid to it."

Hope filled Garth for the first time. "So you know where it is?"

Brennan shook his head. "When I was young, a Council of Druids was called and everyone went except me. I was the youngest—barely past apprenticeship—and I was asked to stay behind and guard the grove.

"At the meeting, all the Druids were poisoned and killed. I was left as the last Druid, though I was barely that. Unfortunately, the location of the Well died with them. I would have searched for it, but the tree was healthy, and I was consumed with finding out what happened to the Druids. I left the mound for many years and lived in the world above."

Brennan fell silent. Garth thought Brennan's eyes looked distant as if his focus had drawn into the past. He waited patiently for him to return.

Brennan blinked and began again. "But that is another tale. In the end, I never found the Well. So now it falls to you."

Garth brought his hand to his neck torque and fingered it. "But Brennan, I'm no Druid, much less an accomplished one. How can I hope to find the Well?"

The old man inhaled deeply through his nose. "It's true, you are no Druid, but I have taught you many things others do not know, nor have they cared to learn. You have the knowledge of the ogam, and you live the values of our people. You are a suitable champion."

Still uncertain, Garth adjusted his brat, widened his stance, and looked Brennan in the eyes. "You could come with me."

Brennan laughed, a slight edge within. "No, Garth. My place is here. This task falls to you alone. I need to defend the tree and give counsel to the king. If Morrigan were to attack the fort, I would be able to at least slow her down."

Garth dropped his hands to his side. "You are right. I apologize. I shouldn't have asked."

Brennan's wide eyes softened, and a slow smile spread. "I understand it is a lot to ask, but you must see it through."

Garth set his jaw and gave a tight nod. "Do you know what the Well looks like?"

"It was never described to me, but I'm sure you will know it when you see it."

He nodded, trying not to get discouraged before the quest had even begun. He tried to focus on what the next step should be. "What kind of clues should I look for?"

"Look for tree clues. Look for ogam letters in hidden places. Trust your intuition."

Garth's breakfast turned to acid and nausea began to gnaw.

"That's not much to go on," he said, settling his hand on his sword hilt trying to bolster his confidence.

Brennan locked his eyes on Garth. "It will have to be enough. You must not fail."

Garth pursed his lips. "I will do it. Come what dangers and difficulties, I will see it through."

Brennan nodded and took a breath. "There may be something that can help you. Do you remember the tales about the four treasures of the Tuatha de Dannan?"

"Yes. From Failas came the Stone of Fal, from Gorias came the spear of Lugh, from Findias the sword of Nauda, and from Murias came the Cauldron of the Dagda."

"Good, good. You remember well. Last night, in my grove, the trees spoke to me of the sword. I believed it was lost long ago, but the trees told me where it is."

Garth blinked hard, struggling to contain his wonder. "They told you where to find Claíomh Solais?"

"Yes, they did. And it is not far from where we stand."

Garth's skin tingled. "Brennan, if what the trees told you was true, it would be a great boon. The sword could make all the difference. Let's go get it!"

Brennan smiled, and Garth followed him out the door.

* * *

Garth and Brennan walked through the morning glow to the front gate of the hill fortress. Guards heaved the heavy timber door open to let the prince and the Druid walk out. The two men walked along a stony path around the fort and toward the towering cliff wall not far from the fortress, then turned south. They walked far from the fort, leaving behind golden fields and green pastures filled with grazing sheep. Brennan said nothing as they walked.

Garth scraped his hand through his long hair and rubbed the back of his neck. "Brennan, do you think the sword could be used to kill the Morrigan?"

"Perhaps, if you could get close enough, but it will be more useful on your quest for the Well. With the Water of Life, we will be able to contain her with certainty."

"But if she was dead, our troubles would be over."

"You must remember there are other mounds, and if Morrigan were dead, someone else would move to take power. No. We must use the sword to get the Water of Life."

"I understand," said Garth. "Can you tell me more about the sword?"

Brennan nodded. "It has many names. It is called the sword of Nuada, Claideb, Claíomh Solais—sword of light. The weapon is said to be inescapable once drawn from its sheath. It is a Druid blade, and it will help you in ways I can't predict."

Though a lightness filled his chest, Garth's mouth was dry. He couldn't believe they were going to get the Claíomh Solais. "The sword will be a great help."

"Yes, it will, but the sword is only a tool. It is your courage and commitment that will see this done."

Garth nodded, feeling the truth of Brennan's words. The sword would not guarantee he would find the Well. Nevertheless, he couldn't help but feel the sword would better his chances.

"One more thing," Brennan said seriously. "The trees told me the sword is guarded."

Garth took a deep breath. "No doubt, or it would have been found long ago. Did they tell you anything about what I might expect?"

"Only that green and strangling block the way."

"So some kind of plant guardian?"

"That is my guess. My advice would be to soothe rather than cut."

Garth nodded and quickened his pace, taking the lead.

After a long hike, they reached their destination, arriving at the edge of a forest marked by a fast flowing brook. Beyond, the vertical stone of the mound wall rose up into distant shadows.

"Now is the time to claim the sword," Brennan said. "This quest you must make on your own. Find your way to the wall and climb to a cave."

Garth took a long breath and looked the Druid in the eyes. "I will find this cave and bring the sword out."

Brennan put a hand on his shoulder and said, "Good luck. May the gods bless you."

Garth nodded his thanks and stepped over the dark water of the stream and into the pathless forest. He put his arm in front of his face and walked forward as best he could through the grasping oak scrub and alder thickets.

Sweat dampened his back, and the twisting forest stretched deeper than he thought possible. The trees blocked him at every turn, made him fight for every step. They pointed away from the wall, their limbs forming barricades. Hawthorne hedges ripped at his skin and cloak, tearing and drawing blood, but he kept on. Finally, he arrived at the cliff wall.

Garth took a drink from his water skin and peered up. The cliff soared above him and disappeared in the darkness. *So now I find the cave and a way up.*

He climbed over the boulders at the foot of the cliff, looking for a clue about where to go. At the wall, he clamored over the loose rocks and moved down the cliff side, searching.

Then he saw it. Up high, a carefully concealed set of stairs led steeply upward. He left his cloak behind and worked his way across the unsteady boulders to the hidden base of the steps.

Garth's hands grew instantly sweaty. He shook them out, took a breath, and started to climb on the loose stone steps as they switched back and forth across the cliff face.

The long set of steps ended at a narrow landing. Light chased away the shadows at the high spot, above the trees. Many orbs hovered nearby, interested in what was happening.

He wiped the sweat from his brow and looked for more clues.

Far above, he spotted the cave entrance, but the stairs ended with nothing but vertical stone above. He looked more closely and found handholds, tracing a way up. Garth climbed his way to the lip of the cave. As he neared the top, he heard a rush of wings. Claws and teeth bit his arms and back. He wanted to pull his sword free, but he was more worried about losing his grip and falling than the faerie menace.

With quivering muscles and sweat in his eyes, he gained the ledge of the cave entrance. He turned on his attackers, and with a few swings of his sword was able to drive off the blood drinkers, but not before they had wounded him. He did his best to stop the blood and turned to see what the cave held.

The grotto brimmed with life. Vines and brambles filled the narrow space, and blue luminous flowers lit the way deeper into the crack.

Green and strangling, huh? I better be careful.

He wormed his way through the tangle, careful not to damage the plants. Up ahead, the light grew brighter, and white flowers joined the blue. Together, they formed a wreath around the goal of his endeavor.

The sword.

Claíomh Solais.

It glowed with its own light as if alive. For a moment, Garth could only stand and stare. It was even more magnificent than his boyhood imagination had allowed. He wondered who had last wielded it or whose eyes had last looked upon it. He thought of the countless years that had passed since the blade was forged and he felt suddenly still, reverence for this ancient blade overflowing.

He stepped forward, only to be grabbed by vines and creepers. They came to life, twisting and climbing around his limbs. He struggled to stay clear, but the more he fought, the farther away the Claíomh Solais slipped.

Garth stumbled on an aged skull and remembered Brennan's words. *Better to soothe than cut.*

He put away his sword, stopped fighting the vines, and slowed down his breathing. Slowly, the creepers let go, but when he started forward, they attacked again, this time with more ferocity. The vines pulled his feet out from under him and he crashed to the ground. They pinned his arms and legs to the ground. Before he knew it, the green tendrils encircled his throat.

Heart fit to burst, he knew he had but one chance. He was no Druid, but Brennan taught him the secret names for each of the ogam plants, and vine was one of them.

He took a deep breath, perhaps his last, and sang,

"Milsiu féraib

Inded erc

Sásad Ile"

His voice echoed in the narrow place, filling it with sound. The vines stopped, but did not loosen. Only after he had chanted the phrases nine times, the vine manacles dropped away. He lay still for a moment, chilled with relief, then struggled back to his feet. He leaned against the wall and put both palms to his eyes. *That was a little too close.*

He opened his eyes, walked forward, and looked at his prize.

A one-handed sword, made of a mixture of silver and gold, it was unlike anything he had seen before. He had expected a bronze blade, given the weapon's antiquity, but it looked more like the iron he was used to, although brighter, like silver. The blade tapered a little from the hilt and curved gradually outward, slightly wider near the tip, in the traditional leaf blade pattern. The hilt, handle, and pommel were bright gold, carved with oak leaves and knot work. Garth had never seen anything so bright and beautiful.

Taking a deep breath, he grasped the sword. True to its name, it shone like a torch. The weapon hummed in his hand, and he knew it had been forged with mighty magic. The ancients had used it in many battles, and now it would awaken again.

Claíomh Solais, the sword of Nuada, was his.

Chapter 14

A blur of painful days passed. After the first day, Logan and his captor left the forest, which had been wet and swampy in vast areas, and now rode through an endless sea of grass. Finally, on the third day, he glimpsed a fortress in the distance. With its many towers, it stabbed upward like obsidian daggers. His stomach clenched; he knew they had reached their destination.

From the stables, his captor prodded and jabbed him through an open area just inside the black walls of the fortress, then pushed him through massive double doors to an interior chamber.

Logan turned behind him. "I'm going, okay? You don't have to keep digging your damn spear into my back."

"Shut your mouth or you'll have worse."

"Someday you and I are going to have a serious disagreement."

The yellow-eyed man put a gag on him and struck him harder. Logan glared back as the man pushed him inside.

He tried to look around, but his kidnaper shoved his head down and told him to look at his feet. A force hit him behind his knees and he collapsed forward onto the hard stone floor. He jerked his head up and stared at the man in defiance. He turned and saw *her*.

Logan's heart raced. He momentarily forgot everything else. His anger and fear evaporated. His eyes widened.

Beautiful in a terrible sort of way, with white skin and long raven black hair, the woman's face was stern and cold with black lipstick and heavy eye shadow. She wore a low-cut black gown with a tall collar and a sword at her hip, its pommel the head of a crow. Silver jewelry adorned her, with a circlet on her brow and long earrings of glittering disks. Her necklace hung low, a blood red stone in an elaborate setting, and her wrists were hooped with bangles of black, red, and silver. But most impressive was the aura of light that shimmered around her in swirls of black. Its purple pulsing energy pressed against Logan.

"You've done well, Ulchabhán," she said, rising from her throne, "capturing him and bringing him all this way. You will be rewarded."

The man bowed.

Logan committed the man's name to his memory. Ulchabhán would pay.

"Unbind him, he is no danger to me," the woman said, walking toward them.

Ulchabhán roughly untied his restraints and the gag. Logan rubbed his wrists. He knew this must be the Queen, but what did she want with him?

"Logan," she said, warmth in her voice.

He stared at her, his confusion deepening. He had been certain his capture was a mistake, but she knew his name.

She smiled. "Do you not know me?"

He struggled to speak. Her presence was unlike anything he had ever experienced. The aura of power radiating from her overwhelmed him. He shook his head, not trusting his voice.

"Stand up so I can take a look at you."

Logan stood, twisted his wolf ring absently, finding it difficult to breathe, taking the opportunity to study the woman more closely. Her features were remarkably similar to, well, his own: long, straight black hair, a thin nose, and high cheekbones. But she was much paler than he.

She circled him before gesturing to a chair. "Sit. I've brought you here to help me, but in order for you to understand why, there's a history to share. In your world, it's told as legend, if it's told at all. And even if you've heard some of it before, I have no doubt it was from the wrong point of view." She flung herself onto her throne before adding bitterly, "History is always written by the victor you overlanders always say. But such revisions don't make it true."

Logan sat in the chair, still rubbing at his wrists. "Where are we?" he asked.

"And who are you?"

"I have many names, but this...*this* is the hawthorne

mound." She spat the words, made them sound like poison. "My people, the Tuatha de Dannan, reigned for many millennia in the world above. We fought amongst ourselves, of course, for there will always be those who are more intelligent and more powerful."

Logan had the feeling she was talking about herself.

"The Celts invaded from Iberia and wanted our land. We fought them, but in the end, we were poorly led and outnumbered. We were defeated."

"The Celts?" Logan rubbed at his temples, having difficulty taking it all in.

"Yes, a barbarous people, dirty and ignorant." She fell silent for a moment, as if reliving the defeat again. Her face was hard and unyielding.

"After the battle," she continued, "the Celt's Druids used magic to imprison those of us considered troublesome in these mounds under the earth. There are multiple mounds, of course, to separate the most powerful of the Tuatha de Dannan."

"So this place, this underground world, is just one of many?"

"Yes, I thought that was obvious." Morrigan frowned at him. "I am one of the most powerful, and yet my power cannot extend far beyond this world. The guardian tree—the hawthorne—keeps me a prisoner and acts as a power filter of sorts, though I can pass above ground at certain times of the year. It gives me a chance to see what the world has become."

She paused, crafted a small smile. "The Celts have kept my people prisoner here for a long time. The people above have grown soft and weak, but here below we've grown strong and multiplied. It is time for our exile to end."

"How long have you been here?" Logan asked, certain he was not getting the whole story.

"I've been trapped here, unjustly, for thousands of years by the count of the world above," the Queen said. "It's been less than that here, because of Druid magic, though it still feels as long."

Logan nodded. A difference in time he found to be the least of the day's oddities. "But if you were alive at the beginning of the exile, that would mean you're over two thousand years old."

She laughed. "I forget you know nothing of the sidhe. We are immortal."

Immortals. Of course.

"Oh, our people can be killed, but we do not age past our prime. I assure you, it is true. I am many thousands of years old. The longer we live, the more powerful we become. It's almost impossible to kill an ancient such as me. But there are few like me anymore, even in the other mounds."

She did not sound boastful, Logan thought. Rather, she sounded so assured of her power and immortality that it was barely worth mentioning. It was a part of her, like her crow-headed sword.

"What does this have to do with me?" he asked.

She smiled, as if she had been waiting for just that question. "The world above has become polluted and diseased. The earth is on the verge of a global catastrophe because of what the humans have done. They kill the trees and blast holes in the ground; they pour toxins into the rivers. They have overwhelmed the earth with their numbers and now many starve to death while the rest grow fat. Can you deny it?"

Logan shook his head. He knew humanity raced recklessly toward the destruction of the entire planet. It was a topic he and Rhiannon frequently discussed. "No, it's true."

She nodded, as if she'd won. "It is time for the Faerie to return; to restore the balance; to heal the earth. To take *our* place under the sun and moon once again." Agitated, she surged to her feet. "The hawthorne is dying, and my power grows again. Soon, the accursed tree will be dead. It will be time to return to the world above and reclaim what is ours."

Morrigan returned to her throne and sat silently for a moment, studying him.

He refrained from pointing out she still hadn't answered his question. He had a feeling she knew it and enjoyed stringing him along.

"You don't look much like your father."

Logan's brows raised. "My father? You knew my father?"

"Yes, you could say that," she said with a smile. "To answer your question, you are special. You have knowledge of the world above, and you have certain talents which could prove very useful. That is why I brought you here."

"What talents?" Logan felt his face flush. He didn't have any talents that would be useful to a powerful faerie, unless she meant the shapeshifting. "I don't know what you mean," he said.

"You have denied your heritage long enough, and you don't need to lie to me. I know full well your abilities."

Logan tried to keep his face blank, but his mind was reeling. How could she know about what he could do? No one outside his tribe knew. Not even Rhiannon. A sudden thought made him smile. Maybe she could teach him how to control it.

As if reading his thoughts, she said, "Soon, you will see there is little I don't know about you. There are many ways we can help each other, Logan."

He shook his head, trying not to appear overeager. "I'm sure there are others with the same talents who have embraced their gift, who would be of better use than I."

"This is true, but none of them have your bloodline. You are unique in that you share both your father's power *and* your mother's."

This time Logan didn't have to fake anything. He had no idea what she was talking about. A sudden tingling traveled through his body. He had never known his mother. "What power did my mother have?" he asked.

She stood and approached him. She grasped both his hands and pulled him to his feet so she could look him straight in the eye.

"My name is Morrigan. I've brought you here because you are my son."

Chapter 15

Logan paced the floor of the throne room, turning to look at Morrigan, considering what she had told him.

"You're not my mother. My mother was a Sioux, and she died when I was born."

"That is what you were told." Morrigan waved a hand dismissively. "Your father and I agreed you should not know the truth until the time was right. I left you in your father's care—as a shaman, he was one of the more powerful men I'd met in the overland. Nowhere near my ability, of course, but I knew you'd be safe. But just to be sure, I've been watching you."

Logan's head swam. He raised his hands showing his palms. *No, it's not true.* Logan had no memory of his mother and had always believed what he had been told about her, that she had died in childbirth. He struggled to regain his composure and stop being the victim.

"If you've been watching me, you will know I've left my so-called talents behind me. I'm an exile from my father's people," he said.

"You are an exile by choice," said Morrigan. "It is time for you to stop running from who you are."

That was exactly what he wanted to do. He wanted to stop running and embrace his power, but he didn't know how to start. "Can you help me learn to control my power?"

"That remains to be seen, but for now you will be given a place of honor here and afforded every luxury. Soon, you will come to realize the truth of my words." The Morrigan turned, walked back to her throne, and reclined there.

"Rhiannon knew in her heart you were born enemies, even if she could not explain it," she said.

"Rhiannon?" Logan's heart caught in his throat. He did not

want her caught up in this. "How do you know about Rhiannon?"

"I told you, I've been watching you," Morrigan said lightly. "Besides, I keep a close eye on my—our—enemies. Rhiannon lured you here to deliver you to her uncle to be used against me."

"Rhiannon is not my enemy." Logan clenched his fists.

"Easy words for a deceived soul. She is on her way here now. We shall see what happens when she finds you."

"She followed me?"

"Indeed," said Morrigan. "She hoped to keep you from me. She cannot use you against me now."

Logan thought back to what had happened. Rhiannon led him to this place? For what reason? Could he even trust Rhiannon? Had she betrayed him? Logan drew in a quick breath, considering. No, he didn't believe any of this.

Morrigan smiled, and Logan realized he'd not been thinking his own thoughts. *She is projecting her thoughts into my mind. This woman who claims to be my mother is indeed powerful, but she doesn't need to know that I can tell.*

"I will think on what you say," he said, trying to keep his voice steady.

"Very well, but in the meantime, I want to introduce you to some people."

"People? What people?"

"You'll see, but first we need to get you cleaned up. The guards will take you to a room where you can bathe and change your clothes."

Logan looked down at his soiled Sturgis T-shirt and jeans and back up at the Morrigan. "My clothes are fine."

The Morrigan's face flushed, just for a moment. "Very well, as you wish. Come with me."

He knew Rhiannon would never betray him. But why was Morrigan trying to make him think so? If he couldn't trust Morrigan's words about Rhiannon, was everything she said a lie? His stomach knotted and his chest tightened.

Maybe this woman could help him with his power, he decided, but he would only take her help under his terms. He refused to be forced to do what *she* wanted. He knew he must tread carefully now. More than anything, he needed information about the Morrigan and this place. Once he had that, if he could learn about controlling his power too, it would help him get free of his past. Then could get free of this place, get free of *her*.

* * *

Logan followed the Morrigan out of the throne room. Strange music echoed up ahead. The Morrigan walked just in front of him, and the aura of her power radiated out behind her. The black nimbus swirled like a cloud of ink stirred in a clear glass of water, strands thick and thin turning constantly around her. The air crackled with energy, like the tension before a lightning strike.

How could he possibly be her son? His resemblance to her was striking, but that could just be coincidence. If Rhiannon was trying to find him, he needed to gather information and escape. If Morrigan considered Rhiannon her enemy, he must protect her.

They walked past rows of armed sentries, standing at rigid attention, dressed in black armor. Logan grew uneasy as he took in the number of guards.

The Morrigan was not going to let him just walk out of here, he decided. He would have to figure out how he could escape. The offer of help with his shapeshifting couldn't outweigh his fidelity to Rhiannon. If he had to choose, he knew he couldn't trade his loyalty for knowledge.

Double doors released as they approached. The room beyond opened like a cathedral, with soaring high arches and a long colonnade of sculpted pillars. Blood red and midnight black marble made a checkerboard pattern on the floor, on top of which every variety of monster and creature Logan had ever imagined, from trolls to ogres, werewolves to goblins, danced. They gyrated and howled in grotesque time to the music. Glimmers of light reflected off talons, bronze armor, and scales.

Plants grew everywhere, from the cracks in the tile, from the walls and the tall columns, emitting a purple and green light and casting bizarre shadows on the stone walls. Glowing orbs floated high above the crowd, and they changed color with the music.

Logan stopped at the doorway, his heart racing. Ulchabhán jabbed him in the back, forcing him forward. Clenching his jaw, Logan walked into the room.

The crowd parted as they approached, and one by one, they bowed to the Queen, but also to him. Unnerved, Logan followed the cleared path, trying to take everything in. Above him, suspended in midair, hung a raised platform with musicians playing. Drums, fiddles, harps, and pipes played, but there were other instruments he had never seen before. The music was terrifying and magnificent at the same time.

Through the crowd at the far end of the massive room, a tall dais rose with a large throne made of black raven's wings atop it. Together they crossed the room to the high seat.

Morrigan sat, leaving Logan standing awkwardly next to her. "Consider this your welcome home party." She looked more imposing now, surrounded by her subjects.

"Thank you," Logan mumbled.

Her features tightened. "Don't get into the habit of thanking people; it's a bad thing to do. Among the sidhe, if you thank someone, it implies a debt. If you thank someone, they can rightly ask you to do something for them, and it would be a severe breach of conduct to refuse them." She smiled mirthlessly. "In our society, much power comes from people owing favors. I can't have my son indebted to everyone when you are supposed to be aiding me."

Logan nodded at the reprimand. "I'm not convinced you are my mother. And I don't know why I should be interested in helping you."

"I like your stubbornness," said Morrigan with a smile. She looked thoughtful, as if trying to decide something. "This might change your mind. A glamour was placed on you to hide your less than human features from the world above. I will now remove it."

Morrigan closed her eyes and waved a hand. In an instant, a strange tingling sensation covered his head, especially his ears. He reached up to feel them and quickly pulled his hand away in shock. Reluctantly, he felt them again. They were pointed.

"They are your true ears. It is a minor change, but pointed ears would mark you for non-human in an instant."

Stunned, Logan tried to process her words. His real ears were pointed? "Let's say you are my mother, that you didn't just create these ears on the spot in order to convince me. Why go to all this trouble? Why bother finding me now?"

"My plan is to reclaim my ancient lands in the world above. Yes, I have visited from time to time, but so much changes between each visit. I chose to have you raised by your father so that you, my son, may guide me when the time comes. I know nothing of computers or engines or electricity, and you must help me."

The word 'must' made Logan bristle. "And what if I don't want to help you?"

"Ah, spoken like a true faerie! In time, you will want to help—once you understand who you are—but I will not force you. In the meantime, there is much you must learn if you are to be a true Prince of the Sidhe. You know little of magic or swords, and these you must master. Tonight, enjoy the festivities, for tomorrow your training begins."

Morrigan gestured to a servant who brought a low bench for him. "Take at seat next to me," she said.

"I think I'll stand," he said.

"I see you don't like to be told what to do. I like it."

Logan shifted uneasily. Once she looked away, he touched his ears again with disbelief. Could they be real? Could she really be his mother?

He looked out on the crowd, and this time saw not just monsters, but also human-type people. They looked like Morrigan, with human features, but they were far from human. Beautiful, even the men, they were dressed in elaborate clothing that glowed and changed with the mood of the music. Some wore bright red, and others purple. Gold and silver jewelry adorned them all, from navel rings to serpentine coils on naked arms. Hair color of every hue crowned the heads of the dancers; some glowed blue, while others were black and shot through with flickering lightning.

"The others that look like us, I mean, um, that look like you, are they the sidhe?" asked Logan. He couldn't believe he had made that slip.

Morrigan smiled. "Yes," she said. "Do you find them attractive?"

"Yes. They are beautiful. Who are the others?"

"We are all faerie, but some have less pure blood and are mingled with elemental blood. You see that tall ogre over there?" Morrigan pointed at the 12-foot tall creature in the center of the hall.

Logan nodded.

"Well, ogres are mostly earth elementals, but with some faerie blood. They make excellent soldiers."

"I can imagine," he said, hoping he would never have to fight one.

"You see the young sidhe woman dancing close to the

ogre? The one in the green gown?"

Logan had not noticed her until just that moment and suddenly wondered how he could have missed her. Nearly naked, with the green fabric accentuating her curves, she had long blonde hair and emerald eyes. He couldn't help but watch her ample breasts and athletic thighs as she whirled to the music. Braids of gold light framed her face and matched the dozens of bracelets on her arms. An aura of summer sunshine encircled her.

Logan stared.

"Would you like to meet her?"

He knew that was a bad idea and managed to say as much.

"Oh, come now. You are a prince, and there are certain advantages to be enjoyed." Morrigan gestured for the young woman to approach them.

Logan watched the graceful woman walk toward them, admiring the way her hips moved. As she got closer, she was even more beautiful than he first thought. Her straight hair hung down her bare back to almost her waist and glowed a soft white-gold. Her lips were full and sensuous, and Logan couldn't help imagining what they would feel like on his body

"Áine, come and sit with us a while."

He watched her climb the stairs. She curtsied to the Queen before turning toward him. He could smell her perfume. It was like vanilla, cinnamon, and honey all blended together and poured over a sun-kissed naked body.

"It is a pleasure to meet you," she said softly, leaning forward to look up at Logan. The thin fabric of her dress shifted, exposing even more of her perfect breasts.

Logan flushed. He tried to summon an image of Rhiannon, but all he could see was the beautiful faerie in front of him. Her presence was overpowering, much like Morrigan, but in a different, seductive way.

"The pleasure is all mine," he stammered.

Áine smiled at him, and the world stopped. Dimly, he knew he had to get free of this situation, that it would only come to misery for him, but it was so hard to think. A small part of him wanted to stand and take his leave, but his eyes could not leave Áine.

"Are you enjoying yourself, my Prince?" she said.

"Yes, I am. A bit too much, I'm afraid."

Áine laughed and took a seat next to the queen.

Logan gathered his resolve. "What food can be had here?" He hoped the blunt question would drag his mind away from Áine.

The Morrigan looked to a servant and nodded. Soon, a tray of steaming food appeared. Logan finally took the offered seat and ate. The tray held bread, mushrooms, and some kind of meat he hoped was beef. He spotted beer and pastries. Famished, Logan ate greedily, satisfying one desire while he kept thoughts of others at bay.

"Would you like to dance, my Prince?" asked Áine when he had finished eating.

Logan swallowed. He had never been much of a dancer, but he caught himself considering it. "I appreciate the offer, but not now," he answered finally.

Áine frowned. "Your majesty, perhaps he likes men?"

He turned at the sound of the Morrigan's laughter.

"Perhaps he does."

Logan frowned. He wouldn't be goaded. If he took one step down that path, it would be disaster. Clearly, he needed to get out of this place before he was caught irrevocably the Morrigan's web. Any chance he had of learning about his shapeshifting was not worth the risk of staying in this place. He could tell even more so now that the Morrigan was dangerous and she could bring to bear strong persuasion to get what she wanted. He knew he could resist…

I'm breaking out of here tonight.
* * *

The party raged, and after one beer, Logan stopped drinking. He would need all of his wits to escape. When he felt like he'd waited long enough, he turned and faced both women.

"It has been an exciting day and I would like to take my leave, if I am truly not your prisoner."

"So soon? I thought you would have more stamina," said Morrigan.

"I am tired and have a lot to think about."

"Very well," she said with a gleam in her eye. "I will have the guards take you to your room."

"I hope you sleep well," said Áine. The young woman stood and offered Logan her hand. Before he knew it, he had taken her hand and kissed it. Immediately, he regretted doing so. Her skin was warm and perfumed, like a summer day, and it was all he could do to not pull her closer. He lowered her hand with great difficulty and walked away.

Logan pushed his way through the crowd of revelers. Once free, he found his mind still disturbed. Despite leaving Áine behind, his thoughts kept straying to her.

He tried to break the flow, thinking about everything that happened that day. He reached up and checked his ears, over and over. How could they be this shape? Maybe the Morrigan used a glamour to make them appear this way now. As soon as he thought of the Morrigan, Áine's image invaded again. His methods weren't working.

Finally, he conjured an image of Rhiannon to counteract Áine's influence. He remembered the look she gave him when he proposed. Her eyes said it all. The blue of them, soft and morning glory bright, whispered of timeless depth, telling him what eternity really meant. The feeling of that look banished Áine's magic and made her seem like a tarnished reflection of true beauty.

Relieved, Logan closed his eyes, took a deep breath, and let it out slowly.

The sound of the guards' boots echoed ahead of him through the stone corridors until they reached his room. Beyond the heavy door, the chamber inside was round, its outside wall perforated with tall narrow windows, and a large bed dominated the space.

Logan exhaled hard as the door closed behind him and the soldiers left him alone. He walked to the dark windows. Outside, myriad lights danced in the elvish night. Pixies and sylphs by the hundreds traveled their highways through the dark dome of the underground world.

Pacing in front of the windows, Logan tried to come up with a plan. If he could get the door open, he could try shapeshifting and see if he could fight his way clear. The hair on the back of his neck prickled. On second thought, maybe that was a bad idea. If he lost control, he could black out, and the Morrigan's guards might turn their crossbows on him.

No, a better idea would be to use his new status to get close to the outer walls. Once there, he could shift and find a way out. The question was, could he get past the guards just outside the door without drawing attention?

Logan walked to the door and pulled on the handle. It was locked. He pounded on it. "Bring me some beer," he commanded.

He was pretty sure these guards knew not to let him out, but surely a request for beer from the new prince wasn't unreasonable.

A short time later, the door opened. Logan stood by the window and held out his hand. One sentry brought him the drink, while the other stayed near the door.

Logan took a drink from the ceramic mug and punched the guard in the face with it. The soldier went down, but the second one fired his crossbow at Logan's leg. Logan dodged the bolt, and before the man could call out, he kneed him in the gut. The leather armor offered some resistance, but not enough. Logan grabbed the back of the helmet and punched upward with his other hand, knocking the guard unconscious. He gagged and tied both men with bed sheets, took the keys, and locked the door behind him.

Logan jogged down the stairs and halted at the bottom to pull himself together. He took a breath and walked out as casually as he could, as if out for a stroll. He made eye contact with a few sentries who looked straight ahead as he walked past.

He remembered the way he had been brought in through the stables and found his way back to an outside door. He waited until the hallway was empty, used one of the keys from the ring he'd stolen, and slipped out into the dark courtyard. Hoping not to draw any attention to himself, he stuck to the shadows and soon neared the gate. So close now, he could almost taste freedom once again. Adrenaline coursed through him.

"Out for a stroll?" Morrigan said suddenly from behind him.

Stunned, Logan turned and the dark Queen stood not five feet away, and behind her a row of armed guards.

"I just needed a bit of fresh air," he lied.

Morrigan raised a brow. "That's not what the guards in your room would say."

"Listen, I'll be honest. I don't want to be here. I don't believe you're my mother."

"Do you think I would treat you so gently if I were not?" the Morrigan said with venom. "You don't know me at all. I could easily make you beg for my mercy."

Logan swallowed hard. He doubted she was bluffing.

The Morrigan sighed and lifted her hand. In response, the soldiers raised their crossbows and leveled them at Logan.

"Whoa, hold on a minute. You're not just going kill me, are you?"

"Well, if you are unwilling to even consider what is being offered to you, I will have to do without you. Painful, yes, but not insurmountable."

"Okay, okay. I'll reconsider. *Really.*"

"How do I know you just won't try to escape again?"

Logan scrambled for an answer she'd believe. "I give you my word I will not try to escape until I've had time to consider what you are offering."

"How long would that be? Five minutes? I have a better idea." Morrigan took a knife from her belt and stepped toward him. "I will take your hair as a pledge." With a quick cut, she held his ponytail in her hand.

"No! What the hell!" Logan shouted. "Why did you do that?"

"Now if you try to escape, I will have this to use magic on you. Besides, you look better without it."

He glared at her, fury on the verge of erupting, but the line of crossbows stopped him. He gritted his teeth and snarled at her. The bitch had cut off his hair. She would pay for that.

"In the morning there is a test you must take. If you succeed, I will give this back to you. Until then, I suggest you get some sleep."

"You are a conniving bitch," Logan hissed.

"You have no idea," said the Morrigan with a laugh.

Logan lowered his chin to his chest and walked into the night. He still didn't know if the Morrigan was bluffing about his cut hair, but could he take that chance? He sighed. It didn't really matter anyway. From what he had seen at the walls, there was no way to escape over the chasm. He would have to come up with a better plan and before he did that, he needed sleep.

Chapter 16

Logan stumbled into his room, prodded by spear point. He turned and glared at the soldier, recognizing it was the one he had smashed in the face. He turned away and gave a small smile of satisfaction, then he saw *her*.

Áine waited for him, *in his bed*.

His blood rose at the sight of the beautiful faerie woman lounging naked on his sheets, holding a glass of red wine. She was truly gorgeous.

"Get out of my bed," he said.

"I was just warming it up for you, my Prince."

Images of what they might do together pounded in his brain. His hands began to sweat. He opened the door and pointed. "Out now."

Logan knew if he gave in, even in the slightest way, he would be in deep trouble. He channeled his frustration over his thwarted escape attempt at the sidhe woman.

Áine swung her legs out and stood naked in front of him. She took a long drink of her wine and slowly licked her lips.

Logan's body responded, blood rushing. He swallowed and pointed at the door.

"You don't want me as an enemy," she said as she walked past him and brushed his stomach with her hand. She frowned from the doorway, still naked and immodest.

Her touch lingered across his abs. His clothes suddenly felt too hot. A powerful lust threatened to overwhelm him.

A fluid movement of curves, she undulated out of sight.

It took all of Logan's will to close the door behind her.

He barely slept, his thoughts chasing each other. He wondered where Rhiannon was, and the thought of not being able to help her made him pound his fist into the bed. Images of Áine lying naked in his bed refused to go away. He knew Áine might make his life difficult, but angering her was a small price to pay for his integrity.

A knock came at the door early, and he was summoned to follow. Guards brought him to the Morrigan in her throne room. Again she wore black, but this time she had on tall, leather boots, black pants, shirt, and a leather jacket. Red lipstick accentuated her pale skin. In her hand, she held a riding crop.

"So you really don't like women, I hear," she said with a smirk.

Logan met her gaze without smiling. "I know what you're trying to do, and it won't work."

"Oh really? What am I trying to do?"

"You are trying to make me forget Rhiannon."

"Surely not. I was just hoping for Áine to give you a warm welcome."

"I will remain faithful to Rhiannon."

"Faithful? What a strange idea. Nevertheless, we have more important things to talk about."

The Morrigan stood from her throne, put down the riding crop, and walked across the room. "I have a question for you." She pulled a .357 revolver from under her jacket and pointed it at him. "How does it work?"

Logan stiffened like a snake just slithered into the room. He stepped clear of the muzzle and held out his hand, hoping she would give him the weapon.

The Morrigan turned it around and put it in his hand.

Could she really be so ignorant? I doubt it.

Logan opened the action. Hollow point ammunition filled the chambers. He raised a brow and his breathing quickened. *Maybe this is my way out? Maybe she really doesn't know how it works.*

"I want you to shoot me."

"What?"

"You heard me. Shoot me now!"

Logan raised the gun and pointed at her chest. His mind raced. *What game is she playing?*

"Shoot now or I'll turn it on you."

He took a breath, and as he exhaled, pulled the trigger. The powder exploded, deafening his ears. Logan couldn't believe his eyes.

Nothing happened. The Morrigan stood smiling at him. "Try it again."

Logan shot until the gun was empty, even at her head, where the bullet disappeared.

He dropped the gun.

"You see, it doesn't work on me. I am immortal, and your feeble technology is no match for my magic."

Stunned, Logan began to realize the depth of the danger. Still a little skeptical, he walked across the room to look for the slugs that must have hit the wall. He found them, embedded in the stone of the wall.

"I see what you mean," he said.

The Morrigan laughed. She returned to her throne and took up the riding crop again. She slapped the whip against her open hand as she studied him. "So you believe me?"

His stomach was in knots. Whether his doubts were shaken or not, he would not admit it to her. "Nothing a cheap stage magician couldn't do," he managed.

"Ever the doubter." She laughed. "It is of no consequence. Today, it is you who must prove yourself to *me*."

Logan sucked in a breath and stepped back a pace. "The test?"

"Magic is what matters here, and this test will teach you more about how to use it—if you live through it."

He scanned the room like a caged animal. "If I *live* through it?"

"Well, there are dangers when learning magic, and we both need to know if you have the aptitude. Son or not, you are of little use to me if you can't use your magic. If you succeed, I will return your hair."

She held out the riding crop with both hands. Before his eyes, it transformed, not a whip anymore. Now she held the long strands of his hair.

Beads of sweat dampened his upper lip, and he felt his eyes widen. *How had she done it?* The sight of his severed hair made his face flush and he started to pace. "If I pass this test, you will let me go free?"

"Yes, *if* you survive."

Logan swallowed hard. He doubted she would keep her

word. "Tell me more about this test."

"I will take you to an ancient place, and there you must find your way to the moonwell. It is a pool where, long ago, the light of the moon was captured and infused with magic. The moonwell is the key to mastering your shapeshifting."

Warmth suddenly filled his body and he felt like he had just taken three shots of espresso. This moonwell might just give him what he needed to clear his name and avenge his father. He took as slow of a breath as he could manage. This was exactly what he wanted. But there was no sense making things easy for her, and he didn't know if what she was telling him was actually true.

"And what if I refuse to play your little game?"

"Then I will have to be more persuasive..."

Logan glared at her.

The Morrigan smiled back at him like a cat. "Very well. Let's make this more interesting. Bring her in," she spoke to the air.

Logan's heart nearly galloped away from him. *Her?*

A door opened. Rhiannon, bound, gagged, and head down, was led to the throne.

Chills ran up Logan's spine, and his mouth fell open. "Rhiannon?" he shouted.

She turned her head and gave a weak smile, and her knees buckled.

Logan ran to her, but spear points stopped him.

"I told you she was coming for you," said the Morrigan.

"Let me help her!"

"All in good time. There is much at stake here. Many will be watching your progress, and the speed at which you finish will mean a lot for your future here and for mine. With a proven shapeshifter standing at my side, none will dare rebel against me."

"Not all your subjects are pleased with you? I don't understand why," Logan said with a sneer.

The Morrigan's eyes blazed. "Return in five hours, or your beloved Rhiannon dies."

Logan felt like he'd been hit in the stomach by a wrecking ball. The Morrigan was going to kill her. Her fate rested in his hands. "Rhiannon, say something," he shouted.

"I'm sorry, Logan. I came to rescue you, but I was caught. Please, Logan. Do what she says."

His spine stiffened. Something wasn't right. Rhiannon would not submit so easily.

He turned back to the Morrigan. "I don't believe this, any of it. Rhiannon wouldn't tell me to do what you say."

The queen shrugged. "It makes no difference to me. Guards, kill her."

Logan's breath caught in his throat. *What if I am wrong?* "No, wait! I'll do it. I don't seem to have a choice."

"Now you are beginning to understand," said the Morrigan with a smile.

"If you hurt her, I will kill you."

The Morrigan laughed. "You can try."

Chapter 17

Surrounded by guards, Logan looked one last time at Rhiannon's crumpled form.

"Don't worry," he said before following the Morrigan out of the throne room. "I'll be back for you soon, and we will get the hell out of here."

"Hurry, Logan, but keep yourself safe," she said weakly.

Logan firmed his jaw and followed behind the Morrigan. Áine joined them when they entered the dungeons and walked with them through a maze of tunnels under the castle. Dressed in black and red with tall boots, Aine's breasts pushed hard against the fabric of her tight shirt.

Logan tried to ignore her and kept his eyes fixed ahead.

Just behind them, Ulchabhán led an entourage of sidhe, ogres, and goblins, who joined them as the unfinished masonry changed to rough-hewn natural caves. At last, an enormous cavern opened up before them. Inside, in a pale purple light, a monolithic stone structure climbed out of the dirt and rose at a steep angle toward distant shadows.

Logan stared at the scene. It reminded him of an Egyptian temple that had been buried for thousands of years in a forgotten underground cavern.

They walked closer, giving Logan had a better view. From the bottom of the edifice, a set of steep stairs rose high above the cavern floor. Halfway up, the steps narrowed, and on either side stood tall stone columns carved to look like oak trunks.

A cramp tightened his gut. The sheer power of the place intimidated him. Logan wondered who built the structure and for what reason. Surely not just for this test?

The idea filled him with dread. What horrors awaited him inside? What if he failed?

Morrigan started up the stairs, a dark hourglass filled with black sand clutched in her hand, and gestured for Logan to follow. He looked at the glass and swallowed hard. The fate of his life—and Rhiannon's—rested on the sand.

He followed, and the two ascended halfway up the grand stairs, the steps darkened by foliage-draped walls.

"This is where you must go on alone."

Logan took off his rings, put them in one hand, and extended them to the Morrigan.

"What's this?"

"If I'm going to have to shapeshift, I don't want to lose these."

The Morrigan nodded and accepted them.

"This is where I will find the moonwell?" he asked.

"Yes...or death for you and Rhiannon if you fail."

Logan swallowed, wishing to be anywhere else.

"Áine will wait for you below." She paused and turned over the hourglass. "Now go!"

Startled, he turned away and ran upstairs to the top. Morrigan may as well have left a viper waiting for him, he thought, but she was the least of his problems now. Either death or freedom lay ahead, depending upon whether he could conquer this place.

Logan reached the top, stood at the edge of long rectangular area. A room filled with tall columns extended before him. He wiped his sweaty hands on his jeans and thought of his other agenda. His goal, ever since his father died, was to find a way to control his shapeshifting. The animal in him had always been too strong.

But if what Morrigan said about this place was true, he would finally learn to tame the beast. Unless there were hidden strings attached. He just didn't know.

Logan set his jaw and looked into the first room; time was wasting. Down the center and on either side of the room stood rows of five monumental oak columns, with no ceiling above, nothing but the distant shadows of the cavern. Ivy clung to these walls too, and they glowed a faint lavender. A pile of dead leaves filled the center of the room.

Logan jogged around the room, avoiding the leaves. He looked up, watching for anything that might harm him. For an instant, he thought something moved off to the right, but when he looked closer he found nothing. Goosebumps rose on his neck. He wished he had a weapon.

At the end of the room, two walls framed the entrance to another space. The thought of entering the dark room made his heart beat faster. Anything could be hiding in there.

He stopped to catch his breath and allowed his eyes to adjust to the inky black. Inside, stone trees filled the room—a veritable rock forest. Crumbled stone debris covered the ground. He stepped inside, feeling like he couldn't get enough breath in the narrowing space.

Across the room, a radiant purple light poured out. Logan peered at it, trying to understand what he was seeing. He decided it must be more of the luminescent plants and walked forward.

At the far edge of the room, the purple light revealed a natural cave inside the farthest wall. Glowing crystals of blue, purple, and white covered every inch of the grotto, shimmering brightly.

Logan gaped in amazement. He had never seen anything so beautiful, as if constellations of millions of tiny stars sparkled all around inside the tunnel, like glowing diamonds covering every inch. A cool breeze met his face and his nose scented fresh water. He took a step into the cave, blinking in the radiance. Farther yet, a dark place in the center of the light revealed itself. A few more steps and an outline of another cave mouth revealed itself.

Logan brought his hand to his chin as he looked around the room. This must be where the test began. The womb-like opening filled him with dread. For a moment, his feet wouldn't move, like they'd fused with the stone of the floor. He exhaled hard and stepped forward.

The strange light from the crystal grotto cast fragmented shadows. Inside the opening, the ground fell away, and Logan realized it wasn't a cave so much as a chute. Far beneath him, he could make out a few rough handholds, but beyond that nothing. Water burbled far below.

Time to begin.

Heart pounding, he looked down into the pit. He sat on the edge of the opening and lowered his feet inside. After one last look back the way he'd come, he found awkward ledges for his feet and hands and slowly climbed down. As he descended, the shaft widened and leaned outward.

Logan paused and rubbed his wet palms on his jeans, one at a time. The smooth quartz stone was slippery, and the terror of the empty abyss below threatened his resolve. He pictured Rhiannon and kept going.

The shaft widened until it mushroomed out into a cavern beneath him. With no more walls for him to descend, he looked up at the distant opening to see if he had missed anything but nothing revealed itself.

Logan felt his grip slipping. He gulped damp air and climbed back up a step where he could rest on his legs.

There must be a way down or this won't be much of a test.

He took a breath and paused to think. In the near darkness, the sound of flowing water grew louder and closer. The water below might stop his fall if he let go, or he might just fall and die.

Mouth dry and stomach tense, Logan took a deep breath and let go. He fell through the open air, wheeling his arms in panic, until he plunged into a crystal-lined pool. He opened his eyes, looked up at the surface, and pulled and kicked his way to the top.

Relief flooded him as he took a sputtering breath. Purple light flooded the rocky cavern, and above him gaped the hole through which he had fallen.

He took a panicked breath. There was no way he could climb back out that way.

Treading water and fighting the weight of his clothes, he felt a current pulling him. He swam hard, parallel to the pull, and soon a narrow shore at the edge of the water appeared. Logan struggled to the stones, climbed out, and stood.

Like the grotto above, the whole room was covered in amethyst of different hues and clear quartz. The moving water cast lavender and deep amethyst shadows and revealed nothing but more rough walls around him.

Logan turned from side to side, searching for where to go next. An idea dawned on him and he knew how he could exit, but he didn't like it. If water flowed out, that meant he could also get out. He squinted beneath the water and a cave plunged down into the ground and disappeared.

Concerned about the current, he walked out of the water, his legs feeling weak. He sat down heavily, trying to escape the dizziness that threatened to overwhelm him.

I can't do it.

He put his head between his knees, his breath suddenly very precious. "Goddamn it. What kind of a fucked up test is this?"

Again, Rhiannon's face came to him. He stood and shook out his hands.

I've got to do this.

Logan filled his lungs with air, dove into the water, and swam into the descending chute. The water turned icy and faint purple crystals lined the deepening tunnel. He kicked hard and pulled at the water with broad strokes. The force of the current raced him along, making the crystals diminish and disappear.

Logan swam for his life in the freezing dark.

His lungs burned.

He prayed for air, just a bit farther, just around the next corner, he needed air. He struggled and a faint light appeared ahead. Too far. He kicked harder, his lungs screaming. It would only be another moment before he involuntarily took a breath, and it would be over; the dark water would claim him, and he would die alone and forgotten.

Logan kicked again, pushing beyond what he ever thought was possible, and finally broke out into the air.

He gasped and gulped for air, shaking as adrenaline coursed through his body. His heart pounded in his temples, rushing precious oxygen to his screaming muscles.

Unbelievably, he was still alive.

That was too damn close, Logan thought. Another few feet and he would've been done for.

Around him, the walls of another cavern rose. He kicked for the shore, pulled himself out of the water, and collapsed on the sand.

Finally, Logan stood, took a deep breath, and let it out. Stars spun in his vision. He took another breath and another. He sat back down and put his head between his knees.

Slowly, his composure returned. He stood again, brushed the sand off his jeans, and looked around. Like the previous cavern, the purple water flowed out through another submerged cave. He didn't see any other way out. Sighing, he squatted down and closed his eyes.

I can't do it. I can't do it again.

After a few moments, Logan opened his eyes and stared blankly at the crystal wall above him. He saw it, far above.

A cave.

He fell back on the sand, shook his head, and laughed in relief. There was another way forward.

Chapter 18

Garth found Brennan again at the edge of the forest.

The Druid took a step back and gave a slow shake of his head.

"You did it," he said finally, his eyes locked on the Claíomh Solais.

"Did you doubt me?"

"No, no. Of course not. And yet to really see the sword of our ancestors…"

Brennan stepped forward and looked closer at the sword, which Garth unsheathed for him. His eyes widened. "Men will be inspired to see such a weapon. Many will want to go with you now."

"I'm in awe of it myself. Please thank the trees and tell them I will try to wield it with wisdom and courage."

"You will have need of it, before all this is done."

Garth sheathed the sword and the light dimmed.

"Have you decided about Niadh?" Brennan asked as he turned to walk back to the fort.

He matched the Druid's stride. "Yes, I have. If he wishes, he may come. He must agree to follow my orders and do what I tell him. On this mission, we will have no room for dissent."

"I'm not sure he will accept your absolute authority, Garth. You will have to be diplomatic with him."

"This is too important for court disagreement."

"It will be up to you to make him understand."

Garth felt his face turning red. "Gods, it's difficult enough without bringing this drama into it."

Brennan nodded. "I know it, but his presence could make all the difference."

They walked in silence for a few minutes.

"When we get back to the hall, let's summon the men to show them the sword," Brennan said. "It should get you some help on your quest."

"Let's hope so. I know many think it is a fool's mission."

Soon, they entered the walls again. On their way to hall, Garth stopped at home and told Deirdre what had happened. She bundled up little Wil and walked with Garth and Brennan to the hall. She quickly found an open seat while Garth took his place on the raised dais. When the hall had filled, Garth spoke.

"Warriors, friends, and family, today I embark on the quest for the Well of Wisdom. I need good men to share in the glory. Who will join me?"

Silence greeted his request.

Garth shifted from one foot to the other. He paused, and his eyes sought out his former friend. Mouth dry, he pushed himself to speak.

"I first invite Niadh. Your bravery and knowledge would be well suited to this mission. Though we've had our differences, the time has come for us to rise above our disagreements and fight our common enemy."

Niadh stood and glared at Garth. "You think a few brave words spoken here will fix what has happened?"

Garth broadened his stance and thrust out his chest. He filled his lungs, ready to wither Niadh where he stood. He let the air pass through his lips, words unspoken.

He took another breath and smoothed his léinte. "You are right, Niadh. I should have apologized for my actions and perhaps spoken to you in private first."

It was Niadh's turn to take a breath. "I will not have it said that I shirked my duty. I will come with you, but when this is over, there will be reckoning."

Garth frowned. "If there is an after, I will be happy to settle our score." He paused and looked around the room. "Beyond the first man, I will only ask for volunteers."

He hoped the initial silence that greeted his request would be forgotten.

Aodhan walked to the front of hall and stood by Garth.

Garth nodded at his friend, slapped him on the back. "Thank you, Aodhan."

He searched the room, looking for any other volunteers. He

addressed the hall again. "I know this is a dangerous quest, and many of you wonder if it can be done. I too have had my doubts, but today something happened that steeled my resolve. Today, Brennan led me to a mighty weapon."

Garth pulled the sword free from its scabbard and light erupted from the blade. He held it for all to see. "Behold Claíomh Solais! The ancient sword of Nuada!"

For a moment, the hall was silent. Then a mighty cheer went up.

Warmth radiated through Garth's whole body as he turned to show his prize to everyone. He could not contain the smile that spread across his lips, but then he sobered.

"This is indeed a mighty weapon, but it will not guarantee success. The journey to find the Well of Wisdom will be fraught with danger, and for that I will need good companions." He looked out over the crowd. "I ask again, who will come with me?"

Many men stood now, eager to join the expedition, more than Garth could accept. Brennan counted out the first six who stood and waved them up to the dais as the crowd cheered. Cathaoir, Bannan, Tuathal, Ronan, Dónal and Croftin were all good strong fighters, and Garth was pleased.

"It is good to see so many willing to brave the unknown," said Conor with a smile. "But a guard of eight men is all we can afford."

Garth nodded and turned to the men.

"Bring your best weapons and say your farewells. We leave today!"

* * *

Garth left the hall, pleased with the result. Yes, things could have gone better with Niadh, but at least he agreed to come. Eight men would indeed have to be enough.

Garth met Deirdre and walked with her back to their home and spent an hour playing with Wil. Though he was tired, he didn't want to waste a second away from his family. He did not know what this mission would bring. He rubbed a hand against the front of his tunic, his chest tight.

Deirdre set a plate of food on the table, roast pork and potatoes covered with gravy.

Garth sat with Wil on his lap and stirred the potatoes.

"I'm sorry for my mood, Deirdre. The food is good, it's

just…"

"I know, love. The quest is the right thing but it doesn't make it an easy thing. The right things are often not."

Garth hugged Wil tight.

"When this is over…"

"You will not leave us again," Deirdre said, her face suddenly red.

Garth frowned.

"I hope there will not be need. You know I'd rather be here with you than anywhere else."

"If you do this task, if you succeed, I'd say you will have earned your place of honor and will be allowed to let others take the risks."

Garth clenched his jaw and shook his head.

"The future is unknown to me, love, and I hope what you say will be true, but honor often has a steep price."

"What about the obligations of being a father? A husband?" she said with heat.

Garth stood, feeling a tightness in his eyes. Wil started to cry.

"You know what I do is to protect both of you."

"Yes, and when it is done, your obligations will be to us. Us alone."

Heat flushed through his body, his muscles tensing. He bounced Wil and rubbed his back.

"Shhh, little one."

He kissed his son and Garth felt the boy's hand softly rub his shoulder. The baby quieted.

"Again, you know I don't know what the future will hold. I am committed to you and you know that."

"Come back to me and prove it."

Garth took a deep breath.

"I will come back to you both, I *promise* you. By the gods I swear it!"

Garth held open one arm and Deirdre came to him.

"I know no one can tell what the future holds," she whispered. "But when you return, you will not leave us again…"

Garth held her tight in response. He pulled back and looked into her eyes.

"It's time."

He kissed Wil again and handed him to Deirdre. He changed into his armor, took his heavy cloak from their trunk. Deirdre pinned it on him with his favorite dragon clasp and kissed him hard.

Garth left the roundhouse. He walked his way through the village, his men falling in with him. At the stables, they mounted. Bagpipers walked ahead of the men, playing out ward tunes. Garth rode at the head of the eight, proud to lead them.

He led the way through the village and down to the gate. Drummers played at the doors with raucous enthusiasm. The front gates were decorated with wreaths of flowers. Everyone in the fort had come out to see them off. The women gave flowers to their husbands and lovers and kissed them goodbye.

Garth made strong eye contact with friends and family in the crowd, sharing a brief moment with each of them. He nodded with confidence. He felt great love for his people and their support of him, but he also felt a heaviness in his throat. He forced a smile and raised his hand in salute to all.

They passed through the gates to a shower of flowers and cheers. Garth pulled his shoulders back, lifting his chest, then looked at Aodhan who rode just behind him and smiled. Outside the gate, the King, Brennan, Bran, and Aron were the last men in line to wish them luck and see them off.

King Conor sat straight on his horse, sword in hand, and saluted the men.

"May the strength of our ancestors guide and protect you," he said. "Remember our code: truth in the heart, strength in the arm, and honesty in speech. May our virtues lead you to victory."

Conor looked directly at Garth. "I'm proud of you, son. Our love, our strength goes with you. Go now, with all of our blessings."

Garth smiled and felt taller and stronger. He nodded and clutched Claíomh Solais tight.

"I will not fail you, father, nor *our* people. Guard the tree well until we return."

Brennan stepped to Garth's side and spoke to him alone. "Remember what you have been taught. Stay true, and you will succeed. May the gods bless you."

Garth felt the love and support of his clan, he felt filled with their good will and felt his eyes brim.

"Thank you, Brennan, for everything. I will not let you down."

Deirdre stood last, just beyond the gate, with Wil. Garth dismounted and hugged and kissed them both with an aching chest. He took Deirdre's face in his hands and looked into her blue eyes.

She spoke quietly, her eyes welling. "I'm sorry about before... We will be here waiting for you, love, and we will face whatever the future holds together." She handed him a black and yellow flower. "Remember your promise and come back to me."

"I will," he said with a clenched jaw as he crushed the bloom in a shaking hand.

Nodding to his men, Garth mounted his horse and spurred him down the road. He set his jaw and tightened his fists on the reins. Nothing would stop him. He would find the Well and save his people.

Chapter 19

Garth took the winding road west with his eight guardsmen following behind. West was really the only direction to go from the hill fort, he knew, since home was so close to the eastern wall of the mound and pretty near as north as he could go without crossing into *her* territory. His plan was to head west toward the opposite wall, looking for clues along the way.

The Silver Rush River bisected the underground kingdom, and Morrigan ruled the northern half. Garth would avoid going there if he could help it. He didn't think the Druids would have allowed Morrigan to live close to the Well. It was too important to let her anywhere near it.

They would check the Black Canyon first. Close enough to home to be a good hiding place, it was also rugged enough to hide a clue. It didn't seem the type of place for Druid magic, but he had to start somewhere.

Aodhan pulled up close to Garth at the head of the line. "You not only chose Niadh to come with you, but you chose him first?"

"Don't take it personally. Both Brennan and Conor asked me to bring him. I respect them both, and I felt I should honor their request."

"I can respect that, but still, he's bad news. You could've warned me."

"Are you really more worried about hurt feelings than getting the job done?" Garth asked sharply. "Can I count on you to rise above this?"

"You know who you can count it when it matters," replied Aodhan.

Garth ignored the pointed remark. "I know. I'm grateful you are here."

Aodhan shifted uncomfortably in his saddle. "When he was younger, I liked Niadh."

Garth gave Aodhan a look of disbelief knowing that even when they were younger, Aodhan only tolerated Niadh because of Garth's friendship.

"No really, I did. He was full of life and was a hearty fighter. But now he has grown old and jealous and has none of the wildness about him anymore. It's as if married life and children have robbed him of his manhood."

"Priorities change when you have a family."

"But you are still the same man though Wil has come into the world. Niadh has changed for the worse. He has lost himself."

"You know I don't respect the choices he made. I would never have refused to go to his wedding over a stupid thing like a horse."

"It wasn't because of the horse. It was because of *our* friendship," said Aodhan. "Niadh knew I lost respect for him. He didn't want to have to deal with me, since you and I are friends. And he affirmed my belief that he was a stinking piece of dung."

Garth snorted. "You certainly are not quiet about your opinions."

"Aye, I do speak my mind, but that is as it should be. Remember, honesty in speech is part of the code."

"Good point. My best hope is that he remembers some of his old self on this trip and can somehow regain what he has lost. I do have more important things to consider, however."

"I will keep my eye on him, and I suggest you do too."

Garth nodded and Aodhan fell back into line, leaving him to ponder the enormity of his duties. For Garth, this quest was about honoring the ancient pledge of his people to hold the gates, but more than that, it was about keeping his family alive.

His words to Aodhan had not been idle; priorities did change. Deirdre and Wil were his primary concern now. If Morrigan's power continued to grow, because of the fading tree, she would soon sense the Celts could not withstand her. She could attack the fort, kill the tree, and regain her full power. She would kill them all. Including those he loved.

Garth fingered his gold torc and adjusted his seat in his saddle. His stomach churned as he thought of worst case scenarios. What if Niadh refused to follow orders and he had to discipline him? What if they never found any clue to where the Well was? What if Morrigan attacked their home while he was far away? He took in a deep breath, set his jaw, and kicked his horse faster.

Today the rolling hills were alive with pixies and orbs. Many trailed the line of armored men and asked Garth questions. A violet colored pixie came up next to him.

"Where you all goin'?"

"It's none of your business."

"Not a normal patrol, I'd say with all the gear you are haulin'…must be something special going on."

Garth glared at the purple glowing pixie.

"I told you, it's not your business."

"I wonder if *she* would find it interesting?"

Garth shifted in his saddle and rubbed at the back of his neck. He didn't want this pixie racing off to tell the Morrigan about them and he had to try to play it off so the pixie wouldn't think the information would be worth mentioning.

"We are just doing a bit of exploring and might be out for a while that's all," said Garth.

"Exploring what?"

"Listen. I've told you what we are doing, now go away…"

"Testy, testy. I'd say the Queen will want to know about this for sure."

"Go on and tell her then," Garth said, trying to appear as if he genuinely didn't care.

"I might just do that," said the pixie with a wink.

Garth watched the pixie disappear, heading north, towards the Morrigan's palace. He gripped the reins tight and swallowed hard. There was nothing he could do about it. He knew they'd run into pixies. Though not aligned as a race with the Queen, many pixies chose to serve her whether by inclination or by persuasion. If this one reported to the Morrigan, it could make things worse, but it wasn't unexpected.

Near dusk, they reached the canyon. Garth found an alder grove near the rim and decided it was a good place to spend the night. The men gathered dead wood and started a small fire for their camp. A few others went in search of game for their meal.

So far, Niadh had not said a word to him. He briefly wondered if Brennan had had to persuade him to come. *No matter*, he told himself. Not everything lay within his control.

While the preparations were being made, Garth walked a short distance to the deceptive edge of the Black Canyon. One moment he stood amid rolling hills and forest, and suddenly a giant rift in the ground descended over two thousand feet. Looking over the edge made him want to step back. It would be a long way to fall.

Garth scanned the rock face opposite him and looked for anything that might suggest a hidden cave or a hint that they were going the right direction. Slabs of different colored rock crisscrossed each other. If he used his imagination, he could almost make out some of the ogam letters, but ogam was such a simple alphabet that it would be easy to see it in every straight rock line that cut across the vertical.

He decided to look closer in the brighter morning light and turned to go. Aodhan approached, Garth stopped and waited for him.

"You call this a camp site? It's all rocks! What about that meadow with the stream? Now that was a nice spot."

"True, but we are looking for clues in the canyon, not in a meadow."

"Ha." Aodhan laughed and slapped him on the back.

Garth looked at him and smiled.

"Did you talk to Niadh?" Aodhan asked.

"No. Not yet. I'll talk to him tomorrow, once we get a little more settled into routine."

"What are you going to say?"

"I don't know. I'll think of something."

"I'm sure you will. Hey, I've got a cask of Brennan's mead that I need to tap. Do you want a horn full?"

"I can't say no to that."

"You know, this is the best time of day. The light is fading, work is done, and it's time for a drink."

Garth smiled. "I couldn't agree more."

The two walked back to camp. Tuathal and Dónal had killed a small deer and were dressing the meat. The Celts drank Brennan's huckleberry mead and when it was ready, they ate a meal of roast venison and herb bread.

The men talked late into the dark, laughing at Tuathal's jokes. Garth set himself aside to get some sleep. The forest ground was hard, but it was dry and the air warm. He ordered a watch be kept all night.

Today was a good beginning, he decided as he drifted off. They had made it to the Black Canyon. Tomorrow, they would search it.

* * *

In the morning, all the Celts ate and they broke camp. Garth's instructions about what to look for were vague since he didn't know himself. He led them as they inspected the canyon from the east rim, then rode south along its edge looking for any kind of portent or sign. Though the cliff walls were riddled with stripes of rock and many fissures, he could not find a clue hidden there. They spent the whole day on the east rim, searching. The men were in good spirits, so Garth took the opportunity to try to breach the gap between he and Niadh. He dropped back in line, drawing close to Niadh.

"I think this canyon holds no secrets, but it's good to be thorough," he said, trying to stay as neutral as he could.

Niadh turned. He glanced first at Garth's horse, Cadifor, and then at Garth. For a moment, Garth thought he might not respond.

"Really? That's how you break the silence between us? No apology, nothing?"

"I already apologized. In front of everyone."

"That was just you playing the big man for the crowd."

"No, Niadh, it wasn't. Besides, if anyone should apologize, it's you." Garth struggled to keep the bite out of his voice.

The two men rode in silence.

Finally, Niadh glanced at him. "I agreed to come only because Brennan asked me. I knew it was a mistake to think you had changed."

Garth took a deep breath. He had tried to see things from Niadh's point of view, but it was hard, too hard. He thought of Wil and he found new patience. He could swallow at least some of his pride for the sake of the mission.

"Niadh, we were once the closest of friends, and I've missed the bond we shared. Both of us feel wronged. Let us agree to drop our argument for now, so we can succeed in finding the Well."

Niadh studied him. "I knew this was a bad idea. Good luck finding your precious Well. I'm done."

He pulled his horse around and kicked him into a gallop.

Garth was stunned. "Wait, Niadh! Come back," he shouted, but Niadh ignored him and disappeared in cloud of dust.

Gods. Now what?

Chapter 20

Garth's gut went sour. He clenched his hands into fists. How badly would it hurt them to be down a man? To have Niadh gone?

Aodhan rode up to Garth as continued forward, his thoughts racing.

"I see your talk went well."

"I don't know what the bastard wants from me," he fumed.

"Well, you didn't kiss his feet, I saw that much."

"I came damn close. What do think, Aodhan? Do I go after him?"

"That piece of dung? No, let him go home and try to explain how he gave up without so much as drawing his sword."

"I'm sure he'll come up with some story."

Garth pulled at his torc. His heart pounded all the way to his temples. "Can we go on without him?"

"We are already," said Aodhan.

His friend's confidence didn't set him at ease. Garth stewed in his thoughts while leading the company along the edge of the canyon. Maybe Brennan's divination had been wrong, or maybe it would work out in some unexpected way.

I did my part, he thought, but it didn't make him feel any better.

Garth tried to focus on what he needed to do. He had to find if any clues existed about the Well. There was still more of the canyon to be explored, and the Well was more important than Niadh.

After riding most of the day, they were almost to the end of the canyon with nothing to show for it. Garth stared into the winding canyon, looking for anything to help them, a strange rock formation or trees out of place, but found nothing.

He rubbed the back of his neck, frustration mounting, but

then he saw something: a shadow where no shadow should be. He kicked his mount into a gallop to investigate closer. Ahead and below them, the shadow turn into a cave in the wall.

Garth felt a lightness in his chest as he turned to face his men and pointed.

"Look, there is a cave."

Garth rode a bit further, dismounted at the edge and peered over. The mouth of the cave had disappeared. Only rock dropped steeply away below.

"What makes you think this has anything to do with the Well?" Aodhan asked.

"It might not, but when I won Claíomh Solais, I found it in a similar cave. This could be another Druid cavern."

"Dangerous climb, Garth," said Aodhan seriously.

Garth felt a tingling in his limbs. He rubbed his arms.

"Yes, but it might be important. I've got to take a look."

Garth opened up his pack, took out a rope and tied it around his waist.

"Lower me down."

Garth put his back to the drop and leaned against the support of the rope, his hands clammy and his heart racing. He leaned back and began the descent, looking at the rock face, concentrating on his footing and deliberately not looking down too far.

Scraggly trees clung to the cliff face, cracking dark stone with strong roots. He dared a look between his feet, searching for the cave mouth. The distant sliver of water at the bottom of the canyon looked impossibly far away. Vertigo threatened. He clung to the rope and closed his eyes to fight back dizziness. He took a breath and continued down. He had seen no opening.

The rope stopped and Garth looked up.

"Give out more rope," he shouted.

"That's all we have," Aodhan replied.

Garth shook his head. He still couldn't see the cave opening. Nothing but scrub oak clung to the rock below. He grabbed the thin trunk of one, tested his weight against it, and found it held.

"I'm untying the rope."

"What?"

"I can't reach the cave. I'm going to have to climb it."

"Take it slow, Garth."

Garth found a place for each foot, hung onto the small tree with his elbow, and untied the knot breathing fast, doubting his own resolve. Sweat flowed from his forehead and he felt adrenaline spike.

With the rope untied, he had a little more to use. He held it with one hand and lowered himself a little more. The opening appeared. Garth took a deep breath with his heartbeat nearly exploding. He would have to let go of the rope and climb just using the trees to gain the entrance.

Lobed leaves and small acorns covered the branches of the short but strong trees. Garth let go of the rope and took hold of the nearest one. He moved across the cliff face using stone and oak to reach his goal. Across the opening below, he lowered himself along the side, looking for a ledge below to stand on.

The tree in his left hand pulled free. He slipped and hung onto a scrub oak by his right hand alone.

His gut clenched and his heart threatened to rip out of his chest. The tree held.

He shifted his left hand to the tree, and let go his right. He scrabbled his feet, fighting for anything to stand on but found just a nub of rock. It might be enough.

You can do this, he thought. He tensed and with his one leg and one arm flung himself around the side of the entrance and into the cave. He fell and his torso landed hard on the floor of the opening, knocking the wind from his lungs. The weight from his lower body pulled him down, the chasm below threatening. He clawed at the rock, tearing a fingernail off, but he stopped, hanging right on the edge of the cliff. He pulled himself up and collapsed on his side.

He rolled to his knees, clutching at his bleeding finger and grimaced. He looked up, anxious to see what all his efforts would reveal.

The cave was empty.

He stood and gritted his teeth. His muscles quivered from exertion and disappointment. He walked further back into the dark cave, stepping over boulders, holding his breath, looking for anything that might help him The light disappeared; all except a faint glowing coming from Claíomh Solais.

He smiled and pulled the sword free. Like a torch it shone,

illuminating the back of the cave.

Carved into the flat surface of the rock was a tree. Limbs circled down and met roots, making a circle. On the trunk of the tree a single vertical line with two horizontal lines jutting to the left had been carved. Garth recognized it as the ogam symbol for oak.

"Thank the gods," Garth said in relief. He pressed his palms against his eyes and studied the picture again.

The Druids had put this here, he was sure of it. But what did it mean? Oak? The oak was considered by the Druids to be a sacred tree, but was this carving part of the Well quest?

He sighed. He had the first clue—maybe. Now he would just need to figure it out, to see if it really could help him find the Well.

He turned, hearing a noise at the cave mouth. A rope made of tied together cloaks lowered. He took one last look at the carving and walked toward the make shift rope, eager to tell his men what he had found. At least they had something to go on; it was more than they had this morning.

Chapter 21

Logan poured the water out of his boots and began the climb up to the cave. The amethyst was slick, and he worked his way slowly upward.

How much time had he used so far? It couldn't be more than an hour. At least he hoped not. If Rhiannon died because he was too slow, he would never forgive himself.

His hands shook as he climbed, the shock of his near death still having its effect, but he pressed upward. At the top, he found a muddy cave. He crawled through the narrow way until he reached the other side, then stood and scraped the mud from his hands and arms while he scanned the space. A large cavern, much bigger than the ones before, spread out in front of him.

Logan blinked in the dim light. Fewer purple crystals illuminated this cavern, but he could still see. The walls—rugged, cracked, and splintered—soared above him, looking like some giant, imprisoned bear used its long claws to scrape jagged channels into the stone.

Logan searched for more caves or tunnels but found nothing. The rough ground tripped him. The shifting stones gave way beneath him as he fell. He slid and caught himself, scraping the skin of his palms and his knees.

He cursed and stood, growing panicked again.

Damn it! I don't have time to waste hunting for the way forward.

He peered up, thinking of his last means of escape, and far above, a tiny tunnel appeared, hidden in the shadows.

Logan took a breath. He walked to the base of the wall, looking for the most direct path, and swallowed hard. The last section jutted out from the cliff making an overhang.

"Well, *that* should be interesting,"

He shook out his hands to get the blood flowing and looked for his first foothold. Working his way up, slowly and methodically, he kept his mind clear and avoided looking down. He found a narrow spot about two-thirds of the way up and braced his back and legs against it so he could rest before the final push.

Once his heart rate was back to normal, he began the last pitch. He made his moves, ever upward, gaining in confidence. Until he saw the spiders.

Logan's skin prickled with fear. He stopped dead.

What the hell are those?

Huge black spiders, with red splotches on their backs, skittered across the cliff face. Every crack and crevice spilled arachnids. He hadn't seen them from below.

He hung on both hands, his left foot swinging in space, wanting desperately to climb back down but it was only a few moves to the top. One handhold and a hole above it marked the way. He thought about putting his hand into the hole and making a fist to hold him, but spiders filled the opening.

Sweat ran into Logan's eye, and he blinked away the burn.

I can't stop now, and I can't stop here.

Clenching his jaw, he grasped the handhold with his left hand, and thrust his right into the hole. The spiders attacked, biting hard. Fiery venom burned, and without thinking, he pulled his hand out.

Heart thundering, he dangled precariously over the drop. He tried again, stabbing his throbbing fist back into the recess. More spiders bit, and Logan shouted but held steady.

Frantic, he looked up, saw another hole above him, punched it with his left, and pulled himself up with both feet dangling over the abyss. His left hand burned as spiders tore into his bare skin, and his right got hit again as he pulled it free.

He reached up blindly over the lip of the wall, felt a narrow indent on the surface, clamped down on it, and pulled himself up by his fingertips. With a groan, he rolled onto his side and stood.

The top of the cliff seethed with eight legged monsters.

He stumbled back, almost over the edge, his legs feeling weak. There were so many of them, he thought, feeling overwhelmed. He turned his fear to anger. Logan stomped, kicked, and ripped them from his clothes until the top was clear.

He took a breath, wiping the sweat from his brow, and

looked at his hands. Nasty swelling already started on both hands. His fingers could no longer bend all the way.

"Damn."

He needed to get moving. Without any idea what the venom might do to him, he had to get to the moonwell as fast possible.

Across from the cliff edge, the tunnel beckoned. Only about waist-high, more spiders waited inside. He could crawl, but his progress would be too slow and the spiders would be merciless.

Logan sighed. The other option was to shift. He weighed the possibilities, not liking either one. The only shape he could take was a wolf. He wished there were others he could do.

Eventually, he would have to shift. That was the whole point of this test. It had just been so long since he had done it.

He stripped off his grimy wet clothes and stood naked atop the cliff. Closing his eyes, he willed the change.

Nothing happened.

Damn. It's been too long.

He clenched his jaw, anticipating the pain, and tried again. His skin burned and heat engulfed him, like someone had poured flaming gasoline all over him.

His muscles ripped, stretched, and tore. His skull cracked and broke, like it had been crushed in a vise. His head shifted and melted into a new form with a long snout and vicious teeth. When the burning stopped, black claws and black fur appeared where his hands had been. He struggled to his feet and vomited.

* * *

The wolf licked up the puddle and stretched, running his tongue over his snout. He sniffed the air and ran into the tunnel. His powerful back muscles brushed the roof of the tunnel, but he had enough room to crouch and run.

The wolf raced through the dark tunnel, and up ahead, he smelled pine and leafmould; he smelled rabbits and water. Spiders crawled on his back and bit, but he kept running. He loped through the tunnel and found a sheet of falling water covering the exit. He splashed out into the open, aware of too many new bites on his back.

The scents of a forest flooded him, loam and the bitter scent of evergreens and so many more. He smelled other wolves, at least a dozen of them, each with a distinctive scent. He knew that other wolves, not of his pack, would not welcome him. They would see his presence as a challenge, a threat.

He found a clear rivulet of water running from the falls at the cave mouth and lapped up the water eagerly. Though he listened intently for any sound that might tell him where the other wolves were, he could not hear them.

He glanced around at the largest cavern he had been in. Luminous trees, shrubs, and flowers blanketed the forest floor in every direction. The wolf in him tried to exert dominance, shoving down thoughts of Logan, but enough human consciousness remained to tell the wolf what he must do. He was supposed to find a pool, a moonwell.

Directly ahead, a path led into the dense oak forest. He sniffed the air again and tore through the trees, eating up ground. He loved the power of his wolf form. It was so addicting.

The human part of him slipped a little more. He realized how easily he could lose his humanity, just let go of all its problems and be content with the simple needs of hunting. He struggled to keep his humanness, to avoid losing consciousness. Somewhere in the back of his mind, he remembered that losing control was why he didn't do this anymore; it was too dangerous.

The wolf's powerful claws raked at the ground, but both of his front feet began to ache. He stopped and licked the feet, remembered the spider bites. They stung, but it wasn't going to stop him. The wolf in him took control. His questions and worries faded. He concentrated on the forest and the run. He was wolf.

The scent was unmistakable; other wolves ahead of him. He must avoid them if he could. The wolf leapt over downed trees and ducked under others, moving fast, moving quiet. This was what he was made for, running through the deep woods, using every sense, every muscle. He loped, pawing at the ground, feeling the air rushing into his lungs with every stride. He stopped for a moment and crouched low, smelling a scent on the forest breeze.

He walked forward, limping. Cautiously, he sniffed the air, listening for any clue of danger. The light from the trees and foliage made it impossible for him to hide; light came from everywhere, left no dark places. He padded forward, keeping low to the ground. Through the trees, a pack materialized, with a huge alpha looking in his direction. The alpha was white and bigger than he was, his mate gray and white and curled up asleep next to him.

Knowing they hadn't see him yet, he sidestepped to his left and kept his eye on the pack as he worked his way around to the side. The alpha gazed toward the forest, but the rest slept. He edged slowly around, not wanting to fight, not wanting to hurt these brothers.

The leader's mate woke. She stood and looked right at him. She sprang into action and the wolf let go of his caution and ran as fast as he could, trying to get around them and beyond. The alpha wolf rallied the pack, and soon they were all in the chase.

The wolf's front paws hurt terribly, which made it hard to run. He ran anyway, but he wasn't fresh like these other wolves. The fatigue of the swim and the climb were catching up to him, not to mention the spider venom. He loped, but he didn't know the woods like the pack. The wolf feared the big alpha was closing in from in front of him. There was no time to think about it. The wolf dug in deep and sprinted.

Ahead, a cavern wall appeared at the edge of the forest and he surged forward harder. The pursuers were closing in. He spotted an opening in the wall, but the tall alpha wolf stood guard in front, teeth bared. If the alpha wolf stopped him even for a moment, the pack would be on him and tear him to pieces.

He heard the female leader close behind him. His front paws had gone from painful to almost useless. Each step felt like stepping on jagged splinters. The chase was almost over, one way or another.

The wolf limped toward the alpha, and when he got close, he feigned a jump up and over, but at the last second, he lunged to the left and knocked the alpha wolf in the ribs with his right shoulder. The alpha was nudged aside, just enough for the wolf to pass.

When he landed on his front paws, pain exploded. He fell to the ground and his momentum carried him across the smooth stone into the room beyond. The wolf closed his eyes as he slid to a stop. When he opened them again, he saw it.

The moonwell.

Ahead of him, a perfectly circular pool shimmered in colors of purple and white, just like the crystals far behind him. A power throbbed in the air of the cavern. It pulsed, as if a great heart were pumping invisible currents of power. He didn't know how power could feel like colors but it did.

The wolf dared a look behind him. The pack had not pursued him but waited just outside. He struggled to his feet and hobbled to the moonwell.

Chapter 22

Logan, in wolf form, turned at the edge of the water and checked on the pack. The alpha male and his mate waited at the edge of the room with the rest behind them. They watched him but came no closer.

Deep down, the wolf knew that he had to become human again, though he regretted the necessity deeply. He needed to think about what to do, and the wolf mind would not be as good at thinking as the man's. He closed his eyes and struggled to regain his human consciousness, to let go of the wolf. He knew it was going to hurt, and with his paws and back so wounded, it would be worse.

A numbing came over him, like something had shoved mud up his nose and in his ears, making his senses dull and flat. He hated it. The transformation came, and with it, cold met his naked skin, and he shivered in the sudden chill.

The shift was easier than the last time, but Logan still felt nauseous and weak. He stretched and looked at his wounded hands. They were swollen and burned, but he at least didn't have to walk on them.

He looked over at the wolves. They snarled but kept back. *Time to focus*, he thought, as he looked more closely at the pool, the edge framed with hand-tooled stones in a perfect circle. Logan peered into the water and was astonished to see a perfect reflection of the moon filling the entire pool, with only a narrow border between it and the edge of the enclosure. He glanced up, almost expecting to see a dark sky and the actual moon above him. Oh, how he would love to see the actual moon, but he only glimpsed the rippling reflections of the waves dancing on the stalagmites above him.

Now what?

Morrigan said only that he was supposed to find it, and he had found it. He touched the water with his left pinky finger, found it cool. He took a drop and let it fall on the spider bites on his right hand. It burned and the water scalded the open redness of the bites, but the red began to fade.

Hopeful, he tried another drop and felt relief flood him. He lathed a palmful over his shoulder and onto his back. The spider wounds at first burned like he'd poured alcohol on them, but the terrible ache disappeared.

Logan reached out with his healed hands and cupped water within. It looked clear and clean.

He decided to drink it.

When the moonwater touched his tongue, he tingled with delight. It was the best drink he had ever had, like liquid joy. He drank deep and sat by the pool, sated and at peace.

The wolves watched him more closely now, no longer growling or pacing. Logan waited for something to happen. He walked around the pool and drank from the other side. Nothing. He approached from all four directions, taking a drink each time, but still nothing happened. Anxiety overtook him, and he paced the floor at the back of the chamber.

Now he was stuck in this cave with no way out. What kind of test was this? Maybe if he shifted back to his wolf form something might happen?

He tried it, but he only felt warmer. The beta wolf licked her lips. He quickly changed back and paced some more.

No matter what he thought about, the sense of foreboding grew.

Something terrible is about to happen. Maybe it's the spider venom? Maybe the pool is poisoned?

His stomach heaved, and he vomited up the water.

Then it happened. A tidal wave of sensation washed over his psyche like a tsunami. Its force stunned him, and suddenly he felt a tremendous unity, an indescribable oneness. Myriad shapes and forms moved in and out of existence—killing, eating, dying and being reborn. His life danced within the larger pattern.

The vision threatened his sanity. He felt the ground of his self being assaulted. His existence assaulted. His very being was nothing but an illusion created on top of the reality of the all, like a bubble on the surface of the ocean about to break. His sense of time disappeared, and he somehow knew that time itself was just a fabrication of his own consciousness, that, in reality, time did not exist, just an eternal now. The truth told him that all the things he held dear did not exist. He struggled to hold on.

The basic particles of existence—DNA, protein strands, atoms, and what he could only describe as vibrating strings—reveled in his consciousness. The strings sang to him, and in their song, he felt new possibilities. He knew that, when he changed from human to wolf, the most fundamental part of him was still intact. He knew that awareness was constant. But now he realized he could take new shapes, he could rearrange the fabric of his physical body to be more than a man, more than a wolf. He could be other things. He could...

The thought stopped. He felt sick again, but he didn't throw up this time. He slumped to the ground, suddenly exhausted. He needed to rest. He needed time to contemplate what he had been shown. He closed his eyes.

When he opened them, he was again just a man. He sat up, head throbbing, and looked over at the wolves. They stared back at him now with different eyes, the eyes of understanding. As he watched, they all shifted and became humans.

He blinked rapidly and stared, momentarily forgetting all else. These were more shapeshifters...shapeshifters like him. He smiled and took in a quick breath.

Watching them, Logan stood. One by one, they entered the room.

"Most can't survive what you just went through," said the alpha wolf, now in human form.

"It was terrible," Logan said, still not feeling right. "Terrible but profound."

"The truth could not be shown to one that was not shapeshifter already. It would be too much. But you have a frame of reference; you know that your basic self, your basic awareness, never changes. Let that be your truth and you can control your form."

"Can I take shapes other than a wolf?"

"The moonwell teaches you the truth, but you must own it. We've not been able to take other shapes ourselves. That is why we are still here, but theoretically you could. We will let you pass for you are one of us, but to finish the test you must find your way back to the entrance. For that, you will need your new knowledge."

Logan swallowed hard. What he had learned was profound, but the practical use of it would be another thing. "Thank you."

Logan shifted to wolf form and so did the others. They moved aside and allowed him to pass. Slowly, he walked back through the forest.

He reached the tunnel leading out and he hesitated. There were more spiders. After being healed, he did not want to get bitten again. He turned and looked back. The alpha wolf had followed him.

"Those spiders are why many of us are still here. The moonwell heals their poison, but there is no sure cure for their bite on the other side."

"Is their bite fatal?" Logan asked.

"We've seen people die, yes."

He bristled. "People who you kept from the well?"

"Only the strong survive. You should know that."

Logan sighed and looked at the tunnel.

"You have earned the right to stay with us here, if you would choose it."

He pressed a hand to his head. Now he understood why there were so many wolves in this place. He suspected the water of the moonwell would keep them alive indefinitely.

He thought of Rhiannon and what would happen to her if he failed. He thought of her blue eyes and the smile she only gave to him. He firmed his jaw and decided. He would save her or die trying.

"No. I will press on. I have too much to live for, and the one I love is beyond these walls. I must take my chances."

"Very well. If you change your mind, you will be welcome here."

Logan nodded and shifted.

He ran as low to the ground as he could, but many bites seared his back. The clock had to be running out. He would have to finish the test fast and get help with the venom.

Once out of the cave, he walked to the edge of the cliff and looked down over the spiders on the ledges below him. He needed a plan. *Wings sure would help*, he thought, and tried to will his arms into wings. Nothing happened. He jumped up and tried to shift in mid-air. No luck. Logan groaned.

He had an idea.

If he shifted into a spider, the others might ignore him.

He tried it, willing the shape of a spider. Nothing.

Logan shook his head, threw his hands up in the air, and began to pace.

Ok, I need to just calm down and think this through, he decided. He walked to edge, looked over and immediately pulled back, his heart quickening. Far below, he had seen the way out.

He crossed his arms and continued to pace. He thought about everything that had happened to him in the temple, the first drop into the water, and the terrible swim through the tunnel, all of it. The whole test had been about being bold. What could be bolder than taking a leap from the cliff and hoping he could fly?

Logan licked his lips and stumbled until his back met the wall. His limbs shook just thinking about it. He took a breath and thought of the hourglass emptying and Rhiannon waiting for him.

Logan inched forward and peered over the edge of the ledge again. The ground was far away, but not far enough. If he couldn't shift, the ground would meet him all too soon.

He threw his hands in the air. This was crazy! He couldn't just jump off the ledge! He swallowed hard, looked at the stone prison around him. If he was wrong, he'd be dead, but if he stood there thinking too long, he was dead anyway, and Rhiannon with him.

Logan paced and kicked at the rocks. He picked up a stone and threw it at the spiders around him. Maybe he should try to turn into something that loves to eat spiders.

Well, Logan, you've really done it to yourself. Drink some psychedelic water and think you can fly.

He paced, waited for a brilliant idea to save him. Instead, the image of the draining hourglass filled his mind.

He had to do it. He had no choice.

But what shape should he take? No, it didn't work that way. The need supplied the form. Yes, that was the key. The need was the key, and he had the need. He couldn't stay on that cliff any longer.

Heart racing, he walked to the edge. He kicked a small pebble, watched it fall and hit the edge of the cliff before finally coming to rest on the floor of the cavern. Stomach in knots and hands wet with sweat, he could hear his heart beating faster and faster. It was time for action.

He stepped back, tightened his muscles for the leap, and looked out. With a deep breath, he sprinted toward the edge and jumped.

Feet first, arms out wide, Logan fell, and the ground rushed at him, too fast. The cliff face raced past in a brown blur, and ebony boulders menaced him from below.

I have to shift!

The air rushed past his ears. The ground came at him. He flailed at the air, desperate to slow down.

And then he did.

Thrilled, Logan felt not arms, but wings, graceful falcon wings. He panicked, pulled them in, and plummeted toward the ground. Terror forced instinct, and he stretched the wings out again, slowed.

He tried to relax. Warm air rising from below lifted him, and he floated, higher and higher. Encouraged, Logan focused on learning about his small and lithe new body. He tried not to think about where all his human mass went, afraid of accidentally changing back mid-flight. He angled his wings, trying different things, and soon discovered control. Flying in wide arcs and steep dives, he landed on the floor of the cavern and shifted back.

Fantastic!

Logan smiled. The power of flight amazed him, and he was alive despite everything. He looked around, feeling the glow of his excitement, and momentarily shifted back into the bird, just to make sure he could do it again. The need made it possible, but once he owned it, the knowledge was his.

He wondered if his father had known such things, or even any of the great shamans of his people. The water of the moonwell showed him how it worked, but maybe there were other ways to the knowledge.

His excitement faded. Another test waited. He walked to the edge of the water and stared at the water filled tunnel. To get out, he would have to find a way up the river, and no wolf or falcon form could help him. He stared down at the purple flow, spider bites burning.

Time to learn to breathe water, he thought with dread.

Chapter 23

Logan's heart beat too fast as he thought about what he had to do. The purple water rushed past his feet, reminding him of the strength of the current. The only way he'd be able to swim against it was to shift.

Just like the last test, if he shifted successfully, he'd be fine—but if not, he'd be dead. He would get washed downstream and never come to open air again. Logan wondered how many people made it this far only to be drowned.

Confidence high from the last test, he knew he didn't have time to waste. Taking a couple of deep breaths, he filled his lungs, steeled his resolve, and dove into the cold water.

The current was stronger than he remembered it, and it swiftly pulled him downstream, the light fading behind him. He reached out and swam, trying to move upstream, his pathetic arms stretched out into the water, not some webbed appendage.

It wasn't working! The water grew colder, and already his fingers and toes numbed. Why hadn't it worked yet? He swam hard, and his lungs burned, but he had no hope of reaching air, none.

He was going to die, he thought. After everything, he was going to die. He fought the urge to breathe, lungs blazing like a forest fire.

Finally, he stopped swimming. The water carried him deeper, despite his best efforts. He concentrated on shifting, eyes closed. A realization hit him. Fish still breathe.

Logan shook his head. He just couldn't do it; he couldn't breathe in the water. The excruciating pain made his eyes bulge. His body took over and water rushed into his lungs. Cold seeped into his chest. He gasped, choked, and more liquid entered him.

Instead of going into shock, Logan felt better. Sweet

oxygen flowed in with the water and relieved his deprivation. He felt a strange pulsing at his neck and tried to touch his throat, but he had no hands.

Shocked, he looked for his arms but found nothing. He turned to looked at his feet and again saw nothing. For a moment, he wondered if he'd died, but he breathed again and understanding flooded him. He was a fish.

Each intake of water brought relief. He'd done it. He swam up current, and his muscular body cut through the clear water, soon passing the cave room and finding the final water tunnel.

Bones reflected in the now purple light, a rib cage and a skull. He thought that should mean something. He nudged the bare bone, finding nothing to eat and felt only disappointment. A numbness crept down the fish's back and he didn't understand why.

Part of him screamed to keep going, to make it to the end, but part of him didn't care. The clean water made him happy. Other fish swam there too. He looked for something to eat again. Maybe he could find a plant growing on the bottom. He dove down to look. The human part of him struggled to connect with his fish body and drive it forward.

The light of the purple and white crystals in the water of the pool reminded the fish of something. Something about the moon. *Yes*, he thought, *there are good bugs to eat when the moon is full.* But that wasn't it.

Moonwell.

The thought of the moonwell cut through the fish's consciousness, and Logan remembered. The brief flash of insight pulled him out. He shifted back to human form through concentrated will. His awkward human limbs grabbed at the water, pulled toward the air, and with great effort, broke the surface and swam for the shore.

He trembled with the terror, overwhelmed by the thought of spending the rest of his days swimming in the underground stream. How many of these fish were not fish at all, but the transformed bodies of people who had failed to remember their human consciousness?

Logan hugged his arms around him for a moment. He wiped the water from his eyes and looked up at the hole in the ceiling. Freedom lay just beyond, and time was running out.

He stood and shifted into hawk form. He circled the large cavern, building up speed, and raced into the narrow chute. His wings brushed the walls, and he was forced to drop back down.

It was too tight to fly all the way up, he thought. He would have to try to shift and grab the rock. Could he do it fast enough?

He circled again and thrust with all his wing power, so he flew high into the hole. He shifted and fell. The wall raced past him, and he turned into a hawk again before hitting the water.

Not fast enough, damn it.

He practiced switching in mid-air. The speed of the transformation was excruciating, but if he couldn't do it fast he was stuck. He must succeed. It was the final test.

He flew higher, higher, and snapped into human form. His hands reached out and slid along the wet stone, but he caught a ledge. His arms shook with the effort. He used his legs and pushed. With a final heave, he was free of the testing grounds

Logan lay on his back, breathing heavily. He struggled to his feet, searching for Áine. His vision blurred, showing him two of everything, and he fell to his knees and vomited. The spider venom roared in toxic force throughout his exhausted body. Forcing himself to his feet, he staggered back the way he came.

His only chance was to reach Áine and pray she would help him.

He crashed into stone trees and groped his way through the dark until he came to the open courtyard just before the stairs. He fell to his knees, crawled to the edge of the stairs, and found her.

In her hands, she held the hourglass. She looked at Logan, then back at the sand. It was almost gone. She shook it to speed the sand.

Logan bared his teeth and pushed back to his feet. He staggered and tripped down the stairs. He reached out with a shaking hand.

"I'll take that," Logan said with a loud voice.

He took the glass, and smiled triumphantly. He had done it!

"Bet you thought I wasn't going to make it, huh, Áine?"

She rolled her eyes at him and frowned.

Despite his terrible fatigue and the spider poison, Logan felt a lightness in his chest. He had succeeded and now if the Morrigan held to her word, he would be free and Rhiannon too.

Logan felt his legs wobble and he sat down hard on the steps.

"Not so triumphant now, huh?" said Áine. "Spider poison is a bitch. I could just leave you here you know."

Logan swallowed and looked up at her.

"You could, but I think the Morrigan might find it strange that I made all the way to *you* before succumbing. I don't think you want to face her anger at letting her son die."

Áine frowned again.

"Okay then, come on, let's get you out of here."

Logan took her hand, stood up, and put his arm around her shoulder for support. He had done it and now he just needed to get rid of the poison. Soon he would be with Rhiannon again and this nightmare would be over.

* * *

Logan awoke, his mouth dry and his eyes burning. He blinked in the purple light and recognized the fabric above him. He sat up and realized he was back in his tower room. Rhiannon sat nearby.

His heart jumped, thrilled at the sight of his beloved. He jumped to his feet and his legs wobbled. "Rhiannon!"

"Shhh, love. Yes, it's me. Sit back on the bed, love, before you hurt yourself."

Logan's skin tingled. He shook his head slowly and sat back down. "I can't believe it. Morrigan really let you go?"

"It's a miracle, I know." Rhiannon walked over to his bed and sat down beside him. She reached out and stroked his hair and kissed him. Logan kissed her back, breathing in her scent. Relief filled him. "What happened? How long was I out?"

"You came back here, they gave you some herbs, and you fell asleep. You've been out for two days."

He took a deep breath and let it out slowly. He brought his palms to his eyes and looked up at her. "Will the Morrigan let us both go?"

"Yes, yes, but don't worry about that now."

She kissed him again and pushed him back onto his pillow. She pulled down the blankets, revealing his naked torso and wolf tattoo. She traced the lines of the tattoo with her finger and kissed them.

Any doubts he had about whether it was really her evaporated. Rhiannon always did that to his tattoo. He pulled her to him, looked into her eyes, and kissed her hard. She was here. He finished the test in time and now everything was going to be all right. He let go of his fears and made love to her.

* * *

Logan opened his eyes as Rhiannon got out of bed. He watched her walk to a water basin, smiling.

"Thank you for that, *my prince.*"

His eyes widened, feeling as though the ceiling collapsed in on him. His mouth hung slack as he watched her put on her clothes. Logan knew the truth. Áine had glamoured herself to look like Rhiannon. The crushing weight of what he had done buried him.

"Rhiannon was never here, was she?" he managed to say.

"No, of course not. The Morrigan got what she wanted and so did I."

Logan's heart turned sluggish, his chest heavy.

"What do you mean?"

"The Morrigan got you to prove yourself in the test so all her followers would be in awe and keep in line. I tried to do things the easy way, but you wouldn't have it, so I had to get creative."

"Why?"

"Royal blood is precious," she said, putting her hand on her stomach.

Logan's head swam, his mind overloaded. He had just cheated on Rhiannon, unwittingly perhaps, but he couldn't believe that he fallen for Áine's deception. "She will understand," he said, with more confidence than he felt.

Áine lifted a brow. "And how will you explain it to her exactly?"

"I'll tell her you used magic on me and disguised yourself as her."

"And she will just accept that you couldn't tell the difference between us? Yes, I'm sure that will go over well. And why would you stop to have sex when you needed to escape so badly…"

Logan rubbed his arms and looked away from Áine.

"Why would you do this? What did I ever do to you?"

"It has very little to do with you actually. You are just a means for me to get that much closer to the throne."

Logan clenched his jaw, feeling heat rising. "What does the Morrigan think about all this?"

"She knows all about it," said Áine with a wicked smile. "We couldn't have you racing back to Rhiannon."

"Rhiannon never needs to know what happened," said Logan with a shaking voice.

"Well you could lie to her of course, but when the baby comes, I don't think I'll be quiet about it. How will it look when she finds you not only cheated on her but also lied to cover it up."

"Maybe there won't be a baby at all."

"Oh, I think there will. I have a sense for these things." Áine smiled and left the room.

Logan lowered his head and looked at his hands. Áine was right. After everything he had been through, he had failed. Rhiannon would never take him back. He would pay the price for a crime he hadn't meant to commit. Logan felt all hope vanish like water down a dirty drain, leaving him weak and empty. Despair crushed him.

Chapter 24

Rhiannon, Tin, Fao, and Flit charged down the hill, stumbling along the steep slope. Through the fog, they spied more soldiers. Like the others, they were spread thin, combing the forest.

Rhiannon swallowed hard, set her jaw, and stormed toward them. *I'm done hiding.*

Tin crashed through the underbrush behind her, with Fao staying at her side. Flit blazed ahead in a blur of blue and rained pixie arrows on the closest soldiers. The fighters swatted away as many of the faerie barbs as possible, but the hail of Flit's attack was relentless. The three closest of Morrigan's soldiers collapsed to the ground, writhing in pain. Their compatriots didn't hesitate. Three of them lifted a net, and two more raised spears.

Riding a rush of adrenaline, Rhiannon shouted out to Flit. "Way to go! Keep it coming!" Vindicated for her original trust in the pixie, her newfound confidence lent her speed.

Rhiannon veered right to avoid the net and spears and jumped a muddy hole to get clear. She blazed through the forest, hoping to get around the end of their line before they closed in on her and her friends. A cry went up, and more soldiers took notice of them. They closed in like the jaws of a terrible beast, all black leather and sharp points.

Rhiannon knew her hope of rounding the end of the line had failed. *Time to punch through.* She picked a spot, raised her magical blue shield, and rushed straight at a spear-wielding fae. The soldier thrust at her, but her magic deflected the point.

She bolted past the guard and kept running, her lungs on fire. From behind her, she heard crunching noises as Tin swept soldiers with his axe. She spotted a clear path; the forest ahead was free of soldiers. They were going to make it.

Fao charged ahead but suddenly stopped and turned back.

Rhiannon whirled to see what was happening. Not far away, Tin stumbled and fell to the ground, caught in a net.

Rhiannon tightened her grip on her sword, and without thinking, rushed back to help.

"No! Run!" roared the minotaur.

She couldn't leave him. Flit appeared, firing blue arrows into the faces of Tin's captors. They batted at their heads and let the edges of the net slump. Fao dove and took one of the fae down to the ground.

Rhiannon raced forward and stabbed her sword at one of the men at arms, forgetting that the shield made her sword useless. Her shield knocked him back, and he dropped the net as he fell to the ground. She didn't dare drop her magical protection to attack.

With two of his captors knocked away, Tin used his brute strength to pull himself free and kill them. For a moment, they stood silently, surveying the damage. The carnage made Rhiannon sick. Split skulls oozed gray matter, torsos were split, and intestines spilled feces. Hand over her mouth, she turned away.

Tin put a hand on her shoulder.

"I know. You're welcome. Let's go," she told him.

If it had only been those few, they would have been clear, but the a dozen dashed out of the trees, some of them armed with crossbows.

Rhiannon gritted her teeth, trying to decide what to do. Her heart hammered in her chest, and she looked around her, desperate for a solution.

The crossbow men quickly encircled them.

An idea came to her. She wasn't sure if it would work, but she had to try. "Tin, Fao, Flit—to me!" Rhiannon shouted.

When they stood close, she expanded her shield to encompass them all. The sphere grew paler and flickered but held. The soldiers fired, and a wave of black bolts came at them. Three darts got through; one cut Tin's left arm, and the other two missed.

The soldiers reloaded, and Rhiannon concentrated and drew in as much power as she could from the surrounding forest.

Her body tensed, and her lips grew into a snarl. She was not going to let her friends die for her. Rage filled her. *I refuse to be a victim anymore.*

The magic swelled inside her, and she held it until the last second. The crossbows raised, and more nets were made ready.

"No!" she shouted, pushing her open hands out as she let the magic rip out of her.

A green wave of energy pulsed, knocking everyone around her flat. The ground came to life. Creepers and roots reached up from the ground and grabbed the fallen, choking and constricting them.

Rhiannon slumped her shoulders and watched with grim satisfaction as her enemies were immobilized. She took a breath and realized her friends were in danger, also enmeshed in her attack. She concentrated like she had with the shield, trying to adjust the strength, but she failed. The magic was no longer under her control. She didn't know what else to do, so she dropped her shield, took her sword, and cut Tin free and Fao. Flitania was back in the air, having squirmed free on her own.

"Come on, let's get out of here," shouted Tin.

From beyond the radius of Rhiannon's attack, dozens more troops came toward them, blocking the way toward their goal.

"No, Tin. I can't. We've got to keep going, We've got to break through."

"Rhiannon, you've proven your determination. Even with your magic, we can't fight all of these soldiers. It's madness. We need to turn back, we need to run."

Rhiannon clenched her fists and turned away from him. She took a step toward the soldiers, and the air suddenly felt too thin. She took another step, but her feet had turned into boulders. She glanced up, and the trees swam around her. "Tin...I don't feel so good." She reached out to steady herself on Tin's arm. "On second thought, we better go back."

"Okay, let me help you."

Her legs buckled, and Tin caught her.

"This is not going to stop us, Tin. We will find a way," Rhiannon said. "But let's get out of here."

* * *

Rhiannon opened her eyes and scraggly trees arched above her. The only sound came from the muddy footfalls and Tin's labored breathing.

"I'm ok now, Tin. You can put me down."

The minotaur looked down at her. "Are you sure?"

"Yes, put me down." He settled her feet on the ground. "What happened?" she asked.

"You blacked out. We barely got clear, and we are still being chased. Can you run?"

"I'm not sure, but I think so. Thank you, Tin."

Rhiannon took a few steps and started running. Behind her, she heard the shouts of soldiers. All around her, Darkin Wood was still. No breeze blew, and no trees swayed. Humid air blanketed everything in a shroud.

Her legs wobbled but held.

Flit buzzed back and hummed along next to Rhiannon. "I'm glad you are okay. I've heard of magic causing people to black out, but we really didn't know what happened or when you would wake up."

"I guess I pushed too hard," said Rhiannon between rapid breaths.

"I found the trail again."

"Good work, Flit. I'm sorry I doubted you."

"It's okay. I probably would have doubted me too. Are we going back to Brennan now?"

Rhiannon wiped the sweat from her brow and kept running. "I don't know. We've got to get away from these soldiers first, and then I'll decide."

Her calf muscle hardened into a cramp, and she was forced to walk. She trudged along behind Tin, who slowed to wait for her. Every step she took brought her farther away from Logan.

Rhiannon stumbled and fell into the mud and, when she looked up, Tin reached out a hand to help her up.

"Where are you leading us, Tin?"

"Back to my cave. I know you didn't want to turn around, but we really had no choice. We would have been captured or killed."

Rhiannon's eyes filled, but she brushed the tears away. Emotion filled her. She hated abandoning Logan. "I know you're right."

They walked in silence for a few minutes. Rhiannon slapped at the mosquitoes and watched for snakes. Soon, Tin and Fao were ahead of her, and she fell again, covering her clothes completely in muck. She ground her teeth and got to her feet.

After hours of running, they came to the edge of Darkin Wood. Tin led them from the old bridge they had passed that morning and back to his cave. The sounds of pursuit had faded away.

Rhiannon followed him inside and collapsed against a wall. "Well, that's not how I hoped today would turn out," she said, managing a weak smile.

"It could've been worse. At least we are alive," said Flit.

She sighed. "Very true."

Outside, the light dimmed and the inside of the cave grew dark except for the faint illumination from the purple moss. Rhiannon took a piece of clean cloth from Tin, dipped it in the water, and washed the grime off her face and hands.

Her thoughts turned to Logan. She'd failed him *again*, but she vowed to free him. *I will find a way.* She forced a calming breath.

Tin emerged from the back of the cave.

"It's not much," he said as he served her some cheese and stale bread.

Rhiannon's mood improved as she ate. It had been a long day in the dark swampy wood, but they had evaded capture and gotten back to safety. She could tell Tin was thinking hard about something from the way he suddenly got quiet. Finally, he asked, "Can you use your power to kill things too? Or just heal and defend?"

The question gave her chills. "The power of nature deals in death as well as life, but I haven't been trained to use it that way. What happened today was new to me, and I barely controlled it."

"In the days ahead, you may need that power," Tin said.

"If it comes to that, I will do what I have to."

"To be such an instrument as that comes with responsibility. It is the dark side of nature, but it is nature nonetheless," Tin said thoughtfully. "You will be clear when the time comes."

"I hope you're right," Rhiannon said.

What if she was forced to use her magic to kill? What would she do if she had to kill to save herself or those she cared about? She hoped Tin was right, that it would be a clear choice when the time came, but even more, she hoped that situation never happened.

She studied him closely. "Do you think there is any chance of getting around those troops and trying again tomorrow?"

"No, I don't think so," Tin said with a sharp shake of his

head. "They will get reinforcements and be looking for us."

Rhiannon stood, clenched her fists, and began to pace. "Gods damn it. I hate to abandon Logan, but I have to admit there is no chance of catching him now."

"It wasn't much of a chance to begin with, but I know we needed to try."

She rested her head in her hand. The choice was clear, but she didn't like it one bit. "I need Brennan's help."

"I tried to tell you that before..." said Flit.

Rhiannon glared at the pixie. "I know, but I didn't trust you and I had to try to get to Logan."

"So do you trust me now?"

Rhiannon took a breath and let it out slowly.

"Yes, despite what it looked like back there in the forest, you did come through in the end."

"You are lucky Rhiannon has a level head," said Tin. "If it was me, I would've smashed you the minute those soldiers turned up."

Flitania put her hands on her hips, her face darkening.

"And you'd have been wrong, minotaur!"

Rhiannon stepped between them, facing Flitania and put her palms up, trying to placate the pixie. "It's been a long day and you *both* have proven your worth and loyalty. Let it go."

Flit let out a breath and gave a curt nod. "I can lead us toward the fort in the morning," she said.

"How do we know the way will be clear?" Tin asked.

"We don't, but once we get closer to the fort, we will be in the Celts' territory and we should be safe from the Morrigan's men," said Flit.

"It's decided. Tomorrow we leave for the fort," said Rhiannon, looking at both of them. Tin let out a snort and nodded.

Chapter 25

Rhiannon awoke, feeling like every muscle in her body had been pounded with a meat hammer. She groaned, stood up stiffly, and looked around. Yawning, she wished desperately for a cup of coffee. Everyone else was still sleeping, so she went outside. She stood in the dim morning light and drew in the life force all around her, the Nwyfre. It healed her tattered body.

Tin emerged from the cave and looked over at Rhiannon.

"Today we need to push hard, Tin. The sooner I get to Brennan, the sooner we can go after Logan."

Tin nodded. "We'd go faster if we could find you a horse."

"Good point, but I don't see any available at the moment."

"If we come across any of Morrigan's horsemen, we'll have to negotiate with them." He patted his axe.

Rhiannon laughed. "I like the way you think."

Soon the others joined them and they left Tin's sanctuary behind. They hiked back through the forest, with Flit leading the way. They passed the archway of trees at the edge of the forest and walked out into the open grasslands, turning east and walking through the long grass toward the distant fort.

Flit, who left them to scout ahead, came back and said, "The way ahead looks clear. I'm going to back track and make sure none of Morrigan's soldiers are following us."

"Be careful," Tin warned. "Morrigan has pixies working for her too, and I don't want them figuring out you are helping us."

"Are you feeling ok?" asked Flit, "Are you actually worried about me?"

"Well, maybe. Don't let it go to your head," said the minotaur.

"When will we get to the fort?" Rhiannon asked.

"Two, maybe three more days," Flit replied. "It depends on

how fast we go."

"And if Morrigan's troops find us?" asked Tin.

"That would definitely slow us down," said Flit with a smirk.

"I know what you mean, Tin." She scanned the way ahead. "We are so exposed on these open grasslands. We could travel at night instead, but I don't want to wait and waste the day."

"Plus, there are things in the dark that can be more dangerous than Morrigan's troops," said Tin.

"It's up to you, Rhiannon," said Flit. "I'll do whatever you want."

"Oh, quit being so accommodating," said Tin with a smile.

Flit glared at him. "I'm just trying to help."

"Speed is our best ally now," Rhiannon reminded them.

"Ok, let's go," said Flit.

Rhiannon hiked forward. The land looked flat, but it was actually made up of many slopes of undulating ground.

Flit returned from scouting behind them. Eyes wide and hands shaking, she gestured back the way she had come. "Bad news. Morrigan's troops have left the forest and are heading this way. There are at least two hundred of them, and they are mounted now."

Rhiannon felt the wind go out of her. "Damn it! How can we hope to outrun them?"

"We can't," said Tin.

"There is one possible way," said Flit. "If we turn north, there is a forest where we can try to lose them. But it takes us out of our way, and it is not a pleasant place."

Rhiannon studied the ground between her feet. She hated being diverted further from her goal. She raised her eyes to her friends. "Okay, let's get to the trees and hope we can get there before we are caught."

They left the trail behind them and cut across country. Rhiannon ran, and even at her best speed, the others had to stop often to wait for her. Though in good shape, she was no marathoner, and she was forced to draw on the Nwyfre to keep going. She didn't know how long she could keep it up.

Praying that they would not be seen, she pushed on. It was the only chance they had.

* * *

After hours of running, they came to the forest. Rhiannon stopped and wiped the sweat off her forehead. She turned around and noticed black dots moving on the horizon. She hunched over, hands on her knees as she caught her breath. "We made it. Let's disappear into the forest before they get any closer."

They crossed under the canopy and looked around. Alder thickets lined the single narrow footpath that led into the dark interior. Spider webs spanned the taller oak trees.

Rhiannon sensed something and closed her eyes for a moment. "There is something foul about these trees."

"You can see why I didn't want to come here," said Flit.

"Yes, I do. The sooner we can lose Morrigan's troops and get out of here, the better. Let's go."

Flit led the way and Fao went with her, scouting ahead. Tin stayed near Rhiannon. The big minotaur took the axe from his back and looked around at the dense forest. The light faded, making it dark as night. The only illumination came from a few moss-covered stones.

"You know, I don't like it here much," said Tin, to no one in particular.

Rhiannon turned his way. "Me neither, Tin. There is something wrong—"

She broke off as a screech resounded through the forest. At first, Rhiannon thought it was an owl, but it sounded more like a braying horn.

From up ahead, Flit raced back toward them, Fao nowhere in sight. "Run!" said the pixie. "It's horsemen!"

"Gods damn it!" said Rhiannon. "Where is Fao?"

Tin was already running the way Flit had come.

"Buying us time," said Flit.

"The hell she is!" Rhiannon said and ran after Tin, determined to not let Fao be sacrificed for them.

"Stop! Turn around!" Flit yelled.

"We have no choice now," said Rhiannon. "We can't abandon them."

Flit cursed but turned around.

In the dim light up ahead, Rhiannon heard growls and shouts and the sound of the blowing horn again. A pack of hounds snarled and circled Fao, and Rhiannon could see the wolf was already bleeding from many wounds. Jumping to Fao's aid, Tin swung his double-headed axe to keep the dogs back. Flit fired blue arrows at the pack, forcing two dogs to cower on the ground.

Rhiannon looked beyond the dogs and green cloaked hunters charged on fast horses. These were not Morrigan's troops. Behind them, an antler-headed man blew the horn. Rhiannon looked closely, expecting the horns to be attached to a helmet, but she saw that wasn't so.

She swallowed hard as he bore down on her friends, clearly ready to slay them all.

The horsemen quickly surrounded Tin and hacked at him with swords. He blocked and attacked, but there were too many of them.

We will not go down so easily, Rhiannon thought. She pulled in power from her surroundings, gasping at the forest's dark power. But her friends were outnumbered and outmatched; she had to protect them.

Rhiannon opened to the dark forest. She pulled in the Nwyfre from the most immediate source, and its anger entered her like a blade. The wrath of the forest's ancient grief, twisted by dark magic, welled up in her. Something happened here, something wicked.

She shook off the fear. She had no choice but to draw on the forest's power. Rage filled her, and she reached out with the power of the Nwyfre flowing in her, out into the tree roots and creepers. They erupted from the ground and twined around the hounds, pulling them all down. Branches of the trees hammered at the riders, dismounting them and tripping the horses. Unlike the first time, Rhiannon felt more control over the plants.

The horned man held up his hand and called out to his hunters to stop.

Rhiannon's legs went weak and her vision collapsed. She took a breath and let the magic go. After a moment, her eyesight returned to normal.

"Who are you?" the antlered man asked.

"I am a daughter of the trees," she said, avoiding the question. "Why did you attack us?" Rhiannon looked closely at the horned man and thought he reminded her of one of the Celtic gods, but shoved the thought down.

"We hunt these woods to keep the dark things in balance."

"We are not them."

"So it would seem."

From behind her, Rhiannon felt the rumble of horse hooves.

Damn, just what we need

"I propose a truce for the moment," said the hunter. "Morrigan's soldiers approach in force. Let us fight them together and settle our differences afterward."

"Very well, but don't think this makes up for what you did."

"As I said, we will have our reckoning."

Rhiannon turned toward the new attack. She pulled in more power and used the vines and thorns to form a wall across the path. She made a funnel on either side of the path to force the soldiers to narrow their ranks.

It's not enough. Not nearly enough.

An idea came to her. She'd never tried it before, but she was desperate.

She drew on the power of the place, again letting it fill her. She thrust her arms in the air in a V shape and shouted, "Nature Spirits, Creatures of this place, I call on you. Come! Aid me against my enemies!"

Silence greeted her.

Damn.

She watched as the first of the horsemen, who must not have had not seen her blockade soon enough, crashed into it, knocking both horse and rider to the ground. Tin, Fao, and Flit raced forward and attacked, but there were more. A horn sounded, and from behind Rhiannon came the thunder of the hunter's men joining the fight.

Her intuition hit hard. In the canopy above, shiny black eyes and huge spider jaws surged toward her.

Sweet Brighid! What now!

The creatures dropped to eye level on heavy cords. She pulled up her shield and raced out from under them. Dozens of eight-legged arachnids landed and rushed toward her.

She panicked and created a secondary shield of vines around her and her friends, but there was no need. The giant spiders leapt over her and attacked Morrigan's troops.

Rhiannon didn't know if she should laugh in relief or be afraid. Had her magic called the spiders?

With heavy webs, the spiders attacked, pinning horses and riders to the ground. They moved in and silenced the yells with quick stings and venom. Morrigan's troops didn't go down without a fight, turning ranks of crossbows on the beasts and leaving many of them feathered with black bolts.

But it was not enough. There were too many spiders, and Morrigan's cavalry retreated back the way it had come, leaving many dead or captured behind them. The struggle was over and the spiders had won; they took their prizes back into the trees.

Rhiannon felt numb. They were safe for the moment, but what a terrible way to die.

The horned man turned to Rhiannon and took off his gloves. "Were those your spiders?"

She shook her head. "I think so. I called for help and they came."

"Why would you call such creatures? They are the ones we hunt and yet you lead them?"

Rhiannon glared at him. "What are you implying?"

"I am a lord of Nwyfre, and I know that such decisions have consequences. Look at your hair."

Rhiannon undid her hair and looked. Her blonde locks now had a thin black streak down one side. She frowned at the man. "It was a small price to pay to save my friends."

"If that is the only consequence, yes. You must be more cautious. There are worse things that can happen."

"Who are you?"

"I go by many names, but you would know me as Cernunnos."

Rhiannon's breath caught. Her guess had been right. She was talking to a god.

"My name is Rhiannon. I came here trying to recapture something that was taken from me. I've had nothing but grief and hardship."

"How did you come by your magic if you don't know the consequences?

"My lord, I am but an apprentice Druid and my teacher, Brennan, has yet to teach me how to fight with my magic."

"You have been lucky. I know Brennan and respect him. You would do well to learn more from him before trying such things again."

Rhiannon looked at her feet, but a flood of feelings came to the surface and she flung her head up. "If he had taught me when I asked, this would have never happened. If he had brought me here with him, instead of letting my fiancé get kidnapped first, things would have gone much better. So I beg your pardon if my methods are sloppy, but I'm still standing and none of my friends have died because of me."

Cernunnos looked at her with calm eyes. "Sometimes, trial by fire is the best way to learn, though certainly not the easiest."

Rhiannon shrugged and took a step back. "I don't know if it is the best way, but it's the only way I have."

"Very well, Rhiannon. I apologize for our attack. We mistook your wolf and minotaur for creatures of darkness. I can see now I was wrong."

Rhiannon's anger cooled. "It is an honor to meet you, Lord Cernunnos."

"For me as well. Now I must be off. We have more work to do. If you keep to the trail, you should find the way before you clear. I would make haste, however, since Morrigan's troops may be back soon and in greater numbers."

Cernunnos put his gloves back on and nudged his horse forward. He took a pair of reins from one of his hunters and handed them to Rhiannon. "His name is Arondale. May he help you on your journey."

Rhiannon smiled up at him. "Thank you, Lord."

"You are welcome. May he bear you to good fortune." Cernunnos nudged his own horse. His troops followed him, and they disappeared into the forest.

Rhiannon brought a shaky hand to her forehead, her thoughts churning. A god had just given her a horse, something she desperately needed, and she'd just used dark magic. A wave of cold washed through her. What she had said to Cernunnos about the magic echoed in her mind. Why hadn't Brennan taught her how to fight? It had always nagged at her and now she was dabbling in magic she didn't understand. It was dangerous. She pulled at the strand of black hair and frowned. It was a lot to take in. She leaned on Arondale for a moment and then mounted.

Despite it all, they were still standing. She had defended her friends, though it had cost her. She took a hold the reins and looked Tin and Flit in the eyes. "Let's get Fao and get the hell out of here."

Chapter 26

Beyond the border of the forest was a field of wild flowers, glowing in the fading light. Rhiannon had Tin lay Fao down amidst columbines and nasturtiums and wasted no time drawing on the good energy found there to mend the tears in the wolf's flesh. She drew directly on the Nwyfre, a vast difference between this place and the forest they just left.

The green power flowed instantly into the wounded wolf. When she finished, Rhiannon slumped to the ground.

"Rhiannon, are you okay?" Tin asked.

"Yeah, I'll be fine," she said without looking up. "Just give me a minute."

Rhiannon felt as though each breath was a labor and closed her eyes. She pulled in some of the good energy of wildflowers and opened her eyes again.

"There was a lot of truth in what Cernunnos said. I don't know what I'm doing, Tin."

"I'd say for someone with much to learn, you are doing a fine job. My gods, those spiders were really something."

Rhiannon smiled weakly. "I'm exhausted. I just need a few minutes to rest."

"I'll make sure the area is secure," Flit said, flying off.

Rhiannon barely heard her. She didn't even realize she had fallen asleep until she opened her eyes. Flit had just returned to camp and it was now night.

"Guess what I found—or should I say, *who* I found?" the pixie said excitedly, flying straight for Rhiannon.

"Brennan?" She jerked into a sitting position, wide awake, but Flit shook her head.

"No, sorry. Not that exciting. But there's a camp of Celts, just on the other side of the clearing."

Tin was immediately on his feet, looking around.

"This far away from the fort?" asked Tin. "Are you sure?"

Flit nodded. "Yes, and I recognize some of them. Garth seems to be leading. It's a small group, but they can give us the latest news."

Tinurion cleared his throat. "Flitania, you seem to feel comfortable with these men, but I don't think they will welcome me, a minotaur, into their company."

Flit crossed her arms. "You are right. The Celts know me, but not you. I can vouch for you if you want."

Tin looked at his feet and nodded. "I can't believe it's come to this, but yes, if you would tell them that my loyalties lie with Rhiannon, I would be in your debt."

Rhiannon slowly stood up, ran her hand through her hair. "Whatever happens, Tin, I won't let them hurt you or Fao," she said as she shouldered her pack. They had earned her loyalty. "Let's go meet these Celts."

Excited to hear any news of Brennan, she hoped these men could reassure her that he was alive and well. If he were truly ok, she could put all her focus on helping Logan.

"Who is this Garth?" Rhiannon asked when Flit had returned.

"He is the youngest son of the king. You will like him. He is a warrior with the heart of a Druid," said Flit.

"Let's go meet him." Rhiannon followed Flit until they found two men standing in the dark.

"Aodhan, you big oaf, what are you doing out here?" said Flit.

"I only know one person who would dare call me an oaf," said Aodhan to the man standing next to him "It must be that damn pixie, Flitania."

"Show yourself," the other man ordered.

Flit buzzed the two guards and turned up her light again so they could see her.

"It is Flit! What are you doing out here? Aren't you supposed to be finding Rhiannon?"

"Found her, and here she is."

Rhiannon fought her nerves and studied the men. They wore plaid trousers and long tunics with wide belts. Long cloaks hung behind them. Both had long mustaches, but the one named

Aodhan was bald. Attached to their belts were sheathed short swords.

She took a breath and stepped out of the shadows. "I am Rhiannon," she said, making direct eye contact with each in turn.

Aodhan introduced himself and Bannan.

"There is one thing you should know. One of us is a minotaur," said Rhiannon, looking carefully for Aodhan's reaction.

The big Celt's eyes narrowed. "Friend or no friend, minotaurs have always been *hers.*"

"He has been a loyal friend of mine," said Rhiannon. "I'm not sure I would be here without his help. I will take responsibility for him."

Aodhan studied the minotaur and exchanged glances with Bannan.

Rhiannon's heart pounded and her hands turned clammy. She wondered if he was considering consulting Garth, but he turned back to her. "Okay, Rhiannon. I will take your word. Bring him up," he said finally.

She let out her breath and smiled at the man.

Aodhan led the weary travelers back to the camp where they could see little due to the lack of a fire. Mounds of sleeping Celts, all covered with cloaks, sprawled on the bare ground.

Aodhan walked over to one of the men and crouched down. Flit fluttering above.

The other man sat up. "Flit? What are you doing here?" he said, rubbing the sleep out of his eyes.

"I found Rhiannon and I'm bringing her back to the fort."

Garth got to his feet. Rhiannon studied the tall Celt. He reminded her of Brennan in a way, but younger and more muscular. His blond hair was long, and he had a bristling brown beard and eyes that looked like they were used to smiling.

"It is an honor to meet you," he said.

"The honor is mine, Prince Garth," Rhiannon said with a bow.

"This is truly a happy meeting. Let us offer you our hospitality, such as it is." Garth spread his cloak on the ground for her to sit on. The big man noticed Tin in the shadows and his hand dropped to his sword. He looked at Aodhan questioningly.

"Flit and Rhiannon said he could be trusted," Aodhan replied.

"I've promised to help Rhiannon," said Tin, "and to help defeat Morrigan. My name is Tinurion and I hope that I can find welcome here with you, but if not, I will retire to the forest until Rhiannon is ready to leave."

At the mention of the minotaur's name, Garth drew his sword. "Don't you know who this is?" Garth spat. "This Tinurion the Destroyer, Morrigan's former captain of the guard!"

The Celts drew their weapons and closed ranks around Garth.

Rhiannon's nape hair lifted and she took a step back.

"Tin, you told me you were a prisoner of Morrigan's, not her captain of the guard."

"I knew this was a mistake," said Tinurion, pulling his axe free.

Rhiannon pounded her fist against her thigh, anger warring with fear. "No! Wait a minute, Tin! Is Garth telling the truth?"

"I didn't lie to you before, Rhiannon, I just didn't tell you all of it. I became a prisoner when I earned the Morrigan's wrath. She didn't like it when I refused to turn assassin for her."

"Rhiannon, this minotaur has killed more of our people than anyone except the Morrigan herself," said Garth stepping forward.

"How would you know?" Tin demanded. "Were you there watching?"

"No," said Garth, "but I've heard the tales and I trust them more than I trust you."

"The Morrigan *was* my Queen. I was exiled here long ago by *your* people, against my will and for no crime of my own. I chose to serve my people and I served them well until the Queen lost her way. She was consumed by thoughts of revenge, and now I serve her no longer."

Rhiannon didn't need to think long. Tin had assisted her at every step. She believed him. She stood in front of him protectively. "Garth, this minotaur has saved my life more than once and has sworn to help me defeat the Morrigan. Surely he can try to make up for what he has done?"

Garth's mouth tightened and his eyes narrowed, staring at Rhiannon. He rubbed the back of his neck. Finally he spoke, his words clipped. "Perhaps. But I will not allow him into my camp. He has offered to wait in the forest. I think that would be best."

Rhiannon felt her stomach drop. Here was finally her chance to learn something about Brennan, but her friend was being told to leave. "Prince Garth, I understand your misgivings, but..."

"It's okay, Rhiannon," said Tin. "I will rest better away from here. I will meet you again in the morning."

"No, Tin, it's not okay. I've given my word and if the word of a Druid is not honored by these men, we will take our leave." She could see Garth's point, but she wouldn't disrespect Tinurion by asking him to leave alone.

Rhiannon glared at Garth and to her surprise, he looked down and nodded.

"Perhaps I was too quick to judge." Garth looked at the minotaur and extended his hand. "If Rhiannon says you can be trusted, I welcome you." Though his voice sounded tense, he motioned for his men to lower their weapons.

Tin lowered his axe hesitantly, reached out his hand and clasped Garth's. "I appreciate the welcome...and thank you."

The words sounded strange coming out of the minotaur's mouth, but Rhiannon knew now Tin understood that difference between their cultures.

Aodhan handed Tin a mug of mead and offered him a seat.

One of the men, Dónal, introduced himself and then knelt down to start a fire. Rhiannon sat down heavily, took a long breath, and watched as the flames grew. She hated that she had had to argue with the Celt, but she would not betray her friends.

"I'm sorry we have imposed on you..." Rhiannon said, her voice trailing off.

"No, I apologize. I let my fear cloud my judgment. You and yours are welcome as long as you would like."

"Thank you, Garth," said Rhiannon sincerely.

"Brennan will be pleased Flit found you and you are safe," said Garth.

"Brennan? I've come all this way to find him..." Her voice trailed off, afraid to ask the question for fear of what she might learn. "Is Brennan ok? Is he safe?"

"Yes, he is. Or at least he was two days ago."

Tears welled up behind her eyelids, and relief made her muscles weak. It was the first good news she'd had in too long. Brennan was alive.

"Thank you. You don't know how important that is to me,"

she said.

She paused for a moment, allowing the good feelings to permeate her. She wiped a back a tear of relief. "Oh, sweet Brighid, thank you," she said quietly.

"Why are you out in this defenseless place?" Flit asked while Rhiannon absorbed the good news. "Why are you not at home?"

Garth looked around and his eyes rested briefly on the minotaur on the other side of camp. "We travel to the Well of Wisdom," he said quietly.

Rhiannon looked up in interest. "Why?"

"Brennan believes the water will heal the hawthorne. The Morrigan has grown too strong. It's our last chance to renew the Druid magic. If we fail, she will try to destroy the fort and all those in it. She will destroy the world above and our sacred trust will have failed."

Rhiannon hugged her knees and tried to swallow, her throat suddenly tight. She took in a shallow breath. "I hope the Morrigan doesn't know you have a way to renew the magic. If she finds out, you'll need more than a handful of men to fight her off."

She studied Garth, a sudden suspicion dawning. "You don't know where it is, do you?"

"We don't," admitted Garth. "We are looking for clues in the land to find it."

"Why didn't Brennan come with you?" she asked.

"He is needed to protect the tree and our homes from the Morrigan. His Druid gifts would be of great use on this journey, but we are too few."

"I could try to help you," said Rhiannon.

"I appreciate the offer, but I believe Brennan has need of you elsewhere."

"I must go to Brennan, of course, but what I meant is maybe there is something I can do tonight."

"We'd be grateful for any assistance you could give us."

She took a small pouch from her bag. She excelled at divination and felt confident she could help Garth. Brennan had often praised her ability, and it satisfied her to use something she knew how to do well for once. She turned her gaze up into the night sky. "Oh gods, let me draw an ogam that will help these men find their way to the Well of Wisdom."

She pulled a set of twenty small twigs from her pouch, put them on the ground and closed her eyes. She hovered her hands over the twigs and after a moment of feeling the energies, she chose one from the ground. It was the oak. She opened her intuition and allowed the message to come.

"The oak is the doorway to the path. Find an oak grove, and it will point the way. You follow a noble path and have the good will of the spirits with you, but beware a foe that appears to be a friend. It could be your downfall."

She opened her eyes and met Garth's gaze. "I wish I could do more."

"You've done enough. It's more than we had to go on before. I found an oak ogam carving in a cave not far from here, but I didn't know exactly what it meant. It makes sense now that it means an oak grove. A circle of limbs and roots surrounded the tree in the carving. We will heed your words and the sign we found and look for an oak grove." He looked knowingly at Aodhan. "And beware the foe that appears to be a friend."

Aodhan nodded. "I told you it was a good thing he left."

"Who left?" asked Rhiannon.

"One of our number left due to a disagreement."

"Do you think he could be a danger to you?"

"I think it's possible. He bears a terrible grudge toward me."

Rhiannon tapped her finger on her lip, thoughtfully. "I'd be careful of him, though my mind is not clear on the matter."

Garth nodded. "So you are heading to the fort?"

"Yes, I've got to find Brennan."

"He will be so happy to see you. Everyone there has heard your name since the day you were born. You will be warmly welcomed."

Rhiannon felt her face flush. After a lifetime of being a loner, the thought of being a celebrity shocked her. "Really? Why?"

"You are Brennan's apprentice, of course."

Rhiannon rubbed her chin. "But aren't there many Druids among you?"

"No. It is only Brennan, and you will be our second."

His meaning made her heart jump. "I don't plan on staying, if that's what you mean."

"Your plans are your own, of course, but you are one of only two. I aspired once to be a Druid, to take my place in the Grove, but my duties were elsewhere. Perhaps if I lived in different times…" Garth's voice trailed off.

She sighed. "We all have our jobs."

"Indeed we do. I thank the gods we had this chance to meet."

Rhiannon was relieved to learn Brennan was well and not in danger. Now she just had to find him and get his help to finally go after Logan. Her thoughts turned to Tin. She had been wary of him, but he had more than earned her faith. Nevertheless, she wondered what else he hadn't told her. She hated the thought, but she knew she'd have to keep up her vigilance despite what her heart told her.

Chapter 27

Garth woke to the sound of a skylark's song as it flew overhead. A mist illuminated by fiery shades of red and yellow surrounded the camp. First glowing radiated, breaking the night.

He got up, feeling tight from his cliff ordeal yesterday. His finger still throbbed. He looked over at his men. Aodhan was already awake and gathering more wood for the fire. Garth stood and stretched before nudging Dónal to start breakfast.

He grabbed a log to throw on the fire. Rhiannon sat next to the flames, wrapped in her cloak.

"You're up early," he said.

"Yeah, I didn't get much sleep. Too much on my mind, I guess. Plus, it's warmer here by the fire."

"Would you mind taking a look at my finger? I ripped the nail off yesterday."

"Of course. Why didn't you say something last night."

"After the rocky welcome I gave you, I thought it might be a bit rude to start asking favors."

Rhiannon smiled. "I understand that, but let me see it anyway."

Garth sat down and held out his right hand. Rhiannon gently unwrapped the blood soaked bandage around his middle finger.

Garth watched as she closed her eyes and a green glow surrounded his wound. The light burned. Garth bit down hard but held his hand still. When she was done, his finger was healed.

"Thank you, much better."

Rhiannon nodded but suddenly looked serious. "Listen, I had a dream last night I think was about the divination I did for you, and I wanted to speak to you about it."

Garth waited for her to continue.

"I don't know what it means, but I dreamt of a black wolf following you. It had a shock of white hair, but otherwise was completely black."

Garth leaned forward. "You've really seen this in your dreams?"

She nodded.

Garth's skin tingled, and his breathing grew short. If Rhiannon had dreamed of the wolf too, maybe she could help him understand what it meant. "My dreams of late have been haunted by the same wolf."

Rhiannon raised a brow. "I sense it is a dangerous foe and you will need all your cunning, wisdom, and strength to defeat it."

"Brennan said I should ask it what it wants."

"Good advice. Did you follow it?"

"Yes, I did."

"What did it say?"

"It wants me to die."

Rhiannon's eyes widened and she stared at him for a moment, then gazed into the fire.

Garth waited for her say something, but she appeared lost in thought so he held his tongue.

"I don't think the wolf is just a wolf." Rhiannon looked up from the flames and into Garth's eyes. "I think the wolf could be the Cailleach, the hag goddess."

"Why do you think that?"

"The wolf is one of the forms she takes and the white hair to me tells me she is old. It's a guess, but the feeling of the dream suggested the Cailleach's energy."

He gazed down into the fire and back at Rhiannon. His stomach knotted and his mouth went dry. "It seems we have our hands full of goddesses intent on our deaths. We must be doing something right."

She laughed. "You are right, Garth."

Garth smiled and decided to change the subject. "Why have you come to our world *now*?"

"I was attacked in my homeland and Brennan vanished. I came to find him and my betrothed was taken."

"The overlander?"

"Overlander? Oh, you mean someone from my world? Yes, it would be him. His name is Logan."

Rhiannon crossed her arms.

"Brennan suspected something like that would happen and sent me to stop the abduction, but I failed and Logan was captured. I was sorry before, but even more so now that I know he was your beloved."

Rhiannon stayed quiet.

Garth poked at the fire and looked her in the eye. "The reason I am here is to try to make up for that mistake."

"I wish you had been successful. He could be dead now for all I know," Rhiannon said.

"The attempt cost many men their lives."

"I'm sorry. I didn't know that. It's a steep price to pay for failure."

"Maybe if you had protected him better none of this would have happened," said Garth, deepening his voice.

Rhiannon stood. "Maybe if you hadn't let the hawthorne weaken, I wouldn't have needed to protect him."

Garth clenched his fists but remained sitting. "You don't know the sacrifices that have been made to protect *your* world, to keep the tree alive as long as we have. We live here away from sun and moon to keep your people safe."

Rhiannon took a deep breath and paused before finally speaking. "You're right. You've sacrificed a lot for us. Your comment hit a little too close to home. I did the best I could to protect Logan, but maybe I could have done more. I never suspected he would not be safe lying in bed next to me. It's still a mystery to me how he was taken."

Garth took a breath. "I shouldn't have blamed you, Rhiannon. It's the Morrigan at fault here."

Rhiannon nodded and sat back down.

They sat in an uncomfortable silence for a while.

"It is hard to know the will of the gods," Rhiannon said finally. "I trust you did all you could to carry out your charge. I do not blame you either."

"That is gracious of you. I swear I will not quit until the Morrigan is stopped and all is made right."

Rhiannon looked into his eyes, and Garth knew she understood the seriousness of his oath.

"Your actions will prove your words," Rhiannon said, not unkindly, and she stood. "It is time for me to go."

"Farwell. May the blessings of the gods go with you," Garth said.

He watched her disappear into the trees toward her other companions and decided it was time to leave the canyon behind and strike out west across the plains of Falcar. He knew they needed to find the oak grove.

* * *

For five days, Garth and his men searched the forests, and Garth knew the men grew more and more discouraged.

"What are we looking for exactly?" asked Bannan.

"We are looking for a grove of oaks. It would make sense for the Druids to hide clues in these groves of trees," said Garth.

"Didn't Brennan give you any hints?" asked Croftin.

"Do you think we would be looking under every shrub if he had?" snapped Aodhan.

"There must be a better way to go about this," said Bannan, his voice just as aggravated. "We left home nine days ago, and all we have to show is some poison ivy."

"I know it's frustrating, but let's keep going," said Garth. "We did find the cave, remember."

"Oh right, the cave. The oak carving could mean anything, maybe it was just some Druid ritual site. We don't know it refers to the Well," said Dónal.

Garth tightened his stomach muscles, feeling his jaw clench.

"I saw the carving, and I say it is a sign for the Well, Dónal. Let it go," Garth said with an edge to his voice.

"Maybe there is no such thing as the Well of Wisdom at all," said Croftin. "Maybe it's just a legend?"

Garth pinched his lips together and felt his temples pound. *I can't let my frustration make matters worse*, he decided. *The men are just as worried as I am about all this.*

"Maybe it's a legend, but maybe not. Brennan never found it, but that doesn't mean it doesn't exist," said Garth. "Rhiannon knew of it, and I believe it exists. I know we will find it. We've eliminated many places already. Rhiannon's divination confirmed what the cave told us, so we keep going."

They spent the rest of the day searching. As the light was beginning to fade, Garth spotted another grove. He reined in his horse and called a halt. "Do you see that grove ahead? It's the first we've seen with only oaks."

"This could be it. We can search one more, right?" said Aodhan.

"Right. Let's go."

The companions rode to the oak grove and dismounted. The oaks formed an almost perfect ring. Garth walked through the towering columns, boots crunching on the dead leaves. No other kinds of trees grew at edge of the grove, and soon, the rows of oaks stopped, leaving an inner circle of the tall trees. He walked into the open glade inside.

Garth felt his skin prickle and his eyes open wide. Green grass covered the ground and, at the center, three stone pillars stood in a triad.

This is it, he thought. He turned and walked back to his men, eager to share the news. Excited, they followed him back and stopped in front of the three standing stones.

Croftin spoke first. "Do you think it has anything to do with the well?"

"Yes, I do," Garth said, walking closer. He noted that each stone was marked with a single ogam letter. Hawthorne, Alder, and Oak.

Garth brought his hand to his chin and rubbed his beard. He thought of all the associations that he knew for each word, and none made any sense.

"What does it mean, Garth?" Aodhan asked.

His stomach tightened. If he couldn't figure it out, the quest was over.

"I don't know," he said soberly. Garth studied the stones, traced the ogam symbols with his fingers, said the names out loud. Nothing happened. He clasped his hands behind his back and circled the stones. "Gods damn it! What am I missing?

The light faded, and he sat, leaned against one of the stones, and closed his eyes, exhausted.

* * *

In the dead of night, Cathaoir quietly woke him. "Riders are approaching."

"Wake the others," Garth whispered, putting on his helmet and grabbing his spear.

He walked through the oaks to the edge of the grove and looked out. In the dim light, he couldn't be sure, but it looked like

Niadh riding hard toward them. As the rider got closer, he confirmed it was Niadh, and he wasn't alone. Behind him rode a dozen of Morrigan's cavalry.

Garth shifted his stance, adjusted his helmet, and narrowed his eyes. Was Niadh leading Morrigan's troops? No. They were chasing him. He rubbed his forehead, unsure of what to do. Help Niadh and risk fighting the cavalry? Or let him pay for abandoning the group? He thought about it longer than he was proud of, but he knew he couldn't let Niadh die without doing anything.

The ground shook as horses approached. His men gathered behind him, ready to fight. Bannan brought Cadifor up and Garth mounted.

"Niadh is being chased by Morrigan's troops. We have to help him," he told them.

Garth pulled Claíomh Solais from its sheath and the blade erupted with light. He spurred his horse forward and his men followed him. They charged straight for the rushing cavalry with swords drawn. Niadh's eyes grew wide in disbelief as he rode through the ranks of the Celts.

Garth attacked, swinging Claíomh Solais at the leader of Morrigan's troops. The blade hit shield as Garth's foe managed to raise it in time, but it didn't stop his attack. The glowing blade splintered the wood, cut through the arm and into the ribs of the leader, who was knocked off his mount by the power of the blow.

For a moment, he gaped at the devastation the sword inflicted, but he didn't have time to marvel at the strength of the weapon. The next soldier chopped at his head. Garth leaned out of the way and sliced down at the helmet of the next soldier, cutting through armor and skull, killing the man instantly.

When he was clear of the soldiers, he reformed his men for another charge, and Niadh joined them. They rode through, hacking and stabbing at Morrigan's riders, but the second charge was not as successful. Morrigan's men were more prepared. Garth's gut clenched as one of his troopers, Ronan, fell from his horse, but still four of the foemen went down.

With eleven riders still opposing them, Garth charged again, attempting to hit one flank and outnumber them at the point of impact. He closed on them and swung, but his enemy ducked and the swing went wide. He was thrown off balance. A second soldier swung at him, hitting him hard on the shield and knocking him off of Cadifor.

The ground knocked the wind out of Garth, and he fought against the panic of not being able to breathe. Blood pounded in his ears as he staggered to his feet. One of Morrigan's soldiers charged him on foot, wielding a sword in each hand.

Just as the soldier came into range, Garth was finally able to take a breath. He feigned a wild overhand hammer swing at the black armored man and let his blade miss. The two-sword man rushed him, just as he hoped he would.

As the foe stepped in close, Garth ducked beneath his shield and thrust his sword up, cutting deeply into the man's guts. Hot blood spurted from the wound, spraying in every direction. Garth spun, used his momentum to pull the blade around his body, and followed through with a swift backhand chop, ending the soldier's life. As his foe slumped to the ground, headless, Garth ran to Cadifor and mounted.

He called for his men to re-group, and the last charge broke their enemies' morale. Leaderless, they rode away. Garth let them go.

He dismounted and walked over to Ronan with a heavy heart. His friend lay sprawled on the ground. Garth winced. Ronan had taken a sword to the neck. He was dead. The men gathered around their fallen companion.

"I've been in a dozen battles with him," Garth said. "He was always a good man to have at your side."

Tuathal nodded, clearly upset. "He's been a good friend."

"It should be you," said Aodhan, glaring at Niadh. "What the hell were you thinking, going out on your own then bringing us this trouble?"

Niadh looked at his feet.

"Morrigan is responsible, not Niadh," said Garth, putting a restraining hand on Aodhan's shoulder. He turned to Niadh. "Why did you come back?"

Niadh stood with slumped shoulders. "After I left and had some time to think about things, I decided that no matter my problems with you I needed to see this quest through. I turned around and tried to find you, but you had left. I searched for you, but I ran into one of Morrigan's patrols. I didn't know you were here. I was hoping to shake them in the grove. If you hadn't come to my aid, I'd be dead. I owe you all a debt of gratitude. I'm sorry."

"Save your apologies, Niadh," said Aodhan. "We saved you, but now you can get back on your horse and ride home and tell Ronan's family what happened."

Garth turned to Aodhan. "Let me handle this. It was my choice to bring Niadh on this quest, and it is my decision if he rejoins us. Ronan would have fought to protect any one of us, and he chose to come on this quest knowing the dangers."

He faced Niadh. "What do you say? Will you put the past behind you and join us again?"

Niadh closed his eyes, took a breath, and opened them again. "Yes, I will take up arms and ride with you again. I should have never left. Garth, I apologize."

Garth nodded and put out his hand. Niadh grasped it firmly. Garth believed that for the mission to succeed he needed Niadh; for that reason he was willing to let things go.

They dug a shallow grave for Ronan near the standing stones and covered it with rocks. Garth gathered his men into a circle around the grave.

"Ancestors of our tribe, we call on you and ask you to welcome Ronan into the Summerland. Nature spirits, we ask for your blessing on our brother as he travels beyond this world. Gods and Goddesses of our people, we ask you to renew Ronan so that, in time, he may return to his people. He honored the cycles, he lived our code, and he died a warrior's death. Ronan, our brother, go now in peace to the halls of our people."

Garth paused for a moment and said, "So be it."

He walked away a few paces, wanting to be alone for a moment. He closed his eyes, deep in thought.

Ever since Niadh had left them, he had worried about Brennan's predictions, that they would need him to succeed. Now Niadh was back. They stood a better chance, but with Niadh or not, they still had the puzzle of the stones to decipher. Without knowing where to go next, the quest would fail. He needed to figure it out.

* * *

Garth and the men walked back toward the oak grove.

"Have you found anything to help find the Well?" Niadh asked.

"We found three stones marked with ogam, but I can't

figure out the message."

"Maybe I can help?" Niadh said.

Aodhan laughed. "You think you can figure it out when Garth can't?"

"I clearly don't know everything, Aodhan." Garth led Niadh to the stones.

"What have you tried?"

Garth explained what he had thought of.

Niadh put an ear to one of the tall stones, tapped his knuckle hard against it and listened. "The stones have a resonance to them," he said. "Listen, Garth."

Garth leaned in and heard what sounded like a tone when Niadh knocked on the stone. "You're right. I remember Brennan saying something about each tree having its specific musical note. I wonder... Did anyone bring a harp?"

The men exchanged blank looks.

"I did," said Niadh.

Garth raised a brow. "I didn't know you played."

"There are a lot of things you don't know about me anymore."

"Can I see it? I don't really play, but I remember the strings Brennan played for each tree."

Niadh handed it to him.

Garth played the C string. The sound met the stones, and the alder stone began to hum and glow. He smiled. "I think we are on to something."

He played a G for hawthorne, and an F for oak. When he played them three times each, all the stones glowed. He played them a total of nine times and let the sound go. The stones grew brighter and brighter.

Garth studied them, and in the glow, more symbols revealed themselves; twelve showed on each of the four sides of all three stones. He stepped closer and the glow began to fade. "Niadh, please play the notes and I'll see if I can read them."

Niadh took the harp and played it better than Garth's plucking.

Garth tried to figure out where to start. He looked at all three stones and all four sides of each. He realized that one of them had huath, -l, at the bottom and decided to start there, translating each letter on the facet. Soon he discovered a message. Excited, he waved his men over.

"We are definitely onto something. When I translate the letters from this first stone, they spell out three words...Heart of Water."

"What does that mean?" asked Bannan.

"I think it means the river's source, but I'm not sure. There are eleven more to figure out."

Now that he had his confidence, Garth worked at translating each side of the three stones, while Niadh played. He knew the ogam, but he didn't use it every day and it took time to piece each part together. Each one had two sides that rhymed, so he kept those together. Each stone also had two sets of words. When he finished the first one, he walked to his right stone, and finally finished the third stone. Together, the three sets read:

Heart of Water
Well daughter
Mists Conceal
Sacred Ordeal

Follow the way
Nine will sway
Virtues Three
Measures Thee

Wise must give
Dead will live
Waters of life
Finish strife

"This is a clue left by the Druids," Garth announced.

"What does it mean?" asked Bannan.

"This is meant to help us find the Well of Wisdom. The Well daughter, I think, means that the Well is the mother of the heart of the water. So, if we find the heart of the water, we will be near the well."

"So we still have a long way to go?" said Dónal.

"What did you think? The Well would just show up here? Come on, Dónal, quit complaining," said Aodhan.

"I'm not complaining, I'm just worried that we won't find

the Well soon enough. You know, before the Morrigan turns up."

"Let Garth finish and we'll get going that much faster," said Aodhan.

Garth looked to the two men, nodded and spoke.

"Sacred ordeal must refer to the Druid test. And Mists conceal must mean that the test is somehow hidden in the mist."

"Seems pretty obvious," said Niadh.

"Like you would know," said Aodhan, glaring.

"Aodhan, I appreciate your support, but calm down," Garth said.

Aodhan's face turned red and he put his hands on his hips. "You know I will follow you, Garth, to whatever end, but having *this* back with us makes my stomach rot," he said pointing at Niadh.

Niadh stepped in close. "You know what, Aodhan? You know what you can do with that comment? Stick it right up your ass!"

Aodhan's hand dropped to his sword.

Garth clenched his jaw and stepped between them.

"Stop it. Both of you. We are all on edge, but we've got to focus here. This is not about our personal feelings, this is about saving *all* of our people."

"This is not over, Niadh," said Aodhan.

"Anytime, Aodhan, anytime."

"I said drop it." Garth glared at the two men, his fists tightening. He needed both of them, and he didn't need this in fighting.

Aodhan stormed off and Niadh frowned and looked at his feet.

Garth sighed and turned back to the riddle.

"Follow the way seems obvious, but nine will sway? I don't know what that means."

"Sway reminds me of trees. It seems like a Druid thing to me," said Niadh.

"Could be, good point," said Garth. "Virtues three could mean anything, but it makes me think of our code—truth in the heart, strength in the arm, and honesty in speech. Though I don't know how those would be used to measure someone. The last part, I think, means that if you give, you will receive the water of life, which will revive the dead—in this case, our dying hawthorne—

and our quest will be done."

Garth smiled and punched Niadh on the shoulder, feeling a lightness in his chest. Niadh looked at him with narrow eyes, but slowly smiled.

"In the morning, we will head north to the river and find our way along to the heart of the water to the west."

Chapter 28

Rhiannon reached the top of a steep grass knoll and took in the view. At her side, Tin pointed out and named the rivers below; the Halcyon River wend its way south from the Silver Rush, meandering through forests and plains in lazy bows. Its broad way turned east at the foothills and made its way, glimmering lavender light, as it approached the home of the Celts.

She stared at the beautiful landscape, eyes a little misty.

Tin put a hand on her shoulder. "There. See that outcropping of rock jutting up from the floor of the mound?" he said, pointing beyond the river.

Rhiannon nodded.

"If you look closely, you will see a great hall sitting on top of it."

She squinted. "Are those walls farther down, and fields too?" Rhiannon grabbed Tin's arm, feeling breathless at the prospect of finally finding Brennan.

"Yes. You will see it better soon."

Together, Rhiannon, Tin, Flit, and Fao continued down the slope toward the Celtic fort. It had been a long day and night of travel since they left Garth's company. Despite their weariness, they had made the long push for the fort, rather than camp on the road.

A fluttery, empty feeling filled her stomach. She kept imagining what the day ahead would hold. All senses heightened, every movement near the distant fort caught her attention. Brennan was close.

They crested another ridge, and Rhiannon could see more. Down below the height, many buildings sprouted from the ground, encircling the burg. A tall wood and stone palisade ringed the fort. At the near end was a tall pair of wooden towers, standing over a massive gate. Fields of crops surrounded the city, and beyond that, large pastures. Cows and sheep grazed on the abundant grass, while herders with their wolfhounds watched them.

Rhiannon held the reins to her horse with sweaty hands and kicked her horse into gallop. The gates stood open.

The urge to find Brennan overwhelmed her. She had been worried about him for so long that she wouldn't believe he was okay until she saw him with her own eyes. After that, she wanted some answers.

Flit raced ahead and made their business known to the sentries.

"You and the woman can come in," said one of the men, "but not the minotaur."

Rhiannon pulled up next to the man, still mounted. "The minotaur is my companion, and I would not be here if it were not for him. I am Brennan's apprentice and you have my word that he is trustworthy," Rhiannon said, feeling her face turn red.

"Aye, and if we let him in, there will be worse for us. We obey the king's order, not yours."

"It's ok, Rhiannon. I can wait out here."

She silenced Tin with a shake of her head. "Gods, no. I won't have you left at the door like some beggar," she said and turned back to the men. "I know you are doing what you were told, but can you check with Brennan to see if an exception can be made?"

Rhiannon sat taller. She wasn't going to leave Tin.

The guard shifted uneasily on his feet and looked up at the walls above him.

A voice shouted down from above. "It's okay, Tierloch. Let them pass and we will accompany them."

The guard stepped aside and led them pass. She dismounted, leaving her horse at the gate. A group of soldiers escorted them along a winding path between roundhouses and workshops, past blacksmiths, weavers, and women dying wool cloth. The air smelled of smoke and horses.

Tiny pixies danced in Rhiannon's stomach as she fidgeted with her awen pendant and glanced around her. She waited for Brennan to emerge at any moment.

Despite her nervousness, she couldn't help soaking in her surroundings. She had never seen such a place, and felt like she had stepped back into history. The smell of roasting meat and baking bread met her as they walked higher. Stairs carved from the rock led the way to the high hall. At the top, Rhiannon turned and took in the view. Many miles stretched across the expanse of the mound. The rolling countryside glowed with the light of myriad luminous, living things, both on the ground and in the dome of the mound far above.

For a moment she paused, forgetting all else. The view revealed the true size of the place, as well as the magic that filled it. It reminded her of the first time she had seen the Grand Canyon. She turned back from the vista and followed Flit across the green lawn, bordered by tall trees, and came to the doors of the great hall. The guards nodded to their escort and let them in.

Her mouth went dry as she bit at her lips. This was it. Brennan must be inside. She took a breath and crossed the threshold.

Inside, tall timbers soared far above them. Far away and through many empty banquet tables, a raised dais stood with a huge tree growing behind it. Many tapestries hung on the walls. They walked past a fire, smoke rising toward the distant ceiling. A whole pig roasted over the low flame.

A raised platform surrounded by a throng of yelling men appeared ahead, and at the very top, sat a tall throne sheltered under an enormous tree.

She searched the crowd, looking for Brenan, and she spotted him standing next to the throne. She covered her mouth with her hand, gave a shaky laugh, and felt tears welling up.

He still wore his blond hair long and kept a bristling brown beard. To Rhiannon's eyes, he didn't look a day older than when she had first come to live with him. His green, hooded robe was belted at the waist, and in his left hand he clasped a tall, gnarled staff. Rhiannon forced her way through the crowd.

"Whether Garth succeeds or not, we must show Morrigan that she is not the one in charge here," said a tall man standing near the throne.

"Our forces are diminished, and it would be a mistake to lay siege to her fortress when we don't have the men," said another.

Brennan looked up and his eyes met Rhiannon's. Her heart swelled and she rushed to reach him. She raised her hand in a wave and pushed her way to the foot of the stairs.

Brennan hurried to her. Rhiannon embraced him fiercely. She closed her eyes and breathed in deeply, soaking in the feeling of relief. Her throat felt thick as she pulled away and tried to speak.

Brennan smiled at her, joy in his eyes. "Come, let me introduce you." He took her hand and led her up the stairs.

Rhiannon looked back at her friends and gestured that they should follow. Tin cleared a path in the throng of Celts. When they reached the throne, she realized the massive tree behind the throne was an ancient hawthorne. It was *the* hawthorne, the one Garth had told her about. The magic tree that kept the faerie prisoner.

It was all but bare of leaves, but its broad trunk supported countless branches that fanned out overhead, as if to shelter the men beneath. Armed guards circled the tree on three tiered walkways surrounding it. Many of the branches were decorated with gold and purple linen. The tree was clearly the heart of the hall.

Brennan held up his hand to silence the debate and turned to the king. "King Conor, this is an auspicious moment, for now arrived is my niece, Rhiannon."

As Tin and Fao reached them, her uncle moved to make room for them too. "Rhiannon is my apprentice, and with her are her traveling companions."

"I welcome you to my hall," the king said.

Rhiannon wasn't sure of the protocol but she nodded deferentially and said, "We are at your service, your majesty."

Tin bowed, showing his gratitude for being welcomed.

"I've brought these companions," said Rhiannon. "Tinurion, the minotaur, and Fao, his wolf companion. If not for them, Morrigan would have surely killed me. On my first night in the mound, she sent raiders to attack us, and Tinurion and Fao both risked their lives to keep me safe."

The king raised a hand in the air. "It is not our custom to welcome minotaurs to our court, but for Rhiannon, I will make an exception. Tinurion and Fao are welcomed guests."

"Thank you, your majesty," said Rhiannon with a bow. "I've come here today to find Brennan but also to ask for your help. The Morrigan has cursed my family and killed all of us except for Brennan and myself. Now, she has captured my fiancé, Logan. I tried to rescue him before he was taken into her castle, but

I failed. I've come before all of you to ask for your help to rescue him."

Though nervous, Rhiannon held her chin up and looked at the king with her feet firmly planted.

"We know about the overlander," said the king. "We are gathered today to decide what is to be done."

"Any aid you can give would be most appreciated."

"What aid would you have?"

"I would ask that some of your men accompany me to steal into the Morrigan's castle."

"Your courage is admirable, but it would be suicide to attempt it."

Rhiannon put her hands behind her back and looked at Tin.

"There is a way it could be done," said Tinurion.

Everyone turned to look at the minotaur.

"Do we dare listen to the council of a minotaur in this hall?" protested one man. "It's one thing to allow him here as a courtesy, but to offer council?"

Rhiannon noticed the man had dark straight hair and a long mustache. He stood taller than all the other men and overflowed with energy and confidence.

"Bran, let us hear what he has to say," said Conor, motioning the minotaur forward.

"I was once a prisoner, forced to fight in the Morrigan's games. I escaped through the tunnels under the castle and have been a fugitive ever since. The way in is through the ruins of Breckdacor and through the old mining tunnels. The way is known to Morrigan, but it is guarded and has never been used against her."

The crowd fell silent for a moment, and then erupted in a sea of questions.

"Can we find this way?" asked a man.

Rhiannon glanced toward the voice. The speaker had short blond hair and was powerfully built. He instantly reminded her of Garth. This must be his brother. He wore a long bladed sword across his back over his long cloak.

The king let them quiet down and turned to the man who had spoken. "Maybe, Aron. Maybe with a small party of warriors, we could find our way in."

"The way is treacherous and would be difficult for many to

traverse quickly," said Tinurion.

"Brennan, have you heard of such a passage?" the king asked.

"No, your majesty, I have not," said Brennan. "But it makes sense that Morrigan would have a secret entrance—or exit, depending on the need."

"There is more." Tin looked down at Rhiannon before proceeding. "I was not alone in Morrigan's prisons. There are many of your people there and others that would join you in your fight against Morrigan if they were liberated."

"Our people?" asked the king. "Can it be true?"

Bran stepped forward, frowning at Tin. "The only thing I believe is true is that Morrigan has sent us her spy to lead our newest Druid into a trap."

Tin's hand reached back for his axe. "Are you calling me a liar?" he spat, nostrils flaring.

Brennan put up his hands. "Bran, you have tarnished the hospitality of your father's hall by accusing Tin without proof or provocation."

"I don't trust him, and that is my truth. We've been taught to be honest in our speech."

"Honest, yes, but needlessly suspicious, no."

"Bran does raise a valid point. How do we know we can trust him?" said the king.

"I trust him," said Rhiannon. "And my life is in more danger than anyone else's."

Aron looked hard at Rhiannon, and she dared not blink. After several seconds, Aron nodded shortly and turned to the king. "I do not know the quality of this minotaur, but when I look at Rhiannon, I feel her integrity. I feel she is one of us, and if she says he can be trusted, I believe her. I will go with you, Rhiannon, and help you free our people."

Rhiannon nodded at Aron. "Thank you," she said with a smile.

"*If* it is true," said Bran, "and I will not believe it until I see it done, the gates could be opened from the inside, and our army could await the prisoners and protect their retreat."

Rhiannon glanced at Aron, who smiled back at her.

"It's just the thing to teach Morrigan a lesson. If we succeed in rescuing them, we would have more people to fight her," Bran added.

"They may not be in fighting shape," Tin warned.

"Nevertheless, I will go," said Aron. "If there is chance any of our people are the Morrigan's prisoners, we have a duty to save them. We know the overlander was taken there. Perhaps my wife is among them too."

"I will bring the army, and see it done," said Bran.

"Thank you both for your help," said Rhiannon. "It means much to me."

"I appreciate your eagerness for this plan that I have not yet approved," said the king pointedly. "But, let us consider the consequences."

"Morrigan will not take the loss of her prisoners lightly and will retaliate," said Brennan.

"If I understand what is happening, in my humble opinion, I believe she will soon attack here anyway," said Rhiannon.

"I agree with Rhiannon," said Bran. "The Morrigan will come soon anyway. When the time comes, I say let her throw herself against our walls and if she thinks she can win, we will make her pay. With our people back, we will be that much stronger. It has taken this minotaur to make it clear. If what he says is true, it would be a mighty feat to accomplish and worthy of much honor."

"It will be risky," said Brennan, after a moment of thought, "but I agree with Rhiannon and Bran. We must do this. It will also draw Morrigan's attention away from Garth, and he may need all the time he can get if he is to succeed with his quest."

"You have said this is an auspicious moment, Brennan," said Conor, "and you are right. We have been stalemated over this issue for a long time and now, with the arrival of our new friends, it is clear what we must do. Aron and Bran, you do our family honor by volunteering. Recruit some men to go with you."

The two princes nodded.

Rhiannon squeezed her hands at her sides, excited and eager. She looked boldly into the eyes of the King.

"Your majesty, I thank you for your aid. It is more than I could have hoped."

"Even if we have only just met, you are one of us, and your need is our need. May the gods smile on you and this task."

Rhiannon smiled, feeling amazed she had received such

help. But now the task lay ahead of her, to lead the expedition into unknown dangers. The reality of it struck her. She stared down at her empty hands, feeling a wave of cold. Before that though, she needed to talk to Brennan. She needed answers and she needed his help if this was going to work.

* * *

Rhiannon followed Brennan through the hall, with Tin, Fao, and Flit trailing. "You are all welcome to my home. I have food and drink for weary travelers, and I would hear the tale of how you came here," said Brennan as they walked through the throng of men.

Rhiannon's smile wavered as she passed through the crowd. Yes, she was relieved to have found her uncle, but a confrontation with Brennan loomed. She was no longer the girl who allowed her needs to be secondary.

Why hadn't he ever told her about this place? Why had he allowed the attack in Colorado? Why had he abandoned her?

She left the hall and followed Brennan to one of the roundhouses.

"I have bread, salted pork, stew, and mead. It's not much, but it will keep body and soul together."

Rhiannon rubbed her sweating hands on her jeans. "Uncle, let's wait for a minute with the food. I need to talk. Tin and Flit would you give us a few minutes?"

"Of course, Rhiannon," said Flit. "I'll show Tin around the fort."

Brennan nodded, opened the door to his home, and let Rhiannon go in first. She took a seat near the low fire inside.

"I came home as soon as Mrs. McBride told me you were missing," she said. "Logan disappeared in the night. I followed his tracks and found the tree open. Why didn't you meet me at the gate?"

"I sent Flit to find you because I was needed here. I also wanted to give you a chance to try your magic. Call it a test. I wanted you to discover that the things I taught you worked so much more strongly here."

"You took a gamble with my life?" she asked, the power of her accusation making her face hot.

"It was a calculated risk, and I can see it paid off. You are here and you have grown. You know I cherish you, and that my intent was only to make you stronger, not put you in harm's way."

Rhiannon widened her stance, feeling anger growing. "Anything could have happened, Brennan! This place is full of danger and it almost killed me, more than once."

"But what happened? You are here and stronger."

"I don't think that's fair. You still gambled with my life."

Brennan frowned. "There was more going on than your arrival here, Rhiannon. Stop thinking of just yourself."

Rhiannon laughed with an edge. "Excuse me? Stop thinking of myself? I dropped *everything* to come help *you.*"

Brennan sighed. "I'm sorry, Rhiannon, you are right. Perhaps I've been a bit selfish, but not without cause. I had to make choices and in the end I think they were the right ones. Again, remember in the end you are safe and have grown."

Rhiannon bit her lip and considered Brennan's words. She didn't like the idea, but she could see how the experience made her stronger. Truly, she would not have discovered her strength if Brennan deposited her safely at the fort.

She took a deep breath and nodded. "Well, the important thing is that we are back together," she said trying to her anger go. "How is it that you are known here?"

"Now that is a long tale, but for now you should know this is my home, and the world above is but a place I visit from time to time."

"How could this be your home?" asked Rhiannon.

"When I was young, I discovered a way to the surface, and because time passes so differently, I could come and go and seem to live two lives. I am your kin, but the story of my life is a long one that will have to wait. The Druids taught me, and when they died I was the last one left. After I had earned it, I took my place at the court of the king. The years passed and no one showed enough of the gift to take my place. Not until you came along, that is. My plan all along has been that you would take my place when my days come to an end."

Rhiannon brought her knuckles to her lips and gave a slight shake of her head. First Garth, and now Brennan, had mentioned her staying in the mound. "Take your place?"

"I am the last Druid, and someone will need to take my place and guard the hawthorne when I am gone. This is what I've been training you for."

She stared at the ground and frowned. "But Uncle, I have plans for my life. I want to finish this business with the Morrigan and then have a normal life. Back home."

He sighed. "It is your choice, of course, but I hope that, before this is done, you will understand the importance of my request."

Rhiannon narrowed her eyes, feeling manipulated. "Maybe what you say will be true, but today all I want is to get Logan back and get out of here. Why didn't you tell me about this place?"

"I couldn't tell you until you were ready. You wouldn't have believed me. Can you understand?"

She rubbed the back of her neck and nodded. "Yes. Though I studied Irish myth my whole life, I would not have truly believed this place existed until I saw it with my own eyes, but it still seems like you could've shown it to me earlier."

"I'm sorry to have put you through what must have been a terrible time. I had confidence in you, and it seems it was well placed. You are here and safe and with new friends as well."

Temper flaring, Rhiannon stepped back. "Not all of us are safe. Did you know I was attacked in Colorado and that CuChulain was killed? "

Brennan frowned. "I did not know that you were attacked. I'm sorry, Rhiannon. Tell me what happened."

Awash with new fury, she told him of the attack on the mountain.

"You are right to be angry," he said. "It is my fault. I came here after I was attacked and thought wrongly you would be safe. The faerie who attacked me in the library came with such force and determination that I knew something had changed. I worried the fort had fallen and the tree had been killed. I left immediately for the mound, pursing my attackers and coming straight to the fort."

His shoulders slumped and he looked at her with sad eyes. "I should have ensured your safety before leaving. I was wrong. I'm sorry, Rhiannon."

Rhiannon pressed her lips together and held her breath, then let it out in a sharp rush. "If you had trained me to use offensive magic, you wouldn't have needed to protect me. I had to rely on iron bullets and a bargain made with Taranis instead."

"I was trying to protect you, Rhiannon," said Brennan with a sigh. "What price did you agree to with Taranis?"

"That is my business. I would say it was worth my life, wouldn't you?" Her voice split the air between them.

"Calm down, Rhiannon. Of course, it was worth your life. The reason I never taught you offensive magic is because I wanted your life to be about more than revenge."

"Don't tell me to calm down. It's time I stop being a victim."

Brennan put his hand on her shoulder but she stepped back.

"I don't want to be comforted, Uncle. I want to end this feud with Morrigan. I want Logan back, and I want to stop having to be afraid all the time."

Brennan looked deep into her eyes. "Very well. I will give you what you wish. It's time for your initiation. If you succeed, I will teach you how to fight with magic."

Rhiannon swallowed hard, then took a breath.

"Just like that? After all these years?"

"Yes. You may not thank me later. It will be difficult."

Rhiannon gulped. This was what she wanted, difficult or not. "Very well," she said. "When do we start?"

"Tonight."

Rhiannon felt a weight lift, feeling pleased that she would finally get more power to help her get Logan back, to protect herself, but her stomach clenched. What would the initiation be? What kind of ordeal would she be confronted with? She didn't know, but she did know she would do whatever it took to succeed.

Chapter 29

Rhiannon rubbed her arms and held out her palms to the fire. Flames leapt up and kissed the metal cauldron, which hung across the blaze. Two iron firedogs supported the rod on which it hung. Brennan stirred the cauldron, tasted it, and gave her a bowl of barley cereal with honey.

"What can you tell me about the initiation?"

"Nothing now."

Rhiannon bit her lip and rubbed at the back of her neck. She picked at the cereal. "I'm not hungry. Can we just get started?"

"You need to eat first. You will need all your strength."

"I'm not hungry."

"This is not an option," Brennan said firmly.

Rhiannon ate a spoonful.

"Tastes good," Rhiannon managed to say. She finished the food and didn't want to admit it but it did make her feel stronger.

"Okay, I'm done. Can we go now?"

He studied her, then nodded. "Okay. Let's go."

Outside darkness encroached. They walked past burning bonfires and glowing torches on their way to the main gate. When they came upon Flit and Tin, Rhiannon let them know she would be gone with Brennan. She left them behind and passed through the gates of the fort.

"Where are we going?"

"To the Druid grove."

Rhiannon's heart raced. What would Brennan's grove be like here in the mound? His grove back at the manor house was very familiar from the many ceremonies they had performed there. She wondered what mysteries awaited her in this new place.

In the low light of early night, they traveled through fields of barley and rows of vegetables, eventually leaving behind the cultivated fields and hiking into the pastures where cattle slept. The realm of men faded away, and all around, nature thrived in its unspoiled grace. Breathlessly, Rhiannon took it all in.

She glanced from side to side, reaching out to touch the tall grasses as she thought about what lay ahead. She knew Brennan loved her and would not intentionally hurt her, but on the other hand, he had left her alone to wander around this dangerous place as a test. Would the initiation be equally as dangerous? It didn't matter. She would see it through so she could rescue Logan and be free of the Morrigan's malice.

Ahead of them, through a mist, the grove appeared. It stood out from the open landscape all around them, an island of trees in an ocean of grass. There, a riot of living things flourished, both trees and other plants and herbs. Vibrant life sprang from the ground.

They reached the grove's border, and there was no path inside. Brennan walked forward, raised his staff, and the tree branches moved aside, forming a tunnel leading deeper into the grove. She took a deep breath and followed her uncle inside.

The skin on Rhiannon's arms prickled, the power intensifying as they meandered through the forest. The quiet and the age of the trees gave her a feeling of ancient peace.

Brennan held up his staff and said, "*Solas.*" A bright light appeared atop his staff.

Rhiannon stopped, her mouth dropping open. "I've never seen you do that before."

"There are many things you don't know. But soon, you will know them."

She looked up. With the light around them, she could now see the tall oaks lining the path, also ash, rowan, and many other trees. Brennan's light not only illuminated them but also woke them up. As they followed the path, the trees began to glow with a light of their own. Rhiannon turned and the trees behind them glowed for a moment, but the light faded as they moved deeper into the grove.

A sound came, and at first she thought the trees moved in the wind, but she realized they were still. The sound of running water echoed ahead. They approached from the west, and soon a sparkling stream appeared. The light, which glowed from the flow, cast silver accents on the hundred green hues of the trees.

Rhiannon felt giddy and took in the beauty of the scene with a smile.

Three square, flat stones rested in the flow with water falling between them, making a bridge. Rhiannon followed Brennan across. At the far edge of the stream, a smaller stone sat. A deep groove descended around it, spiraling downward from the tip.

Her uncle stopped and removed a jar from his robe, then poured the contents of the container onto the top of the carved rock.

"A gift for the spirit of the grove," he said, answering her unspoken question.

The amber liquid flowed down into the groove and spiraled down to the earth beneath. Brennan crouched down and put his hands on the soil. He took a pinch of it and approached Rhiannon.

With the soil on his first three fingers, he rubbed them downward on her forehead. "May the blessings of the sacred earth of our mother grove bless you."

He marked his own forehead before walking forward.

Soon, they reached an opening in the center mostly covered by the tree canopy. Faint lights darted high above, and an occasional glimmer found its way down. A soft green luminescence came from the grass at their feet and from the low shrubs. Brennan extinguished his light.

In the center of the grove, a slab of stone resting on two upright supports made an altar. Celtic knot work bordered the blue gray surface, and carved ogam letters decorated the center. Beyond the altar, a fire pit ringed with stones sat, filled with logs ready to burn. On the opposite side of the altar, a large boulder jutted, also carved with ogam. Beyond the trees, lying on the ground were piles of furs as well as ceramic jars and sacks of grain. A breeze greeted them from the east, making a wind chime sing.

"Welcome to my *true* home," said Brennan.

Rhiannon slowly shook her head, taking it all in. "This is amazing," she said in a hushed voice. "It's so beautiful and peaceful."

"Yes it is, though not always. Sometimes the trees are wild and sing in the wind; then you can really feel the power of this place. Long ago, a group of Druids used to meet here to work powerful magic. Now it is only me, and *hopefully* you. It is time for your initiation."

Rhiannon swallowed hard. "What do I need to do?"

"You will be tested. If you succeed, you will be shown a great secret, and that secret will give you power."

Her hands turned clammy, but she took a deep breath and nodded.

"If you pass the test, I will teach you how to fight with magic. Do you freely choose to be initiated as a Druid?"

The idea of being a Druid made her heart swell. It was as if her whole life led to this moment. She knew she wanted this more than anything. But, she also knew there would be no turning back. That thought gave her pause.

"If I do this, Brennan, am I committing to staying in the mound?"

"No. But being a Druid brings great responsibility. How you choose to use your knowledge will always be your choice. The time for talk is done. What do you choose?"

Rhiannon nodded. She knew that whatever the future held, she could better face it with the wisdom and power of being a Druid.

"Yes, I do so chose to be initiated as a Druid," said Rhiannon solemnly.

"Then follow me."

Brennan crossed the glade toward the shadowy far edge. The forest opened to allow them passage, and Rhiannon followed closely. This part of the grove felt different; there was a certain haunted feel to it. The trees stooped down, and tendrils of moss made them look like old Druids themselves.

Tingling all over, she bit her lip and wrapped her arms around herself as she walked.

Brennan led her in silence until they reached a cliff wall. "Here is where you must go on alone," he said, pointing to a narrow crack in the wall.

The tingling intensified. "What will I find inside?"

"Follow the cave down until you come to a pool. You will meet no foes here, other than what you might bring in your own mind. The pool is a sacred place. When you find it, you must enter it and recline in the water. It will support you. Float and wait for a vision. It may take hours or days, but you must stay in the dark until it happens. You can either leave as a Druid with a vision, or without one and go no further in learning the Druid ways."

"If I don't have a vision, will the power I already have be stripped away?" Rhiannon said, studying his face.

"No. What you have learned will always be yours, but you will not learn more. This is the way it has always been done. Come away with a vision, and your power will grow. Fail to open to it, and you consign yourself to the life of an apprentice only."

"You did this test?"

"Yes. All of the Druids of my lineage did so. If you choose to do the same, go now."

Rhiannon swallowed hard and looked into the cave. She was afraid, but she knew she had to do it. She had been born to be a Druid. She must gain a vision or not come out at all.

She gave Brennan a curt nod, edged her way through the crack, and climbed through the narrow space beyond. The walls were covered with amethyst crystals that glowed pale purple. The way led deeper and deeper.

She picked her way carefully, descending into the earth. Sweat ran down her back, not from exertion, but from the humidity in the air. Soon, the crystals grew fewer and fewer. Near pitch black surrounded her, and the cave continued to drop.

Just as the last of the crystals gave out, she noticed a faint glow ahead. The tunnel twisted and shrank. She dropped to her knees and crawled up an incline, through a narrow passageway. She wriggled her way into the shaft and squirmed forward on her stomach until she forced her way through.

Rhiannon emerged from the tight confines, muddy and covered with sweat. One look told her she'd found the right place. The small chamber, filled with stalagmites and stalactites, held the pool. The cave reminded Rhiannon of a predator's jagged maw about to close, with countless points stabbing into the space. Moist air surrounded her, and the only light came from inside the amethyst colored pool.

She fingered her awen pendant and rose to her feet, stepping forward to look at the water. The purple liquid filled a shallow and smooth basin. The clean water swirled slowly, radiating lavender light. She paused for a moment and took a breath. Something about the pool made her uneasy.

She stepped back, clenched her jaw, slowly relaxed then removed her clothes.

Rhiannon stepped into the pool and lay back. She tested the water and released all of her weight on it, feeling it support her completely. The warm fluid enveloped her as the crystals below her went dark. Suddenly, she was lost in the darkest pitch she had ever experienced.

She calmed her mind with her breathing, just as Brennan taught her. In the water, she heard her heartbeat and the clear sound of her breath. She inhaled the warm air and exhaled back into the inky dark, feeling her body awareness recede into the background as her mind and thoughts came to the fore. She thought about Logan; she thought about Brennan; she thought about Morrigan. Her mind circled the same thoughts over and over.

I hope Logan is safe. I wonder if Brennan is guarding the entrance to the cave. Does he know what is happening to me? Does Morrigan know about this place? Could she reach me even here?

She clutched her hands into fists and bit down hard, her thoughts rambling on and on.

Focus. Go deeper.

Rhiannon concentrated as she had learned to do when doing healing magic, but taking her time, really focusing. She drew in energy from all around her and controlled her breath, taking in a slow inhale through her nose to a count of three. She breathed out through her mouth, also counting to three. Finally she held her breath, again for a three count. Nine times she repeated the pattern. She slowly envisioned each of the energetic cauldrons, starting at the lowest one, the cauldron of formation, in her belly. She imagined a spark of fire kindling, then jumping to the middle cauldron, the cauldron of motion, in the region of her heart. She felt the energy rise, but it wasn't easy. It didn't leap upward like usual, leaving the top cauldron untouched, blocked from her.

She shivered in the black water, curled her toes, and felt nauseous.

I'm failing. Please, Brighid, help me.

Maybe she needed more energy, but there wasn't much to work with. Because there was no plant life? Surely energy existed even in the cold dark.

She returned her awareness to simple breathing. She lay in the stillness, a pain in the back of her throat. It felt like she had been floating for hours. Time stretched eternally.

Maybe a vision won't come, she thought with panic. Maybe, after all she had been through, she would not pass this test. She tried to let go, tried to relax, tried to not struggle. And then she just stopped trying.

Time lost all meaning. Rhiannon floated on and on. She passed into a void space, like a deep, dreamless sleep. She regained awareness on the other side and knew that she had been gone.

In the dark, she felt her body moving, slowly turning in the stillness of the pool. For a moment, she grew alarmed, but she relaxed. The vision was coming. She calmed down, and as her body rotated in the pool, she was sure.

She let go and moved toward the end of the pool, but instead of hitting the wall with her head, she found herself in a tunnel, moving faster. She put out her hand, felt the wall racing past, and she could sense a drop coming.

She fell. Through the dark pit, Rhiannon tumbled, falling and spinning into the blackness. She prayed the vision waited for her there.

* * *

Moments later, Rhiannon found herself standing in a dark tunnel. She didn't remember how she got here. Was she in the place of visions? Had she succeeded by getting here or was this place just some sort weird hallucination?

Suddenly, the darkness around her attacked. The blackness pressed in like a rapist, whispering that the world had never existed; only the abyss was real. A terrible certainty, that the endless night was all that existed, filled her, overwhelmed her.

Rhiannon shrank to the ground, hugging her arms around her, rocking back and forth under the crushing weight of oblivion. Alone in the deepest dark, her breath would not come and she silently screamed.

Closing her eyes, she pulled at her hair, focusing on the sensation, trying to get out of the black. The pain said she existed.

I am not alone, she though desperately. She pictured Logan, Brennan, her mother, and the love she felt for them summoned memories to her aid. She remembered the time Logan brought her roses just because he was thinking of her. She remembered when Brennan hugged her after she fell out of a tree and broke her arm. She remembered when her mom tucked her in at night. The love she felt lifted some of the weight, and she was able to stagger to her feet.

Only love has the power to lift the darkness

She stumbled forward, desperate to get free. She leaned on the wall, pulling herself forward and trying to breathe. The darkness clung to her like black mud as she fought her way through the tunnel. She turned a corner and froze. A massive black door stood just ahead, menacing her.

Rhiannon stared at the iron handle and the heavy hinges. Her leg muscles felt shaky and weak. Dread washed over her. She didn't want to see what was behind that door.

She turned and saw the darkness behind her, knew she had to keep going. She took a deep breath, set her jaw, and pulled the door open.

Dead leaves covered the floor inside. Decaying body parts were strewn about like a pack of animals had feasted there. Beyond the mess, Rhiannon saw *her*.

Heart nearly exploding, she stumbled backward against the wall, shaking her head in denial.

Morrigan, dressed in black, had come for her at last.

Her whole body shook as she reached out, seeking power to protect herself. Nothing came to her, no power, and no help. The earth was dead. Rhiannon's strength left her, and she crumbled to her knees.

Thousands of the blood-drinking faeries, the same kind that had killed her mother, hovered around Morrigan. The Faerie Queen pointed a finger and shouted, "Kill her!"

The swarm came at her.

Rhiannon struggled back to her feet as the creatures attacked. She tore and punched at the faeries, but there were too many of them, and she felt her life draining away. She screamed her outrage. This goddess had caused so much damage; killing all that she loved.

Her blood flowed, from a hundred lacerations, onto the ground. Body weakened, she slipped to one knee. Rhiannon stared defiantly up into the Morrigan's cold gaze but she collapsed to the ground. She felt her heartbeat turn sluggish and her body dropped away, but not her awareness.

In the darkness, she rose above her shredded body, moving closer to the Morrigan, and looked into her face. The blue eyes drew her in. What she saw there, struck her like a cold slap of water. The Morrigan's face was her own.

No! How could it be?

The pain of the realization overtook her. Her fear of Morrigan had transformed her into the queen herself.

Never! I will never be like her!

All went black again and she drifted.

I still exist. I still exist. I still exist. Somehow, her awareness remained.

Rhiannon rose higher and higher through the stone, and she found herself melting and merging into everything. Light filled her, showing her she was at one with the *all*, that she was connected to everything, that her "death" hadn't meant anything. She was one with the stone of the earth, and the flowers of the fields, and fire in the heavens; it was all part of her and she part of it, even the Morrigan herself. She knew in that instant that nothing ever truly dies in the circle of life.

Death touched her psyche. All things that live must die and be reborn again; that which kills and that which dies are the same.

After what seemed like an age, she opened her eyes in the purple-lit cave of the Druids. Her mind stood still, absorbed in the quiet. Slowly, she awakened and her thoughts turned to what she had learned.

Only love lifts the darkness and my relationships give value to life. I must not let my fear and anger twist me to become like the Morrigan, to turn hurt into rage. I must remember how we are all connected and how death and life are part of the same cycle.

After a time, Rhiannon stood. Her body felt weak and heavy. She brought her shaking hands to her temples, wondering how long she had been gone.

A resonant humming permeated the stone of the cave, subtle and yet powerful. The sound, just at the edge of perception, came from within. Her mind, still and clear as a lake, hummed with new energy.

Rhiannon climbed free from the pool and found her clothes. Dizzy, she used the stones to support her as she dressed. She staggered slowly through the cave and found her way back to the cave entrance, where Brennan waited.

Chapter 30

Rhiannon crawled from of the cave and fell, panting, against the outside wall. As profound as her vision had been, she still didn't see how it would help her in her struggle with the Morrigan. Yes, she needed wisdom, but she also needed power.

Brennan sat cross-legged on the ground, chanting in a low voice.

"I did it," Rhiannon said and slumped down to the ground.

"I know," he said.

Rhiannon raised a brow. "You know?"

"I went inside, connected with you, and learned that you were successful."

"Then you know what I experienced."

"Some of it. The vision comes to us all in different ways; we must face our greatest fear, and through that, face the reality of death.

"Did you know it would be the Morrigan who came to me?"

"Not specifically, but it makes sense. She has been the source of all your pain."

"I will never be like her, that much I've learned."

Brennan nodded.

"I've believed in reincarnation all my life," Rhiannon continued, "and this experience has confirmed it. But is there an end to all these lives?"

"Some say that creation has no beginning or end. That it is an ever-turning wheel, where we move from the source, from a place of unity with all that is, and back to that unity again at the end. We live to add our distinctive experience to the all."

"Do you believe that?"

"I believe it is a simple way of trying to express the great

Mystery. I believe the truth of it is beyond what words can express."

"Brennan, I don't see how what I experienced gives me any more power. Wisdom, yes, but power to stop the Morrigan? No."

"Why are you so eager for power, Rhiannon?"

Her stomach hardened. "I would think you'd know that better than anyone. I want the power to get Logan back and to keep the Morrigan from hurting us anymore."

Brennan stared at her. "You've never been patient, always wanting more."

Rhiannon clenched her jaw so hard it hurt. She ran her hands through her hair and took a breath. "I admit, I've been eager to learn, but you don't know what it has been like for *me* to always be dependent on *you.* You learned how to harness the magic before you had need of it, but I've been vulnerable, terribly vulnerable, and helpless to protect myself."

Brennan put his hands behind his back and pinched his lips together. "Rhiannon, I know it's been hard on you. Come with me. We are not done yet."

Her uncle turned and walked away from the cave, and Rhiannon followed. Still discombobulated, she tripped over a rock and Brennan caught her. She leaned on him for support as they walked back to the grove.

In the distance, a fire burned through the trees. The light danced amidst the boughs and cast sharp shadows. They entered the grove and she moved to the tall blaze.

"This is a sacred fire, built from the wood of all the sacred trees. I built it to commemorate this special day when you become a Druid. Kneel now and take the oath."

Rhiannon knelt by the roaring flames as she was told and repeated the words as Brennan spoke them.

"Oh gods of my people, I, Rhiannon O'Neil, call upon you to witness my Druid oath. I vow before you to deepen my understanding of the Druid way, to seek virtue in my life, and to keep the rites and honor the gods. Oh, gods and goddesses, hear my vow.

"Ancestors, I call you forth today to witness my oath. Standing here before you, I vow that I will live a life of service to our people, to do right by my kin, my friends, and my community. Ancestors, hear my vow.

"Spirits of Nature, I call you forth today to witness my oath. Standing here before you, I vow that I will heal, nurture, and protect the earth and be her champion. Spirits of Nature, hear my vow.

"These things I swear to the gods as my witnesses. So be it."

Rhiannon's breath came easier and lightness spread from her chest as the words resonated out into the night. The weight of new responsibility settled on her shoulders as well.

Brennan studied her and bent down and took from the fire a gray pile of ash, still warm from the blaze. He took some of the ash onto his finger. "I mark you with the sign of the Druids, with the ogam symbol for oak, *duir*, to imbue you with power and strength."

Brennan traced a vertical line down the center of her forehead and then two horizontal lines branching off from the first line to the left.

The mark burned Rhiannon's skin, but she let it sink in.

"Now, I must teach you the words of power. Until now, you have drawn on the power of the earth and directed it with your mind alone. That is good for beginners, but with more power comes the need for more control. Listen, and I will teach you how to use the words of power."

Rhiannon worried her mind couldn't take any more knowledge, but she had been waiting so long for this, what she craved since the night her mother was taken from her. Finally, she would be able to fight back.

"As you know, our power, Nwyfre, comes from the source of all creation. The Source is known by many different names: God, Brahman, the Great Spirit, Kether. It is the divine ground of all matter, energy, time, space and being.

"In the beginning of creation, the Source manifested out of the void in its first and original form as sound. The primordial sound, some call it the Oran Mor, still hums through all of creation and that is why we chant, to align ourselves with the sounds of the Source. Sounds can summon different attributes of the Source, and each word I teach you, when combined with intention and power, will cause magic to happen."

Rhiannon listened carefully, sitting back on her heels and feeling the wonder of what Brennan was teaching her. Rushing blood made her body hot. She leaned in and waited for Brennan to continue.

"Now I must teach you the words you will use from this day on. With the words of power, you can focus the Nwyfre to achieve different effects. It is a powerful technique, and you will need it."

Rhiannon's breath stalled, and her whole body tingled. She sat up straighter, eager to take in all of Brennan's teachings.

In the light of the sacred fire, Brennan leaned forward and whispered the first word. As he spoke, a breeze blew through the treetops and the grove began to sway. Everything around them moved in the dance of the wind, and no one but Rhiannon heard the words as they were taught to her.

She felt them enter her consciousness and make a home within. They vibrated inside her, waiting to be unleashed. They soaked in, becoming her knowledge. They empowered her. Terrified her. Humbled her.

She would never be the same.

* * *

Rhiannon touched her temples and closed her eyes. When she opened them again, she stared into the sacred fire, resting, trying to process all that had happened. The words of power hummed inside her, ready to erupt, to aid her.

Brennan disappeared into the trees and came back with bread, cheese, an apple, and a mug of water. He handed her the food and drink. "You need to eat something," he said.

Rhiannon nodded and bit into the apple.

"For a long time, I have been content to guard the hawthorne and rely on its power," said Brennan. "Even now, I rely on Garth's successful quest to save our future. But there is something more we can hope for."

"What is it?"

"There have been no new Druids for a long time, partly because the talent for the art is rare, but also because the staff of the Arch Druid was lost to us."

"I've never heard of it," said Rhiannon.

"It is called the Faillean Duir and it was created by the first Druids. It is said to be older than even the Tuatha de Dannan."

Rhiannon opened her eyes wide. "Older than the Tuatha de Dannan?"

"Yes, and it represents our relationship with the earth, our bond and our covenant, if you will. It is a symbol of our faith."

"What happened to it?"

"It was carried by Gweneira, my Arch Druid, until she was murdered and the staff was stolen by the Morrigan. She hoped that concealing it would weaken us. She was more right than she knew."

"How do you know she didn't just destroy it?"

"Because the Faillean Duir is part of the World Tree. It could not be destroyed without causing damage to the very fabric of existence. The Morrigan would have learned this if she attempted to damage the staff. No, she would have had no choice but to keep it locked away."

"Are you sure she kept it in her castle?"

"I'm not positive, but I think she would want to keep it close enough to keep an eye on it.

Now that we've learned of a way to get into Morrigan's castle, we can find out. If I'm right you will be able to reclaim the Faillean Duir."

The blood rushed to Rhiannon's face. She clenched her hands into fists as she looked up at Brennan. "I need to get that staff."

Brennan nodded. "If you reclaimed the staff, you could avenge your mother's death."

Rhiannon's lips parted, and she leaned in closer to Brennan. "The staff could kill her?"

"It's hard to say, because it's never been tried, but I believe that it could. I think Morrigan believes that too."

Rhiannon stood and looked up, awash in a floating sensation. Tears welled and spilled down her cheeks.

There is a chance I can finish this.

"Thank you, Brennan. You've given me hope."

She bowed her head, letting the news sink in. She had never thought to confront her mother's killer. Her best hope was to be strong enough to defend herself, to perhaps reach a compromise that would keep them safe. Now she was being handed a chance not only to end the feud, but to take revenge. The thought tantalized her, but at the same time she felt hesitation.

"What Morrigan did was wrong, but killing her won't bring my mother back."

Brennan nodded. "Vengeance is never a good reason to kill. However, when the time comes, we may have to stand against her nevertheless. We may need to protect others and to protect the hawthorne. Having the Faillean Duir will give us a chance to defend ourselves."

"I must get started. Can you give me any advice?" asked Rhiannon.

"Go with Tinurion as we planned, but when you are inside the castle, you must find the staff and take it. Use your pendulum to locate it once you are inside."

"It will be guarded."

"Of that you can be sure."

"What if Morrigan herself guards it?"

"You will have a difficult time."

Rhiannon's stomach turned sour. "The power words will have to be enough."

"Before you go, I have some parting gifts." Brennan pulled a green robe from behind him and handed it to her. "This robe was made from the bounty of the earth. May it protect you from heat and cold, weapons and spells, and keep you safe to do the work of Mother Earth."

"Thank you," said Rhiannon. She took the precious gift with careful hands.

"Now, take your staff." Brennan walked to the edge of the clearing and removed a tall staff decorated with red ribbons. "This is your Druid staff made of wood from the hawthorne. Use it to focus your magic, and it will protect you and cause your enemies harm. Never use it in anger, only to protect the weak. Remember that you came from the earth and there you will return. Keep this truth clear in your mind whenever you have need of protection."

Rhiannon took the staff and turned it in hand. Beautifully crafted, all twenty ogam letters were carved along its length. She felt power in its core. Somehow, it was still alive.

"Thank you, Uncle," said Rhiannon again. "These are mighty gifts and I will use them well."

"You will have need of them," he said.

Rhiannon gripped her staff hard, her fingers turning white. So much had happened, the initiation, the power words, the Faillean Duir and the hope that it could be reclaimed and with it, finally end her troubles. Much still stood in her way but at least now she had a plan and hope. Now she needed to get started as soon as possible, to gather her friends and leave for the Morrigan's castle, to rescue Logan and reclaim the staff. Rhiannon relaxed her grip, raised her chin, and strode forward with wide steps.

Chapter 31

Logan pushed the door of the throne room open. Inside, the Morrigan stood from her seat on the dais and smiled.

He looked up at her. "You called for me?"

"Yes, yes. I've heard you are finally able to move around again."

Logan glared, feeling his anger simmer.

"What's wrong? You should be very proud of yourself. I didn't want to weaken your confidence beforehand, but no one has survived that test in a very long time."

"I faced danger only to falter at the end."

"What are you talking about?"

"Áine."

"So you had a little fun, so what? You will have to learn that faerie morals are quite different than human ones. What matters is you survived the test and have grown in power."

Logan studied the Morrigan. No doubt she was behind Áine's affections, using the faerie to trap him. How could he leave now? Where would he go? He couldn't go back to Rhiannon, not after he had been unfaithful. The trap had been carefully laid, and he fell right into it.

The Morrigan smiled as if reading his thoughts. "I can see you are distressed. Trust me. In a few decades, you won't even remember what the problem was. You are a prince of the sidhe. You need to embrace your glorious future."

Logan looked at his feet, feeling sick.

"I have some of your things." The Morrigan held out her hands, palms up. In one was Logan's ponytail, and in the other, his rings.

He stepped forward. If nothing else, he had his possessions back. He put on each ring, thinking about each. They all had significance; the claddagh ring from Rhiannon, the skull ring from Sturgis, the wolf ring from his father, and the turquoise ring.

"I've added a little something to them. They will now stay with you when you shift so you won't lose them."

"Can I learn to keep clothes too?"

"Don't want to be naked all the time?" Morrigan laughed. "Yes, I will teach you that too. Now come sit next to me. We have work to do. There's nothing better for a broken heart than keeping busy."

Logan's gut sank, heavy with self-loathing. He had been manipulated at every turn. He bore the responsibility for his mistakes, but it was the Morrigan who had orchestrated it all. Heat rushed through him and he clenched his jaw as he climbed the stairs toward the Morrigan. "You might think I'm a fool to have fallen so easily into your trap. But I'm not a fool, and I will find a way to be free of you."

Morrigan's eyes burned into him. She laughed. "You can try."

She stared hard at him for a moment longer daring him to try something. Logan burned with frustration but looked away. Despite the power he had gained, he knew he was still no match for the goddess.

Morrigan turned and spoke. "Ulchabhán, let in the Cailleach!"

The soldier opened the doors. In walked an old woman with a stooped back and gnarled hands. She walked slowly but confidently to the throne of the Queen.

"I have a task for you, Cailleach. I think you will enjoy it."

"What is it, my Queen?"

"A prince of the Celts has left his lands with a small force of men. I would know what their mission is, and then I want you to kill them."

"How shall I know them, your majesty? They all look alike to me."

"You've seen him before. He was the one who led the attack on my soldiers when they tried to capture my son."

"Oh yes, yes. The blond one. Garth, they call him, yes?"

"Yes, he is the one. Find him, learn what he is up to, and then kill them all."

"It shall be so, your Majesty."

Logan wondered how this old woman could ever be a match for the warrior with the blue face paint.

The Cailleach shapeshifted before his eyes, becoming a black wolf with a single streak of white fur on its forehead. As big as Logan's wolf, the creature turned and loped to the door. He bet she was just as strong, despite her age, and no doubt more cunning.

"See, now wasn't that fun?"

Logan simply nodded. He knew he was on the wrong side in all of this, but he was trapped. His own lack of vigilance had been his downfall, but there must be some way he could make it right.

"There is more to magic than shapeshifting, and it's time you begin to learn. You must learn how to use power words, and when you have learned that, you must learn how to fight with weapons. You can't be a prince and not be able to defend yourself."

It was as if the Morrigan knew just what to say to woo him. He had always wanted to learn how to use his power and become stronger, but there had never been anyone to teach him until now. He had no idea how to fix the situation with Rhiannon, but until he did, the more he could learn, the better off he would be.

"There is someone I want you to meet. Don't be put off by his size. You will find he is quite formidable." The Morrigan shifted in her throne. "Nyx, come," she said to the air.

From a high window flew a pixie glowing dark purple. He circled the room and landed at the feet of the queen and bowed. "I am here at your command, my Queen."

"The time we have talked about has come. I want you to train my son in both power words and swords."

"Yes, your majesty," he said with eyes still downcast.

Logan looked at the Morrigan with a questioning glance. How could this pixie possibly train him to fight?

"Nyx, demonstrate what you can do."

The pixie flew up and in a loud voice shouted, *"Fuinneamh!"*

From the tiny man's hands, a bolt of purple black energy erupted and struck a stone statue near the far end of the hall. The stone exploded and fragments filled the air. A few stray stones skittered to Logan's feet. Nothing remained of the statue.

Logan looked at the pixie with newfound respect.

"You see, Logan? He's small, but very powerful."

"I can see that," he said.

"When shall we begin, your majesty?" asked the pixie.

"Take him with you now. He is going to need everything you can teach him for when the war comes."

Logan thought the Morrigan must be blind to the possibility he would never be hers, but as long as she kept teaching him, making him stronger, he would let her, until he was strong enough to defy her, to get free of her web. He would learn all the pixie would teach him. He would find a way to beat her at her own game.

Chapter 32

Rhiannon walked through the barley fields with Brennan, wearing her green robe and carrying her staff. A new day glowed and the terrors and mysteries of the night were now behind her. Thoughts of her initiation and the power words replayed in her mind. The mantel of Druid responsibility lay heavy on her shoulders. Today she needed to leave on her quest to rescue Logan and find the Faillean Duir.

Men worked the fields and tended the cows as they made their way back to the fort. Rhiannon rubbed at her eyes and stifled a yawn. She felt exhausted from the long night but she needed to get started. Sleep would have to wait.

Rhiannon found Tin, Fao, and Flit near the mead hall.

"Time to face our fate?" asked Tin.

"I look that grim?"

"You look like you've been up all night and have a score to settle."

Rhiannon laughed. "That's a fair assessment."

"Prince Aron is gathering a few other Celts to go with us and will meet us at the gates."

Rhiannon nodded and turned to lead the way, but Tin stopped her with a hand to her shoulder. He bent to her ear and spoke in a hushed voice. "Rhiannon, you need to know it has been many years since I escaped through the tunnels. I know it's possible to get through them, but things may have changed, and I might not remember everything."

She rubbed the back of her neck. "How many years, Tin?"

"Two hundred."

Her mouth fell open. "How old are you, Tin?"

"I came from the world above two thousand years ago, and I was not young then."

Rhiannon reached out and touched his hand. "Tin, I had no idea."

"Long life is a blessing, but it can also be a curse. Many memories lie heavy on me, and I've lived many years alone."

"Someday, I want to hear the story of your life."

"It would do me good to tell it someday, but not today. I wanted to tell you how long it's been since I used the caves because a lot can change in that many years."

Rhiannon swallowed hard, crossing her arms. She wished he had mentioned it earlier, but there was nothing she would change now anyway. She looked up at Tin. "If there is a chance we can make it through, we have to try it. Thank you for being honest."

"I'm ready to go," said Flit. "The sooner we get this done, the better."

The four of them walked back through the village and stopped at the front gate.

Aron brought three other Celts. He gestured to his men and said, "Let me introduce you. This lad is Conlaodh."

He pointed to the man just behind him, tall but thin and lean with long red hair and a full beard. Many tattoos covered his bare arms and he had smile lines around his eyes. He wore a sword on each hip. The man stepped forward at the sound of his name and bowed to Rhiannon.

Aron waved over the other two men. "This is Eamonn," he said, gesturing to a Celt with long jet-black hair and a full mustache. The man carried a long shield painted with a golden wheel against a blue background. A single leaf bladed sword hung from his hip. "And this wall of a man is Goban, he's one of our blacksmiths." The tall bald headed man hefted a two handed hammer and grimaced. "Don't let his size lead you to think he is only along for his strength. He's a good man to have in a tight place; strong and sly as a fox, this one."

Rhiannon nodded. "There is much at stake in this mission," she said. "I don't know if we will survive. I don't ask you to come, but if your courage and honor do, then I thank you."

The men looked at her with firm eyes. She did not blink as they weighed her words.

Brennan approached them, accompanied by the king. "You will be in good company with these men," Brennan said. "I've known them all since they were boys, and you'll find none better."

The Druid reached into a leather pouch that hung from his belt.

"I made this for you," said Brennan as he held out a turquoise, obsidian, and silver bracelet.

Rhiannon took it from him and noticed the turquoise bits were carved into the shape of tiny skulls.

"Skulls?"

"It's a protective bracelet I made that will make your shield stronger. The turquoise is a stone for physical protection and the skulls will keep harm away. The obsidian is for absorbing spells."

"Thank you," Rhiannon said as she put it on her left wrist. "It's beautiful, Brennan."

She felt an ache in her chest as she looked up into Brennan's eyes. "I've found you only to leave again. I wish it were otherwise."

Brennan put a hand on her shoulder. "Me too."

Her uncle embraced her and called all of the companions to stand together. He raised his hands and spoke a blessing on them.

"Gods of our people, I call upon you now to bless these companions. Protect them in their struggle, and if skill and fate will it, bring them back to us. May the blessings of ancestors and the spirits of the earth go with them and lend them wisdom and strength for the road."

When Brennan finished, the king gave them his blessing and said farewell. The Celts and Rhiannon mounted their horses and the eight companions left through the gates.

Rhiannon touched the new bracelet on her wrist and blew out a series of short breaths. This is it, we are on the way, she thought. For better or worse, there is no turning back now.

* * *

Rhiannon crossed the Halcyon River, leading her company. Beyond, they rode through field and forest, and after two days, crossed the Silver Rush River. Finally, they crossed a sea of grass until, at last, they crested a hill and found ruins spread out below. Tin explained to Rhiannon that these were the remains of the city of Breckdacor. Long ago a battle was fought here between different factions of the sidhe. Now little remained of the once great city. Below the tumbled stone, lay the secret way into the Morrigan's castle.

The view made her stomach clench. The long miles of hard riding brought them to the entrance to the tunnels, and presumably, a way to Logan and the Arch Druid's staff, the Faillean Duir. Here she would have to go deeper underground, something she dreaded. The depths of the mound above her already made her long for blue sky. Now, she needed to go deeper into the earth, taking her farther from the free air and the light of sun and moon.

More than that, here her new power would be tested. Would the power words Brennan taught her work when she needed them? Would they be enough to accomplish her goals? Would they keep her and her companions alive in the dangerous depths that awaited them? She didn't know. Rhiannon stretched her neck and looked closer at what lay ahead.

The long straight way approached the entrance where two shattered towers framed an open gateway. The large fortress had clearly been impressive in some long forgotten day, but now only six towers, some roofless buildings, and a few crumbling sections of the walls remained.

Rhiannon rolled her shoulders as they approached the gate. She called a halt and dismounted. She surveyed her surroundings and rubbed her arms. The crumbling ruins made her uneasy. "Is this the right place, Tin?"

He nodded.

They took their gear from the saddlebags and released the horses.

"It doesn't look so bad," said Goban, glancing around nervously. "Just a bunch of rocks."

Conlaodh snorted at his friend.

Rhiannon led the way through the debris-strewn gateway, stepping cautiously over shifting slabs of stone. Inside, the foundations of a large central building stood with a great hall in its center. Blackened stones hinted at the demise of the once great stronghold. Broken bronze blades and bleached bones littered the debris.

"The entrance lies under the floor of the tower in the north corner," said Tin.

They turned and walked past a row of roofless stone buildings. Broken pottery littered the streets.

To Rhiannon, the whole place felt haunted, like the dead inhabitants were busy baking bread and sewing new clothes, like death came so suddenly they still carried on as if nothing happened. She held her awen pendant as she walked.

The north tower was the most intact part of the whole castle, with only a section of the roof gone. Clear light spilled in from above, illuminating the remaining stone structure. A few stout wooden beams remained, crossed over the wide circular opening, the shadow of their length casting cross-shaped darkness onto the debris below. Rhiannon looked carefully around. A skeleton hung suspended above them by iron manacles. A mound of rocks littered the floor where part of the roof had collapsed.

"The roof must have caved in since you escaped, right Tin?"

"Yes. None of this was here before. Let's see if we can find the door under all this debris."

Tin began to heave the larger stones away. Rhiannon and the Celts helped, and Flit supervised. Fao watched their back while they worked.

Soon, they found what they were looking for. A metal trapdoor rested in the middle of the floor. Tin lifted the heavy portal and looked inside. Down below, a narrow spiral staircase disappeared into the pitch below.

"Let me go first," said Tin. "I've been here before, and I know the way."

"No, Tin. I brought you all here. I will lead the way." Rhiannon lit a torch. "Just tell me what to expect."

He nodded. "Just follow the steps down."

She looked down into the darkness and swallowed heavily. Lit torch in hand, she took the first step. The curving spiral passageway made it difficult to see more than a few feet at a time. Tin and Aron followed directly behind her, then came Conlaodh. Eamonn followed after him, and then Flit and Fao. Goban stepped in last, pulling the door closed behind him.

The steep narrow stairs, made of gray flagstones, dropped quickly, and Rhiannon had to go slowly to keep from falling. She brushed through tangles of spider webs, pulling the sticky strands off her face and hands as she went farther down. Her muscles tightened and her hands turned more clammy with every step.

The spiral descent wound counterclockwise and ended after thirty steps. She pulled her cloak closer to protect her from the cold damp air and the spider webs. The stink of death lingered in the air, as if the moldy moisture of the caves preserved the memory of death.

"What do you make of the smell?" Conlaodh asked from behind her.

"It's Morrigan's lair. What else would it smell like?" Aron answered.

"Well, it reminds me of Goban's feet."

Aron chuckled.

"I heard that, Conlaodh," said Goban from the back.

A corridor led straight ahead, away from the stairs. The smooth walls and ceiling looked solid and stable. Up ahead to the right and left appeared the rusted metal bars of prison cells. A long row of them lined both sides of the tunnel. Rhiannon held her torch up high, peering into the shadows beyond the illumination. Just before the cells, a corridor led off to their right.

"Which way?" asked Flit. "I can scout ahead."

"Straight," said Tin. "I don't know what is down to the right."

"I say check to the right before going forward," said Aron.

Flit looked at Rhiannon.

"I think we need to get through here as fast as possible," she answered.

"Rhiannon, I know you are in charge here, but if we leave unknown corridors behind us, we could be in for a nasty surprise."

"Not if we are not around long enough for anything to catch us."

"Ok, Rhiannon. But I don't like it."

She looked at Aron and frowned. "I know what you mean, Aron, but I think speed is our best ally."

Aron shrugged, and she turned back and nodded to Flit, who disappeared down the hallway. Rhiannon walked forward and looked into each cell. All were empty, nothing but cold stone and rusted bars.

A stench assaulted them as they neared the end of the row of cells.

Rhiannon brought up her cloak up over her mouth and nose to cut the foulness. "My gods, what is that smell?"

Tin pointed to the farthest cell. A pile of corruption littered its floor. They quickly moved past, noticing only briefly the bones and rot filling the room. An open doorway led out of the passage, and they quickly stepped through and closed the heavy oak door behind them.

The next hallway stretched beyond the limit of the torch light until it ended at a door.

Conlaodh moved forward and listened at the door. "All's quiet," he said.

"Tin, do you remember what's here?"

"I was running for my life when I came through here, and it was many years ago, so some of the details are fuzzy. I don't remember anything about this room."

"Well we don't seem to have a choice. We have to go through here. Is everyone ready?" Rhiannon scanned their faces.

Everyone nodded.

"Let me get the door," said Aron.

"I can do it," said Rhiannon.

"I know you can, but I'm wearing armor and you aren't. Let me help you."

Rhiannon sighed, knowing it was foolish to bring people along if she wasn't going to let them help. She stepped aside and motioned him forward.

Aron smiled grimly, then pulled the handle.

A blast of cold air greeted them, and all the torches went out. They could still see in the light of Flit's glow, but just barely. Rhiannon moved forward and sensed a black hovering shape advancing from the corner of the room. Aron took a step forward.

The hair raised on her neck and arms. "No! Wait. Something's in there." She blinked rapidly, trying to see.

He stepped back and the shadow raced forward. Aron drew his sword and attacked as the darkness rushed him. He swung his blade, but with no effect. The wave of night hit Aron like an avalanche of darkness. He was thrown to the ground, and the thing fell on him.

"No!" shouted Conlaodh, racing forward and stabbing at the man-shaped shadow with his two swords.

Rhiannon brought up her staff and shouted, "*Solas!*"

Light erupted and the shadow shrieked and pulled back into the room. Conlaodh chased the wraith deeper, attacking with his twin swords. Goban rushed past Rhiannon and joined Conlaodh's attack. Eamonn grabbed Aron and dragged him back down the hall. The Celts' weapons had no effect on the wraith, meeting only air. Tin joined the fray, swinging his axe, but his weapon met no resistance when he hit the astral shroud of the spectre.

Rhiannon's heart hammered in her chest. Aron was down and their weapons were useless. They must depend upon her magic. "Tin! Get out of the way!" she shouted.

Tin dared a look back, and Rhiannon gestured desperately for him to move. He took a step to the side, giving her a clear view of her target. She closed her eyes, drew on the power of the source, and channeled it up through the energetic cauldrons and out through the hawthorne staff.

"*Dóiteán!*" she shouted.

Nothing happened.

"Gods damn it." Fear crawled up her spine as the wraith turned toward her.

Goban dove, trying to tackle the shadow, but instead sailed through it. The wraith used Goban's momentum and threw the Celt against the wall, where he hit hard, slumped to the ground, and lay still.

Tin backed up and stood between the wraith and Rhiannon, with his head lowered and his horns pointing menacingly.

The wraith came at them. A rush of icy air hit first. The blackness hit Tin like a tsunami. The force knocked him from his feet, pushing him nearly into Rhiannon. She staggered back, but felt little impact as Tin had blunted the blow. The insubstantial shadow condensed and fell on Tinurion's prone form, appendages tipped with claws raised to shred the fallen minotaur.

Panic gripped her. Her fire attack had not ignited, and three of her friends were down. She couldn't let Tin die. Desperation sharpened her need. "*Dóiteán!*" she shouted again, with razor focus.

The air crackled, and a green light erupted from her staff, lancing out and striking the wraith like a bolt of lightning. The force of it blasted the black shadow back against the wall. It shrieked its frustration. Enraged, it came at Rhiannon again.

She drew a shield of protection around her and attacked. "*Dóiteán!*" she shouted, and the green light ripped into the black thing, like a cat's claws through fabric. It hissed, but didn't stop its attack, hacking viciously at her.

Fao and Flit swarmed around Rhiannon. Flit fired blue arrows at the swirling darkness, and Fao moved to guard Tin as he sluggishly clamored to his feet.

Talons tore at the blue light of Rhiannon's shield. It flickered as her focus shifted to drawing in more power. *"Dóiteán!"*

A burst of green light punctured the shadow, ripping a hole in the center. The edges of the tear crackled with jade fire, and the ring of destruction roared outward, consuming the blackness. In an instant, the wreath of druid fire devoured the undead menace and the wraith disintegrated, like the night at the sun's first light.

Rhiannon put her hands on her knees, feeling the sudden drain. She took a few breaths and sighed with relief. She had done it. She had saved her friends using her magic. The power words worked.

"What was that thing?" she asked.

"It was a wraith," said Conlaodh as he sheathed his swords and relit the torches.

"That wasn't here last time," said Tin. "I hope we don't run into any more of those."

"No wonder Morrigan doesn't worry about this back entrance; it's guarded well enough," said Eamonn.

Goban sat up and rubbed his head. "Damn thing hit hard."

Back outside the room in the hall, Rhiannon knelt next to Aron. His chest rose and fell. She exhaled hard. She had feared the worst.

Blood covered his left arm. Rhiannon took a flask of water from her pack and washed the wound. She touched the arm and it felt strangely cold. She drew back her hand, confused.

She closed her eyes, put both hands on his arm, and sent healing light into Aron's arm. His eyes flew open and he winced as the energy knitted his flesh back together. When she was done, she looked down and nodded. It was better, but far from healed.

"I'll want to keep an eye on that. That wraith might have done more than scratch you."

"What happened?" he said as he sat up.

"A wraith tried to eat you," said Goban.

"Rhiannon destroyed it," said Eamonn.

Rhiannon stood and a wave of dizziness overcame her.

Tin reached out and steadied her.

"I'm not used to drawing so much power," she said, putting a hand on Tin's arm. "I'm okay now."

Eamonn helped Aron to his feet.

"Thank you, Rhiannon," Aron said.

She nodded.

"How did you create that green fire?" asked Tin. "I've never seen you do that before."

"Brennan taught me how during my initiation."

"Well, I, for one, am glad he did," said Conlaodh.

"That was very impressive," Tin agreed.

"We better get moving," Rhiannon said. "We've made it this far, but we still have a long way to go."

Chapter 33

Rhiannon dimmed the light of her staff to save her magic, relying now on the flickering torch light to illuminate the walls of the hallway. She was ready to go. A sound stopped her. Back the way they had come, they heard a door opening on rusted hinges, the metal sending shrieks of noise at them. Her heart stopped. *Maybe it was something from that corridor that Aron had wanted to explore?*

A growl of many voices echoed down the hall. Her feet refused to move and a surging mass of corpses, wearing tattering clothes and rotten flesh, rushed down the hall, moving faster than she believed possible. More undead were coming for them. Terror broke her hesitation.

"Back into the room now!" shouted Rhiannon.

Inside, they barricaded the door, using wooden benches they found inside.

The dizziness came back from her use of the magic. She felt like her insides were quivering. She set her jaw and fought back the anxiety. "Let's get out of here!"

Rhiannon led the way out the opposite door. Beyond, a set of stone stairs climbed down into the darkness. Behind her, the pounding on the barricaded door echoed. She wondered what would happen if those things broke the door down. She didn't think she could offer much resistance as tired as she was. Using her magic on the wraith had drained her. Knowing they had to get away, she shoved the thoughts down and raced down the stairs two at a time. The steps ended at a landing and more stairs.

A crash came from above, and Rhiannon's adrenaline spiked. The door had been breached.

"Go! Go! Go!" she screamed.

She ran down long flights of stairs, leading her friends with the pursuit gaining on them. They reached another door.

"I hear something," she said, listening at the portal. "Maybe a waterfall, but I can't tell if there's anything else."

"Whatever it is, it's better than what's chasing us. Weapons ready," said Aron.

He stepped forward, drawing his sword, and resting his hand on the door pushed it open.

The access opened into a large, natural cavern. It ran about a spear's throw and then descended steeply. Flit shot ahead and the rest followed. They closed the oak door behind them and piled up some rocks to brace it as best they could.

Heart racing, Rhiannon squinted into faint light ahead.

The corridor angled downward leading them toward the ever-growing crash of water. She led them, and the hallway opened up into an even bigger cavern, with rough edges and an uneven floor.

Against the far left wall, water rushed from a mouth near the spiked roof into a pool far below. A mist sprayed their faces and the yellowish-brown walls all around. The pool overflowed into a deep stream, which cut the room in half in front of them. A stone bridge crossed the dark bubbling flow and gave access to the far side of the room.

"Let's keep going," said Rhiannon at the sound of pounding behind them. "That door isn't going to hold for long."

Flit scouted ahead with Rhiannon leading the rest. On the other side of the bridge, a narrow passage, rough cut and braced with large aging timbers, dug deeper into the earth.

When she stepped into the new passage, dust fell from the ceiling. Rhiannon peered up, shielding her eyes from the fine particles.

"I don't like the looks of this," said Flit.

"I agree." She looked behind them. "But I don't see that we have a choice."

She pushed forward until the tunnel opened up into an enormous cavern. An old wooden bridge began at the lip of a deep drop-off. Rhiannon hoisted the torch as high as she could but barely made out the distant roof.

She glanced down below the bridge. Even with the additional light, she could not see the bottom. Only darkness stretched beneath them. She took several cautious steps onto the bridge, but paused when it groaned beneath her weight.

"Flit, maybe you should scout this out for us. Crossing will be precarious at best, and I want to know what's on the other side before we attempt it."

The pixie's glow receded into the shadows.

Rhiannon looked back at the tunnel. Timbers now groaned, more dust fell, and the pounding of fists on the door echoed.

"Rhiannon, something's not right," said Tin. "This is not how it looked when I came through. I've never seen this cavern before."

Her chest tightened, and she bit her lip. "What do you mean, Tin? How could you not have seen this before?"

"I'm starting to wonder if you really have been telling us the truth," said Conlaodh. "Did you come this way or not?"

Tin glared at the Celt, nostrils flaring, then turned to Rhiannon. "I know my lack of memory is not helping, but I'm telling the truth. I think we missed something back by the waterfall."

Rhiannon put her hands on her hips and looked up at Tin. She took a deep breath. "I believe you, Tin. Let's wait for Flit to come back and then we will go back."

A groan and a creak brought more rubble into the passageway behind them.

"We better wait for Flit farther back. I don't want to get trapped in here."

"Flit!" Goban bellowed, "Where are you?"

Rhiannon winced as Goban's shout jarred more debris loose. Just as they were about to pull back, Flit darted toward them. "The cavern narrows farther down and then opens to the outside," she said breathlessly. "Beyond is a great chasm and nothing but the ruins of an old collapsed bridge. We can't go that way."

"Let's go back and figure it out," said Tin.

Rhiannon turned and ran back to the waterfall room. She stood on the curved stone bridge and looked for what they might have missed. The door groaned from the attack of their pursuers.

"Hurry, Tin. We don't have much time," she said.

Tin looked carefully at the bridge and frowned. "It's the water."

"What do you mean?" she asked.

"The last time I was here, it was dry. The way down is over there." Tin pointed to the wall. "This wasn't a stream when I was here. Look, you can still see some rotting timbers, just like in the other passageway."

"So you're saying the way down is now a stream?" asked Rhiannon.

"Yes, exactly."

"And it's more than half filled with water," groaned Flit.

"It's time to get wet," said Aron.

"That's easy for you to say," said Flit. "You're not six inches tall."

"Can't you just fly over the water Flit?" Rhiannon asked.

"I could, but there is so little room, if I dropped too much the water would take me."

"You can ride on my shoulders if you want, Flit," offered Tin.

"No, thanks. I'll let you do the scouting this time and I'll watch from here."

"Okay, Tin," said Rhiannon. "Let's try it."

"Wait a second. Are you saying that you came up through that hole?" Conlaodh looked at Tinurion suspiciously.

"Yes, that is what I'm saying. I'm sorry I didn't recognize it at first. The water has changed things."

"I hope that is not all that has changed," said Eamonn. "I will go, but I don't like it."

Behind them, the door crashed open. The horde shouted with glee and raced toward them. Creatures with pale skin and covered with dirt, dried blood, and the rotting stench of death charged at them with gnashing teeth and hands.

Rhiannon's knees wanted to buckle but she steeled herself. "Oh, gods. We've got to go! Flit, fly up above them, and if we don't come back, leave through the cavern, find your way out, and tell Brennan what happened here."

Flit glanced over her shoulder and gave Rhiannon a hard look.

"I understand," Rhiannon said. "Now go!" She jumped into the water, which came up to her armpits and stole her breath with its chill. She strode forward through the dark stream, the ground beneath her feet gravelly and uncertain. Behind her, the Celts sucked in sharp breaths as the cold hit them.

Rhiannon regretted leaving Flit behind, but she knew the pixie would be able to get clear and the rest of them wouldn't. It was the only decision she could have made.

She surged forward, using her staff to stay on her feet. The heavy backpack made it difficult to balance in the strong stream. She prodded the ground carefully, feeling for any holes or large stones, and then touched nothing ahead of her. Poking the ground desperately, she found only deep water. Panic filled her as she heard her companions behind her, struggling to get away from their pursuers, and now there was no way forward.

Rhiannon shivered and tried to decide what to do. She scanned the roof. It sloped down and stopped at the surface of the water. There was no way they could go down into that tunnel and not drown. They would have to turn and fight, she decided.

As she turned to go back, her feet slid on the gravel and she lost her balance. The force of the current knocked her from her feet, and she fell face first into the icy flow. She rolled onto to her back, sputtering, and the water pulled her under, the tunnel suddenly angling down, turning into a chute.

Rhiannon sluiced through the airless void. It happened too fast. She held back the scream that wanted to erupt and tried to think, to plan, to do something to get free, but the power of the water overtook her.

The water grew colder, deeper. Her hands and feet went numb and she flailed aimlessly, knowing there was no hope of rescue. Her lungs burned like no other pain she had felt. Death reared its ugly head and she fought against that vision.

Wait, if Tin came up this way, there must be an outlet somewhere.

The thought did little to relieve her panic, and her lungs burned stronger than ever. All around her was nothing but cold, black water. She swam furiously now, deeper and deeper into the tunnel. Soon, she would need to take a breath, and it would be over; she would die. She wasn't ready, but the water didn't care.

Please, Brighid! Help me!

As fast as the water had pulled her under, it spit her out. The blackness shattered, and she cascaded into open air. Rhiannon gasped a deep breath and watched with dread as the black surface beneath rushed at her. She hit the pool so hard it almost knocked her senseless. It felt like she'd hit concrete, and she wondered if she cracked her ribs.

Water surrounded her again, but she knew that there was air above. Kicking and grabbing armfuls of the water, she pulled toward the surface. Finally, she broke free into the air.

Gulping in great gasps, she looked around, grateful to be breathing, grateful to be alive. Before she could act, Aron splashed down nearly on top of her. He struggled to the surface just as she had.

"Are you okay?" she asked, swimming closer.

It took him a moment to respond, but he nodded. "I think so," he gasped finally. "I didn't think I was going to make it."

"Yeah, me too," said Rhiannon. The fear that had gripped her eased, but the taste of death was still fresh.

The others followed, with Tin and Fao last, all landing heavily in the deep water. Fao swam to the surface. Tin took the longest to rise because of his weight.

Rhiannon peered around in the low light of the glowing purple crystals far above. The Celts struggled to stay afloat. Tin fought against the water with his heavy gear pulling him. She paddled to stay afloat when a terrible realization hit her. Her hands were empty, which meant she must have lost her staff on the way down.

Panic gripped her. Without the staff, her magic would be weaker and she needed the strength it gave her. She scanned the dark water, eyes darting. A glint of red ribbon caught her eye. She had left the decoration on it to remind her of Brennan, without it she never would have seen it. The staff bobbed and floated just out of sight. "My staff!" she shouted. "Help me get my staff!"

Rhiannon knew in an instant that Tin and the heavily armored men would be of little help. Her pack weighed her down as well. She shrugged off shoulder straps, let it drop into the depths, and swam.

"No, wait, Rhiannon!" Tin called out. "You might get sucked into another hole. It's not worth it."

Rhiannon ignored him. Without the staff, she would have less focus for directing the energy from the power words. She wouldn't just be weaker, she would also have less control. No, she would not give up her staff without a fight.

Rhiannon squinted and could barely see it as it moved away. Her cloak dragged on her. She pulled it off and kept swimming. The current grew stronger.

Desperately kicking and pulling at the water, she almost grasped it, but not quite. Fatigue caught up with her. Her breath came too hard and her muscles burned. She lifted her head to take a breath. Splashing made her turn. Fao surged forward through the water. The big wolf swam past her. Rhiannon gave a shout of triumph as Fao took the staff in her powerful teeth.

Rhiannon laughed in relief. She stopped pulling forward and treaded water, catching her breath. Fao swam back against the current and dropped the staff in front of Rhiannon.

"Thank you, Fao," she said breathlessly. "Now, let's get out of here."

Together, they swam perpendicular to the flow, hoping to find the edge. As they went, Rhiannon paused to listen for her friends but heard nothing. Her legs threatened to cramp, tightening involuntarily. She rolled over and floated for a moment, letting her muscles rest, but the current pulled her too fast to stay that way for long.

Frustrated, she held up her staff. *"Solas!"* First, there was a loud crackle, and then a bright pop. It was as if the darkness had not been disturbed for so long that it refused to give up its secrets, but then the stunning blue orb flared into full strength. The orb illuminated the edge of the shore and a cavern wall to the right, but nothing beyond that. The ceiling and the opposite shore were lost in shadow.

Rhiannon kicked the rest of the way to the rocky edge of the water. She collapsed on the rocky ground; rounded pebbles embedded themselves in her arms and back, but she didn't care.

When she caught her breath, she stood to look for everyone else. Fao already walked back the way they had come. Rhiannon stood and wrapped her arms around her, shivering as she moved. "Tin! Aron!" she shouted.

She hoped they made it to the shore and that nothing bad happened to them. Fao looked back at her and then ran ahead. Rhiannon staggered after her. From the shadows, her friends emerged, stumbling toward her.

"Thank the gods you are all okay," she said, hugging each in turn.

"I didn't know how we were going to find you," said Tin. "But your staff lit up and showed us the way."

"Fao saved the staff. Without her, it would have been gone." Rhiannon knelt down and hugged Fao too.

"I'm sorry we had to leave Flit behind. She never would have survived the water. Let's hope she can find a way out of the tunnels."

"There was nothing else we could have done," said Aron.

Rhiannon nodded. "Okay, which way, Tin?"

"Wait a minute. Are we still going to trust *him*?" said Eamonn, eyes bulging. "Coming down that tunnel almost got us all killed."

"It was our only choice," said Rhiannon.

"So let me guess, you swam up that tunnel before?" said Conlaodh.

"I remember this lake, but it was smaller and the tunnel was dry." Tin put his hands on his hips.

"A lot sure has changed since you were here last, *minotaur*," said Eamonn.

Tin clenched his fists. "Are you calling me a liar, Eamonn?"

"*Yes*, that is what I'm saying. For all we know, you just brought us here so Morrigan would be done with a prince and a Druid in one easy deception."

"Whoa, whoa, hold on, Eamonn." Rhiannon stepped between them. "If Tin wanted me dead, he could have easily done it long ago. He saved me from Morrigan's troops, when he could have just stood by and watched."

"I'm just saying that, if he is telling the truth, he is the worst guide I've ever had."

"You can't call me a liar to my face and get away with it." Tin growled.

"Listen, Tin," said Rhiannon, putting a hand on his forearm. "We just almost died and tempers are bit a short. I'm sure if Eamonn had led you to that fall, you wouldn't have been very happy with him either."

Tin stared at her, and nodded. "You are right, of course, but I don't want to hear any more complaints about my lack of knowledge. I told you, it was a long time ago."

"We know, Tin," said Aron. "Eamonn will keep his mouth shut about this, won't you, Eamonn?"

Eamonn looked at his feet. "That tunnel just made me think

I was going to the Summerland today. And, well, I'm not ready yet."

Rhiannon nodded. "None of us is ready for that, Eamonn. Now, let's get going."

They hiked along the lake edge, which met the vertical wall at several points, causing them to wade through the cold water. Fortunately, the water got warmer as they went. Though damp, cold, and hungry, the only hope of safety lay in moving forward. They could not turn back.

The silence was whispered away, as the sound of falling water again grew nearer. Rhiannon tensed, certain she would rather do anything than go through another water-filled tunnel. The icy chill was still too fresh in her mind.

A drop-off, at the far edge of the lake, roared. The water crashed into a large canyon below. Across the plunge, she spotted a distant cliff connected to them by an old bridge. The shore edge ended at the near end of that bridge.

The seven of them stopped at the brink and looked down into the depths. Rhiannon could not see where the water stopped falling, but she heard a thunderous roar far below.

"I remember this place," said Tin. "Beyond the bridge are more caves, and we will go deeper yet."

Rhiannon swallowed and rubbed her neck. "When will we start back up again?"

"Not for a while."

She nodded and led them across the bridge and into a large cavern on the other side. She could vaguely see the roof of the enormous space. The floor, clear and free of debris, sloped downward, leading deeper into the earth.

Rhiannon's light easily lit the walls around them, but above hovered patches of darkness the light did not reveal. Despite the openness of the corridor, she felt increasingly aware of the weight of the earth above them and fretted that the way out was blocked.

They plodded onward till their stomachs began to rumble. Just as they were about to stop for a rest, the corridor made a sudden hairpin turn and descended much more steeply. A sickly sweet smell and a warm breeze rushed upon them. The scent of decay found their nostrils.

Rhiannon stroked her throat and grimaced.

"I hope that smell doesn't mean more wraiths," said Eamonn.

Goban looked over at him and said, "Don't worry, I'll protect you."

Eamonn groaned and kept walking.

They stopped just out of the foul breeze at the top of the next descent. Dripping water echoed from below. The steep path made Rhiannon feel like she couldn't breathe.

"We need to eat," said Goban.

"Okay, let's take a break," said Aron.

Rhiannon dimmed the magical illumination while they rested. They sat in the dark, drinking water and eating apples and soggy cheese.

"When I was away with Brennan, he told me about an ancient Druid staff called the Faillean Duir," she said, breaking the silence. "Brennan thinks we could use it to stand up to Morrigan. She stole it away and has it hidden in her castle. When we get inside, I need to find it."

"Wait, I thought the plan was to free the prisoners," said Goban.

"It is. This will be a side mission for me alone."

"Do you know where this staff is?" asked Aron.

"No, but I have to find it. If we are to have a chance of defending the fort from Morrigan, we will need it."

"We won't have much time once we free the prisoners, but I will do what I can to help you," said Aron.

"That's all I can ask," said Rhiannon.

* * *

Rhiannon's boot crunched and she stopped. They had only traveled a short way since they ate. She looked down. A cracked and yellowed thighbone jutted from under her foot. A chill ran through her as she noticed bone after bone scattered around them on the floor. They were clearly humanoid skulls, ribs, and arm bones.

"This doesn't look good," she said.

"I wonder what happened here," Aron asked.

"I don't know, but we should get through fast," said Eamonn.

Rhiannon lengthened her stride and walked quickly among the remains. A chill crept into the air again, and she wrapped her arms around her as she walked. More bones littered the floor, and here and there lay rusted weapons. The corridor widened into a cavern, and the remains of what must have been a large battle came into their view. Broken helms and rusted axes, blackened bones and crude earthworks showed the remains of a fierce struggle.

"Tin, what do you think this place is?" asked Rhiannon

"I remember it, but I don't know what happened. I wondered last time why the dead were just left here."

"Do you see the bright metal in the walls? It looks like gold," Aron said.

"That might explain what the battle was about, but whoever won didn't care about the ore. That worries me," Tin said. "The faerie love their gold even more than humans, if that's possible. I wonder what drove them off so completely?"

Rhiannon led them carefully through the battlefield, wary of hidden danger. The shadows played tricks on her. Every movement seemed to be mirrored by something just out of sight, something in the shadows.

She continued until they reached the end of the chamber where three corridors exited the cavern, all narrow and low. The middle way sloped upward. The right tunnel was level and turned sharply away to the right, and the left passage dove steeply downward, disappearing into the black.

"Which way do you think, Tin?"

"They all look about the same," he answered. "I came out from one of them, but I'm not sure which."

Rhiannon shook her head and put her hands behind her back. It made sense he wouldn't remember which cave he had come out of, but it was still frustrating. The fact he remembered so little weighed on her.

She tapped her finger on her lip, looking at the options. In the deep silence around them, she suddenly heard a scrabbling noise coming from the center and the right tunnels. It clicked and scraped, quickly approaching. Only the left passage remained quiet.

"There is something coming," said Conlaodh.

"I don't know what that is, but I don't want to stick around and find out," she said. "I say we take the left one."

Tin nodded.

Rhiannon led the way into the descending cave. Tin followed her, then Fao, Aron, Conlaodh, Eamonn, and Goban.

The round wormhole descended quickly and deeply. Many smaller tunnels branched off to either side, but all were too small for Tin, so they kept to the main passageway.

Soon the tunnel widened into an enormous cavern, the biggest she had seen yet. She exited the cave, and in front of them more remains of a battle lay. Broken bones and skulls lay everywhere, along with rusted weapons. The cavern stretched as far as she could see, nothing but battlefield.

Rhiannon rubbed the back of her neck, crossed her arms, and turned to face the others. "Tin, does this look right?"

"Yes, it does. I think you picked the right one."

Rhiannon walked forward through the bone yard, with Tin close behind. The ground was soft, and her boots sunk six inches into the soil with each step. Up ahead, the distant edge of the battlefield showed, and beyond it an enormous staircase leading steeply upward.

She stopped and took a step back. "Finally, a way up."

"Yes, we are almost there," said Tin. "But there is one thing. This place is different."

"What's different?" Aron asked.

"Well, this room used to be like the last one, lots of bones and hard soil, but now there are less bones, and this ground is too…"

He was cut off as grasping bony hands shot out of the loose soil and snatched at their ankles and legs. Pale limbs, streaked with blood and dirt, clawed at all of them and pulled down hard.

Rhiannon's pulse exploded, and she attacked with her staff. There were too many of them, and they were too close to her friends to use her green fire like before. She stabbed down hard, but as soon as she hit one grasping hand, three more popped up from other spots.

Cold fingers encircled her calves and pulled her down into the dirt up to her knees.

Her breath came too fast, and she began to hyperventilate. "Tin!" she managed to call out.

He turned away from his chopping, grabbed Rhiannon's arms, and pulled. She stopped sinking but she didn't come out of the dirt. Aron and Goban fought their way to her aid and, together, they were able to free her. No sooner was Rhiannon clear than Eamonn and Conlaodh sunk down to their waists. Tin leaped to their defense and soon pulled both of the Celts up.

Dirt-covered humanoids, howling with rage, broke the surface and attacked the group with claws and fangs.

"More undead!" Aron shouted. "These are fast and strong."

"We need to get out of here," shouted Eamonn.

Only tatters of clothing remained on the corpses, and none of them held any weapons. Their hands ended in long black talons, and sharp teeth snapped at the air as they tried to bite the living.

Rhiannon knew she had to do something. There were too many creatures, and without her magic she and her friends would all die. She raised her staff and drew on the power of the earth.

"*Balla Dóiteán*," she shouted.

In a wide circle from the ground, flames rushed upward creating a wall of green fire around them. Its heat and light pulsed with power.

The undead shrank back from the flames, and though some burned, more rose up from under the ground. The group fought inside the circle of fire, hacking at heads and arms as the animated corpses crawled to the surface.

"There are too many of them," shouted Aron. "We need to get across!"

"Follow me!" shouted Rhiannon. She ran as fast as she could without leaving anyone behind or tripping over the outstretched hands trying to pull her down. Tin charged along on one side of her, and Fao took the other. Together, they kept Rhiannon free.

"Stop, Rhiannon! We need help!" Aron shouted.

She slowed and turned. Eamonn had been pulled into the soil to his neck. Aron, Conlaodh, and Goban dug frantically, trying to free him. A rotting head with gnashing teeth emerged from the ground and bit into Eamonn's throat.

He yelled in anguish. "Get me out of here!"

"Tin, help them!" Rhiannon shouted, but he was already on his way.

Rhiannon's flames roared around them, and Fao protected her. By the time Tin reached the Celts, all that showed of Eamonn was his black hair. He dug down into the earth. His hand came back with a fistful of hair and covered in blood.

Rhiannon stomach tightened fighting back the terrible nausea she felt.

"No!" she shouted, desperately concentrating. She wanted to rush to her friend's aid but she couldn't let the wall of fire drop or else they would be over run.

Aron, Conlaodh, and Goban clawed the earth with frantic hands and found nothing but more dirty hands reaching out for them, trying to pull them into the ground too.

"It's no use, Conlaodh," said Aron. "He's gone. Run!"

"No!" shouted Conlaodh. "We can't leave him."

"We will all be joining him soon if we don't get out of here," said Goban, turning to fight another grasping undead hand.

Growling, Conlaodh fought to help Goban. "Okay, you're right," he said. "Let's go."

Rhiannon's hands shook, and for a brief moment she closed her eyes. Eamonn was gone. *What a terrible way to die*, she thought, to be a feast for these creatures. A wave of cold ran through her, deepening her nausea.

She swallowed hard and resolved to not let anyone else suffer Eamonn's fate. "Follow me," Rhiannon shouted. "We need to go."

She rushed forward, using the fire wall to burn the ground clear as they went. Tin chopped at anything that crawled to the surface, and the Celts unleashed their rage on the foul things when they erupted out of the soil. Sweat, smoke, and black blood covered them all when they finally stood on solid rock again and the undead attacked them no more.

Rhiannon let the fire wall down. Her mouth was dry and her muscles weak. Tears welled up behind her eyes.

The horror of what happened to their friend stunned them and they stood together, unable to just leave him behind.

Finally, Rhiannon spoke. "Gods of our people, please accept Eamonn into the Summerland," she said with a bowed head. "May the ancestors welcome him to the halls of his fathers."

All fell silent for a moment.

"Eamonn deserved a better death than that," said Aron as he looked up.

"We all knew the risks," said Goban heavily.

Rhiannon watched him struggled to maintain composure.

"He will not be forgotten. He died a hero's death, and

though his body is now food for those things, his spirit is free," said Aron.

"He said he wasn't ready for the Summerland…" said Tin, his voice trailing off.

"Who is ever ready? None of us." Rhiannon's anger rose.

She turned and looked up the stairs, realized how close they were to rescuing Logan and the other prisoners. She clenched her jaw and pointed upward. "Eamonn died so we could save our people. Let's go do him proud," she said as she started up the stairs.

Chapter 34

Rhiannon's muscles tightened as they ascended. She pushed up the sleeves of her robe and led the group forward, determined to finish what they set out to do. The death of Eamonn hung heavy on her heart. She had failed him; what if she failed them all?

At the top stretched a tunnel. Aged timbers supported the roof of the passageway beyond, which led deeper into the earth. She paused and turned, pressed her lips together and made steady eye contact with each of them as they finished the stairs. She turned and led them deeper in.

Loose soil fell on her as she walked into the passageway. Boulders jutted into the path, and behind her, Tin had to squeeze through some spots. Upward the tunnel climbed, and then it opened into a small cavern.

A pool of clear water sat at the center of the room. Rhiannon crouched down, dipped her hands in it and washed them. "Any idea how soon we will reach the dungeon?" she asked, looking up at Tin.

"It's not far now," he said.

"So what is the plan when we get there?" asked Goban.

Rhiannon looked at Tin. "You know what we'll encounter. What are your thoughts?"

"When we come out in the dungeons, there will be guards close by. We fight them, take the keys, and start unlocking cells. Then follow me out of the castle. We lower the drawbridge, get everyone across, and pray that Bran is there to meet us."

"He will be there," said Aron.

"If he's not, it's going to be a blood bath," said Tin.

"It will probably be one anyway, if I know Bran," said Conlaodh. "He will want to stick it to Morrigan as much as he can."

"We all do," said Goban. "They've been killing off our men for too long. It's time we had a victory we can celebrate."

"Tin, do you think Logan will be in this dungeon?"

"It's the only one Morrigan has, so I'd say yes."

Rhiannon's skin tingled all over. She bit her lip, wrapping her arms tight around herself. She couldn't believe, after everything she had been through, that she was finally going to find Logan. It felt like a lifetime since they fallen asleep together in the manor house. He was close now. She could feel it. Her heart raced, and she imagined the expression on his face when they were finally reunited.

Suddenly self-conscious, she took a breath and anchored herself in the present. "Let me see that arm of yours," she said to Aron, wanting them all at full strength before they opened the door.

"It's fine."

"No, really. I need to see it."

Aron rolled up his sleeve. The flesh around the wound was gray and white.

"Why didn't you say something?" Rhiannon said with alarm.

"We've been a little busy. Can you do anything?"

"I've never seen anything like it. Let me try."

She had him sit down next to her, and as she got a closer look she grew more worried. She didn't want to alarm anyone else, but it looked like undead flesh. Closing her eyes, she prayed silently.

O' Brighid, goddess of water and fire
I call on you now for aid,
Help us in this hour most dire
Let this evil be staid.
Oh Brighid, let your power show,
Remove this unnatural blight.
Heal him like Nuada of long ago,
Make his arm pure and right.

She concentrated her power and poured green light into the wound.

Aron jumped to his feet and shook his arm.

"What is it?" Rhiannon said, startled.

"It wasn't like before, when you healed my arm. That hurt,

but it was bearable. This time, my arm burned like a forest fire."

Rhiannon stood and looked at his arm again. If anything, it was worse. She crossed her arms in front of her, feeling her mouth go dry. What was going on? Was Aron being turned into one of *them*? The thought was too terrible to contemplate. Her healing skills were not enough to help him now.

"When we get back I can try some herbs, but there is nothing else I can do now."

Aron nodded and rolled down his sleeve, then drew his sword. "We have some prisoners to save. Let's go."

Rhiannon nodded. *If* they made it through what was to come, she hoped Brennan could help. She didn't want to voice her fears. That would only weaken their resolve, and they had enough to worry about.

She started forward again. The winding tunnel climbed higher and higher, and soon, she found herself scrambling up rocks more than walking. Finally, it leveled out. Tin stopped them with a gesture and waved them back.

They retreated a short distance and quietly whispered.

"It's the entrance to the dungeon," said Tin.

"Is everyone clear on the plan?" Rhiannon asked.

They all nodded and drew their weapons.

"Before we go, I just want to say that I may not have asked all of you to come on this journey, but I want thank you. Whatever happens when we open that door, I want you to know it's been an honor," she said.

"You can thank us when this is done," said Tin with fire in his eyes.

Rhiannon smiled. "Okay. Here we go."

Tin moved out into the hall and opened the door. Inside, a short corridor ended at a T. Rhiannon followed Tin past three prison cells on each side, and the people within began to stir. Beyond the cells were two doors on either side and one more straight ahead. The five rescuers moved silently behind Tin, who gestured that behind the door would be their first fight.

Tin opened the door and rushed in swinging. His companions dashed in behind him and slammed the door. Six black leather armored fighters, some standing and others lounging unsuspectingly in chairs, turned to gape at the group.

Tin's massive war axe swept into two of the sidhe on the

right, and they fell immediately. Rhiannon blasted two others on the left with Druid fire. The Celts moved in to attack the others. Fao finished the two that Tin had felled. Aron fought another guard, and Goban ended the man's life with a heavy two-handed swing of his hammer that crunched his helmeted head. Soon, the six lay unconscious or dying.

Rhiannon searched one body and found the keys. She first went to the five pits and unlocked them all. Conlaodh stood at the door with his ear pressed to it. Tin helped open the heavy grates, while the Celts lowered ladders down and looked eagerly for familiar faces. In minutes, the captives stood in the large room, blinking with disbelief at their rescuers.

"Nemain!" shouted Aron. "I hadn't dared to hope that I'd find you here."

The last to climb out of the pit, Nemain ran her fingers through her short red hair. She looked bruised and weary, but smiled at Aron. "It's about time you came for me," she said quietly.

Rhiannon looked at Aron questioningly.

"This is my wife, whom we thought lost to us," he said as he stepped forward and embraced the woman. He turned back to them with a beaming smile. "I want you to meet Rhiannon and Tinurion. Rhiannon is our newest Druid. And Tinurion is our guide and trusted friend."

"Minotaur, huh?" Nemain asked. "Pleased to meet you both." She nodded at Conlaodh and Goban and said, "Many thanks to you all. Now should we go?"

"I agree. We need to get moving," Rhiannon said. She looked at the dazed prisoners. "Follow as best you can. We are getting you out of here!"

"We got company," said Conlaodh, who had been listening at the door.

"This way!" Rhiannon led the way out into the hall.

More guards had gathered, but they didn't seem aware of the attack. Taking advantage of the surprise, Aron charged past Rhiannon and struck. The Celts went directly behind their prince. The rest followed, gathering in a tight knot near the door.

"Intruders! Sound the alarm!" a guard shouted.

Aron killed his soldier and moved to take out the sidhe who had shouted. Tin pushed his way through and bull rushed half a dozen of the leather-armored fighters. He knocked them back, and Fao moved to attack the downed men. Rhiannon fired bolts of green fire from her staff, tearing into them.

Goban took a hit to the ribs, but the big man fought through it. Aron thrust with his bastard sword and came in under the shield of the man in front of him. His foe crumbled to the ground.

The able-bodied prisoners jumped in to help Fao. Rhiannon tossed the keys to Nemain, who unlocked the other cells. Floods of dirty, scared men and women poured into the hall. They quickly armed themselves with dropped weapons, and some even took the time to strip armor off the corpses and don it in a hurry.

"Tin!" shouted Rhiannon. "Push them back to the door! We need to get through before they can lock us in."

The minotaur broke off and made a rush for the door. One guard took a look at the charging bull-headed man and dove out of the way. Tin reached the door and pushed his way through. Aron followed, helping hold the door open.

Rhiannon grabbed keys off a downed guard and helped Nemain open the next set of cells. She moved to the rear, where arms and legs stuck eagerly through the bars, people pressed close to see the fight. She put the key in the first lock, and soon they had a horde of 50 more allies in the fight.

Looking frantically for Logan's face, she tried to imagine how he would look after weeks of being a prisoner. She pictured him dirty and still in his jeans and Sturgis shirt. He was not there. She raced to the next cell and unlocked it. No Logan. Where was he? Fear gripped her. What if the Morrigan had killed him?

"Logan!" she shouted, hoping he would hear her.

She looked around her. Despite their numbers, they were not faring well. The knot of sidhe warriors fought viciously, even though they were heavily outnumbered now. Their training and discipline was wreaking havoc on the mob, taking many of the prisoners down.

Goban charged, shouting a battle cry. He ran into the guards, his heavy hammer cocked to crush them, but his wild swing left him open, and a spear thrust caught him in the throat. Without a sound, he sank to the ground, his hammer falling from his hand.

Rhiannon raced to his aid. She grabbed the big man and tried to drag him clear, but he was too heavy and the sidhe fighters came at her. Aron tried to fight to their side, but there were too many guards in the way.

"*Dóiteán!*" Rhiannon shouted, firing into the closest soldiers, who screamed as the green fire engulfed them, but there were too many. She attacked with terrible ferocity, but she couldn't fight them all and heal Goban at the same time.

Deciding to take a chance, she brought up her shield and knelt next to Goban. Weapons glanced off the shield, but it took too much concentration to keep it up. She put out her hand to Goban's throat, trying to stop the flow of blood. She dropped her shield for an instant and rushed healing light into the fallen Celt.

A club glanced off her head and landed hard on her shoulder. She fell forward over Goban, stopping before his face. His eyes dimmed and glazed, his life fled.

"No!" shouted Rhiannon. She put up her shield again and struggled to her feet. Still under attack, she turned on the soldiers and blasted them with Druid fire.

"We have to get out of here," shouted Aron.

"To the door," said Conlaodh.

Rhiannon fell in behind them as they raced to join with Fao and Tin at the door. The mob of prisoners followed, attacking the guards and quickly overwhelming them. Rhiannon winced, afraid to know how many of the prisoners also fell in the attack.

Tin had cleared the guards from the room ahead of them, and now they faced another door. A hefty group of freed prisoners stood behind them. It had cost Goban his life, but they were that much closer to freedom.

Rhiannon caught up to Tin, who opened two doors in succession and led them to the palace. The hall was empty. Rhiannon's mouth fell open. How could that be?

Tin turned left and ran through the broad hallway hung with tall tapestries. Rhiannon followed him. She looked behind her but could not see any of the Celts. Fao was with them, but not her friends.

"Tin, stop! We have to wait for Aron, Conlaodh, and the rest of the prisoners."

Tin stopped, and the sea of escaped people swarmed around him, followed by Aron, Nemain, and Conlaodh.

"We've got to get out the front doors now!" Tin said.

"Not yet," said Rhiannon. "I have to find Logan, if he is

still alive, and the Faillean Duir too."

"There's no time," he told her.

"I can't leave without trying. Go on without me. Tin, lead these people out and I'll catch up."

Tin reached out, hugged Rhiannon, and turned to Aron. "Follow me," he said and ran down the hall.

Eyes desperate, she glanced around her. Everything rested on her now.

* * *

Rhiannon raced down the empty corridor. There were so many doors, so many corridors. She didn't know which way to go. After a moment, she decided to use her divination skills and pulled out her pendulum.

"Oh Brighid, my matron and protectress, I call on you now and ask that, through this pendulum, you show me the way to the Faillean Duir."

The pendulum reacted right away and swung, clearly pointing down the hall toward the set of stairs. She ran down the broad hall and mounted the steps, climbing them two at a time. When she reached another corridor at the top, she looked around the corner. The hall was empty. She ran again, knowing from the pendulum that the Faillean Duir was above her somewhere. She considered trying the pendulum again, but the thought came to her that it was higher up.

"Thank you, Brighid," she whispered to the air.

Down the corridor she raced, looking for some way, any way, to climb higher. She found a door guarded by two sidhe fighters.

"*Dóiteán,*" she shouted without hesitation.

Green Druid fire engulfed the fighters, and they collapsed in a blaze of green agony. Rhiannon pulled the door open and raced up the narrow stairs beyond. The spiral staircase was tight, and she used the walls to help her speed.

At the top of the stairs, she reached the highest floor of a tall narrow tower. Low crenellations surrounded the diameter. Far below her, she glimpsed a battle at the gate. Glancing around, she saw no way to go any farther.

Rhiannon clenched her jaw and started pacing, trying to figure out where to go next. Her chest grew tight. "Damn it! Think, O'Neil!"

She rubbed her temple and her eyes darted around, looking for any clue. She tilted her head back. Directly above her was another tower, but this one hung down from the ceiling, with a downward pointing cone for a roof and a narrow window in the tower's rounded wall.

Rhiannon took a deep breath and sighed. She'd found it. It didn't make sense to her rational mind that she would know where the Faillean Duir was, but she trusted her intuition. How could she hope to get up there, though? It was at least thirty feet above her. She paced, staring upward, tapping her finger to her lip.

Desperate, she pulled at her pendant and studied her surroundings. The black stone reflected in the purple light of the luminous plants. A slow smile spread across her lips.

That was it.

She stepped between the plants and raised her staff. "*Ag Dreapadh, Ag Dreapadh, Ag Dreapadh,*" she chanted, drawing on her power.

The purple plants began to grow and climb. The four plants wound around each other, forming a single twisting cord. They grew and grew, anchored in the rock of the tower. Fed with Rhiannon's magic, they raced upward and finally reached the pointed bottom of the tower. They climbed up the steep reverse spire and disappeared inside the narrow window.

Rhiannon thrust her staff through the front of her robe, securing it awkwardly at her waist, and began to climb. She pulled herself slowly upward, keeping her eyes on her goal and trying not to look down.

Her hands went clammy and her fingers turned white with the effort of holding on. The vines swaying under her weight. She made an effort to slow her breathing and focus on each handhold, each foot rest, until she reached the window.

The arched aperture was made of gray stone, and it was too narrow to squeeze through. She shook her head and bared her teeth. "Gods damn it!"

Peering inside the window, the sight astounded her. Leaf-winged pixies, the same kind that had killed her mother, the same ones that had killed her in her vision back in the cave, filled the room.

Rhiannon lowered herself down so they wouldn't see her. Her already pounding heart raced faster. She knew the staff would be guarded, but she never imagined this. There were hundreds of them, and for a moment, she was a ten year old girl again. Helpless. Afraid. Alone.

Mom. Brennan. Logan. Where were they? She shrank back from the window, wanting nothing more than to hide. She knew these faeries would bleed her to death if they got to her.

She swallowed hard, remembering she had the magic now and that she could make all the difference. Without the Faillean Duir, all her efforts would be wasted. Morrigan would come and kill the tree. Brennan might slow down the goddess, but what chance did they stand without the staff?

Firming her revolve, she freed her own staff from inside her robe. She had to get inside. She could do this.

Rhiannon hung onto the vines with one hand and leaned as far away from the narrow window as she could. She pointed her staff at the far edge. *"Fórsa!"*

The power erupted out of her and blasted the hard stone. A spray of gravel hit her, followed by disappointment. The hole still wasn't big enough, and now the leaf pixies knew she was there. A flutter of leaves rushed out the window and leapt onto her. She couldn't use the shield and open the wall at the same time. She let them bite her while she drew in her power again.

"Fórsa!" she yelled with more conviction.

This time, the blast weakened the wall enough that two blocks fell into the tower. The debris sprayed her and the pixies. She slipped on the vines but caught herself by clinging to the vegetation and hugging both arms around, still holding her staff, while the attackers stabbed her. She took a breath and ignited her shield. The leaf monsters shrieked, and some of them disintegrated from the power.

Rhiannon clutched the vines and caught her breath. She climbed back to the opening and wormed her way through, eyes on the impressive sight inside.

A silver tree glowed above her. It floated in midair, with a long thin trunk. From the top and the bottom, limbs and roots extended out, filling the room.

The vines she summoned had grown through the hole and still climbed the limbs of the silver tree and the walls above it. Rhiannon scaled the vines, trying to hold onto her staff at the same time. She slipped and had to let go of the staff to keep from falling.

"Gods damn it!" She couldn't believe she had dropped the staff. The situation had been bad enough before, but now her hawthorne staff was gone. The focus the staff lent her made her magic easier to maintain and stronger.

Her shield dimmed, and the vicious faeries rushed her. She strengthened it. It was strong enough for the moment, but she didn't know how long she could keep it up. It was hard to concentrate on the shield and climb. If she halted either, she was dead.

Without her staff, Rhiannon's power faded. She looked down, and for an instant thought of going after it, but then she realized what waited at the bottom of the tower. In the dim light, she hadn't seen them before. Below the pixies, the floor moved in undulating shapes, sliding and hissing over one another, enveloping the carved shape of her hawthorne staff.

Her breath caught in her throat, and the hair rose on her arms and neck.

Snakes. Mounds of snakes covered the not-too-distant floor.

Rhiannon closed her eyes, took a breath, and climbed toward the silver tree above her. Power radiated from it, reminding her of what she felt in Brennan's grove, but even more so. The silver light entered her skin and her bones.

Pushing on, she climbed, and the onslaught of the leaf biters broke through her shield. They swarmed her, and she batted at them with her one free hand. There were too many of them.

"*Balla Dóiteán*," she shouted, and a wall of flame surrounded her.

Just powerful enough to push back some of the winged menaces, but the ones on top of her were not affected. She felt her body weakening from using so much power, and also from blood loss. She had no choice but to pin her hopes on the staff and climb.

She reached the trunk of the silver tree and grabbed it. The moment her hand touched it, the light surged, almost blinding her, and the limbs and roots of the tree retracted into the trunk. The silver tree disappeared.

Rhiannon gasped. In her hands, she held the staff. What she thought was a narrow trunk was really the Faillean Duir!

The vicious fae circled madly, stabbing and biting with renewed desperation. Rhiannon called up her shield again. The

Faillean Duir responded immediately, glowing silver. A rush of what looked like tree limbs erupted from the staff and encircled her in a protective arbor. The leaf biters were thrown from her into the wall of flame just beyond, freeing her. She drew on the power of the staff to close her wounds, to stop the bleeding.

A rush of warmth radiated throughout Rhiannon's body, and happy tears ran down her cheeks. The Faillean Duir was hers.

She smiled and took a moment to look at her prize. The staff seemed to be made of living glass filled with the silver glow. She expected to see ogam symbols carved on it, but it was free of any markings. Exactly her height, it had shrunk to match her size exactly. The sight filled her with renewed purpose and strength.

She took an easy breath and a new calm filled her. Her goals could finally be accomplished. With the staff, she now had a chance to stop the Morrigan and rescue Logan. The relief made her laugh.

Rhiannon climbed down the vine and out the window. She looked back into the tower and shouted, *"Dóiteán!"*

A blast of fire erupted from the staff and engulfed the hollow of the tower in an inferno.

She opened her eyes wide and her mouth fell slack. The power that blasted the tower was beyond what she thought possible. The flames roared, consuming everything inside.

Rhiannon grasped the vines with one hand and tucked the Faillean Duir inside her robe. She hugged the plants and lowered herself down. Daring a glance downward, she swallowed hard. Vertigo threatened. She closed her eyes, to regain her composure. She continued down carefully and when she grew close enough to the tower below, she let go and dropped the rest of the way.

She ran back the way she had come, exhaustion threatening to overwhelm her. She drew on the power of the staff, and it hit her like four shots of espresso. As her energy surged, she ran faster.

Rhiannon had the staff, but she had not found Logan. If he was still here, why wasn't he with the other prisoners? Where was he?

She decided to use her pendulum again and track him down. She didn't have much time before the Celts retreated. If she took too long, she would be trapped. It was time to find Logan and get out.

Chapter 35

Garth pulled in the reins and slowed as he came upon some rough ground. They'd spent the last two days traveling north, aiming for the Silver Rush River. It was the source of all water in the mound, and Garth hoped it would lead them to the Heart of the Water. He looked back at the men and briefly made eye contact with Niadh. He would not have believed it, but he was relieved Niadh had returned; it had only been because of him that he'd been able to decipher the ogam stones.

Garth surveyed the ground ahead as Aodhan pulled up next to him.

"Do you think we can expect another attack from Morrigan?" he asked.

"I'd be a fool not to. I don't know if that patrol that chased Niadh was out looking for us, but I think there is a good chance they were."

"They were far into our territory. It does seem they must have been there with a purpose."

"I agree. We must outride them if we are to succeed."

Ahead, the trees grew more prominent, and soon they came upon a large forest filled with tall oaks, ash, and rowan. A road had been cleared into the forest.

Garth kicked Cadifor into a gallop and rode hard down the clear way, with his men following him. Dappled light from all around played across the polished metal of their armor and weapons as they rode.

Twilight grew, and Garth noticed a black shadow moving through the forest. He rubbed at his eyes and blinked. Perhaps the fatigue of the journey made him see things. Off to the left, in the trees, a black shadow raced along with them. When he tried to see what it was, it disappeared again.

As the light began to fade, they came upon the Silver Rush River. The clear blue water glowed with its own light and illuminated the rocky shore. A stone bridge curved up and over it, and the road continued beyond it, heading into Morrigan's territory. Last glowing was upon them, and Garth called a halt.

He scouted the perimeter of his intended campsite. He had never been to the headwaters of the Silver Rush, and he hoped that was what the riddle meant by the Heart of the Water. In the morning, they would turn west and see where the source of the river was.

The sound of a twig breaking grabbed his attention. He stopped and crouched, looking in the direction of the noise. Silence. He waited, holding his breath.

A black wolf with a white streak of fur across its face glared at him.

Garth's muscles tensed for action and his heart hammered. He recognized the wolf immediately. It was the wolf from his nightmares.

He stood and shouted, "What do you want?"

The wolf turned and bared its teeth then disappeared into the shadows, leaving no trace.

Garth drew his sword and took off in pursuit. He caught one more glimpse before the wolf vanished entirely.

"Gods damn it!" He clenched his fists and turned back to the camp.

Dónal sat near the fire, cutting potatoes for their stew. Aodhan fed small twigs into the blaze.

Garth called the men together. "There is a wolf prowling around in the woods, just beyond the camp."

"By itself?" asked Aodhan

"Yes. It's been following us all day."

"Really? Why didn't you say anything?" asked Niadh.

"I wasn't sure at first. I thought it was just shadows, but now I'm sure."

"Should we go hunt it?" asked Aodhan.

"No. I don't think it is just a wolf. It could be the Cailleach in disguise, hunting us."

"How do you know, Garth?" asked Niadh.

"Before our quest started, I had a recurring dream of a black wolf with a white stripe hunting me. I told both Brennan and

Rhiannon about it. Brennan confirmed the importance of the dream, and Rhiannon believed that it is the goddess Cailleach."

"The Cailleach?" asked Tuathal.

"She is a hag goddess who can appear as a wolf or raven. She is one of the Morrigan's assassins."

Tuathal opened his eyes wide.

Bannan stood and put his hands on his hips. "What can we do? How can we hope to defeat a goddess?"

Garth looked up at him. "We have Claíomh Solais and our wits."

"Tonight, let's build up the fire and keep it burning bright. We will plant our spears pointing out in a ring to slow her down if she comes at us. We will double our watch, with two men on guard at a time. And no drinking."

Bannan sat back down.

"I know I won't be sleeping tonight," said Tuathal.

"I doubt any of us will, but we've got to try to get some rest. Tomorrow we have to ride hard to find the Heart of the Water."

"Garth, do you really think our best plan is to sit here and wait?" asked Niadh.

"I don't want to go out in the dark to hunt this thing. We don't know what we are up against, and it would be too easy to get separated and be more vulnerable. We stay together in a place of strength and wait."

Niadh nodded. "How long do we follow the river?"

"Until we find its heart," said Garth.

"How do we know the pillars were even a clue meant for us?" asked Croftin.

Garth frowned. He didn't have patience for such questions. "I don't know for sure. But I believe they were."

"You knew that this would not be a straightforward hunt, Croftin. Why don't you let Garth do his job?" said Aodhan.

"Why don't you stay out of it, Aodhan?"

"Because it's my hide too if we fail, and you are not helping things," said Aodhan.

"I just want to know we are going the right way," said Croftin.

Tuathal got up from the fire and walked toward the woods.

"Where are you going, Tuathal?"

"Take a piss, if you don't mind."

Garth nodded. "I know everyone is nervous, and we have little to go on, but we are on the right track. We will find the Heart of the River."

"It is late and we are all tired and need sleep," said Niadh. "Garth's plan is a good one. Everything will look better at first glowing."

"I agree. We need to rest. I will take the first watch with Tuathal," said Garth. He stood and started planting their spears around the camp. A flash of movement caught him. He turned, drawing his sword. First, he saw nothing, but then realized what he had seen was Tuathal's back as he disappeared farther into the trees.

He shook his head and sheathed his sword, feeling the attention of his men on his back. "Sorry, I'm jumpy, lads. It was Tuathal."

Garth drove another spear into the ground. The other men helped, and soon they had a hedge of leaf bladed spears pointing out into the night. Tuathal returned from the dark, threading his way through the points. They ate a quiet meal and found their bedrolls. Garth sat opposite the fire from Tuathal.

He felt Tuathal's stare and looked up at the man, who turned his gaze to the fire. Garth stood, crossed his arms tightly over his chest, and began to circle the fire.

"Sit down already. You are making me dizzy," Tuathal said suddenly.

Garth stopped and looked at him. "What did you say?"

"I'm sorry. I'm nervous enough without you pacing around."

Garth looked over his shoulder and back at Tuathal. "You are not the only one on edge," he said as he continued to pace. "What are those daggers in your belt? I've never seen them before."

"Oh these? I took them off of one of Morrigan's troopers."

"Can I see them?"

Tuathal shrugged and handed them across the fire without a word.

Garth looked at the daggers carefully. "I've not seen workmanship like this before. They look almost like pottery, not like forged metal. There are no hammer marks."

"Thought they'd come in handy," said Tuathal.

Garth handed them back and gazed at the embers. His nerves felt raw, every sense heightened, and his intuition screamed danger but he couldn't figure out why. He took a breath, rubbed the back of his neck, and continued to circle the fire.

Bannan and Aodhan appeared for their shift. Tuathal left the fire and Garth pulled Aodhan aside.

"Wake me if anything unusual happens," he said in a whisper.

Aodhan raised a brow. "What's going on?"

"Something's not right. I just can't decide if I'm being paranoid or if there is really something going on. Tuathal has this pair of sidhe daggers I've never seen before tonight and he claims to have gotten them from the fight two days ago. I know it's not much, but there's something...I just can't place it. Anything sidhe puts me on edge."

"Okay, I will take care of it. Now get some sleep," said Aodhan, narrowing his eyes.

"That's probably all it is. I just need some sleep."

"Maybe. I will keep an eye on him anyway."

Garth walked away. He trusted Aodhan; they had been on many adventures together and always had each other's backs. It had once been the same way with Garth and Niadh.

He returned to his bedroll and lay with his back to the fire, looking out into the dark forest. He knew he'd get no sleep this night. He watched the shadows.

He was still awake when the next shift started. Cathaoir and Niadh took the watch. Garth worried that Aodhan wouldn't have passed on his concerns when he heard Cathaoir shout. "Hey, Tuathal? Did you fall in the river?"

Garth sat up. Cathaoir took a few steps into the woods.

"What are you up to? Get back here," said Cathaoir.

Garth stood.

"Wait, Cathaoir. Don't go out there," said Niadh.

"What's going on?" Garth asked.

"Tuathal got up to go again and he hasn't come back. Cathaoir left to go find him."

"We better wake the others, something is wrong," said Garth.

"I agree."

He drew his sword and watched the trees where Cathaoir disappeared.

After all the men were awake, Cathaoir returned. "I couldn't find him. It's like he just disappeared," he said, shaking his head.

"We better see if we can find Tuathal. Cathaoir, come with me. Niadh, you stay here. Aodhan, Bannan, and Croftin, go south along the river."

Garth led the way down a slope closer to the water. He kept Cathaoir next to him. They searched and found a pool of blood on the forest floor. Garth bent down and put a finger in the pool. It was still warm.

Suddenly a smothering hand covered his nose and mouth, nails digging into his cheek drawing blood and pulling his head back, exposing his jugular. The smell of decay and sweat filled his nostrils. Instant adrenaline hit his blood stream. His eyes bulged, and before he even had time to think he rolled forward, tearing from the grip. He hit the ground hard and gasped for breath. His attacker was on him again, landing on his chest.

A hunched crone crouched on top of him, with one eye drooping below the other and a single white patch marking the ragged black hair. She hissed and raised two daggers, aiming at his throat. He yelled and tried to jerk free but his arms were pinned. Despite his strength, he could not throw her off.

The crone lunged. Garth bucked with all his strength and knocked her off balance just enough that the blades hit his neck armor, instead of his throat. She attacked again, striking at his ribs. One blade cut through the leather armor and pierced his side.

The puncture burned, and his blood flowed. Garth shouted again, but this time from pain and frustration.

Cailleach raised her daggers, ready to stab him again. She dodged to one side as a spear blade sliced passed her head. She looked up, hissed, and in a cloud of black feathers, shapeshifted into a raven. She lifted off from the ground just as a second spear blade point passed under her wing.

Garth sucked in a breath and let it out with relief.

She was gone.

He rolled off his back and turned, expecting to see Aodhan.

Niadh reached out to help Garth up.

"What are you doing here?"

"Saving your hide, you ungrateful ass."

Garth stood slowly, felt his wound tearing. He winced and brought his hand to his side.

"We better take a look at that," said Niadh.

"It can wait until we are back at the camp. What happened?" asked Garth. "I couldn't see."

"I followed you from the camp. I felt something wasn't right. Cathaoir changed into a hag right before my eyes. It was the damnedest thing I ever saw. And then she attacked you."

Garth swallowed hard. It happened so fast. "It was the Cailleach."

"Must have been."

"What made you suspect Cathaoir?"

"I don't know. Maybe it was the way he walked, but something told me to follow you. I wish I had been closer. I almost didn't get to you in time. It was a hell of spear throw."

"I owe you my life, Niadh. Thank you." Garth held out his hand.

Niadh clasped Garth's hand and smiled. "You would have done the same for me," he said.

"Cathaoir is dead, no doubt, and probably Tuathal too," said Garth soberly. "I thought Tuathal was not right either, but I couldn't figure it out. I told Aodhan before his watch that Tuathal had two daggers I'd never seen before. My guess is he was the first victim, and then Cathaoir. If it wasn't for your good thinking, I would probably be dead now."

"Just doing my part," said Niadh.

Garth's mouth went dry thinking about what had happened; two men dead and he almost joining them. If the Cailleach had taken him, the quest would have failed and with it the death of all his tribe. It was a narrow thing, too narrow, but a sudden lightness filled him. Niadh was back, at least for now, and they could be allies again.

Garth put his hand on Niadh's shoulder. "Let's get back to camp."

Near the fire, they took off Garth's breastplate. The wound was deep and oozed blood. Niadh washed it and Garth took some dried marigolds from his pack and pressed them to the puncture while Niadh wrapped a linen bandage around his waist.

Niadh called out for the rest to return to the camp. Garth

told them about the attack, and together they searched for signs of their fallen companions but found nothing but more blood.

Garth paced, clenching his jaw. "Gods damn it. We've lost three good men with nothing to show for it but a poem." He took a deep breath, looked them each in the eye.

"Listen, no more wandering off alone. Even if you have to relieve yourself, take someone with you. We sit tight until first glowing." He crossed his arms across his chest. "We are down to six and the Cailleach is still out there. In the morning, we ride for the Heart of the Water."

Chapter 36

Garth awoke to a silver radiance coming through the alders, from the river. He stood carefully, mindful of his wound from the crone, and walked to the fire to warm himself. Bannan and Croftin were sitting watch.

"Any more signs of the Cailleach?"

"You know how it is. Every shadow seems a monster, but nothing definitive," said Croftin.

"I do know what you mean. Bannan, will you come with me down to the river?"

Bannan nodded and stood.

Garth walked to the rocky edge and looked out at the water. The Silver Rush River leapt at its banks, gushing through boulders and fallen trees.

"This whole situation has me on a knife's edge," said Bannan.

Garth turned and put a hand on his shoulder. "I know it; you are not alone."

Garth dipped first one water skin, and then another into the clear water. Something caught his eye, a brief flash in the water. He looked and pointed. "Do you see that gleam?"

"Aye, it looks like bronze."

"Like a piece of armor..."

Garth swallowed hard. He took a branch from the bank and fished the metal out. He took the small plate in his hand, seeing the holes where the rivets used to hold it to a leather breastplate.

"Tuathal's?" said Bannan quietly.

Garth clenched his teeth. "Yes. The hag must have put the bodies in the river, that is why we couldn't find them." He punched his open hand, feeling his face redden.

"Gods damn it. She is going to pay."

He put the metal in his pouch and they walked back to camp.

Garth paced, flexing his fingers while he waited for the water to boil. The yellow moran reisc blooms began to glow, adding their light to the morning. He made some healing tea and drank it quickly, anxious to put this place behind him. "Let's get everyone up and get going."

Alder and willow grew in abundance along the Silver Rush, and there was no easy way to ride next to the flow. The ground grew rockier as they rode west and the land rose. Garth rode away from the river to get to better terrain. They topped a ridge and found it clearer.

In the shadows of the forest, Garth sensed movement. He halted his men. His heart leapt when he saw the wolf again. "There it is," he said, pointing.

"I don't see it," said Aodhan.

"Nor I," said Niadh.

"It was there, but it moves fast and quiet. Keep alert."

They rode on again, and only the sound of bridle and reins broke the silence. The wind was still, and even the trees seemed to be listening.

At last glowing, as the light began to fade, a fog rose around them.

"We better stop here," said Garth.

"I can't see anything anyway," said Aodhan. "I'll get a fire going."

"No. Not tonight. The fog may help us stay hidden from Cailleach."

Aodhan nodded and looked around nervously.

The men dismounted and made camp.

Garth's head throbbed. He held his hands behind his back, gripping his own wrists. *Another day gone and a dangerous night ahead*, he thought, feeling his frustration rise. "Let's put up our ring of spears again," said Garth.

The horses stomped their feet as they ate. It was a still night, with the mist hovering near, and the men gathered together and ate a cold meal of smoked pork and apples.

"Niadh, I could almost think of you as respectable after your heroics last night," said Aodhan.

Niadh snorted. "Almost, huh?"

Aodhan nodded, his expression grew serious. "Garth related his worries about Tuathal. I didn't notice anything wrong, but you were sharp as a blade and came to the rescue. Good work."

Niadh shrugged as if it was nothing.

Garth relaxed just a little and gave a small smile. He knew Aodhan was sincere in his praise and the fact Niadh didn't attack Aodhan in response was a good sign. They would need to be as strong as they could for what lay ahead.

All of the men sat with their backs to each other. Garth scanned the forest around them and sat up straight. Lights appeared in the fog. They started slowly, flashing red, blue, and green. Similar to the orbs the men were used to, they were smaller and there were many of them. Garth pointed out the dancing spheres.

"I've never seen lights like that, not after last glowing," said Aodhan.

"Nor have I," said Garth. "I think it we should investigate."

"It could be a Cailleach trick to get us lost and separated," said Niadh.

"Very true, and normally I would agree with you, but what if it is a sign that Brennan talked about?"

"We could always walk farther in once first glowing dawns," said Bannan.

"By then the lights could be gone," said Garth. "I say we risk it."

"This is one of those times when I know you are right but I don't want to do it anyway," said Aodhan with a frown.

Garth's chest tightened and his hand rose to finger his torc. "I know it, but we could be close to the Heart of the Water, and this could be the way in. Plus a camp without a fire is no good anyway. Let's leave two men with the horses and the rest come," said Garth. He didn't know if the lights were anything, but he didn't want to sit stewing in his frustration and fear if there was a chance they could improve their situation.

Bannan rubbed the back of his neck and looked toward the lights. "I will stay," he said.

"As will I," said Croftin biting at his lip.

"Thank you," said Garth. "Now, let's go. Stay close and follow me."

The light from the spheres glittered and danced on the still leaves and bark, making it difficult to walk straight. Garth stumbled on hidden tree roots and pointed them out to Niadh just behind him. The orbs found the men in the fog and danced around them. Garth turned to look behind him and could see Niadh but no one else. He stopped to wait for the rest to catch up and, after a brief pause, began to get worried.

"Aodhan! Dónal! Can you hear me?"

Garth held his breath.

Silence.

His legs felt suddenly weak. He shoved his hands into his armpits. "They were just behind us," said Garth.

"I know it," said Niadh.

"Let's give them another moment."

Garth blinked rapidly feeling cold spread.

The lights moved less now that they were still.

Garth drew his Druid sword, and when he did, the glow from the blade shot out like beacon around them. In the golden light, a footpath led deeper into the fog. He turned and looked at Niadh. He opened his mouth and closed it again before speaking.

"What do you say?"

"We should regroup," said Niadh.

Garth scratched at his cheek and looked once more at the illuminated path. He turned back. His stomach churned and he thought about what might be happening to his men. Had this been a trick of the Cailleach to separate them? Were they even now dead behind him? "You're right. We need to find the others."

Garth and Niadh carefully worked their way back toward camp, shouting for their companions along the way. Not only did they not find them, they could not find the camp. They tried calling for Bannan and Croftin too, but no answer.

Garth stopped, turned, and brought a shaky hand to his beard. "We should be there by now." He looked all around him, especially behind him. "We're lost."

"We could stop and wait for first glowing," Niadh said.

Garth took in a deep breath and let it out slowly. "Or we could find that path again," finished Garth.

"I don't know that we can, but anything is better than just waiting for the light," said Niadh rubbing his shoulders.

They retraced their steps as best they could and to their amazement found the single-track footpath again. They followed it amidst tall alder trees and rowan. It traced a never-ending route through the mist. The light of first glowing grew and Garth turned to ask Niadh something.

Niadh was gone. The cold he had felt now froze him completely. He pulled his cloak tighter. "Niadh!" shouted Garth. "Where are you?"

Silence.

Garth's stomach felt rock hard. He held his breath. *This is an enchanted place,* thought Garth.

He searched and shouted but to no avail; he was alone in the mist. Up ahead, he heard a quiet lapping of waves and soon the shore of a lake appeared.

Garth rubbed the back of his neck. His men were lost in the fog behind him, the Cailleach lurked nearby, and in front of him could very well be the Heart of the Water. He rubbed at his wrists, trying to decide what to do. *Do I turn around and try to find the men or do I push on? If I leave this place, will I be able to find it again?*

He walked to the water's edge to investigate. There he found a gray coracle banked on the sand. Oval in shape and only large enough for one person, it was made of interwoven willow rods tied with willow bark. Animal skin made up the outer layer and a thin layer of black tar made it waterproof.

Garth brought his hand to his torc and fingered it. The boat seemed an invitation for one, not for six. The men had got him this far, and his intuition told him now he must go on alone. He swallowed and took a breath. This must be the Heart of the Water.

* * *

Garth firmed his jaw, looking out at the lake. Whatever lay beyond would lead him that much closer to his goal.

Resolved, he looked closer at the boat. There was no oar. Though he could make something that would work from the trees around him, he wondered if the absence was intentional. Without any way to paddle, he would be at the mercy of the currents and the wind. Perhaps that was how he would get closer to the well, to trust in nature to take him. Maybe this was the first test.

He pulled the coracle a little more onto shore and placed his pack into it. With a short running start, he skimmed the boat out and jumped in. The lake was still covered in mist and he could not see how far away the opposite shore might be, but in the near distance he could hear the sound of water breaking. Garth guessed it was the water leaving the lake to feed the river below.

The shore disappeared. In the near silence, his hearing was keen and behind him he heard a shout travel over the water. It sounded like his name. His heartbeat kicked up as he listened carefully.

"Garth!"

Chills climbed his spine. It was Niadh, he was sure of it.

"Niadh! I'm on the lake!"

He held his breath and listened. No more sound came. He let out his breath and brought a knuckle to his lips. The shore was quickly falling away. Should he try to get back? He remembered that he had no oar. He could try to swim it, but with all his armor he doubted he could fight the current enough to make it. The decision had already been made. *I should have brought an oar*, he thought as he dragged a hand through his hair. He closed his eyes and prayed that Niadh would be okay. He needed to press on.

He trusted the current that pushed him along through the mist and gazed as far ahead as he could see. The first glowing was brighter now, and the gray fog had turned to gold, but still all around him was nothing but water. Waves lapped quietly on the hull, and he felt an unusual calm descending on him. The mist comforted him like a warm blanket on a cold day. The silence soaked into him as he drifted across the endless lake.

Garth lost track of time. When he glanced behind him, now there was no sign of the shore from which he had come. His still mind let go of the questions about what he might find out on this misty lake. Waves guided him until, at last, a gray shape appeared in the golden fog. He couldn't make it out at first, but now an island appeared in the middle of the lake.

He blinked rapidly, taking in what was in front of him. He rubbed his hands down his legs. The poem said, "Mists conceal sacred ordeal." *This must be the place.*

The island was tall and tree-covered. The sandy shore was clear of trees for a short while and then they grew up like a fortress. He noticed piles of rocks made to look like eggs along the beach. The sculptures stood as tall as he, made of many fist-sized stones, fitted together carefully.

Garth pulled the boat out of the water and hid it in the nearby trees. He walked up the shore, hearing the sand crunch beneath his wet boots. The golden mist thickened, becoming even more impenetrable now.

As he walked the beach, two rows of the stone eggs pointed into the woods, like a funnel. He followed the corridor of rock markers to the edge of the forest and a footpath cut through the trees. This path was paved with gray stones with moss and lichen on the surfaces and in the cracks.

At the edge of the trees he found a stone portal. Two large bluestones of irregular shape stood on either side of the path, and across the top was a third lintel. The stones framed the entrance to the forest and summoned him inside.

Garth shook out his hands, trying to warm them. He knew he was in the right place. He had crossed the Heart of the Water and now the ordeal would begin. *The Well is close now*, he thought as he walked forward with wide steps.

Chapter 37

Garth stepped under the entry and walked into the woods beyond. The light of his sword cut the mist so he could see a short way ahead. The stones beneath his feet were damp, and Garth walked slowly to keep his footing. Winding around trees and boulders, the path disappeared into the net of the trees.

His pounding heart was the only sound in the forest. He took a breath, trying to calm himself as he walked forward.

The path ahead suddenly split, heading right and left. A large, round gray stone stood at the divide, covered with green lichen. Garth studied the stone carefully. He took off his glove and felt its surface. Under the lichen, he felt the faint remains of a carved letter. Clearing the moss away, he saw the ogam letter for birch; a single vertical staff bisected by another single horizontal line pointing to the right.

Garth stroked his chin as he considered what to do. He tried to remember Brennan's teachings from years ago. He knew birch trees colonized bare ground first after a mature forest died, making it a symbol for new beginnings. Looking right, at the edge of his vision a small grove of silver birch grew. He looked to the left and saw nothing but the same chaotic mix of trees found all over the island. *Right it is.*

Garth's chest thumped and his mouth felt dry. It started with birch and ended—he hoped—at his goal, the Well of Wisdom. He hoped his limited Druid knowledge would be enough.

Raspberry thickets all but blocked the narrow way, but with a careful eye he was able to find the stones of the path. The birch trees beyond the undergrowth thrived here, and soon they surrounded him. Towering a hundred feet over his head, their silvery white bark shimmered with its own light. Garth watched his footing and listened closely. A distant rustling met his ear and soon a squirrel appeared, leaping from branch to branch high above him.

The path climbed higher, winding through rocks and fallen trunks. Ahead of him, at the top of a rise, another small grove of trees sat, growing apart from the chaotic mix of the rest of the forest. At the foot of them, the path split again. The new trees were rowan trees, and they stood less than half as tall as their birch cousins. Garth studied them closely. They were in full fruit. Their red berries reminded him of something Brennan had told him once.

From the air above, Garth heard the croak of a raven. The sound reverberated ominously and he drew his sword. The Cailleach had escaped from Niadh by turning into a bird. Maybe he'd heard just a normal raven, but his gut told him different. Even on this holy island, he wasn't safe. He held his breath and listened, but now only silence met his ear.

He turned his attention back to the rowan trees and tried again to remember what Brennan had taught him about them. It must have been something important, but for the life of him he couldn't recall. He took a long drink from his water-skin and decided to walk forward to the intersection to find clues about which way to go. The path was obscured by leaves. Without warning, the ground vanished beneath his feet and the void grabbed him. He dropped into a hidden pit, shouting in surprise.

Garth frantically reached out, trying to catch the edge. His hands came back with only leaves. He pulled roots out as he dropped, trying desperately to slow his fall. He bumped against tree roots and ledges on the way down and landed hard in a pit of leaves. Agony burned through him as his puncture ripped open and started to bleed.

He lay motionless, clutching at his side and biting his lip with closed eyes. With a painful effort, he stood with a grimace and brushed himself off. Above him, he heard the raven again.

"Gods damn it!" he hissed. His heart raced. He was hurt, trapped, and he suspected Cailleach flew above him somewhere.

Garth scanned his prison. The roots of the rowan trees had explored this dark cavity for many years. He reached for the closest root and pulled. It held his weight, but the pain from his stab wound ripped through him and he let go.

Clenching his jaw, he started to climb. Each pull brought fresh pain. He gasped with the sharpness of it. Agonizingly, he worked his way back up, sweating and biting back curses.

When he reached the top, he collapsed on the ground, holding his side. The pain surged in excruciating intensity. While he rested, a memory came to him. Brennan said the rowan berries were used as bait to trap birds. He should have remembered. That alone should have warned him.

I'm failing this test.

He wanted to just lie there, to have a brief respite from the pain, but the Cailleach could be close. Garth struggled back to his feet, head swimming. He took off his breastplate. A bright spot of red seeped through his bandage. Grimacing, he unwrapped the linen. The puncture wound oozed blood.

He reached into his pack for a fresh bandage. Before he found it, a black cloud of noise ripped through the trees above. An unkindness of ravens, with black eyes and talons, sliced the air on powerful wings, diving for him. He drew his sword, cursing that he had dropped his breast plate. He brought up his shield, and spun. Claíomh Solais cut the air, shredding feathers and muscle. The cloud of black engulfed him, blocking all the light. Sharp beaks bit and pecked, wounding and shredding skin. *Run!* his brain screamed, but which way? He couldn't afford to fall into another pit or worse because of a bad decision now.

The right path led to an alder grove, and the left to a hawthorne grove.

Alder followed rowan, not hawthorne.

Garth turned to the right and sprinted, swinging his sword and protecting his face with his shield. The path narrowed, and alder brush closed in around him. Through a storm of black feathers, he barely made out a ring of tall trees ahead of him.

Claws raked at his unarmored back, tearing his skin. He flinched, the clinging alder roots tripped him, and he went down. He rolled, crushing some of the birds, came back to his feet, looked ahead again. The path disappeared into a knot of alder thickets.

Garth ran, hoping the tightly woven trees might give him some protection. The path faded altogether, and the land dipped down so he could only see a dozen feet or more directly ahead of him. He raised Claíomh Solais, intending to cut a way inside, but the canes parted and let him in.

He crashed to the ground and fought the birds pecking at his face, cutting them viciously. He turned to look behind him. The alder saplings had closed in behind him, blocking any more birds from attacking him. The Druid blade glowed.

Garth's muscles quivered, and the torn, aching flesh on his back enraged him. He took deep, heaving breaths and looked around, safe for the moment. When his breathing calmed, he turned in the direction he wanted to go and focused his mind on the saplings. Slowly, they parted for him. He crawled forward and stood.

With each step, the trees grew denser around him, protecting him, and he soon walked on their roots more than on the ground. His feet crunched down into the tangle, like walking in a net. Each step took effort, and he grabbed at alder branches to catch his balance.

Sweating profusely now, his face and hands sliced with small cuts from the rough bark, he came to the edge of the thicket. He wiped the sweat from his forehead to keep it from running into his eyes and took a draw from his water skin. Once he left the safety of the thicket, he would have to fight the ravens again. He needed a plan.

I can't out run them, but I have to keep going.

Garth peered through the tangle. The ground rose ahead of him. The small alder trees dropped back before their larger brothers. At the top of the rise, an opening appeared. That would be his target. He knew what he would do.

He took a deep breath, and using the sword to open the way ran out from his cover. The ravens attacked immediately. He ran up hill, trying to gain some distance, fighting them as he ran. Across the grove, the opening led downward into the forest.

Garth ran with the scything raven beaks cutting and stabbing at him. Gravity pulled him. He struggled to keep from losing his balance as he plummeted downhill.

Using the magic of the sword, he made an archway in the alder thicket and ran inside. A narrow way opened for him, and when he was far enough in to have drawn in most of his attackers, he sealed the corridor behind him. Running with a frenzied black cloud just behind him, he made a small opening in the branches ahead and dove through, willing it shut behind him, trapping most of the ravens inside. He hit the ground, rolled, and turned to face what remained of his attackers..

Garth whirled, slicing at the ravens. Seeing that the

advantage of their numbers was gone, the birds turned and flew high into the trees. One of them, the largest, sat on a limb and cawed at him loudly.

Garth took aim with his spear and threw. The weapon would have hit the bird, but it rose up again and flew away. Watching, he gave a slow smile and stumbled back a step, his mouth dry from the exertion.

He took another draw on his water, emptying it, and looked up at the ridge above him. Another stone portal sat at the crest of the ridge. He ticked off the ogam trees. Birch, Rowan, and Alder done. *Six more to go*, he thought. More determined than ever, he retrieved his spear and began the hike to the gateway above.

Chapter 38

Rhiannon pulled her pendulum free and crouched on the floor at the bottom of the stairs in Morrigan's castle. She had won the Arch Druid's staff and now she needed to find Logan. She prayed silently to Brighid to help her find him while she watched the pendulum. It didn't move. She tried to relax, to let the information flow, but the pendulum hung stiffly on its chain. Now was not the time for the pendulum to fail her.

Rhiannon's throat closed and her stomach hardened. Was he already dead? She stood, clenched her fists, and looked around. Going back the way she had come held little promise. There was only one way to go.

She turned right and ran down the empty corridor. Immediately, she stopped, stunned.

Logan.

Rhiannon brought her hand to her throat, suddenly short of breath. Dressed in the clothes of the sidhe, he was clean and had a sword at his hip. At his side, a beautiful woman with long blonde hair grabbed his arm when Rhiannon appeared.

"Rhiannon?" he whispered.

"Logan?" She couldn't believe it was really him. Logan threw off the other woman's arm and stepped forward and embraced her.

He smelled different, like cinnamon, and he felt leaner. She pulled away and looked up into his eyes. Relief was suddenly mixed with anger. "Who is your *friend*? And why are you not a prisoner?"

"There's no time to explain that now. If Morrigan catches you, she will kill you. You need to go!"

She reached out for him. "Come with me, Logan!"

He pulled away. "I…I can't."

"What? Why?"

"Rhiannon…I love you, but there is something you need to know."

She swallowed hard. "What is it?"

"The Morrigan is my mother." He looked up at her as the words left his mouth.

Rhiannon stepped backward and felt her legs go weak beneath her. "No. It can't be. She lied to you."

"I'm *sure,* Rhiannon."

Her pulse throbbed in her throat. She shook her head. "No, your mother was a Sioux."

"It was lie to protect me."

She rubbed her eyes, hiding her tears. "I don't care, Logan. What the Morrigan did has nothing to do with you. Come with me now."

"Rhiannon, we can't be together. I know everything now. How our families are at war with each other. I don't want to believe it, but it's true. Morrigan killed your mother, and she will stop at nothing to kill you too."

Hot tears burst onto Rhiannon's face, and she raised her hand to slap him.

He caught her hand, kissed it.

"He's mine now anyway," said the blond sidhe behind him.

"Stay out of it, Áine," Logan spat.

"Logan, what does she mean?" Rhiannon pulled her hand free and brought it, shaking, to her forehead.

"It's complicated, Rhiannon. You have to trust me that I still love you, but…"

"You are too late," said Áine. "Logan has accepted his place here with *me.*"

Rhiannon turned her gaze to Áine and glared at her. "I'm not talking to you."

"Rhiannon, I'm so sorry. I tried so hard to get back to you, to get free of this place, but the Morrigan ensnared me. Her tricks and deceptions were too much."

"I think you rather enjoyed some of the illusions. Like when you were *tricked* into sleeping with me," Áine said and gave a wicked smile.

Rhiannon's whole body grew weak. She stumbled back another step and held up her palm to stop him from coming closer.

"You slept with her?" she said.

For a moment Logan didn't answer, but when he met her eyes, his were wet.

"I don't expect you to believe me, but Áine used magic to make me think she was you."

Rhiannon looked down at her hands. She wanted to collapse. How could she believe him? Even if it was true, how could he have not known it wasn't her? A heavy weight crushed her chest, and her breath wouldn't come.

She looked up at him, searching his eyes. "I gave up everything to find you..." Her words trailed away to a painful silence.

Logan looked at her with red eyes. "I'm sorry, Rhiannon. I never meant for any of this to happen." From behind him came the sound of stomping boots and the shouts of soldiers. "Go now. I'll try to stop them," he said.

Heat rushed into her body, her grief turning to anger. "I believed in you, Logan." The words turned to ash in her mouth. "This is not over," she said, pointing at Áine who just smiled back at her.

Rhiannon turned and ran. Her thoughts tumbled over each other in confused chaos.

How could Logan be Morrigan's son? It was impossible.

Oh, sweet Brighid, it must be a lie. How could my one true love be the son of my enemy? And how could he have slept with that bitch?

She heard shouts and raised voices, followed by the sound of the soldiers turning away. Logan led them off. She sighed, the sound low and sad.

She couldn't stay here. She had to get free of this cursed place.

* * *

On the main floor, the fight raged between the Celts and Morrigan's army. Bodies littered the area, many sidhe. Rhiannon spotted Tin and fought to reach him as he cleared huge swaths of the enemy with his axe. She suspected many of the dead were from his efforts to hold them off while she'd retrieved the Faillean Duir. Aron, Nemain, and Conlaodh fought near Tin and Fao. The main door was closed, and her friends no longer had any reason to stay and fight. And neither did she. Logan was lost to her now.

Blocking the thought, she ran, knocking aside anyone in her way to reach her friends.

"Follow me!" she shouted, charging the gate and fighting her way to the door. She pushed it open. Outside, beyond the courtyard, the drawbridge was down!

We can do this!

"There is the way out!" shouted Aron, pointing at the gate. "Let's go!"

Aron and Nemain led the charge for the gates, passing Rhiannon, and the mob followed them. Tin and Fao turned to leave. Another troop entered the great foyer. Tin turned and attacked, trying to buy his friends the time they needed to get clear.

Rhiannon squeezed her fists tight and clenched her jaw. "Tin! No!" she screamed. They had to leave, and Tin needed to come with them or be overrun.

It was too late—he was engaged and Fao was at his side. They fought the new attackers fiercely.

"We have to go now or we are finished," said Conlaodh, standing next to Rhiannon.

Tears in her eyes, Rhiannon turned and looked toward the gates. Against all odds, a band of Bran's Celts had seized the gatehouse. Though they were heavily engaged, they were still holding the way clear for escape. Despite her heartache, part of her wanted to cheer.

Rhiannon turned. Tin and Fao still fought Morrigan's soldiers. "Tin! Fao! Come *on*! The way is *clear*!"

It was too late. Even as she shouted, another cohort join the others, and the minotaur went down. Fao, too, disappeared from sight.

Her stomach clenched into a knot and her breath froze. "Tin! No!" She took a faltering step toward them, drawing on her power. She couldn't leave her friends to die.

Then she saw *her*.

The Morrigan.

Rhiannon held back a scream, feeling her adrenaline spike. Her mouth dropped open as the Morrigan lead a huge force of soldiers into the hall, not more than thirty feet away.

The faerie queen's black robes flowed around her like a nimbus of power, and she radiated menace. Rhiannon recoiled. Here was her mother's killer, in the flesh. Her confidence turned to water as the goddess strode forward.

Directly behind Morrigan lumbered ogres carrying clubs and axes. Behind them, green trolls, complete with long limbs and wicked two-handed swords. Foolishly perhaps, Rhiannon had hoped they'd be able to escape without having to face Morrigan. Even now, she could follow the others and make a run for it. Hands shaking, Rhiannon hesitated. Morrigan hadn't seen her yet.

But she couldn't leave Tin behind.

She stood face to face with her mother's killer, and she had the power to fight her. Nearly overcome, she tried to decide what power word to use. What would have a chance of taking Morrigan out?

In the split second of hesitation, Morrigan focused on Rhiannon through the chaos of the fight. "No!" she shouted, eyes focusing immediately on the Druid staff. Fury etched in every line of her face.

"*Fiachra!*" the faerie queen screamed, pointing her crow pommeled sword at Rhiannon.

Rhiannon's shield flared to life instantly. The roots and branches erupted from the staff and encircled her in a sphere of living silver-white tendrils. The sickly black light probed her shield, but it held. Her bracelet, the one Brennan made for her, grew hot on her wrist.

In a flash, the black spell light disappeared. Her bracelet and the staff had saved her. Rhiannon felt quick satisfaction and gave a crisp nod. She had with stood an attack from the Morrigan.

Outside her shield, she watched in horror as the black energy enveloped the throng of fleeing people, both Celts and Sidhe, around her. She watched them shift, against their will, into a murder of crows. The screams of agony as their bodies morphed made her cringe. The crows circled Rhiannon and attacked her, obeying Morrigan's will. If it were not for the shield, she would be one of the crows.

The urge rose to use her fear and anger against Morrigan. She wanted to unleash all the pain that roared raw in her psyche. The pain of Logan's betrayal, still hot. She longed to just channel it all and level it at the Morrigan, to kill the one who had ruined her life. The dark impulse whispered that Morrigan's death would fix everything, make her life right again.

Faintly at first, but then stronger, she fought against her

reaction. She remembered the lessons from her initiation, that all of life is sacred and magic should not be used in anger. She pulled power in, more than she had ever pulled before, from a place of protection, not anger. She would need it all for destroying the Morrigan.

Rhiannon planted her staff on the stone of the ground and shouted, "*Airgead!*"

The ground rumbled beneath her feet. A bolt of silver light erupted from the orb of branches and roots around her. The flash roared, and all nearby were momentarily blinded; all except Morrigan, who swept her sword across her body to deflect the impact of the strike.

The energy ricocheted off into the ceiling and imploded. The roof shuddered and cracked under the impact. A shower of stones fell. In almost one piece, the roof fell with a thunderous crash.

Behind the wall of gray dust and stones, Rhiannon lost sight of Morrigan and her troops. Her shield shed the stones as they fell, but a large piece of the ceiling collapsed on top of her. Her bracelet, which was already burning her, suddenly glowed bright and reinforced her shield, keeping her safe as the large stone slab split around her protection.

She ran forward, looking for Tin and Fao in the debris, but she couldn't find them. She shouted their names, but there was no answer. The ground began to roil. She didn't want to leave Tin and Fao, but she feared they were dead. And that she had killed them. Her chest tightened. There was nothing more she could do. If she stayed, she would be killed too.

The shield stayed around her as she dodged falling columns and blocks of stone. Rhiannon found Conlaodh just outside the gates in the open yard. He fought for his life, wielding his swords against many foes.

Exhaustion threated Rhiannon. The silver bolt had taken almost all she had left, but she could give a little more.

"*Dóiteán! Dóiteán! Dóiteán!*" she shouted.

Green fire cut, laser-like, around Conlaodh, with more control than she had ever had with her old staff, freeing him of danger and shredding all his foes to ribbons. He looked at Rhiannon and gave her a tired nod. His face was covered with dirt and blood, but he was alive.

They shared a smile, but then his faded and his eyes widened. Rhiannon turned and saw the enemy troops regrouping behind her. She grabbed his arm and pulled him across the drawbridge and out into the field beyond. They had to get free of the Morrigan's soldiers and get everyone back to the Celt's fort, back to safety, which she was sure would be short lived. The Morrigan would no doubt be coming for them, to finish them. Rhiannon must be ready. She had to be able to kill the Morrigan.

Chapter 39

"You know you didn't have to say anything about us sleeping together," Logan said, staring out the window of his tower room at the retreating Celts. Rhiannon was down there somewhere, leaving him. He had to find a way to make it right with her.

Áine raised a brow and looked at him. "What did you expect? That I was going to just let you two kiss and make up?"

Logan's stomach hardened and his throat tightened up. He turned away from the window. "Why are you ruining my life?"

"I don't want anything from you, not anymore, but you are still the Morrigan's precious little investment in the future."

"Then why stand in the way of my leaving?"

"The Morrigan would not be pleased if I let you slip away."

"So you are my guard?"

"In a manner of speaking, yes."

Logan tightened his fists and felt his face flush. "I will find a way to make it right, to get free of the Morrigan and you. You've taken everything from me."

"But we've also given you much."

"I earned what I learned in the caves; that was no gift, and precious little it has done for me."

Áine walked over to the wardrobe and took out a harp.

Logan watched her.

She began to play, and the sound that came from the gold instrument hit Logan like a slap. The music was the same that had lured him away from Rhiannon on that terrible night. The ache of it overwhelmed him.

"It was you that brought me here."

"It wasn't my idea, but yes, it was my magic you found so irresistible." Áine put down the harp and looked over at the closed door, and at the window. She stepped closer to Logan and whispered into his ear. "Perhaps I can make it up to you."

Logan frowned, but lowered his voice as well. "I doubt it."

"There is a way we can help each other. I know what the Queen doesn't—you will never be loyal to her."

"Surely she must see it."

"No, she doesn't. She is blinded by her affection for you."

Logan snorted. "That's affection?"

"If you knew her the way I do, you would know what I'm saying is true."

Áine pursed her lips and narrowed her eyes, considering him. Finally she whispered, "There is one more thing I need from you."

Logan laughed. "You've got to be joking."

Áine frowned and shook her head. "I know a secret that could set you free, could solve all your problems, and only I know it. The Queen would kill me if she found out I know."

Logan swallowed hard, wondering what it could possibly be, but he had been fooled enough to not take the bait. "So, this is the part when I ask what it is, right? I don't care. I don't want anything more to do with your deceptions."

Áine shrugged and leaned in, caressing his neck. Her voice was so low that he barely heard it. "I know how to kill the Morrigan."

Logan eyes widened. Despite himself, he felt a sudden lightness; a feeling of hope filled him. He did his best to hide it from Áine. "If this secret is so powerful, why don't you use it yourself?"

"Because she doesn't trust me."

"And you think, because she is blinded by her affection for me, I could do it?"

"I think you might have the opportunity I will never have."

"And you think I am capable?"

"If it would save your little Druid friend, yes, I think you are."

Logan knew she had a point. "Okay, I'll bite. What is this secret?"

"First, you must promise me that, when I tell you, you will do as I ask."

"I'm not sleeping with you again, if that's what you mean."

"Ha! I wouldn't give you the pleasure." Áine laughed. "No, what I mean is that, when I tell you, I will free you and you will kill the Morrigan."

The thought of freedom and the power to kill Morrigan was a powerful motivation. Logan stared at her, awash in skepticism. "I'm not a murderer."

"Perhaps not, but if it came down to killing Morrigan or letting Rhiannon die, what would you chose?"

"If it came down to that, I would protect Rhiannon."

"That is not so much to ask, is it?"

"What about the Morrigan's displeasure if you let me go?"

"If you agree to our bargain, I will find a way to manage the situation. She will be leaving soon and perhaps we could both disappear for a while. She won't have time to look for us now that she will be attacking the Celts."

Logan crossed his arms, forming a barrier between himself and Áine. "No, I won't do it. I agree, it is tempting, but I don't trust you."

Áine put her hands on her hips and glared at him. "You are *her* son, *so* stubborn."

Logan smiled, feeling a moment's satisfaction at thwarting Áine.

"There is just one more thing…" Her voice trailed off.

Logan clenched his jaw, waiting for it.

"By killing Morrigan, you would not only be protecting Rhiannon, but also would be protecting our son."

The ground dropped away from under Logan. He stared at her. She must be lying. "Let's say I believe you, which I don't. Why would Morrigan hurt her own grandchild?"

"She would see him as a threat; a nearly full blooded sidhe with both of our bloodlines could take her throne."

"No more than you could."

"You underestimate yourself, Logan. Together, we could defeat the Morrigan and rule in her place, and our son after us."

"Why would you risk it?"

"You try serving *her* for a couple thousand years and then you will know."

"I don't like this at all. What if I just tell Morrigan of your plan?"

Áine laughed. "I would deny it convincingly, and you would be expected to travel with her and fight the Celts."

Logan opened his mouth, shook his head, and let out a long breath. "You've thought of everything, I see."

"Yes, including this. If you kill the Morrigan, Rhiannon will be so relieved that, despite your transgressions, she will forgive you and take you back."

Logan's limbs tingled, thinking about the possibility. She offered the most important thing he wanted—getting Rhiannon back—but he still didn't trust her.

"I will *not* promise you anything, but if you tell me this secret, I will do all I can to protect Rhiannon, and if in the process of doing that Morrigan is killed, then you will have what you want."

"Not good enough. I need your promise."

Logan looked at his hands. Áine offered him the key to fixing everything, and he could hardly refuse, but he knew she knew that. "Very well. I promise to protect Rhiannon, and if Morrigan attacks her, I will kill her."

"It's not the same as promising to kill Morrigan." Áine looked at Logan with fiery intensity.

"No, it's not, but it's the best I'm going to give you."

She stepped back from him and put her hands on her hips.

Logan knew it was the right decision, making the offer in the way he had. He would not promise to murder anyone, even the Morrigan, and he wasn't going to be coerced into it. If he could use Áine's knowledge to protect Rhiannon, however, he would do so.

Áine nodded finally. "Very well. I will accept your promise, but if somehow the Morrigan survives the coming battle, I will kill you."

Logan swallowed hard. Áine was a powerful magic user, and she would be a dangerous enemy. "If Morrigan lives, I will probably be dead anyway."

Áine nodded grimly and leaned in. Logan held his breath, not wanting even the sound of his breath to keep him from hearing. Did she really know? Áine's breath brushed his ear. She whispered the secret to the Morrigan's death.

"The Morrigan can be killed in only one way. She must be stabbed with her own sword."

Logan's eyes grew wide, and he clenched his jaw. Could it be that simple?

"How do you know this?"

"When she had the sword made, long ago, the enchantments used bound it to her, in essence making it a part of her. All of her defenses protect her from others but not from herself. The sword will kill her."

Logan fingered his wolf ring and nodded. "I don't think she will just give it up."

"No, she won't, but you can find a way to get it away from her."

Logan put his hands on his hips. "If it means saving Rhiannon, you're damn right I will."

"Good. It is decided. When the time is right I will arrange your escape and you will kill *her*."

Logan tightened his stomach feeling the reality of what he was going to face. Killing the Morrigan, his own mother, would be no easy thing, but for Rhiannon he would do it. Now he would have to learn as much from Nyx as he could to make himself as powerful as he could before his escape. He didn't like colluding with Áine, but perhaps her wits would truly help him. They could beat Morrigan at her own game, using cunning to defeat her.

Chapter 40

Logan followed Áine to a high tower door. He hadn't known how long it would be before Áine released him and was surprised when she came for him the next day. She opened the lock, stepped aside, and signaled for him to exit. His pulse quickened as he faced freedom, even now worried that it was a trap. But it was a risk he must take. He needed to protect Rhiannon.

Áine stepped in front of the opening. "There's just one more thing," she said.

Logan shook his head. "What is it now?"

"When the Morrigan is dead, you must return here."

Logan felt his stomach tighten. "You know the reason I'm doing this is so I can be reunited with Rhiannon, plus I have other business in the world above to finish."

"You can save her, that should be enough. Your problems in the world above no longer matter. This is where you belong."

Logan tensed his body and felt heat building. He pointed at her and shouted, "I'm not coming back here!"

"You are a *fool* to throw away so much for someone who will die so soon, if not at the hands of the Morrigan, then when her short mortal life ends. Let her go, Logan."

"That's not how love works, Áine, at least not for me."

"Love? Oh, come on, Logan. What is love to power? Nothing. A sentiment for fools."

"Think me a fool if you will, but my heart is Rhiannon's."

"What about our child?" said Áine, putting her hand on her hips.

"I don't know that you are pregnant first of all." He opened his mouth and closed it again.

"Yes?" Áine asked.

Logan clenched his jaw as a headache roared to life. "If you really are carrying my child, I will take responsibility for him—or her—even though I was tricked by you."

"You will come back?"

"If I learn you have had our child, I will do my part to see to his or her welfare, but I'm not going to live here with you."

"Not good enough, Logan. You are either with me or not."

Logan squeezed his fists and looked down at his feet, hoping to lower Áine's defenses, then he rushed forward, knocking her to the side and leapt out into the air.

He shifted and in an instant was flying in falcon form, speeding away to freedom. A shriek behind him made him turn; he feared it was Áine. A great golden eagle dove for him. *Damn, it must be her*, he thought, wishing for nothing more than to get away. Instinctively, he turned, caught a thermal, and began to rise higher. His lighter body gave him an advantage in the heights.

The eagle followed him, eyes narrowed and strong wings pulling its heavier body higher and faster than Logan believed possible. He reached the roof of the mound and found a rock ledge. He landed and shifted into his human form.

The eagle landed and shifted back into Áine's shape.

"I don't want to fight you, Áine, if only because you *might* have my child, but I will if you don't let me go."

"You can't win, Logan. Accept it. Give me your word to return, to rule with me and help raise our child, and I'll let you go."

Logan's tensed and heat coursed through his body. "That I can't do," he said.

Logan shifted to wolf form and lunged at Áine. The sidhe woman became a golden mountain lion and took a swipe at Logan, who ducked under the cutting claws. He bit at the neck of the lion but missed. Áine reared, swiping at Logan, forcing him to back up.

His hackles rose as he growled at the cougar. He looked behind him and saw no escape. He shifted back to human form, drew the sword at his hip, and pointed it at the cougar.

"Leictreach!" Logan shouted.

A mass of blue fingers of power struck the lion, knocking her back to the edge of the cliff. Only the long claws dragging on the stone kept Áine from going over the edge.

Logan's heart pounded. In the time before his escape, Nyx had taught him the secret of power words, but he had not needed to use the power words to actually defend himself, and the power that flowed out of him left him breathless. He walked forward, pointing his sword at Áine.

Áine changed back to his sidhe form and glared at Logan. "Stop this! You are making a mistake, we could be so much *together.*"

Logan ignored her plea. *"Leictreach!"*

Áine whipped her sword clear and deflected the energy of the spell with her will. *"Draighean!"* she countered.

Logan blocked, again using what Nyx taught him.

Áine's spell reflected away from Logan and struck the stone above him. Thorns erupted from the rock and spiked tendrils exploded outward. One tendon grabbed his left arm and pulled him from his feet.

Things were happening too fast. He was a novice spellcaster. Áine exceeded him in the use of magic by many years. In fact she surpassed his abilities in every way. Her spell held him tight. Logan shook his head, then realized his sword arm was still free. He closed his eyes and drew in his power.

"Forsa!" Logan shouted. Instead of aiming at Áine, he aimed the force at the thorns holding him.

The thick sinews shredded, and the rock above took a direct hit and crumbled. He fell to the ground. Fist-sized rocks fell on him, but also on Áine. The spell bought him precious seconds.

Logan scrambled to his feet, feeling blood flowing from his forehead.

Áine stood and brushed the dust off. "You can't defeat me, Logan. Accept your fate." She attacked. *"Bogach!"*

The solid stone beneath Logan's feet turned to muck, and he sank down to his knees and then his hips. He fought to pull himself out, when he couldn't do it, he attacked again. This time, Áine blocked the spell. Logan fought the mud, trying to get out, but the more he struggled, the more he sank. The mire solidified again, trapping him in the stone.

Áine put his hands on her hips and smiled. "That should hold you long enough to change your mind."

Logan pounded on the rock, his face hot with frustration. "This is not over. I will get free."

"I seriously doubt it. Change your mind and I will set you free. Otherwise, when I return, I will kill you." Áine shifted to eagle form, dropping away, leaving Logan trapped in the rock far above the floor of the mound. Soon the fight would begin, and he was sunk to his waist in solid rock.

He rubbed the back of his neck, shaking his head. He had to get free. He tried shape-shifting, but the stone adjusted to his every shape, the magic holding him tight.

He thought through everything Nyx had taught him, but nothing worked. He stretched out his hands, splaying them wide and relaxing them. There had to be a way out.

***

Two days passed and Áine didn't return. He still didn't have any idea of how he was going to get free. If he was still here when Áine returned he would not agree to her plan, of that he was sure. He also knew she would hold to her promise and end his life.

His hunger left him a day ago, but his thirst cried out incessantly. His throat ached terribly and his lips had grown crusty with dried skin and saliva. He had tried shapeshifting into something that would help him escape, but the only forms he took stayed firmly anchored in the rock.

He decided to think about the fight again, for the hundredth time, to see if there was anything he could learn from what had happened. He stopped thinking about what Áine had said and focused on her magic. An idea came to him.

What if he could use the same spell Áine used to trap him and loosen the stone enough for him to pull himself out? The thorn vine that had grabbed him from Áine's spell was still there, only a few feet away, still anchored to the ground. If he could loosen the stone, he could pull himself out.

He brought his knuckle to his lip, concentrating. What was the power word? He relived the fight in his imagination, seeing each spell and listening for the exact word.

Was it *Bogach?*

After a moment, he nodded, drew in his power and released it, saying the word.

The stone shimmered and liquefied. Logan swam toward the edge, reaching for the vine, his hand fell short and the mud-like stone only sucked him deeper. Now he was up to his shoulders. "Damn it!"

His chest tightened and his breath came hard. Any deeper, and he'd be unable to breathe at all. His right foot tingled and he wasn't sure why.

He took in a slow breath, filling his lungs, and glanced around him. At least the spell had worked, but he was in worse condition than before. He guessed that his foot tingled because it had come out the other side of the thin shelf of rock.

Logan laughed. His hands shook with the possibility. If he was right, he could use the spell again and sink out through the other side, but if he was wrong, he would sink over his head and be trapped in the stone. He wouldn't be able to cast the spell again to free himself if the stone closed over him.

He bent his head forward, looking at the stone. He drummed his cold fingers on the surface of the cave floor, trying to decide. He knew he couldn't wait. If Áine came back, she would kill him. And he feared that Rhiannon could already be fighting for her life, maybe she was already dead, because he had not been there to save her.

"No!" he shouted. He refused to accept that option.

He had already tried all the spells he knew. No other magic would save him. This was his only option. He took a deep breath, closed his eyes, and shouted the power word.

The stone turned to mud as before, and Logan ducked his head into the mire. He knew he only had a few seconds before it solidified again. He swam down through the gritty muck as hard as he could. He pulled in armfuls of mud, each second promising to entomb him, but he couldn't find the edge. Panic gripped him and he blew out his breath into quagmire. He surged forward, kicking. His face broke through a membrane of muck. He sucked in a breath and got a mouthful of mud but also sweet oxygen. He blinked his eyes, fighting to clear them. He had reached the other side!

The rock solidified as the spell ended and pressed in on his chest, forcing his lungs to contract. He fought the crushing pressure, refusing to give up after such a struggle. His face alone stuck out from the stone. He concentrated and built his power, and then shouted the power word one last time. The granite released him, and he dropped into midair. He tumbled in free fall towards the ground.

Elated, Logan shifted and soared free once again. He floated, letting the relief sink in. A few more inches of rock and he would have been buried alive. But now he was free.

He looked carefully for any sign of Áine and didn't see her.

He wheeled and turned south in the direction the Celts had withdrawn. Toward Rhiannon. Lightness filled him as he soared high above the ground, finally free of the Morrigan's castle, free of Áine, finally free to win Rhiannon back. Áine had been wrong to think he wouldn't find a way free and both she and the Morrigan had been wrong thinking he would ever abandon Rhiannon. Now he just had to find her.

Chapter 41

Garth walked through the standing stones, and looked down from the ridge. A steep slope fell away beneath him, leading to a distant stream. He stood, fingering his torc and taking in the lay of the land.

He believed Cailleach was behind the raven attack, and had probably been among them, shapeshifted into their form. He decided that the Cailleach was acting on the Morrigan's behalf, as her ally and that the Morrigan couldn't let him retrieve the water of the Well. That must be why she wanted him dead. He was confident she would send more creatures to kill him.

He had to be prepared for whatever she would throw at him. His wound had stopped bleeding, but he still felt weaker than he liked to admit. Even at peak strength, he wondered if he'd be a match for the crone. But there was nothing he could do about it now, other than be alert and ready to defend himself.

He needed to focus on finding the Well, the one thing that would save the hawthorne and fortify the mound. Garth hoped he was getting close. He followed the trail through the trees until he drew close to the water. He knew his water skin was dry, and he needed more. The bubbling sound of the stream made his mouth feel even more parched. Amidst the litter of rounded stones and broken trees, a willow grove grew on both sides of the water. The rough bark was gray and wrinkled like an old man.

Willow was the next tree, so Garth knew he was on the right path. Garth's chest tightened, and he rubbed his arms, looking around. The willow was a tree of watery death. What danger would threaten now?

He studied the situation and nothing revealed danger. He walked cautiously to the water's edge, his thirst overriding patience, and squatted down with his water skin. In the glow of the willow trees, he could see down to the bottom of the stream. His breath stopped short.

Bones and skulls reflected the green light of the trees from the bottom of the creek. Garth jumped up and stumbled quickly back from the edge, his water skin still empty. Suddenly, the trees awoke. The long willow stems thrashed, reaching out for him.

His heart raced, and he swallowed hard.

The willows whipped the air.

Do the willows pull people under and drown them?

In his mind, he reached out to the trees, and rather than malice, he detected a sense of duty from them. He didn't know what it meant, but the fact the trees were not blindly aggressive gave him an idea. He searched the ground near the trees and found a downed branch. Green leaves still grew on the long stem, like it had just been blown off the tree not moments before. He picked it up and held it in his shield hand.

From behind, he heard a raven croaking again. It must be the Cailleach he decided. She was answered this time, not by more birds, but by howls.

Wolves.

Garth's hackles rose and his stomach tightened. He needed to get moving and test if his hypothesis was right.

He ran toward the bank, toward the boulders jutting out of the clear stream. The willow branches lashed around him. He jumped to the first stone. The willows flailed at the air but ignored him.

Garth leapt to the next stone, and the trees must have realized something was wrong. They reached out and grabbed at the branch in his hand, tried to rip it free. He dodged the whipping limbs, leaping for the opposite bank. Just as he landed on the far shore, the branch was ripped from his grasp, and the agitated trees entangled him. One branch grabbed his right ankle and pulled hard.

Garth stifled a yell as he fell and landed face first in the dirt. He scrabbled, reaching for a handhold, but found none. The limb pulled him back toward the water. With a mighty groan, he drew Claíomh Solais and struck at the grasping branch, cutting himself free.

More limbs gripped him. The twinning ropes tightened, and he felt his muscles being bruised. Things moved too fast. Water chilled his legs with icy fingers. There were too many roots and branches to cut away.

Panicked, Garth writhed and twisted. He took a breath as the water moved to his waist. The weight of his gear and the strength of the trees would soon have him submerged. He tried frantically to think of something that would let the tree know he meant no harm, something that would calm them. He remembered how he had soothed the vines in the cave where he had won his sword.

What were the kenning words for willow? His mind raced; he couldn't remember. He tried to envision sitting with Brennan by his fire, to remember the night when the Druid had taught him about willow but failed. Desperation forced his focus. In his mind's eye, Brennan finally appeared. His face and his lips formed the sounds of the kennings. Garth heard and remembered.

Lí ambí
Lúth bech
Tosach mela

The words came, almost of their own accord. The words resonated in the air. Garth's windpipe choked closed. He flailed as the water covered his shoulders. He slipped beneath the surface.

He tore at the woody grasp around his neck. The words hadn't worked. Kicking frantically, his feet found a rock to push on. He pushed hard and felt iron resistance. His lungs burned and death loomed.

Willow branches and roots softened and the killing grasp let go.

Garth flexed his leg muscles and wrenched himself free of the willow net. With his last effort he broke the surface and gasped for air.

He was free.

The chant must have finally worked, he thought with gratitude, though almost not soon enough. Weighted down by the armor, he struggled toward the shallower water. Clamoring out of the death trap, he lay still on the shore, breathing hard and letting the relief sink in. "Thank the gods. That was close."

Time to go.

He stood, and his ankle nearly dropped him back to the ground. "Gods damn it!"

He tried using his spear as a crutch and found he could hobble forward, barely. Determined, he climbed the path, struggling with every step to put more distance between him and the coming assault.

He swallowed hard, clenched his jaw, and struggled his way up the steep hill, determined to defeat the next test. Willow was behind him and he was that much closer to his goal. Willow was the fourth ogam tree. The poem had said, "nine will sway." He understood now that it probably meant nine trees.

Five more to go.

* * *

The path climbed toward a high ridge. From behind him, he heard wolves cry out, not in anticipation of an easy kill, but in unexpected pain. He turned toward the cries. The first of the pack had made it to the stream. Far below, the willows entwined and crushed them, pulling them down into the water. The pack drew back and paced along the water's edge, not daring to attempt a crossing. Finally, the Cailleach cawed, and the wolves turned and followed her away from the ford and deeper into the forest.

The willows had bought him some time, but Garth feared that the wolves would soon find another way across.

He turned and hobbled up to the ridge, where a single row of ash trees grew at the top. Beyond the trees, the ground fell away and disappeared into a haze far below. *This must be the next test, to find a way across.*

A chill rose. He kicked a pebble over the edge and shook his head when he heard nothing. Taking the weight off his right ankle and setting his spear on an ash trunk, he leaned on a tree and clutched Claíomh Solais in his shield hand. With the light from the blade, he looked out into the fog, and far beyond, the edge of the canyon cut the gray.

I've got to cross.

Garth sighed heavily and he looked down. A huge boulder was wedged between the walls of the ravine, creating a way to the other side. On top of it lay the broken lattice of woven wood that used to be a bridge.

Garth stepped back from the edge and leaned on the tree.

Can I climb it? The boulder is not too far, but if I slip...

He shifted, brought his hand to his wounded side, and bit his lip. He sheathed his sword, put his shield on his back. He lowered himself to the ground and slid his way down the slope, using his spear to slow his momentum. Small cracks and fissures scraped at him, but also gave him something to hang on to.

His fingers turned white as he clutched at his spear. Every time he pulled it free, he slid a little faster toward the boulder and the gaping canyon under it.

Above him, the Cailleach's cry ripped through the air. He couldn't tell where the sound came from. The chorus of wolves erupted all around him, behind and ahead. His skin prickled.

Sliding faster, he jumped the last crack to land roughly on the slick surface of the boulder. He tried to land on just his good leg, but he failed and his bad ankle took some weight, making him collapse. He slid toward the abyss.

Panic grabbed him. His sweat-soaked hands streaked across the smooth rock, and his left boot caught a crack close to the edge arresting his decent. Garth paused, not daring to move. A sapling grew just above his grasp, jutting up from the rock itself. He lunged for it and it held him.

He climbed away from the edge, breathing heavily, and dared a look behind him. A dark wave of fur and fangs crested the ridge above him.

Garth scrambled across the rock and reached the far wall. He paused, putting hands on hips and catching his breath. He looked up, and glimpsed the top far above him. He tied his spear between his back and his pack and climbed. With his arms and one good leg, he worked himself up. He pulled his weight, arms shaking with the exertion, clinging to the wall and scraping skin until he reached the top.

Another tree test behind him. He was getting closer to the Well and he hoped the ravine would stop the wolves from getting to him. He knew there was no way they could make a climb like he had just finished.

* * *

Garth listened as he shook out his arms. He heard wolves all around him, on *this* side of the ravine. "Damn it! How did they get around the drop?"

It didn't matter. He pulled his spear free and limped forward, rejoining the stone path again. Blowing out a series of short breaths, he fought to hold his courage. The howls made him realize how so many of them were coming for him.

Panic threatened to overwhelm him. The hawthorne would be next, he thought, the tree of terror and despair. A tree the color of bruises; just what he needed when surrounded by wolves.

Ahead, the path split. To the right was a corridor of hawthorne trees, their white flowers in bloom. He looked up the trail, and in the dim light shadows darted amongst the trees.

Looking behind for any sign of the wolves, Garth didn't see anything but his own blood on the ground trailing him. He glanced down. His bandage was gone and his puncture wound leaked blood down his side and leg. He stopped to tend the wound, but a crashing noise ahead interrupted him. The sound grew louder and he abandoned his first aid to face the new threat.

Darkness all around, Garth drew his sword. *To courage I must hold.* He limped forward under the boughs of the hawthorne branches. The trunks grew so close together that there could be no penetrating them. The path led him up a hill, darker with every turn.

He moved his spear, ready to cast at an instant's notice, and brought up his shield. In his left hand, Claíomh Solais glowed brighter.

The path rounded a steep corner, and at the top he found a broad clearing encircled with tall hawthornes. At the back of the grove stood a tall open way framed by monolithic blue gray stones; two up right and a third across the top. Light radiated out from the portal, and his heart thrummed at the sight of the largest black wolf he had ever seen. It crouched in the glare, and behind it stood eight more.

These were not normal wolves.

Immense, they had glowing red eyes and long black teeth. Holding his ground, he waited for a moment to see what they would do. Slowly, they came for him.

Garth steeled himself. He knew he had little chance against nine wolves. He would have to act quickly or die. He needed to better his odds before they closed on him.

He took aim at one of the smaller wolves, hoping he could take it down with one good throw. He aimed and the spear flew, striking true and landing in the ribs of the wolf, which collapsed to the ground. Garth switched Claíomh Solais to his right hand.

The pack closed around him, snarling and baring fangs. Garth attacked the wolf farthest to his left, swinging his glowing blade, and struck the black wolf in the shoulder, cutting through fur, bone and heart. The monster fell.

Another wolf attacked, aiming for Garth's throat. He turned, and the bite landed on his hard alder shield. Garth flung the wolf off, but a terrible weight landed on his back, knocking him to the ground.

He knew if he stayed down, he was a dead man. He rolled and sliced at the air above him, hoping to wound one of the wolves and get out from under the weight. Claíomh Solais caught one wolf in the ribs, and hot blood splattered, spraying Garth and blinding him. The wolves ravaged him, biting and tearing at him while he struggled to get back to his feet and clear his vision. Wolf fangs met thick armor, but some bit flesh.

Garth shouted as blood flowed from his left leg and right arm. He was weakening quickly.

I must get back to my feet.

He punched out with his shield, knocking a wolf off his leg. With great effort, he pulled himself up using one of the hawthorne trees, regaining his feet. His blade crushed the skull of the closest wolf, but two more grabbed his legs and tried to pull him down again. If he went down, he knew he would never get up again.

The power of Claíomh Solais glowed stronger and brighter as he swung down and killed another of the massive wolves. Jaws grabbed at his bad ankle and tripped him yet again. Garth fell to one knee and turned just in time to bring up his shield and defend his throat from a new attacker. He punched out with the shield and caught his assailant in the throat, crushing the larynx. The wolf that had hold of his ankle let go and leapt for the nape of Garth's neck. He impaled the wolf through the lungs with the Druid blade. The creature fell heavily to the ground.

Garth slowly regained his feet. Six dead wolves lay on the ground. The leader was unharmed, and two wolves flanked him. As one, the three attacked.

Garth dropped to one knee and brought up the point of his blade. The top wolf landed on the razor tip and was impaled. The weight of the wolf pulled Garth's sword down, and he couldn't free it before the two remaining beasts attacked him. He raised his shield, blocking one, but the leader grabbed his right arm and bit through the thick leather vambrace, drawing a spout of blood.

Garth screamed, feeling his tendons shred.

He used his shield to pummel the wolf on his left and he rolled that direction, throwing the other wolf off as he rolled free.

On the ground with only the lead wolf left, his sword was lost to him, but, even if it hadn't been, he doubted he could hold it. His right wrist pulsed blood. He staggered to his feet and faced the wolf.

The wolf bared its teeth, looked at its fallen pack, and took a step backward.

"That's right, go!" Garth stood as tall as he could and hid his bleeding hand behind his shield.

The wolf snarled.

Garth waited for the lunge he knew would come, and when it did he hopped back and brought down the metal edge of his shield, chopping. His alder shield was less effective than his sword, but it still had crushing power. The edge caught the leader on a foreleg and Garth heard a satisfying crunch as the bone was broken.

The wolf circled him, limping.

Garth glared at the wolf and shouted. "Come on!"

The wolf turned and looked back.

Garth followed the wolf's gaze and there sat the Cailleach, in raven form, perched on the bluestone trilithon. She croaked loudly, urging the wolf to fight.

The wolf turned back to Garth, lowered its shoulders, and limped off into the trees. The Cailleach screeched, lifted off, and disappeared.

Garth stumbled back and closed his eyes. The wolves were defeated, but the Cailleach was still out there. If he could face her alone, get her to stand and fight him, he could end all these attacks and focus on finishing the tests and get the Water of Life, finally. His body was ravaged, but his determination still firm. He would find the Well and nothing was going to stop him.

Chapter 42

Garth examined his wounds. The wrist was the worst, bleeding freely. He took some herbs from his pack and tore a strip of linen from his tunic. He cleaned his wounds as best he could, pressed dried flowers to his wrist, and did the same with his left thigh. He tried to get water from his skin before he remembered it was empty. He took a breath and thought about what to do.

He had trapped the ravens and killed most of the wolves. He knew now that he must kill the Cailleach. He needed to get her to stand and fight. He knew he didn't have much left in him, so he needed to kill her before she summoned more creatures to attack. Then he could finish the tests and get to the Well. Garth knew he must keep moving.

He stood on weak legs and swallowed hard, feeling the terrible dryness in his mouth.

If I don't get water soon...

He wiped black blood from his sword and sheathed it with his left hand. He limped toward the stone portal across the grove. When he reached it, he leaned on the cool stone and looked beyond. A path lined with oak trees led into the forest.

Garth staggered wearily into the oak corridor. Up ahead, the line of trees opened up into a ring. He entered the grove and peered up. The oaks towered over him, the gray bark cracked and furrowed from the long years of their lives. Green light glowed softly all around. The ground was covered with acorns and leaves, and in the center sat a huge silver cauldron. The metal gleamed with designs of animals, plants, and knot work.

Garth blinked and looked again. He shuffled closer and looked inside the container.

Was this the oak test?

He grabbed a stick from the ground and touched it to the surface of the liquid inside. When he pulled it free, a clear drop fell from the tip back into the basin. Tucking his gloves into his belt, he licked his dry lips and tried to think about why the water would be here. Finally, his need outweighed his caution. He cupped his hand and lowered it into the cauldron, the liquid cool against his skin. In his hand, he saw clear water.

Carefully, he brought it to his lips then stopped. "Gods of my people, I offer you this libation in thanks for your blessings," he said and poured the water on the ground.

The oaks stirred and creaked. Garth looked around, startled. Had the trees been watching him? After what he had seen with the wolves at the willow grove, he had new respect for what angry trees could do. He slowed his breath and tried to connect to the grove. He sensed satisfaction.

He reached in for another handful, and the cool, clean water crossed his lips and soaked into his mouth before he swallowed it. His swollen tongue slowly softened as he brought his palms to his eyes, sank to his knees, and took another drink.

Garth shrugged off his pack and again filled his palms with water. He filled his water skins and drank deeply. Closing his eyes in relief, he slumped forward, forehead in hand.

The cursed croaking of the Cailleach broke the silence.

Garth looked around, heart racing, hoping to finally face Cailleach, but she did not come.

He gathered his things and hurried as best he could out from the oak grove, toward the sound and closer he hoped to the well. He hurried along a short path ahead, which led to holly trees with abundant sharp, glossy leaves and red berries. He remembered Rhiannon saying holly trees represented mastery and wondered what challenge he faced next.

He was in no shape to prove mastery of anything. But he knew that a warrior doesn't have the luxury of facing challenges only when rested and whole in body, he must face what confronts in him in whatever condition he is.

At the entrance to the grove, he saw her. The Cailleach, finally come alone to face him. She stood before him in her crone guise, a wicked dagger in one hand and her other hand clenched into a fist. She wore all black with tattered ragged edges. Her face lined and bitter, with one eye drooped low over a bristled cheek.

"Look at you. *Pathetic*," she croaked, much like a raven's voice. "You can barely stand, and I bet you can't even hold your sword after what my wolves did to you."

Anger warmed Garth's face. "Come and see just how much life I have left."

"A brave boast for one about to die," she said, showing her yellowed teeth.

"Before I kill you, I want to know why."

"Why?" The Cailleach cackled. "It's simple. The Morrigan sent me to track you. I know of your plan to save your *cursed* tree, and I am here to make sure it doesn't happen. With your death, hope dies for your pathetic race. But more than that, you disgust me. I'd kill you just for my own satisfaction, to snuff your existence. So proud and noble, and never embracing the darkness. You don't deserve the air you breathe, vain false idiot."

Garth knew better than to make the fight personal. Her insults would not unbalance him. Her words confirmed his suspicion about her motives. It mattered not though, she must die for the deaths of his men regardless of other considerations. "Let us end this." Garth pulled Claíomh Solais free, held it steady in his *left* hand, and moved forward.

The Cailleach shifted, her body morphing to a black wolf. She bared her fangs and bit at Garth's bad ankle. He dropped to his left knee and brought his shield across his body, striking the canine skull with force and defending his injury. The wolf staggered back. Garth wished he could close in on her, but his ankle wouldn't hold.

The Cailleach-wolf circled, then charged, jumping at his shield. He turned, sliced his blade out, and took a step back. The blade grazed ribs, drawing fist blood, and the wolf landed to Garth's right.

Sweat dripped from his brow. He took careful breaths and waited for the next attack. With his mobility gone, he had little choice but to use defensive tactics.

The Cailleach shifted again, taking on her crone aspect, and glared at him. She brought a hand to her ribs and it came away red. "You are going to pay for that."

"I'm waiting," said Garth grimly.

The crone raised her hands, and the air grew still. "*Camanfa!*"

A blast of wind raced from the goddess's hands and swirled

around the Celt, picking up first leaves, then twigs, and finally rocks. The whirlwind moved faster and faster. Garth covered his face with his shield and held Claíomh Solais up as a talisman against the spell.

After a few seconds, he realized that all was still. Mouth dry, he swallowed hard and lowered his shield. The Claíomh Solais glowed brightly in his hand. A golden aura surrounded him, and the lacerating wind didn't touch him.

Garth smiled. The sword had saved him again.

The Cailleach screamed her frustration and the wind died.

Garth grinned at her. "Is that all you've got, Cailleach?"

The hag yelled and pulled a handful of something from a pouch at her waist. She raised her left hand and threw a cloud of black powder at his face. Garth turned his head to shield his eyes, but not fast enough.

Terrible pain burned, and darkness enveloped him. He swung his blade in a broad arc while trying to blink away the dust.

The Cailleach's blade serrated his thigh, cutting through his armor.

The slice burned, followed by the warm rush of blood.

Grimacing, Garth pivoted and chopped down with his blade, but he met only air.

"The darkness is closing in on you. It won't be long now."

He swayed on his feet and knew she was right. He had to take her down now, but how? He backed up, hoping trees waited behind him.

"I'm going to enjoy this," hissed the Cailleach.

A blade carved his left thigh again, right above the other wound, cutting through leather and skin. Garth bit down hard at the sharpness of it. He dropped down onto his right shin and punched with his shield, hoping to catch her with its hard edge or at least knock her back. Again he found only air.

"Too slow," laughed the hag.

Garth leaned forward, taking in every stir of wind, every creak of branches. If he couldn't see, he had to be able to hear her coming.

Without warning, her blades double cut his left leg.

He screamed in terror and pain as he collapsed and fell back into a holly tree.

"I could end you now, but I'm enjoying myself too much.

What should I take away next..."

Garth's whole body shook. His breath rasped in his throat, and he shook his head in defiance. His heart beat irregularly from the blood loss.

From his desperation, an idea came to him. New strength blazed through his body.

With all the will he had left, he reached out to the trees around him and felt a tingle of connection. Reverently, he asked for help.

To his right, a branch snapped. He crouched behind his shield and stabbed blindly at the air.

"You'll have to do better than that," cackled the hag.

The voice sounded close, and this time, he could tell its direction. He concentrated his will, and through the power of Claíomh Solais, he willed the trees to attack.

A slashing storm of whipping branches erupted around him. Garth heard a scream as the Cailleach was caught in the fury. He blinked as a pinprick of light appeared, then a narrow tunnel of light.

Garth took a deep breath, trying to calm his body and keep it from going into shock. His vision cleared enough for him to see that tree roots had grabbed the Cailleach's feet. She swatted fiercely at the thick branches.

One branch and another caught Cailleach's wrist, pulling and stretching her away from the ground where her feet were firmly tangled. A scream of pain tore from her. She tried to shift to her raven form, arms turning to wings, feet to talons, but the tree held her fast. Black feathers filled the air.

Garth crawled forward, with his sword gleaming. "It is done, Cailleach," he said as he raised Claíomh Solais.

"Never!" she shouted.

He struggled to his knees to strike the killing blow, but his left leg wouldn't hold him, and with the sword in his left hand, he couldn't swing. Blinding pain brought stars to his vision.

Grimacing, he closed his eyes and poured all that he had left into the magic. He drew on his deep reserves, the love he carried from his family, his clan, his race. He focused his outrage and his fury, poured it all into the attack.

Cailleach's eyes opened wide. The holly trees pulled at her, and tendons shredded, cartilage cracked. Muscles stretched and popped as they came apart. The Cailleach screamed in pain and frustration, cursing him. "Damn you, Garth, may you die a fool's death far from your loved ones." Her words shattered into an incompressible scream of agony and her body ripped apart into a hundred pieces. Blood spattered the foliage, and roots pulled and drank what was left of Cailleach back into the earth leaving nothing but darkened soil behind.

Stunned and spent, Garth collapsed. He lay heavily on the ground, staring up at the swaying trees. He took a deep breath and let it go.

The Cailleach was dead.

Chapter 43

Garth blinked, too numb and exhausted to move. It felt like every inch of his body was ravaged. Anxiety washed over him. *If I don't get up, I will die. Only the Well can heal me.*

Garth crawled slowly clear of the holly ring, trailing blood behind him. His goal was close now; he only needed to hold on a little longer. Wincing, he rounded a corner and rubbed his eyes at an astounding sight. After everything he had been through, he'd found the Well.

Gray stones jutted up from the forest floor, framing the trail and extending in a broad circle. Trees of all kinds grew with wild abandon amidst the rocks, creating a natural grotto. Closer in, nine hazel trees ringed the edge. Golden light radiated out from them, like nine suns.

The rays fell on a pool of water in the center, sending an aura of reflected gold into the green of the trees. The deep green pool rippled in small waves that lapped at smooth stones at the edge. Like adding fragrance to jewels, the sight was beauty on beauty and beyond anything Garth could have possibly imagined.

Flush with joy, he sat back on his right leg again and let out a huge breath. With a slow smile, he brought a hand to his heart and looked up in gratitude. "Thank the gods."

Garth looked closer at the pool. In the depths, something moved. A single hazelnut fell from one of the trees, and before it met the water, a huge salmon leaped, caught the nut, and disappeared back into the depths. Five glittering streams flowed from the pool and poured over rounded stones of many hues— amber, jade and granite—before disappearing into the dense forest beyond.

He breathed in the scent of loam, clean water, and the sweet fragrance of gardenias and white roses that grew around the pool. Their open blooms dotted the green like stars. Using his spear, he pulled himself up and took in a deep breath.

Garth took a step forward. From out of the dense growth of trees, a man appeared. With long brown hair and a beard that grew past his belt, he wore the green robes of a Druid. Green light glowed from him.

"I am Nechtan, the guardian of this place."

Garth gasped and lowered his eyes out of respect. He knew the legend of Nechtan and realized he was in the presence of one of the gods. "Greetings, lord. My name is Garth, and I've traveled through many hardships to reach this sacred place."

"Welcome, Garth."

"I ask your permission to drink and to take away some water."

Nechtan cast a steady gaze upon Garth and frowned. "I cannot agree. I alone may approach the Well of Wisdom."

"I would ask, for the sake of my people, that an exception be made this one time."

Nechtan eyes shone with bright intensity. "There is one way."

"My lord, may I humbly ask what it is?"

"I will question you, and if I am satisfied with your answers you will be given what you ask. But if you fail, your life will be forfeit."

"Without the water, I will die anyway," Garth said. "Very well, ask your questions."

Nechtan nodded solemnly. "Young man of instruction, where did you come from?"

Garth started to answer that he came from the Celtic fort, but bit back his words. There was a trap here. The question was too simple, and the language too formal.

He remembered Brennan telling him a story about two Druids, an older and a younger, and a series of questions to prove the younger Druid's worth. The dialogue started with Nechtan's very words. He thought back hard, seeing Brennan sitting by the fire. It was so hard to stay conscious, much less concentrate, but the words came to him.

"This is not difficult. From the heel of a sage, from a confluence of wisdom, from perfection's goodness." Garth paused, feeling weak.

Nechtan put up his hand. "A moment's rest, perhaps?"

Garth nodded and took a draw from his skin. "From the brilliance of the rising sun, from hazel trees, from poetic art…"

He trailed off again.

Nechtan waited.

The water hit Garth's stomach, and he felt like he was going vomit, but he fought it down and continued. "From circuits of splendor, through which the true is measured according to excellence in which the untruth is placed, through which the colors are seen, through which poems are renewed. And you, my elder, where did you come from?"

Garth watched Nechtan's expression. He knew he had repeated word for word what Brennan had taught him. In fact, Brennan insisted he memorize it long ago, but he wasn't sure if he told Nechtan what he wanted to hear.

"This is not difficult," Nechtan answered. "Along the columns of age, along the rivers of Leinster, along the magic hill of my wife, along the forearm of the wife of Nuada, along the land of the sun, along the dwelling place of the moon, along the umbilical cord of the young man."

Garth's skin prickled. He had gotten it right.

"What is your name?"

Garth knew this part too, and his confidence grew. "This is not difficult: very small, very big, very firm, very brilliant, ardor of fire. Fire of words. Sound of knowledge. Source of wealth. Sword of singing, direct art, with the bitterness of fire. And you, my elder, what is your name?"

Nechtan nodded. "It is clear to me you know the tale and are no stranger to poetry. I have one final question."

Garth clenched his jaw and looked at the god.

Nechtan paused and took a breath. "What are the names of each of the nine hazel trees that surround my well?"

Garth felt his eyes stretch wide.

I've never heard them named.

He looked at his feet, at his blood-stained boots, and felt his confidence draining away into the soil at his feet.

"What are the names?" Nechtan demanded.

Garth heard the wind blow through the hazels.

"A moment, I ask, Lord."

Garth knew Brennan had never taught him this. He knew

the names of the five sacred trees. He knew all the ogam songs. But *this,* he did not know. Garth lowered his chin to his chest and shook his head.

After all I've been through, to come this far and to be defeated with such a simple question.

The hazels swayed and a wind rustled their leaves. He heard something.

Was it a name? Could it be? Did the sound come from the trees themselves?

Garth looked up and spoke the word. "Sall is the first one."

Nechtan nodded. "And what are the rest of them?"

He listened to the trees again, and miraculously, they whispered three more. *"Fall, Fufall and Finnam,"* he said reverently.

He sent his thoughts to the hazels. *Thank you, mighty ones. Please share the rest of your names.*

The trees answered, and Garth spoke two more. *"Fonnam, Fofhudell,"*

Oh generous trees, what are the last three?

There is a price…

Garth swallowed and pursed his lips. *Name it, wise ones.*

You must take his place and become the new guardian.

The whisper faded, and Garth recoiled as if he had been struck. *I must return or none of this will matter*, he said to the hazels.

Nechtan pulled his sword free and looked at Garth. "What are the last three?" he demanded.

The trees swayed. *What you say is true. With a promise to return alone, we will agree. Take one year and a day to honor your word, or suffer the wrath of the trees.*

But what of my wife? My family?

Choose now.

Garth made a curt nod and dread descended on him. A life in this place, alone, with no Deirdre, no Wil, no tribe, was a terrible sacrifice. But without consenting, they would all be dead anyway.

He took a deep breath and let it out slowly. *I accept your terms.*

The trees swayed, the leaves fluttered, and finally a whisper came to him. He spoke the final names.

"Cru, Crinnam, and Cruanblae."

Nechtan sheathed his sword.

A terrible weight settled on Garth. Yes, he would live, and so would his people, if he made his way home in time. But those he loved most would be far from him until the end of his days.

"You have the blessings of the grove. None but the hazels can reveal their names. I am pleased with you."

"They have agreed to let me drink, but I must return and take your place."

Nechtan took in a breath and let it out slowly. "It has been countless years…"

"What of your family?"

"They cannot approach this place."

Garth swallowed. His throat tightened. "It is as I feared."

"Take what you will and return here again."

Garth walked forward with Nechtan's help, to the wide stone lip surrounding the forest pool. Covered with ogam script, all the trees were represented. The stone was aged and warm to the touch, and he pulled himself to the brink.

With a shaking hand, he took a palmful of water. He looked into his cupped hand and drank the luminous liquid. Cool and sweet, it trickled down his parched throat like the first drink after a month of dust. It soaked into every part of him.

Garth felt his skin began to knit back to together, closing off the many cuts and punctures. The water restored his blood, which flowed strong again, and refreshed his sluggish heart. His ankle tendons throbbed as the sacred water healed them. His side and wrist, his shredded thigh, all of him blazed with fire. He dropped to his knees and closed his eyes, enduring the healing blessing.

When he opened them, Nechtan was gone, but he spoke from somewhere hidden. "Remember your promise. Return in a year and a day."

Heart heavy, he nodded. "I will honor my word and return as I have promised."

Garth took off his backpack and found the crystal vial he brought for just this purpose. He unstopped it, put the container under the water, and watched the air bubbles escape as it was filled. The water glowed inside the flask as he wrapped it in heavy cloth and put it away in his pack.

Whole again, he rose, feeling greatly restored. He took one last look at the Well of Wisdom. The glowing light danced in the leaves of the hazels, each tree radiating healing and beauty. The green was so bright, the light made it nearly yellow. He wondered what tales those trees could tell. He took a deep breath, filling his lungs with the sweetness of the place. He turned and left the pool behind him.

The Cailleach was dead and he had succeeded, but he would have to return to the Well of Wisdom, to live out the rest of his days beside it. The one thing he wanted most was to save his family. They could now be saved, but he would have to live without them.

Now the fate of all rested on him bringing the water back in time to save the tree. With strong strides, Garth headed for home.

Chapter 44

Rhiannon and Bran lead the refugees across the plains and forest. There had been no pursuit from Morrigan's forces, but they knew it was only a matter of time. Rhiannon's thoughts preoccupied her. She felt powerless to make sense of her confrontation with Logan. That he was her archenemy's son was one thing; that he admitted to sleeping with a sidhe was quite another. One was out of his control and the other—she wanted to believe his words that he'd been tricked, but the violation wounded her deeply.

After many days, they reached the Celtic fort. She walked through the open gates to cheers from the guards. She smiled with relief, pushing her personal thoughts aside and setting her mind on finding Brennan. She needed answers; they had to be prepared for Morrigan's counterattack.

Rhiannon threaded her way through the throngs of people and finally found Brennan inside his roundhouse. A sudden lightness filled her at the sight of her beloved uncle. She hugged him tightly.

When she pulled back, Brennan smiled at her. "I knew you were alive," he said, "despite what Flit said."

"So Flit made it back. That is good. Many others were not so lucky. We lost Tin and Fao, as well as Goban and Eamonn."

Brennan shook his head sadly. Rhiannon put a hand on his shoulder to comfort him. "It is a heavy loss," he said in a low voice.

"There is more." Rhiannon knew they had no time to dwell on what they could not change. "Aron made it back, but he has been afflicted with some kind of undead disease."

"Tell me what happened."

Rhiannon told Brennan about the fight with the wraith.

"I will see to Aron as soon as we are done. Where is he

now?"

"He's talking with the king about where to find housing, food, and clothes for all the people that followed us here. Some are Celts and can return to their families, but others are overlanders. We'll need to figure out what to do with them. We did rescue Nemain, Aron's wife."

"Ah, that is good news. It will give the people hope to see her again. We need that now."

"We also need to decide what to do with this." Rhiannon pulled out the Faillean Duir, which she had kept concealed behind her.

Brennan looked at it with reverence. "The Arch Druid's staff," he said, eyes wide. "I never thought to see this again in my lifetime. You did it."

Rhiannon smiled and told him the tale of finding it in the high tower and fighting the Morrigan.

"Your success against Morrigan proves both your ability and the power of the staff. The staff is yours. You've earned it."

Rhiannon started to protest, but Brennan shook his head. "Truly, only one who is destined to be the next Arch Druid could have accomplished such a task. The Arch Druid is not chosen by seniority, but by strength."

Rhiannon suddenly had difficulty breathing. Her ears rang. She took a seat across from Brennan and spoke in a quaking voice. "I owe it all to you, Brennan. Without your care and instruction, it never would have been possible."

"The power of the staff will be of great service in the coming days, I am sure."

Rhiannon warmed her hands with the fire and let the weight of Brennan's words sink in. She would be the next Arch Druid; in charge of all who came after her. It was her destiny to take a place of leadership.

Darker thoughts settled, and she gave her head a hard shake. That was the future, if there was a future. For now, she had more pressing matters to consider.

"Is it true Logan is Morrigan's son?"

"So he told you."

Rhiannon stood and put her hands on her hips. "Why didn't *you* tell me?"

Brennan raised his palms. "I had hoped we would capture

him and keep him from her. He was not like her in spirit, and I hoped we could have won him to our cause."

Rhiannon's throat closed. "I don't care about *that*," she said, pointing a forceful finger at him. "I was going to *marry* him and you never told me?"

"I thought that, if the two of you did get married, maybe we could end this war with Morrigan's people. I didn't want you to feel pressured, despite what it might mean for our people. I hoped you would be a bridge to a lasting peace."

"You still could have told me," said Rhiannon.

"Don't look at it that way. I was doing what I thought was right for all of us, yourself included. I didn't bring you two together. You chose to have him move in with you and accept his marriage proposal despite me telling you to wait."

Rhiannon rubbed at the back of her neck. "But I didn't know who he was then."

"And yet somehow you were drawn together."

"It seems the gods wanted us to meet."

"Yes, I believe that is true."

Rhiannon sat back down and stared into the fire, eyes stinging. "But if that is so, they why has he chosen to abandon me?"

"Is that what he said?"

Rhiannon nodded, then shook her head. "Yes—no—I don't know. He would not come with me. And it was clear he had chosen another path." She wiped a tear away, firmed her jaw, and stood. "But that is behind. There must be no more secrets between us. I'm no longer a child. I'm a Druid like you.

"I've done what I thought was right to protect you. I will be honest, there is one more secret I've kept from you."

Rhiannon raised a brow. "What is it?"

"You have more at stake here than you know. Your mother was from this place, and your father too."

Rhiannon's mouth fell open and her heart raced. "What? How is that possible?"

"When you were born, your mother decided to take you to the world above to keep you safe. She didn't want to do it, but she understood the importance of keeping you safe despite the grief it would cause. We suspected your Druid gift and believed that one day your power could make all the difference in keeping the hawthorne safe."

Rhiannon's head swam, and she clutched the Faillean Duir to steady herself. "But I was told my father left us when I was born."

"Well, he wasn't the one who left. Your mother and you left him here."

Rhiannon took a step back, her blood rushing. "Is he still here?" she asked, her voice shaking.

"Yes." Brennan paused, as if weighing the right words to use. "He is the king."

Rhiannon pressed her palms to her cheeks, on the verge of hysterical laughter. She took a deep breath and finally smiled. "King Conor is my Father?"

"Yes, and Bran, Aron, and Garth are your brothers."

Rhiannon pressed a hand to her chest. Euphoria filled her. She wasn't an orphan anymore and she had three brothers. The sensation stole her breath and made the room feel like it was closing in on her. It was so much to take in.

She sat down and looked up at Brennan. "It is really true? I can't believe it."

"It's true, but no one but us knows it. The king knows now—I told him after you left—but your brothers don't know."

Rhiannon smiled widely, stood, and hugged Brennan.

"It must be our secret for now," he said.

Her happiness deflated. "But why can't we tell?"

"If the Morrigan is defeated and Logan is restored to you, there will still be a chance for a lasting peace. A marriage between the royal bloods of both groups would join our peoples, but it would have to be handled delicately. I ask you to trust me to handle it."

She sighed. "Ok, Brennan, but I don't see how it could ever happen. Logan has chosen to stay with Morrigan, and he has been unfaithful to me. There is no future for the two of us."

"Nonetheless, we must keep this secret until all is played out. Much may happen to change things. Unless Garth returns with the water, we will be doing little more than slowing the Morrigan down, even with the Faillean Duir."

Rhiannon swallowed hard. A sudden realization hit her. She was already invested in this fight but now she had even more a stake. These Celts were *her* people. The king, her father; the princes, her brothers; and now Morrigan was coming to kill them all.

She nodded, understanding Brennan's point. "Let's go find Aron," she said. "We will need us all to be in fighting shape."

* * *

Rhiannon and Brennan emerged from the roundhouse. A crowd of people pushed through the streets leading toward the mead hall.

"What's going on?" Rhiannon asked.

"A meeting must have been called. We should go. We will find Aron there and see what has happened."

She fidgeted with her awen pendant and wondered what was so important that everyone in the fort rushed to the hall. She doubted it was good news. She rubbed her arms and looked around at the sea of people, *her* people. Some were dressed in Celtic finery with gold jewelry and clean clothes, but many were the refugees she had helped rescue, all of whom wore proud faces and determined glances even if their clothes were tattered and dirty.

Inside the hall, Brennan parted the crowd and Rhiannon followed. Her uncle mounted the steps to stand by the king.

When Rhiannon hesitated to join them, Brennan turned and spoke to her. "You have earned your place here. Come and join us."

She looked at the king with new eyes. He smiled at her. It was all she could do to stop herself from racing up to him and hugging him. She looked at his eyes and his hair color—yes she could see herself in him.

He was her father. The man she thought barely existed, whom she always believed had abandoned her. Worry tempered her exuberance, however. To have gained so much and then have it threatened was terrible.

Rhiannon climbed to the dais and stood next to Brennan. She looked through the gathering for Aron but didn't see him. Before long, a haggard soldier parted the crowd and approached the throne.

"I have news of Morrigan's troops. May I address the hall?"

Conor nodded.

"I bear ill news. My men and I were out scouting this morning when we came upon a high ridge with a view to the north.

We found a patrol of Morrigan's soldiers almost on top us. And beyond them, the whole of Morrigan's army. We tried to escape unnoticed but without success. We retreated but lost many good men on our way to report that Morrigan will be here soon—before the light wanes."

Rhiannon's stomach clenched into a knot, and she shifted her feet uneasily. She drew in deep breaths, trying to control her anxiety. The confrontation with Morrigan that she both dreaded and hoped for was now imminent. She had won the staff and now had more power than she ever thought possible. But would it be enough?

The crowd mirrored her sentiment, shouting and making their anger and fear known.

The king raised his hand, and the hall fell quiet. "That is ill news," he said. "You have made a heavy sacrifice, but your warning may save many lives. Thank you, Ardanach."

"We must call in allies and all our troops, and prepare to fight," counseled Brennan. "We must be ready to withstand Morrigan's wrath until Garth returns."

"Are you sure of this?" asked Bran. "We have many men scattered throughout the mound making the way safe for Garth's return. Father, we need to keep them in the field."

The king looked at Brennan then back at Bran. "I agree with Brennan, Bran," he said. "Garth is resourceful, he will find a way. We can't weaken our defenses by hundreds on the chance that he will need them."

Bran's face reddened, putting hands on hips. "I know I have often spoken against the quest for the Well, but now that we've committed to it, I think we need to see it through. We can't leave Garth alone. Do you take the counsel of your Druid over that of your son and heir?"

The king stared hard at Bran, vein pulsing in his forehead. "There is no way we can know what route Garth will take, and we can't have enough men in the field to cover all the approaches. Garth will have to make his own way, though I wish it were otherwise. And yes I will take Brennan's view on this. As the king, I must listen to many voices and then *I* choose what to do. Listening to wise counsel is something *you* need to learn, Bran, *if* you will ever be king."

Bran opened his mouth and closed it again, frowning.

"Surely a few men can be spared to aid Garth. Perhaps just one troop?" asked Aron from near the back of the hall.

Rhiannon smiled at finally spotting him.

The king took a breath and brought a hand to his torc. "Very well, one troop may stay in the field on the off chance they find Garth. Aron, you decide who it should be."

"Very well, Father. I will," he said with a nod.

Rhiannon looked at her brother, the one who had traveled with her through so many dangers, and felt great love for him. She needed to try and heal his arm as soon as the meeting was over.

The king turned his attention back to the crowd. "Glaisne, send out riders to summon the host of men back to the fort. Accalon, see that food is brought in for a siege, and get men to check the walls for weak places. There can be no chink in our armor. Brennan, summon what friendly sidhe will aid us. Bran, see to it that the able-bodied among our returned kin are armed and fed."

Rhiannon turned to the king. "Your majesty, strength of walls and of arms will not be enough. We must use cunning to slow down Morrigan. Everything hangs on Garth's return. What he needs is time."

"What do you suggest?"

"Meet her at the river. Use the river crossing to slow her down. Don't let her march right to the gates unimpeded."

Conor brought his hand to his chin and stroked his beard. "A good idea, but we are too few, and our walls give us the protection we will need. We will fight from a protected place and not dilute our strength."

Rhiannon gave a curt nod. She trusted her father's judgment.

"The King has spoken," said Brennan. "Let us make haste to prepare for the attack."

She looked for Aron again and kept her eye on him as the crowd dispersed. She could help first of all by taking care of Aron's arm. Then she would see what else she could do to help the defense of the fort.

Chapter 45

The crowd quickly dispersed. Rhiannon and Brennan worked their way over to Aron, who was talking to Glaisne about which men to leave in the field. When Aron was finished, he nodded to them and descended the steps of the hall.

"Aron, I'd like to have Brennan take a look at your arm," Rhiannon called.

Aron looked at her grimly and nodded. "I'd be grateful for anything you can do, but I suspect it's nothing that the next few days won't take care of."

Rhiannon frowned. "Well, let's hope it doesn't come to that," she said. "Come back with me to Brennan's house."

Aron nodded and followed them.

Inside the roundhouse, he took a seat on a stool near the fire and rolled up his sleeve to show Brennan the wound. Rhiannon's breath caught in her throat. The arm looked worse than before. The skin was not only white, but now it was rotting.

"I've never seen anything like this before," said Brennan.

Her chest tightened. She hoped that Brennan would at least be able to diagnose Aron's condition. If Brennan couldn't help, what could she do? He studied it for many minutes, prodding it with different spells, but nothing changed.

"I'm sorry, Aron," he said, "but I know of no herb or stone to use."

"It is as I feared. The wraith has cursed me, but at least we set our people free. It's a small price to pay to save so many."

"The only option I can see is to take off your arm," said Brennan seriously.

Aron blanched and he looked down.

Rhiannon brought her hand to her lips, thinking. "Wait, I have an idea," she said. "You said the wraith cursed you, which means it's not a disease as we would normally think of it. Whatever created the wraith used a curse to make it live when it should have been dead long ago. It's an aberration of nature, and as such it is outside our normal healing powers."

Aron nodded. "But how does that help?"

Rhiannon looked over at Brennan. "The Faillean Duir is ancient, and in fact, was part of the great world tree when the world was made. So it is also outside of nature in a way, because the natural world as we know it did not yet exist when it was created."

Brennan raised a brow and nodded for her to continue.

"The Faillean Duir draws on power that underlies nature, and with it I might be able to heal you. Though it's not really a healing. It's more of a remaking," said Rhiannon.

"So instead of trying to knit things back together, you will rebuild my arm from the ground up?" Aron asked.

"That is what I was thinking," she said.

Brennan frowned. "What you said makes sense, Rhiannon, but nothing like that has ever been tried before. You are talking about working with the very forces of creation themselves, not just drawing on the Nwyfre that already exists."

"I know, Brennan, but I might be able to make it work."

"Or it could go terribly wrong," he said. "Toying with that kind of power can have dire consequences."

"I'm willing to bear the responsibility."

Brennan gave her a small smile. "You never cease to amaze me, Rhiannon. Now you are pioneering a new kind of magic."

"Let's try it," said Aron.

"It's going to hurt. A lot," said Rhiannon honestly. As she spoke, her hands tingled and her mouth went dry. What if she failed? What if she killed him? What if she killed her own brother?

"It can't be worse than chopping it off though, right? So let's do it." Aron rolled his shoulders.

"Well, it actually it might be worse, and I'm not sure if it will work," said Rhiannon.

Aron swallowed hard and paused. "Maybe we should wait until the battle is over. Despite what it looks like, I can still fight with it," he said.

"I don't blame you for wanting to wait. I don't like it either." Rhiannon looked him in the eye. "There is something else.

I'm afraid if it spreads much more you could become a wraith yourself. At the moment, the curse is only in your arm, but I fear soon it will travel into your shoulder and chest, and it will be too late. I don't want to take the chance that you never recover from this. If I fail, we still have a chance to take the arm and pray the curse will go no farther."

Aron looked at his hands and raised his eyes slowly. He said nothing.

"We have to do this, Aron. I wish there was another way. It's either amputate it, or use the Faillean Duir."

He took a deep breath and let it out slowly. "I know you can do this, Rhiannon. I trust you. Use the magic."

Rhiannon's stomach churned, and she shoved down her worries. Rubbing her arms as if a sudden chill embraced her, she looked over at Brennan.

He nodded, and Rhiannon picked up the staff. Her hands grew cold at the thought of what she was about to attempt. "You better lay down," she said.

When Aron was ready, Rhiannon planted the staff in the ground and drew in a deep breath. Instead of drawing in power from the surrounding Nwyfre, she envisioned the staff reconnecting with the world tree, the primordial power. She reached beyond time and space to the place of beginnings, the place of non-dual awareness. With the help of the staff, she made contact with the world tree, the mighty ash grown so long ago.

In response, silver roots grew out of the staff and disappeared down into the earth. Silver branches spread out from the top of the staff, and they climbed upward to the roof of the roundhouse and grew around until Brennan's house was part of a great tree.

Rhiannon's eyes opened wide, and she sucked in a quick breath at the sight.

From the tree came a sound, a subtle hum, and the room vibrated with it. Ceramic jars fell from their shelves and cracked on the floor, bundles of herbs swayed, and the fire crackled noisily.

Her knees went weak, and her body tingled all over. Power flowed around her and through her. She forced herself to concentrate, to remember what she was trying to do. She firmed her jaw and focused.

Rhiannon took the silver light into her body through the

staff, and then, with her left hand still on the Faillean Duir, she reached out and put her right hand on Aron's arm.

She let the light flow up and cover the plagued part of his arm, and she unleashed the full power of the tree. Aron's arm dissolved into a mist and was gone.

Aron shouted with the shock of it.

Brennan held him down as best he could. "Aron, you have to stay still or this won't work," he shouted above the roaring.

Aron grimaced, grabbed the bed with his right hand, and held still.

"Hurry, Rhiannon," shouted Brennan,

She focused on bringing in the intelligence of the tree, the intelligence of the universe, and let it work on the subtle energy where Aron's left arm had once been. Aron bit down hard, and sweat poured down his face. Blood flowed from the stump of his arm, pooling on the bed.

It's not working, Rhiannon thought. She was going to kill him if she couldn't do this faster.

Suddenly, the mist began to take the shape of an arm, swirling with motes of light. Aron convulsed and stopped moving.

I can do this. Just a little bit longer, thought Rhiannon, praying she was right. "Oh, Brighid, first born of the earth, I call on you now to aid me in my work!"

As if in response, the light began to solidify in Aron's arm. Slowly, sparks of light wove together. Each mote found a place, and an outline of bones appeared and thickened. Next came tendons and arteries, then veins and skin. The light intensified, melding it all together and it was done.

Stunned, Rhiannon let the energy return to the tree and then the staff. The leaves and roots retracted. The sound stopped and all was quiet.

She looked down and an arm of silver existed where the plagued arm had been. The room shrank, and a terrible chill filled her. As the walls of the roundhouse fell in on her, she vaguely remembered something about paying the consequences of the magic, and she sat down heavily.

Rhiannon watched Brennan as if he were lost in a blur. She sensed an aroma of herbs and felt a warm cloth on her forehead. The light grew and hurt her eyes. When the energy of the tree left, Rhiannon immediately felt her own cost. She had been filled with so much light and power, but it died and left her empty, dark and powerless.

"Sip this, it will help," said Brennan as he offered her a mug of tea.

Rhiannon slowly took the brew with shaking hands and drank.

Rhiannon looked over at Aron." How is he doing?"

"I think he will be fine, but this is the first time we've tried anything like this."

She studied Aron, who seemed to be sleeping peacefully. His arm still glowed with some light, but it was much dimmer now. She wondered if the arm would work, or if it would just be a silver sculpture attached to his shoulder. Time would tell. They needed to find Nemain and get her to keep an eye on him while he recovered.

"If nothing else, the magic stopped the curse," said Rhiannon with a quick nod. "And I've learned a new magic to help us."

Brennan put his hand on her shoulder. "You never cease to amaze me, Rhiannon."

Rhiannon felt the herbs working, and Brennan's words brought a smile.

"Thank you, Brennan. I could have done none of this without you."

"Whatever happens, Rhiannon, I want you to know how proud of you I am, no matter how this ends."

Rhiannon felt her eyes fill and her throat thicken. "I want you to know, uncle, that I am so appreciative of everything…" Her voice trailed off. She took a breath and smiled.

"I need to stand. I need to pull in some Nwyfre," she told Brennan.

He reached out and steadied her as she stood. She kicked off her shoes and let her feet contact the earth of the floor. She closed her eyes and let the energy of the earth flow into her. It rose like a white light through her feet and nourished her depleted body.

She steadied herself and embraced Brennan. "I love you uncle."

Brennan returned the embrace and Rhiannon felt full and yet terribly afraid.

From outside the house, pounding drums suddenly broke

the silence, like a hammer striking smoldering metal. The sound reverberated off the high ceiling of the mound. Battle horns answered from all around, and the ground trembled under the weight of Morrigan's approaching army.

Rhiannon's heartbeat leapt and she felt weak in the knees. "Somehow, I thought we had more time," she said in a breathless whisper.

Brennan nodded grimly.

Rhiannon looked Brennan in the eye, lifted her chin. "The real test is about begin," said Rhiannon as she walked to the door. "Time to finish this."

Chapter 46

Rhiannon emerged from the roundhouse and Brennan followed her. They walked together in silence through the village. The Nwyfre had restored her some, but she was not at her full strength. Rhiannon sighed. It would have to be enough.

On their way to the wall, they found Nemain. They told her what had happened and she turned and ran back to Brennan's roundhouse to sit with Aron and help him when he awoke.

Rhiannon reached the walls and climbed the ladder. From the top, the first of the dark armored troops crested the distant plain at the edge of the forest. Black Crow pennants flew in the breeze. Trolls and minotaurs came first, carrying massive shields. Winged creatures came behind them, flying overhead. Crows, wyverns, and rocs spread out to encircle the fort.

Bran sounded the horn of the Celts and roused all the remaining troops to their posts. King Conor emerged from his hall clad in his armor and with his bodyguard all around.

"I wish there was a better way to settle this than fighting," said Rhiannon with a frown. "I have as much reason as anyone to want to see Morrigan dead, but it seems such a waste."

"This struggle has gone on for a long time, and it seems we have little choice," Brennan said. "Unless Garth returns, we have no hope of stopping her and she knows it. She will press us hard now and hope to destroy us."

The black wave of troops advanced across the fields. A silence fell over everyone as Morrigan made her first appearance. She moved forward through her ranks in her raven chariot. Her black dress blew out behind her as she rode.

Rhiannon looked for Logan, but if he had come with his mother, he was not by her side now. She hoped that maybe he stayed behind and refused to fight. In the distance, she thought she saw him, dressed in black and looking like Morrigan.

Her body tensed. What would she do if she was forced to fight him? Could she do that?

Rhiannon looked more closely at the advancing troops and tried to spot him again, so desperate for answers. Why had he protected her back in Morrigan's castle? If he was really on his mother's side, why didn't he just capture her or let the troops find her?

Her knees buckled. The realization that should have been hers days ago finally hit her. He protected her because he still loved her. What did that mean for them? She knew she would never fight him but beyond that she didn't know.

Rhiannon looked out on Morrigan's army. They stopped and spread out. A team of horses pulled something through the dust. Finally, she was able to make it out. A tower rolled on giant wheels.

There was more than one. Teams of horses pulled towers with black raven banners flying. They spread out along the entire perimeter of the fort. Rhiannon's stomach knotted. What was Morrigan doing?

The king left his place on the opposite wall to come talk to the Druids. "What is this?" Conor asked.

Rhiannon shrugged. She had never seen anything like it before.

"Whatever it is, it can't be good," Brennan said.

In the distance, they watched as Morrigan's army parted to allow her black chariots access to the front. Drums pounded a steady beat as the towers moved.

"We can't just stand here and let her do what she will," said Rhiannon.

"I agree," said Conor, "but they are too far away for spears, and I don't dare lead the men out from behind the walls until we know what she is doing."

Rhiannon looked out, worried a trap was closing in all around them, but there was nothing they could do. Morrigan's plan proceeded without the least bit of resistance from them, and it made Rhiannon's blood boil.

The drumbeat stopped. The towers appeared to be in place around the fort, spaced evenly around the entire perimeter. Morrigan raised her arms, and the black metal columns glowed blood red. A stream of red light erupted from her sword and shot out to the two closest towers. From those two, red energy joined the rest of the towers together in a vast circle. From the ring of red light, a wall rose upward and curved inward until it created a single red dome over their heads.

The sky above the Celt fort grew dark as midnight. A blood red rain began. It fell from the dome above in thick droplets, and red liquid stuck to everything it touched, coating people and buildings. The substance turned black as it dried, drowning out the bioluminescence of everything. Glowing trees and flowers darkened as if the blood had poisoned them.

Rhiannon gasped. A few sputtering torches still cast eerie shadows across the open spaces, but only on the walls could anyone see well. Atop the rise where the tree was guarded, a faint glow radiated out from the protected plants inside, like a beacon of hope amidst a sea of darkness.

And then the drums started again.

Rhiannon and her allies stood atop the wall with no choice but to wait.

In the dark, men stomped their feet and called out to one another, and banged their swords on their shields. When the blood rain stopped, a cheer went up from the men who hated the black goo covering them, but soon their relief was met with further dread. At the edge of the ring of towers, bonfires began to kindle. A veritable ring of fire erupted from the ground.

Rhiannon looked closely. The flames of the fire that surrounded them were tinged with green, and a billowing smoke of the same color rose into the air from the blaze. An almost imperceptible breeze picked up, and a wall of sickly green roiled across the open ground toward the waiting Celts.

"That is no normal fire!" she said. "There is some enchantment at work. We must do something before it reaches us!"

Rhiannon concentrated and tapped into the earth below them. Nothing. There was no power to draw on. It was wrong, terribly wrong. Instead of tapping into a deep source of magic, she was somehow cut off. Only a trickle energy was available.

"Gods damn it," she shouted. "That's what that damn sphere is for. It's cutting us off from our power. It must extend down into the ground too."

Brennan tried to pull on the elements and discovered

Rhiannon was right. They were cut off.

She had barely enough for a little magic.

"*Gaoth!*" she shouted and conjured a wind that blew in a circle around them, but it wasn't big enough to protect them all. The smoke crept closer.

"That's the best I can do," said Rhiannon. "We must find another way to stop it. The blood sphere is isolating me from the earth's power."

"She has trapped us, and now she hopes to finish us with her poison gas," said Brennan.

Rhiannon looked out and in the dim light and her mind lit up. Morrigan may have cut her off from the power of the four elements, but she didn't know about how the Faillean Duir worked. Rhiannon would have to use what she had learned in curing Aron, even if she didn't know what it would do to her. It might kill her, but she had to try or they would all be dead.

Chapter 47

Rhiannon looked at Brennan and Conor. "We need to pull back to the courtyard outside the hall. It is the highest place and will protect us the longest from the smoke."

Conor nodded and gave the order to pull back.

The timber walls stopped the mist, but only for a moment as it found cracks in the wood and then flowed up over the palisade. Panic followed. People started to choke and collapse.

Rhiannon mounted the stairs two at a time and Brennan followed her. She drew what power she could for one more push of air, but it did little. The dome was filling, and there was nowhere for the poison to go.

The fires outside the circle still burned and the smoke continued to flow into their enclosure. It was only a matter of time before every man, woman, and child would be dead, and all without one sword being swung. It was an ingenious plan, but Rhiannon could find no admiration for her terrible enemy.

Now or never, she thought as she coughed from her first lungful of the smoke. She looked at Brennan, who tried desperately to conjure more wind, and closed her eyes. Again, she envisioned the staff reconnecting with the world tree and the same silver roots and silver branches appeared, spreading out from the staff until she and all near her stood in the center of a great tree.

The light of the silver tree illumined much of the inside of the dome, casting stark shadows with its brilliance, and in its light revealing what they had feared. Wherever the green fog had touched the barley fields around the fort, the grass had withered and died.

From the tree came a sound, a subtle hum, and the ground rumbled. Rhiannon took the silver light into her body through the staff. With her left hand still on the Faillean Duir, she reached out with her right hand, pointed at the creeping green mist, and turned slowly in a circle, driving the poison gas back.

Seeing the toll the poison had taken, so many people prone on the ground, Rhiannon realized the wind would not be enough. She had to take out those towers or they were lost. Drawing more deeply on the magic, she let it build, growing more intense. It made her bones ache, threatened to make her explode.

"Fáinne Forsa!" she shouted finally and let the power go.

It erupted from the staff in a blinding circle of silver light that radiated out across the barley fields to her targets. Waves of power poured from the staff, like pulsing circles of lightning. The spell struck the towers, the silver and red contended, swirling together. Magic warring with magic. The silver flared, consuming the red glow. The enchantment on the towers evaporated as if it had never been. The silver quieted and faded, its work done. Above, the blood dome shattered, raining a last gush of liquid down on them.

The power of the staff started to fade, but Rhiannon clung to a small portion of it, praying she wouldn't lose consciousness again. The force that had rolled through her was tremendous, and she didn't know what the long-term effect would be, but she knew she had to stay on her feet.

The dark menace was gone, but so was her light, her power. It was like the after effect of healing Aron, but worse. Despair filled her, like nothing would ever be right in the world again. Rhiannon dropped to her knees and the light of the tree went out. Rhiannon felt Brennan's hands on her shoulders supporting her. She had broken the dome, she had removed the killing smoke, but she had left nothing for herself.

She stared at her hands with a bowed neck, feeling every ache in her body. She brought a hand to her face and felt wrinkled skin. She pulled her hand away in horror.

What had the magic done to her?

Chapter 48

Garth returned from his ordeal at the Well to find his men waiting for him back at their last camp. The mysterious fog had lifted, and each man made his way back. Together they had waited, while going out in pairs to look for Garth. He met Niadh and Bannan in the woods, and soon the remaining six were reunited. Jubilant at obtaining the Water, they now bent all their efforts on returning to the Fort. Together, they rode home, bearing the precious water of life.

Garth rode to the top of the valley, and at the ridge he pulled Cadifor to a stop. Niadh and Aodhan reined in next to him. Down below, a sea of Morrigan's troops crashed against the log palisades of the fort. Trolls, ogres, goblins, and sidhe fighters swarmed the walls. Fires burned and smoke billowed high into the air.

His mouth went dry. He had to get through to the hawthorne with the Water of Life. Everything depended on it. They had come so far and now an army stood between him and his goal.

Garth turned Cadifor and looked at his companions. "We can finish this. We are not expected. We can ride fast and cut through the Morrigan's troops from behind, then reach the wall before they realize what's happened."

Bannan shifted in his saddle. "There are only six of us, Garth."

"What's a few fighters to *us?*" said Aodhan. "We can do this."

"It's not a few, Aodhan. It's an *army*," said Croftin.

Garth nodded at his friend. "Listen, I know the odds are not good. But if we fail, if we turn away, all of our people, down below and up above, will die. Today we have a special privilege.

Whatever happens in the next few minutes, if we ride down into *that*, we will be welcomed as *heroes* in the halls of our fathers. They will raise high a toast to our deeds, and we will drink deep from the horn of victory."

Bannan smiled with bright eyes.

"We are with you, Garth," said Niadh.

Croftin closed his eyes and took a breath. "I will not stay when my brothers ride to battle."

"Today, we are all heroes. Now let's ride! Follow me to the wall!"

Garth spurred Cadifor into a charge, and the six of them raced down the hill. Ahead, a ring of strange towers encircled the fort. Whatever they had been, they were ruined now, and he raced past them.

They met a thin line of infantry. The six horsemen burst through the line and hit the rear left flank of Morrigan's army. Garth led them, fighting toward the walls.

Between attacks, he looked up at the palisades, searching for his brothers. Where were Bran and Aron? Where was his father? The sea of monsters closed in behind them.

An 8-foot tall green monstrosity of muscle and claws turned, showing a mouth full of black teeth. The creature crouched and sprang at Garth. His adrenaline spiked as he brought up his shield. Razor claws sliced the wood of his defense.

Garth swung Cadifor around, knocking the troll back, and swung Claíomh Solais. The glowing blade took an arm off the troll, but the other arm raked down across Garth's head. The ridge brow of his helmet deflected the claws from his eyes, while the tips caught his chin, cutting three grooves. Garth shouted with sudden pain and thrust with his sword, catching the troll in the throat.

The creature clutched at the blade. Garth pulled it free, cutting fingers on the way out. The troll sank to its knees, clutching its throat. Garth took its head with a single chop.

He looked around for his men. Out of the corner of his eye, he saw Bannan get pulled off his horse. Niadh and Aodhan fought near Bannan, but where were Croftin and Dónal?

Garth rode to Bannan's aid, killing two goblins. All around him, a mire of death clawed and stabbed at his men. A minotaur trampled Dónal. Garth spurred his horse to drive the minotaur back. Just as he did, something struck Garth on the right side and unseated him.

His ribs roared with pain and he hit the ground, making it worse. His vision filled with stars. Clenching his jaw, he struggled to his feet.

Garth knew he had to get back on Cadifor. To stay on foot in this melee promised death. He spun around, looking for his horse and trying to avoid what had attacked him. A creature, massive with muscle and covered with fur, raised its head from Cadifor. Blood and entrails covered the thing's face. It bellowed, showing yellowed teeth and the tusks that had just gutted his horse.

"No!" Garth yelled, fury erupting at the sight of Cadifor's blank eyes.

Claíomh Solais hummed with power, and Garth attacked, slicing into the ribs of the fur-covered beast, drawing a spatter of blood. He brought up his shield as a cudgel-bearing fist swung at him. The strike pounded his shield, like a mountain falling on him, breaking the wood and bone beneath.

His left arm snapped, sending a wave of agony through his body. He staggered back, his arm hanging useless at his side. The wereboar came at him, jaws wide to bite. The beast roared. Garth spun and kicked the legs out from under his attacker. He stepped in and stabbed the creature in the chest.

Niadh appeared and took the creature's head. "That's for Cadifor," he said.

Garth nodded. "Let's get out of here."

Around him, only Aodhan and Bannan still fought; the others dead or lost. He must get free now or die. The walls were close enough that he could run. "Niadh, Aodhan, Bannan! Follow me!"

Garth ran, fighting his way through anything between him and the walls of the fort. The Druid blade burned, and none stood against the Celtic prince. Finally, Aron appeared atop the walls, defending a large section of the wall by himself. A ring of fallen bodies lay heaped around him.

Garth blinked, not quite believing what he saw. A silver glow radiated from his brother, centered on his left arm. Aron fought with terrible power. In the old legends, Garth knew it was called the hero light, and Aron was aglow with it, like a torch.

Garth rushed the ladder, and with vicious strokes cleared the way. Aodhan climbed the ladder first, pulling sidhe warriors off as he went. Garth went next, using his one good arm to climb, and Niadh followed.

Aron's eyes grew wide when the Celts appeared. He put down the spear and reached out a hand. "Took you long enough, little brother," he said with a smile.

"I ran into a bit of trouble," Garth said, looking back at the army.

"A small inconvenience, I'm sure."

"Nothing we couldn't handle."

"Did you get the Water?"

Garth nodded, feeling taller, and gave a satisfied smile.

"What about your other men?"

He frowned. "They died like heroes."

Aron nodded grimly. "Let's get you to that tree, then."

Garth peered down from the walls. The defenses had been breached in many places and between him and the mead hall, where the tree lived, stood a sea of Morrigan's soldiers.

His stomach knotted. He took in a short breath and blew it out, then shook his head. There were so many. "All right," he said finally. "Let's finish this."

Garth moved toward the ladder to climb down. He felt a rush of air from above and looked up. A giant black bird, with a wingspan more than four spears wide, descended toward him.

He swallowed hard and picked up a spear. He drew back his arm, ready to cast it at the new threat, when his mouth fell open. The minotaur riding the giant bird looked familiar.

The rider waved at him and shouted. "Garth! It's me, Tinurion!"

Recognition flooded him. It was the minotaur that Rhiannon traveled with. What was he doing here?

"Need any help?"

Garth put down the spear, feeling hope fill him. Maybe Rhiannon's trust had been well placed, maybe there was still a chance. "If you could take me to the hall, your help would be most appreciated, Tinurion," he shouted as the bird landed on the wall.

Tin reached out a hand and pulled him up.

"Let's get this done," he said.

The bird lifted off the ground and circled up high over the fort. Garth swallowed hard seeing so many fallen Celts, so many of his people dead. Where were Deirdre and Wil? Were they all right?

He felt his balance slip, and his breath caught in his throat. He pulled himself back straight and firmed his jaw, knowing he had to stay focused. Everything depended on what was about to happen. There would be time for other things later, *if* he succeeded.

Chapter 49

As if from a long way away, Rhiannon heard drums pounding, shouting, and the clash of weapons. An aura of green light flashed into existence, surrounding her. In the sphere, leaves of all the ogam trees whirled in a translucent orb. She felt Brennan's legs against her back. His shield protected them both.

She looked up. The sky above seethed with the flying minions of Morrigan; crows, ravens, pixies, and sylphs. She tried to get up, but her muscles refused. She leaned forward and put her hands on the ground, feeling like all her muscles had turned to goo.

Rhiannon reached out with her Druid senses and felt an ocean of Nwyfre all around her, the life force of trees and grass, streams and light. The blood dome was gone. She opened her hands to the energy and drew it in, feeling her strength coming back.

The energy grew, filling her, restoring her. She felt her face as the Nwyfre flooded her. The wrinkles faded a little.. She took in a breath and let it out sagging against Brennan. She searched her face again, and felt lines around her eyes that hadn't been there before, and hadn't been removed. A small price, she thought, giving them a fighting chance. She clenched her jaw and looked up, aware of her surroundings again.

She looked beyond Brennan's green shield at the stairs at her feet. She rubbed at her eyes, not believing what she saw.

At the bottom of the steps a giant bird landed, and from the saddle two riders dismounted. The first was enormous, holding a two-handled axe, and the other, a blond-haired Celt. Her heart pounded.

She looked up at Brennan. "I can stand," she said in what she thought was a normal tone, but it came out as a whisper.

Brennan must not have heard her in the tumult. She spoke

again, stronger this time. "I can stand."

He heard her this time. With a smile, he lowered his shield and helped her to her feet. Below, the two riders ran up the stairs, and her mouth dropped open. Tinurion led the way up the stairs, with Garth just behind him. How was that possible? Tin *and* Garth? She didn't know the answer, but the sight of them both filled her with relief.

"Brennan, look!" she shouted.

Brennan turned and gave a shout of triumph.

Tin and Garth reached the top of the steps, and she joined them in making the last dash across the courtyard, while Brennan fought off the incoming attacks.

From the morass of swirling wings above, a single giant raven pierced the avian curtain and landed at the doors to the hall, behind which the dying tree awaited. The black corvid shifted, and the Morrigan faced them.

She smiled. "So here we all are, and none of you between me and the tree. How delightful. All I have to do is walk through this door, cast one spell, and it's all over."

Rhiannon's hope turned to fear. She knew Morrigan was right, but maybe if she kept her talking for just a little longer, she could recover enough to stop her. "You think no one guards the tree inside?" she said.

The Morrigan shrugged. "It doesn't really matter. Whoever, or whatever, won't stop me. It's time for the hawthorne to die and for the faerie to have their revenge."

"Not all the faerie," said Tin, scowling at the Morrigan. "You are only queen to those who are cowardly and wicked. All the free fae despise you."

"Oh? Who are you again? Oh, right. You are that minotaur who killed more in my games than anyone else. You even killed humans. You have no moral ground to stand on."

"I was forced to fight, you know that as well as I do, Morrigan." Tin turned to Rhiannon. "I've been trying to make it right. But *she* has had choices and *she* chose to do terrible things." He pointed his axe at her.

"He's right. Morrigan, you could still stop this fight," said Brennan.

"I know, I know. We could all become one big happy family." She threw her arms in the air. "Enough talk! It's time for the hawthorne to die!" Morrigan turned and pulled open the doors to the hall.

"Cré Dorn!" Brennan shouted a power word Rhiannon had never learned.

From the earth below the Morrigan's feet, a giant fist of rock and soil erupted. It caught Morrigan and began to squeeze. Her shield of black light crackled and held, but Morrigan was stopped, her own shield making her a prisoner.

She turned back toward the Druids. *"Fuarán!"*

The ground of the courtyard rumbled, and from the hole where Brennan's earth fist had emerged, a rush of water blasted upward and encircled the clenched fist and the Morrigan both. The swirling water turned faster, and when it dropped away the fist was gone and the Morrigan stood glaring at them.

"Really, Brennan? Is that the best you've got? I expected so much more from you."

Desperate, Rhiannon drew in power to attack. Tin and Garth stood on either side of her, with Brennan just behind. She knew they had to take down the Morrigan, but just as importantly, she had to get Garth to the tree with the water. If Garth went down and the water was destroyed, their hope was gone.

Morrigan narrowed her eyes at Rhiannon. "Just because you have *that* staff doesn't mean you can stop me, little Druid."

Rhiannon clenched her teeth. "Time to find out, Morrigan." She braced herself. *"Gabha Casúr!"*

Light surged from the Faillean Duir, and as it crossed the space between them the comet of power took on the shape of a giant hammer. The magic weapon smashed against Morrigan's shield, and the sound of it exploded like thunder. The Morrigan, however, was untouched.

"Fuinneamh!" the faerie queen countered, and a black bolt of energy leapt from her hands at all of them.

Rhiannon jumped in front of Garth, blocking the spell from hitting him. The energy hit harder than she expected, but her shield held. Tinurion dodged to the left, far enough that the spell swished past him. The power hit Brennan's shield, but he turned as it hit, deflecting most of it back into the ground.

Rhiannon attacked again. *"Reoite!"*

A lance of white energy struck the Morrigan's shield, and frost crystals covered half of the shield, giving Rhiannon the chance to move unseen for a brief moment. She moved to her left, trying to flank Morrigan, while keeping Garth safe behind her.

Brennan countered. *"Dóiteán!"*

Green fire blasted toward the goddess, but Morrigan knocked it away with one hand. "You'll have to do better than that," she hissed before she disappeared inside the hall.

Tin charged forward and jumped the chasm in front of the doors. He too disappeared inside the hall.

Rhiannon sprinted for the door, with Garth and Brennan just behind her. She jumped the crevice using her power to strengthen her leap. Behind her, she heard Brennan land, but not Garth. She turned. He stood considering the jump. Her pulse stalled. Without her magic, she would not have attempted it.

"Go on!" shouted Garth. "Stop the Morrigan!"

She nodded, turned, and pulled the doors open. Far away, at the end of the hall, where the hawthorne used to stand unprotected, now stood warriors guarding it. Overlapping shields held by the fighters lined newly constructed tiered walkways that surrounded the circumference of the tree. A hatch had been lowered over the opening above, with a concave shield attached to the bottom that now covered the top of the tree, forming an unbroken shell. The king, just outside the barrier, stood in front of his throne.

Rhiannon swallowed hard. She knew the men wouldn't slow down the Morrigan for long, and that the man standing there bravely, defending the tree with no protection from magic, was her father. Her head spun. The goddess would only need two spells to finish the job.

She tried to decide what to do. She was too far away to get to the tree before Morrigan attacked. Her best option was to attack. She hummed with power and got ready to blast the Morrigan, but Tin stood in the way. She ran forward to get him out of her line of sight.

Tin pulled back his axe and threw at the retreating Morrigan. The weapon struck the Morrigan's shield and glanced off, embedding itself in a wooden upright.

Tin lowered his head and charged.

Morrigan turned, drawing in her power. *"Fiachra!"* she yelled, gesturing and pointing at Tin. He yelled in protest as the magic swirled around him. He crouched down, his massive form shrinking, and in a burst of black feathers, he was transformed into a crow.

"No!" Rhiannon pulled in more power, pointed the Faillean Duir at the Morrigan. It happened too fast. There was nothing she could do to help Tin, not now. The bird flew up and out of the way, giving Rhiannon a clear shot. She focused and attacked.

"*Airgead!*"

A crackle of energy, and then a blinding flash. The silver bolt ruptured the air as it sliced across the mead hall.

"*Dealán!*" Brennan intoned the power word at the same instant as Rhiannon, and a flash of lightning seared the air.

Rhiannon's silver ray and Brennan's lightning bolt impacted the Morrigan simultaneously. The combined attack ripped Morrigan into the air and into one of the hall uprights, breaking it in half with a spatter of splinters and smoke. The debris filled the air, and for a moment, Rhiannon was blind to what was happening.

From the haze, the Morrigan reappeared, no longer laughing. A volley of spears from the tree's guardians cut the air and struck Morrigan's shield as she staggered forward. The spears fell as if they struck rock. She ignored them.

"You Druids are so annoying," Morrigan hissed. "No more games. Time to die!"

She drew in her power and the light faded from the room. Black energy roared out of her. The wave of energy struck them both with terrible intensity.

Rhiannon clenched her jaw, feeling the impact like a tidal wave breaking all around her, trying to crush her. Behind her shield, her feet slid against the floor, and she crouched to let the wave break over her. The deafening sound roared, and fingerlets of power slipped through the branches of her shield, finding skin, cutting. Blood flowed as the flames of black fire lacerated everything they touched.

She turned and looked over at Brennan. His shield flickered. "Hold on, Brennan!" she shouted above the tumult.

Brennan's bracelet shattered, and the green orb of light in the sea of darkness disappeared. The dark magic struck. A purple and black bolt impaled Brennan's chest. He stumbled back, collapsed to the ground, and lay still.

Rhiannon's throat swelled, her chest fell in, her heart sank. "No, Brennan! No!" She clutched her hands into fists. She shoved down her anguish, and her grief turned to rage. She was not going to let the Morrigan win.

Rhiannon pulled in power to attack again. Out of the corner of her eye, Garth came in from behind her, his sword glowing bright. He ran past her, charging the Queen.

Morrigan turned all her focus on the Celt. *"Sracadh!"*

Garth brought up Claíomh Solais, trying to deflect the spell. Some of the black light reflected off the Druid blade into the thatch above, catching it on fire, but the rest got through to Garth. He fell to his knees, and his momentum made him skid forward and tumble to the ground. He screamed in agony, clutching at his head.

Rhiannon shook her head, not believing it had come down to this. Brennan was down, badly wounded or dead. Garth immobilized, and Tin gone. Her breath ragged, she braced herself as her nemesis focused on her alone. Knees weak, she brought a shaky hand to her forehead.

Morrigan laughed mercilessly. "I suppose you think you can stop me by *yourself.* Look what happened to your precious Brennan, to Garth, and that stupid traitor minotaur."

"It's time for you to pay for all the blood that you've spilled," said Rhiannon. "You've taken too much from me and it stops here. It stops *now.*"

The Morrigan attacked again. *"Duine a thriail!"*

Rhiannon poured Nwyfre into her shield, blocking the attack, but her strength was fading, her breathing labored. She stumbled. The magic penetrated her defenses, not completely, but enough to do harm. Blood already seeped from a hundred small cuts, and with it, her life force.

A wave of cold filled Rhiannon's body. She looked up at the Morrigan, and the room began to spin. Impossibly, Morrigan looked fully refreshed.

Rhiannon knew that the Morrigan had simply blocked everything they tried. She drew on the power and struggled to hold it and stay upright.

Morrigan smiled again, toying with her. She attacked again. *"Éadóchas!"*

As soon as Rhiannon heard the word, she felt what it meant.

Despair.

Her stomach sank and all hope left her. She looked down at her feet, drew a deep breath, and let it out. What was the point of fighting anymore? It was impossible to win. It had been a fool's hope all along. The hope that she could defeat a goddess was blatant stupidity.

Her wrist burned. She looked at her bracelet and then looked up at the Morrigan, who turned away to face the tree.

"*Fiachra!*" the goddess yelled, pointing at the men surrounding the tree. A black cloud enveloped the defenders, and in a terrible sound they all shifted into crows, like Tin had done. Spears and shields clattered to the ground. The hawthorne stood undefended.

Rhiannon clawed at her temples and screamed.

Her bracelet grew hot and exploded in fragments of turquoise and obsidian, spraying her face and cutting it. Morrigan's spell vaporized, and the fog lifted. Grief and panic filled her. Her father and his men were all turned to crows, and the Morrigan was about to kill the tree. The sound of her heartbeat thrashed in her ears.

For Brighid's sake, think of something, O'Neil!

Finally, an idea came to her for a new attack, something that might just work. She remembered when she and Brennan had hit the Morrigan together it had done the most damage of any of their attacks. Maybe if she could use three different energies at the same time, it might work. Rhiannon took a deep breath and released it into three power words. *"Léas Solas Tri!"*

From the tip of the Faillean Duir, three cords of light emerged—emerald, azure, and gold—each with its own power; the power of land, sea, and sky. The living tendrils of light arched across the battleground and blasted into the Morrigan's shield. The black orb shimmered, flickered, but then reflected the green and blue assault. The gold current, the light of radiant sun, shredded the darkness of Morrigan's shield. It obliterated the Morrigan's defenses, striking the goddess with full strength. The sun was the only cord that worked, so she let the other two drop.

Rhiannon poured every ounce she had into Morrigan, letting the power of the sun blister her enemy. Finally, she could give no more and slumped on her staff, spent and barely standing. Pain from the extreme drain on her body ignited. Her chest, lungs, and throat burned. Her legs turned to water.

The roof above Morrigan collapsed, letting in the purple light. Debris covered the goddess, but Morrigan rose to her feet. Still smoking, she walked toward Rhiannon.

Rhiannon's vision collapsed to a tunnel. Shame overtook her, shame that, despite everything, she had failed and soon the Morrigan would be free to have her revenge. She shook her head and held up her staff in front of her, defying the Morrigan with what little energy she had left. Her eyes burned as she watched Morrigan come.

Rhiannon blinked hard. Behind the Morrigan, a shadow descended through the open roof. It looked like a falcon.

"Die now!" Morrigan said as she reached for her crow-handled sword. But her hand grasped air. With a cry of shock, she looked down at the empty sheath, then turned. Logan stood behind her, holding the sword.

"Looking for this?" he said.

Rhiannon took a sharp breath.

"*Sceach!*" Morrigan shouted. Black energy erupted from her hand.

But she was too late. Logan stabbed his mother as the spell hit him. The blade punctured the Morrigan's chest.

A flash of light erupted from the mead hall. At the end of the hall, Garth stood triumphant in front of the hawthorne, his father holding him up. Somehow, the king had resisted Morrigan's spell, and in the confusion had helped Garth finish the quest.

"No!" Morrigan screamed, clutching at the blade. The tree contained her power and she shrank.

From the stab wound, a black light spider webbed outward, drawing lines of destruction all over the Morrigan. The streaks grew in intensity, pulsing purple. Her body shredded with a ripping and tearing noise, and with a scream of agony she vaporized into a cloud of black smoke. The crow-handled sword clattered to the ground.

Rhiannon staggered to grab Logan, who collapsed against her. He looked up at her, eyes wide with terror. She couldn't believe what she was seeing. Black thorns erupted from his body, from the *inside*. His skin ripped, and thorns flew out.

Rhiannon screamed, her heartbeat thrashing in her ears. She tried to pull in some power, to try and stop the thorns from doing any more damage, to stop Logan from being ripped apart before her eyes, but the strain was too much; she had nothing left. Logan's face, drained of blood, turned ashen. His eyes opened wide and the light went out.

Logan was dead.

Rhiannon brought a shaking hand to her forehead and let out an uncontrollable scream. Her body shook all over, eyes flowing with hot tears. Her ears rang and she pulled at her loose hair, turned gray from extreme magic use. A terrible keening rose from her throat.

The Morrigan was dead, but at a terrible cost. The ones she loved most were dead.

Chapter 50

Someone put a hand on Rhiannon's back.

"You can save him," said a familiar voice.

She heard but didn't understand. She opened her eyes. Garth stood there, covered with the stains of battle, and leaning on their father. In his outstretched hand, he held a vial of glowing water.

"Take it and save him," he said. "I had a little extra."

Rhiannon held her breath, lightness flooding her. She fixed her eyes on Garth and bit her lip. "You have extra?"

"I poured half on the roots of the tree, and it seemed to be enough. I didn't want to waste the water, it being so precious."

Rhiannon sat up and put her hand on Logan's arm, feeling for his pulse, praying to Brighid that somehow he was still alive. His wrist was still.

Hot tears flowed down her face. Logan was dead, and probably Brennan too. She struggled to her uncle's side. His face was drawn and wrinkled, and his once blond hair was silver gray. She touched his cheek and it was cold.

She glanced up at Garth. "Is there enough for both of them?"

"That I don't know. You need to choose quickly."

How could she choose between Logan and Brennan? She'd rather die and they both live than have to pick one of them. She looked at both men, searching their faces.

"It's your choice, Rhiannon," said the king.

Her stomach ached. The decision was too terrible. Brennan meant so much to her and to these people, but Logan, for all his faults, gave his life to save hers. They both deserve to live.

Rhiannon pulled at her hair. "Please, Brighid. Help me to make the right choice!"

She clenched her fist, feeling her nails break the skin. She reached up for her awen pendant.

Better a chance at one living than both dying, she thought soberly. She closed her eyes, feeling the tears streaming down her face, and looked down at her uncle. "Forgive me, Brennan."

She sat and put Logan's head in her lap, and took the bottle and poured half of what remained slowly into his mouth.

She waited.

Nothing happened.

"Gods damn it!"

Perhaps it was too late. Maybe he was too far gone. Maybe the thorns had done too much damage.

She looked at the last of the sacred water, looked at Brennan and back at Logan. She could use the rest on Brennan, but maybe it would not be enough for either of them. She'd already made her choice. She poured the rest of the water into Logan's mouth and closed her eyes.

Oh Brighid, if I ever had need of you, it is now. Please allow this sacred water to heal Logan. Please bring him back to me.

She waited for a moment, not wanting to see. She opened her eyes. The black thorns under his skin faded. His color began to return. Rhiannon held her breath.

Logan stirred and opened his eyes. He looked at Rhiannon. "What happened, where am I?"

Rhiannon hugged him feeling comfort in the embrace. "Thank you," she whispered to the air.

Garth leaned forward. "The Water of Life has brought you back to us from the Summerland."

"What happened to the Morrigan?"

Rhiannon looked over at the crow-handled sword still lying on the ground. "After you stabbed her, she disappeared in a cloud of smoke. She's dead."

Logan clenched his jaw and nodded. "I learned that Morrigan could only be killed by her own sword. Áine told me the secret."

"Who is Áine?"

"The woman you saw me with..." Logan looked down.

Rhiannon's past anger faded. Yes, he had made mistakes, but without him, she would be dead. She was sure of it. "It's in the past now."

Logan looked up, gave a short nod, then smiled. "But where is Brennan?"

Her eyes filled with tears. It had been a terrible choice, and she would miss her uncle forever, but he had trained her for this day. Maybe he even knew what would happen, that for the hawthorne to be restored, he would have to die.

"She chose you over him," said Garth.

Chapter 51

The smoked curled up from the funeral pyre, leaving the confines of the Celtic fort and traveling up to the roof of the mound. The wind blew from the west, making the flames sputter and snap. The oak logs burned hot, and Rhiannon's tears fell down her cheeks. Logan held her hand and stood with her.

Nearby, Tinurion stood with his head bowed, with Flit on his shoulder and Fao at his feet. The king, her father, and his three sons, her brothers, stood on the other side of her, with faces grim and blank stares. Rhiannon had reversed the Morrigan's crow spell, restoring Tin and the other Celts.

The survivors stood around the fire. Rhiannon turned full circle looking at them, at *her* people. The death toll had been terrible. Many were dead, but those who lived stood strong and proud.

Rhiannon swallowed and cleared her throat. "Spirits of the ancestors, I call to you and ask that you welcome home to the Summerland all of our beloved people, those who have died in this terrible conflict. They have served you well. Embrace them and welcome them to your halls.

"Gods of our people, long have our people honored you through rites and actions. Now I ask that you honor our departed kin and if they choose, help them to return to us once again.

"Nature spirits, I pray you honor our beloved dead, as they have honored you. In love and respect, I ask that you strengthen their spirits and give them rest."

Rhiannon fell silent, the back of her throat heavy. She was not alone in her grief. Many others said their farewells in their own way, but slowly they drifted away, leaving her alone.

The fire burned through the long night, and Rhiannon kept vigil. When the first light began to glow, she took some of the gray ashes from the fire and marked her forehead with three lines. She took ashes from where Brennan's body had been and put them in a small metal urn.

Alone, she mounted a horse and rode to the druid grove. The twilight air rushed past her, feeling cold after the long heat. A feeling of connectedness filled her as she rode, having no wish to be anywhere else, without a thought of what was to come or what had happened. Ahead, the grove loomed.

She dismounted, and when she approached, the trees parted for her as they once had for Brennan. She crossed the stream and stood under the arching trees, greeting them.

Inside the sacred enclosure, she dug a hole in the earth with her hands, and when it was deep enough, she placed the ashes inside. On top, she placed the roots of an oak sapling and filled the hole with good black earth. Around the tree she piled stones in a ring and finally poured water from the river onto the ground. It was done. Brennan was gone.

Rhiannon took a deep breath and let it out slowly. She brought her hand to her awen pendant as she looked around. This was now her grove, her home, her responsibility. But for now, she would not take on any added burden. This moment was for Brennan alone. She built a fire, sat for a while, and listened to the trees sing. She sang the songs Brennan had taught her until her voice gave out. First glowing was past, and the full light of day came upon the grove.

Rhiannon rose stiffly, put out the fire, and left the oak sapling behind in the grove. So many thoughts passed through her mind on the way back to the fort. She let them come. It was time to start living again.

As the last Druid with her enemy vanquished, the future had been saved, but at a terrible cost. The tree could live for another two thousand years and the world above kept safe. But now she had some decisions to make.

Rhiannon dismounted and found Logan inside the Druid roundhouse. The fire burned in the center and water boiled in the cauldron that hung over it. She took down a bundle of herbs drying near the door and picked a stem. She crumbled the agrimony leaves into a ceramic mug and let it steep.

When it was done, she added some honey and sat staring into the flames, sipping at her tea. She knew the herb would help lift her sorrow, and it would help her move on. She looked across the hearth at Logan.

"The cycle turns," she said finally.

"Why did you choose me?" he asked. "Brennan is so much more important to these people. To them, I am nothing."

Rhiannon put down her tea, walked around the fire to Logan, and took his hands. He stood and looked into her eyes.

"I chose you because I love you."

"And I love you," he said, his eyes sparkling like lights on new-fallen snow.

She leaned in and kissed him, letting the feel of him fill her.

She pulled back and paused for a moment, deep in thought. "From death comes new life, and so the circle turns."

"The circle turns," he agreed.

She took a deep breath and put her arms around him, feeling all the tension drain from her body, and for the first time in a long while, Rhiannon smiled. A feeling of gratitude rushed through her. She closed her eyes and let out her breath.

The End

Thank you for reading Hawthorne! Book Two of the Druid Spirit Chronicles is in progress. The working title is "Rowan." It begins where Hawthorne ends. If you enjoyed reading Hawthorne, Please consider leaving a review where you purchased your book. Thank you!

About the author:

Kevin grew up in Michigan and Florida, but you could equally say he grew up in Tolkien's Middle Earth and C.S. Lewis's Narnia. From the first time he walked through the wardrobe into Narnia, he knew he loved fantasy fiction. It allowed him to dream of bright places and also the dark and mysterious.

After finishing his English degree, he moved to Colorado and worked for Barnes and Noble. He managed four stores over fifteen years and during that time he worked on Hawthorne, hoping to one day have his own work on the shelves.

He lives with his family in Denver and is now dedicated to working full time on writing.

Find him on Facebook
http://www.Facebook.com/kevinfuryauthor/
Follow him on my website http://www.kevinfury.com

Pronunciation Guide

Ag Dreapadh	Og-DRAH-pah
Aghamore	Ag-ha-more
Aíne	AN-ya
Airgead	Ar-ged
Akecheta	AHKE-shetah
Aodhan	Aid-en
Cadifor	KAD-i-for
Cailleach	Kal-e-ach
Camanfa	KamA-nfa
Cathaoir	KA-hear
Cernunnos	Kern-noo-nos
Claíomh Solais	Kleve Sol-ish
Conlaodh	Kun-lee
Cré Dorn	Cray Door-un
Dealán	Jee a lawn
Dóiteán	DOH-chahn
Dónal	DOE-nul
Draighean	Dray Un
Duine a thriail	Din-a a THREE-all
Éadóchas	A-dov-us
Faillean Duir	FAE-le-an Doo-r
Fáinne Forsa	Fona Forsa
Fiachra	Fee-a-kra
Forsa	FOR-sa
Fuarán	FOR-awn
Fuinneamh	WIN-yuv
GabhaCasúr	Go KAS-ur
Gaoth	Gwee
Goban	Gub- awn

Gothfraidh	GOT-hfraidh
Gweneira	Gwen-IE-ara
Kohana	Ko-hahn-ah
Léas Solas Tri	Lease SUH-les Tree
Leictreach	Let-tro
Lugh	LOO
Niadh	Nee-uh
Ogam	O-am
Reoite	ROY-cha
Sceach	SKach
Solas	SUH-les
Sracadh	SHH-racka
Tuathal	TOO-hal
Ulchabhán	Ul-ka-vawn